EROWINA

Tom Mallin

VP Festschrift Series:

Volume 1: Christine Brooke-Rose
Volume 2: Gilbert Adair
Volume 3: The Syllabus
(Edited by G.N. Forester and M.J. Nicholls)

Reprint Titles:

The Languages of Love — Christine Brooke-Rose
The Sycamore Tree — Christine Brooke-Rose
Go When You See the Green Man Walking — Christine Brooke-Rose
Next — Christine Brooke-Rose
Xorandor/Verbivore — Christine Brooke-Rose
Three Novels — Rosalyn Drexler
Knut — Tom Mallin

other Verbivoracious titles @

www.verbivoraciouspress.org

EROWINA

or

L'ETERNELLE BLESSEE

(The Everlastingly Wounded One)

A SEXUAL NOVEL

Tom Mallin

Verbivoracious Press

Glentrees, 13 Mt Sinai Lane, Singapore

This edition published in Great Britain & Singapore

by Verbivoracious Press

www.verbivoraciouspress.org

ISBN: 978-981-09-4470-4

Printed and bound in Great Britain & Singapore

First published in Great Britain by Allison & Busby 1972.

Introduction

NATE DORR

A BIOGRAPHER OF FICTIONAL PERSONS

Tom Mallin's novels, at least the five that reached publication across the 1970s, could be taken as a series of biographies. Life stories, centred around a single character whose name adorns the cover, typically spanning decades, often encompassing a number of different "sources". They vary wildly in particulars, level of detail, and formal design, but seem, at least among those I've read, to be unified in tragedy.

The most comprehensive is certainly Mallin's first, *Erowina*. Completed as early as 1962, the same year that Mallin quit painting to devote his time to writing, it went unpublished until 1972 — by then his third novel, preceded by the slighter and more narratively streamlined *Dodecahedron* (1970) and *Knut* (1971). Overambitious as often only first novels can be, it's not so hard to see why publishers may initially have baulked, but over-ambition may be a great asset, and it remains his most complex. The novel addresses the entirety of a life, from coroner's report to swirling early memories — not backwards as that suggests, nor forwards, nor exactly out-of-order, but following elaborate cadences of interrelation and personal narrative — in twenty chapters each covering a different subject and composed in a wildly different style or technique.

In hindsight, *Erowina* seems to function by an almost Oulipan system of constraints and categories, but was probably composed more in parallel with early Oulipo than actually influenced by it. In all probability, the culprit progenitor (as always) of such high formalism in encyclopedically recording a life (as no contemporary reviewer of the novel could resist noting) is Joyce, whose *Ulysses* even gets a direct nod, though oddly it's to the "yellow smellow melons" line.

THE STORY OF A LIFE IS MAPPED IN BLOOD AND FLESH

Why that bit in particular? Well, perhaps because this is a lifetime told almost entirely across the congruent subjects of body and eroticism. At first with complete clinical detachment in the opening portrait of the deceased's physical specifications, whose marks and traces of past affliction actually offer a map of the novel's emotional and psychological course. Later chapters quickly fill in these cold details with the body's other meanings: ribaldry, passion, sex, anxiety, sensuality, and transgression, all those events that a life may encompass for better or for worse. This is a book about the erotic body.

It is certainly not accidental that the titular heroine's name suggests Eros, though Mallin offers the redundant explanation on the title page: "A SEXUAL NOVEL". Perhaps of more interest is the secondary title in French: "L'ETERNELLE BLESSEE (The Everlastingly Wounded One)." Here again the body, but now as vehicle of scars and unhealing injury, whether physical or psychic. This is a book about pleasure and pain.

On the other hand, "Erowina" also suggests "eroina", the Italian word for "heroine". Erowina is then the most essential and archetypal of the many identities by which the protagonist chooses to denote herself throughout the twenty chapters and near as many reinventions: Emily, Emma, Eunice, Evelyn, Esmeralda, Erica, Esbiel. One is her given name, one an occult alias, others seem to be generated following the severance of various significant relationships — a method, like altered hair colour, of self-renewal and forward momentum. It is important to note that all of these transformations are driven, by all accounts, by Erowina herself throughout her life. None are applied via the altering gaze of outside observers. This is a book about identity.

Such, in one of the novel's greatest assets, is Mallin's consideration for his heroine. Entirely unlike Dodeca's rigid course in *Dodecahedron*, travelled with a bitter determinism, Erowina here reshapes herself along much her own path (at least to the degree that such self-determination is possible amid the eternal forces of memory and possibility pushing all of us along). The tragedy is that despite this, her path remains troubled and troubling. Still, it's all given from warmly, empathetically close to her perspective.

This is a book about making sense of your own life.

In fact, much of the text is presented as her own.

In fact, it's rarely that simple.

CAN ANY LIFE BE RESOLVED WITH ANY CERTAINTY TO A SINGLE CLEAR CHRONOLOGY IN THE POSTMODERN ERA?

Much of the text is presented as Erowina's own.

"I stole all of her diaries," Tammy Lamlin tells Gloria Sansum. They are both significant ex-lovers of the bisexual Erowina. "They are not all diaries. Erowina wrote essays, short stories — plays even. They're all there."

And so: Erowina's words, in both fact and fiction. But which may be the truer? This self-explanation of the text occurs at the end of the third chapter, 'Black Swan Wake', a marathon pub-bound mourning process, thoroughly steeped in alcohol and memory. The preceding chapters are the coroner's report and a description of the funeral itself. Certainly none of these chapters could have been written by Erowina herself. Whereas that first section is entirely impersonal, professional, the earthly remains excised of the human, devoid of identity or name, in the latter sections our heroine gains a retrospective summary identity as "Erowina" in Tammy's first-person narration. And so we come to know her first as he does. Whether we ever know her otherwise may be somewhat ambiguous. Whatever I said about her apparent agency last section.

As Tammy tells us, Erowina's chapters that follow take a variety of formats: first-person stream-of-conscious confessional, symbolic-surreal stories like 'Father's Skin', in which a young Emily attempts to fit into the shape of her forebear for unsettlingly ambiguous purpose, distanced third-person descriptions of encounters, two theological dialogues under very different circumstances, and, at several points, complicated *mis-en-abyme* cross-cuttings of the entire chronology. One period is conspicuously absent: Tammy's own relationship with Erowina.

"I lie," Tammy admits. "The years fifty-two to fifty-six are missing."

"Convenient," says Gloria.

"I watched her burn them," Tammy offers.

Can this be trusted? It is tempting — Tammy is another sympathetic narrator, and closest to our reader's position outside of Erowina's own life, especially if he has become *de facto* executor of her manuscripts and legacy. But it is awfully convenient that he alone escapes her scrutiny. Or, perhaps that's not entirely true — we see a third person Esmeralda ending the relationship with Tammy, and burning her diaries, in a brief stretch of one of those odd time-collapsing chapters, a detailing of a life of allergy to roses. (Why exactly, whether the affliction is real or metaphorical, is one of the novel's key puzzles.) In any event, he is mostly excised, supposedly by her hand. But we also learn that Tammy, formerly a doctor, has quit in order to write (in this shifting of profession, not to mention by anagram, he is also identified with Mallin himself). Since he has written at least two chapters (quite eloquently at that, in fluid voice and dialect), can we ever be sure that he hasn't written them all? Or barring that, modified and edited her originals, for style or content, subtly or grossly? He is even seen (in that brief view in 'Allergy') burning his own autobiographical novel at her request, so destroying that side of their collective memory as well. But if this section is one of those attributed to her and fully credible then why, after fainting, is she "drawn into awareness by (my) concern and tenderness", a sole intrusion of Tammy's first person into her ostensible narrative sections. The placement is highly deliberate, the questions it raises are integral. Can we even be sure that he burned his own manuscript? That we're not reading it *right now*?

Furthermore, I have said before that certainly none of these chapters occurring after Erowina's death could have been composed in her own words. But is there really any way to know that the scope of her fiction-spinning couldn't extend beyond the horizon of her own life? If Erowina could be Tammy's construction, he could, just as easily, be hers.

I should mention that the actual experience of reading *Erowina* is not actually this kind of arid intellectualising, but more a foray into elegant storytelling and emotional involvement. Yet these mysteries add a cryptic embroidery that should not be ignored for a full appreciation.

A COMPLICATED MIS-EN-ABYME CROSS-CUTTING OF THE NOVEL'S ENTIRE CHRONOLOGY

Especially considering that even Erowina's self-understanding, if we take any of this to be her own story, is so thoroughly postmodern.

Besides 'Allergy', the other major self-summary comes in the form of Erowina's seemingly final work. Tammy again: "And the newspapers? On the day Erowina died, she ringed various headlines in the Sunday newspapers and made marginal comments."

These headlines (real? invented?) become a vast framework to join together sequences that echo, illuminate, or rewrite the rest of what precedes them in a gruelling self-interrogation. Conspicuously absent are reference to events that immediately precede — an Usher-like familial collapse, a revelation, a moment of calm — and the present moment itself, in which the heroine is all but invisible. Perhaps she is in a state, flashed forward to much earlier, of "having no identity". And so left nameless and blank, a condition that persists into the opening autopsy.

But aside from these more elaborate cases, the fluidity of Erowina's identity allows for subtle self-evaluation throughout. Witness how a key bathhouse sequence opens on Erica, recomposes around "the girl with the beautiful green eyes" after a fateful encounter, and finally stabilises on "I", the first point at which Erowina allows herself a full self-identification with her character within her text. It's a moment of convergence, of psychic wholeness, of health. She'll remain so for only a time, but the state will last at least through the beautifully internal centrepiece love scenes, where self and other move in perfect balance towards some kind of total understanding. It's as much as anyone can hope for, perhaps.

At another point, confusion of identity will tilt events the other way, towards destruction.

AND WHAT OF

I've really only scratched the surface. My intent here is not to explicate or summarise, but simply to suggest some of the twisty paths through a reading of this book. There are others, and they lead through yet-unsuggested highlights (a dream recounted, a madness, a demonic ritual, a whispering of tumultuous thought such as we have all likely experienced at one time).

Actually, let me spend a moment on that ritual, which, in fitting into the course of the novel is grotesquely bodily in its specific terms. Here again an unexplained external voice enters, seemingly an outside historian referring to the writings that we, readers, are only about to encounter. Which suggests publication post-text, or perhaps, again, Erowina's own postmodern sense of self-analysis in composing her less directly autobiographical "stories". (Which, even so, could not be taken as anything but autobiographically insightful, perhaps even moreso than the the direct relation of factual events. Which is as good a justification for exploratory fiction as any. I'm paraphrasing David Foster Wallace, Mallin would seem to have agreed.) In any event, it seems that these layers of self-fictionalisation are also the best way to resolve the sharp contradictions in Erowina's apparent theological positions.

But that, as I said, is just one of the many pleasures and frustrations along the tricky course through this book. Importantly, the formal and conceptual puzzles are only a background machinery designed to animate an entirely human story. Mallin's following work would favor mechanism over empathy or psychology, the next sentiment over form and development. Both would spiral in single-minded decline. But here, a life in full: warm, convincing, desperate and vital.

EROWINA

A PARTICULAR DESCRIPTION

E.

Female. Chromatin count normal, tending towards minus.

White Europiform.

Weight: Nine and a half stone, or one hundred and thirty-three pounds.

Apparent age: Thirty. Chronological age: Thirty-six years, one hundred and nine days — having been born on the fourteenth day of June, nineteen hundred and twenty-seven.

Height: Five feet seven and a half inches.

The measurement from the apex of the sagittal suture to the seventh cervical vertebra (vertebra prominens) is nine inches;

to the articulation of the clavicle to the sternum, eleven and a quarter inches;

to a transverse line through the nipples, eighteen inches;

to the umbilicus, twenty-seven inches;

to the anterior superior spine, twenty-nine and a quarter inches; to the upper border of the symphysis pubis, thirty-three and three-quarter inches;

to the head of the femur or to a transverse line through the lower fold of the groin, thirty-six and a quarter inches.

to the gluteal fold of the buttocks, thirty-seven inches and to the lower limit of the patella, fifty and a half inches.

The upper limb, from the middle finger to the acromion, measures twenty-eight and a half inches.

The measurement from the tip of the acromion to the olecranon is the same as from the olecranon to the head of the third metacarpal — which is twelve and a half inches.

The width of the shoulders is twelve inches and the width of the hips, measured between the two great trochanters of the femurs, fourteen inches.

FAT DISTRIBUTION

The cervico dorsal accumulation:

A large collection in the region of the vertebra prominens, over a diamond-shaped tendinous area of the trapezius, produces an accentuated hump. (This probably became exaggerated when the subject was standing or showed signs of fatigue or tension. It would also have been noticeable when her stance was bad.)

THE POST-DELTOID COLLECTION

There is an increase in the antero-posterior diameter at the root of the limbs which is consistent with the subject's age. It covers the upper and back part of the arms behind the insertion of the deltoid and upper part of the triceps. This is much in evidence when the arms are raised sideways.

THE FAT OF THE FLANK

This is limited by the groove from the subscapula region and, although there is a generous collection as typical in women, it is by no means gross. The fat has no lower limits but continues into the buttocks and is not broken by the iliac furrow — which is completely buried. It also obliterates the upper two dimples at the outer border of the erector spinae but makes the lower dimples over the posterior superior spine conspicuous.

THE FAT OF THE GLUTEAL REGION

There is a generous accumulation on the buttocks. The fat bulges formed on the fibrous shelves attached to the ischial tuberosities are ample, forming two deep transverse gluteal folds. The fat is more abundant on the inner sides where the furrow is deepest.

THE SUBTROCHANTERIC ACCUMULATION

A large amount of fat is situated on the upper and outer part of the thigh. A prominence begins at the level of the great trochanter and quickly reaches a maximum diameter. The slight furrows between and below the extensors and flexors are filled above with subtrochanteric fat. It is continuous from the front of the thigh, running round to the fat of the buttocks. A number of faint depressions can be seen where the skin is tied to bands of underlying deep fascia. The inner side of the legs have a poor fat covering which accumulates slowly towards the knees.

THE FAT OF THE MAMMAE

The accumulation in the breasts is average, overlapping the seventh rib and extending from the sternum to the mid axillary line. From the side, the open angle or groove between the lower curved plain and the region below is non-existent, there being a fatty overhang of half an inch.

THE ABDOMINAL FAT

A small accumulation below the umbilicus and above the pubis forms a crater for the navel approximately three-quarters of an inch in depth.

PREPUBIC ACCUMULATION

There is a marked protuberance, forming a triangular prominence, situated in front of the symphysis pubis bounded by a furrow separating it from the abdomen and on either side by the deepening folds of the thigh.

HAIR

The pigmentation is brown with curved hair follicles giving rise to wavy hair, approximately twelve centimetres long. There is evidence of a previous, longer growth, from the extended follicles in the subcutaneous tissue; possibly when E. was a child. The loss of pigmentation is apparent when the hair is parted and the growth seen nearer the root. There is no evidence of dye having been used. A current accumulation of secretions from the sebaceous glands makes the hair greasy. The growth is thick and very resilient.

EARS

The ears of the subject are of a small ovoid form with a characteristic depression in the external prominent rim of the auricles, so that the helices appear dented or pinched. The absence of lobules is very marked although there is evidence of areolar and adipose tissues. Only on close inspection can hair be seen on the tragus. A few sebaceous glands are partly blocked in the right ear in the areas of the concha and scaphoid fossa, forming comedones.

It is not recorded that the subject's hearing was in any way impaired by otitis (May 1934) which was accompanied by a purulent discharge.

Both ears were pierced in 1948. There is evidence of keloid in the auricle round the closed punctures. Although the subject E.'s Aunt was committed to an insane asylum in 1936 there is no evidence in the subject E. of an excessive blood collection between the cartilage and the perichondrium (Dr M. D. Shaw).

EYES

The eyes have green pigmentation. Dolland and Aitchison record vision as R.6/24, L.6/5 without glasses in 1951.

The only visual characteristic aspect of the eyes is that when they are fully opened there is a tendency for the upper palpebral portion of the orbicularis palpebrarum to disappear under the arched eminence of the integument over the orbital portion which, obliquely, supports the growth of sparse, thick brown hair. There is evidence of cutting and plucking this hair in order to shape the supercilia.

The pigmentation of the skin around the eyes is brown and very apparent.

In 1947 repeated styes, resulting from blockages of the meibomian glands in the right eye, caused blepharitis (Dr Borges). Associated spasms, probably due to irritation of the fifth or seventh cranial nerve, and repeated quiverings were attributed to the orbicularis palpebrarum by the opthalmologist (Alma Judd) who discounted refractional error. The apparent fear of the subject E. of ptosis, imagining possible, impossible congenital atavism because her Aunt who, at the time of her restraint, was suffering from this disease, was, according to Dr Borges, very great.

There is evidence of recent and copious rheum extrusion.

NOSE

The nose is small and hyporhined. The cartilage of the septum appears slight when viewed from the side and the dorsum nasi, in direction and shape, conforms proportionately to the septum. The number of stiff hairs, with golden pigmentation, growing on the margin of the nares, is not excessive. They are unobtrusive and uncut. The activity of the sebaceous follicles is poor and the temperature of the nose was probably low.

Dr Urquhart reports that in 1931 he anaesthetised E. and, using the left forefinger in the naso pharynx to prevent a possible blockage of the air passages, he removed, through the anterior naris with forceps, a pencil stub, coloured yellow, measuring sixteen millimetres in length.

A previous irritation and interest was shewn in the nose because of slight, untreated, epistaxis (Dr Urquhart).

LIPS

The orifice of the mouth is bounded by fleshy folds of the labia oris. They are full and the external integument is covered by a pale, luminous pink lipstick which is varnished, giving the lips an illusion of moistness. The corners of the mouth correspond to the outer borders of the canine teeth. Although the teeth are large, the alveolar arch is small, making the mouth when closed proportionately small, contrary to the size of the mouth when fully opened. The largeness of the mouth cavity when open is probably due to the deformed articulation of the condyle with the glenoid cavity of the temporal bone.

TONGUE

The tongue is wide and thick. The dividing raphe is shallow. The anterior fungi form papillae which are smooth and pale but healthy in appearance. A surprisingly long frenulum linguae allows an excessive protrusion of the tongue. Very much in evidence, when the tongue is rolled to one side, are lacerations of the frenulum together with considerable scarring. This was probably due to repeated extrusion of the tongue and crushing the frenulum on the incisors of the lower jaw, causing slight bleeding and soreness.

Between the posterior and anterior pillars of the fauces there is also scarring, tonsillectomy and adenoidectomy having been performed on the twelfth of June, 1935.

TEETH

These are large, white and even with only slight deposits of tartar. The gingiva is highly coloured and very healthy in appearance.

Teeth present:

	87654321	12345678
	876 4321	12345 78
Decayed teeth:		
	2	2
	6	
Fillings:		
	21	2 6
	6	

There are marked abrasions labially on all the anterior teeth, especially 321⌋ and 43⌐. There is some supra-gingival calculus on the palatial surfaces 21⌐12 but with little staining. There are no recent extractions.

8⌋ is over-erupted. This tooth bites on the surface of the mucous membrane behind 7⌐ over the unerupted 8⌐. Irritation — oedema, and subsequent pericoronitis — is not sufficient to have caused E. enough pain that she would have sought dental advice.

6⌐ is restored with class two, mesial-occlusal silicate filling, of a type not allowed under N.H.S. regulations for this situation.

Traumatic toothbrush abrasions occur at the cervices of the anterior teeth on their labial surfaces, but a marked grooving shows on 3⊥3 and 3⌐3 which was developmental in origin but which is exaggerated by brush trauma. It is possible to indicate from these abrasions that the subject E. was left-handed.

There is moderate staining on the palatial and lingual aspects of all teeth which is consistent with smoking in moderation.

Further to the filling mentioned above the remaining restorations are of the following types:

21⌋ are both lingual with amalgam fillings.

⌊2 is lingual with gold inlay.

⌊6 distal occlusal with gold inlay.

NECK

This is slender and lined. The thyroid cartilage is small and unobtrusive and probably unnoticeable during deglutition.

ARMPITS

Neither axilla is deep and both are free from a vigorous growth of hair. Deposits of ammonium chloride and aluminium acetate evidence the use of a deodorant. A small developing keratosis lies just outside the right axilla, towards the right breast.

BREASTS

The mammae are both well-formed hemispherical eminences which have returned to the weight and dimensions previous to a period of lactation in 1953 (Dr Gordon Oswell, Middlesex Hospital). The left breast is a little larger than the right and this can be determined by careful visual observation. The conical nipples are raised on a non-existent fatty region and are opposite the fifth rib interspaces and are directed forwards, upwards and outwards. Both nipples give the appearance of having undergone mechanical excitation and of maintaining a full erection upon their raised areolae. This was apparently natural in the subject E. and a further apparent erection with a comparative hardening was possible — thus eliminating the probability of a spheroidal-celled cancer (Dr G. Oswell). The colouring of the nipples is very dark as is the surrounding areolae. About fifteen non-pigmented nodules, composed of raised sebaceous glands on each areola, are clustered round the base of each nipple as well as being scattered over the said integument. A few dilated veins radiate from each nipple. Prolapse is negligible.

Although the subject E. was concerned lest the growth of hair round the areolae was excessive, there is no evidence that she suffered from hypertrichosis of the breasts. The small amount of hair was kept depilated.

In 1953, the subject E. was the basis of a lecture at the Middlesex Hospital where both breasts were examined and E. demonstrated to the assembled doctors and students an almost excessive expression of colostrum corpuscles, together with an abundant fatty extrusion from the Montgomery glands (Dr Oswell). This excessive extrusion was more than sufficient to keep the whole of the integument bathed and protected whilst being sucked.

Recent albolene deposits on the mammae indicate a self-administered salve in order to counteract dryness.

Owing to a miscarriage in 1953, E. was a nullipara.

UPPER LIMBS

Neither have distinguishing features other than those listed under "Fat Distribution". Both carpals are somewhat thickened, but this is consistent with the subject's age. The hands are well cared for, the nails being neatly trimmed and coloured red. There is no evidence of a ring having been constantly worn.

UROGENITAL REGION

The urogenital cleft is covered with strong, crisp hair which extends from the posterior boundary of the vulva orifice, over the fatty collection of the mons veneris and upwards, evidencing by its strong growth and extended borders persistent depilation. There is, in this urogenital region and in the post-anal furrow, an almost excessive bronzing of the skin which one would normally associate with the later stages of cancer, but there is no evidence of this. The linea nigra, running up to the umbilicus along the mesial line, is very marked, broad and bronzed. There are some areas of striae albicantes on adjacent parts of the buttocks, thighs and below the umbilicus. These cicatrical indentations are consistent with abdominal distension during pregnancy.

The clitoris is well developed. A flattened vestibule, with a short sagittal cleft and the raised margins of the urethral orifice, is pierced by the mesial slit of the vaginal orifice. Traces of the small membranous fringe of the hymen remain as rounded elevations. The bodies of the bartholin glands, opening into the groove between the hymen and the labium minus, appear enlarged.

The interval between the posterior commissure and the anus is reduced to under one inch. This is probably due to the laceration of the perineum during childbirth when the subject E. was not placed in a correct lithotomy position and the parts exposed for accurate suturing; with the resulting consequences that only the anterior edges of the perineal body were thought to be implicated. This has resulted in a partial prolapse and might be the pointer to the rectal costiveness as reported to Dr Borges. There is no relaxation of the vaginal outlet.

There is evidence of albolene and ammonium acetate deposits in this urogenital area.

The uterus, measuring 13.5 x 10 x 7 cms, contains a foetus measuring 7 ems and weighing 29 gms. Placental, chorionic and decidual tissues are present. There is no blood in the vaginal vault nor is there evidence of seminal fluid or sperm in the vaginal secretions.

LOWER LIMBS

Both legs are well formed. The skin of the thigh, especially in the hollow of the groin, is thin, very smooth and elastic. It contains few hairs, except in the vicinity of the pubes. Towards the outside, the skin becomes thicker and the hairs more numerous. The skin over the buttocks is fairly thick, although soft, and has low vascularity. The buttocks are destitute of conspicuous hair except towards the anal furrow where a sparse growth is evident. The skin over the knee is covered by a thickened epidermis whilst that of the inner leg is thin and, prior to depilation, haired. Although the various fat distributions contribute greatly to the shape of the legs, the gracilis controls the outline of the upper, inner leg to a great degree, except when the adductor longus is activated and ridged.

The varicose condition of both legs is fair. A deterioration was aggravated by phlebitis during pregnancy (Dr Oswell), and by tight gartering during the years 1950-52 (Dr Borges).

The soles and heels of both feet have a great thickness of discoloured skin. The extent of the thickening of the stratum lucidum is such that the nails are extremely horny. Trimmed straight, all nails are painted red. There are indolent scaly patches between all toes of the right foot but these are not evidence of eczematoid ringworm.

In both feet, the inferior calcaneo-navicular ligaments have yielded, allowing the head of the astragalus to press downwards, inwards and forwards, causing pes-planus. This must have been apparent when the subject was bare-footed and standing. With the distension of the synovial sacs in both feet there is, combining with flat-footedness, bulging occurring posteriorly and fluctuating, thus causing a swelling on either side of the tendo-Achillis.

There is a contusion on the left shin, consistent with a fall.

ANALYSIS OF BRAIN TISSUE (Dr M. D. Shaw)

" . . . these comparative tables show that the concentration of potassium is significantly lower than would be normal, that the water content is higher and that there is a slight increase in the sodium content. The loss of chloride in comparison with the potassium loss is insignificant and in no way reflects that the patient was an alcoholic, as the sodium increase would have to be gross. I am therefore of the opinion that, because of the imbalance of electrolytes around and in the excitable tissue submitted for analysis, the subject was disturbed.

If at all possible, I would be very interested to know the level of cortisol in the plasma. Body weight would also be most helpful.

Etc.

P.S. I understand that Dr Gunter Veitch saw the patient prior to death and I would appreciate any information you may be able to elicit from him regarding mental state of patient prior to death, especially if Veitch thinks he/she was a depressive. If this can be done without exciting Borges, so much the better."

DISTINGUISHING MARKS

On the left leg, a transverse discoloration of the skin forming a dark brown nevus, measuring three inches by one inch, runs transversely between the legs. It is invisible from the front but is in evidence when viewed from the rear. It lies approximately one inch below the gluteal fold.

There are two small but deep cicatrices above the right eye —possibly the resulting scars of chicken pox contracted in 1932.

Partially hidden under the hair on the back of the neck is a large scar which may or may not be the result of a furuncle inexpertly lanced.

The only other cicatrix measures three-quarters of an inch and "brackets" the right-hand corner of the mouth; it is obliterated by make-up. This scar, according to Dr Urquhart, was the result of an accident in 1932 when the subject's father attempted to wrest a knife from her in order to prevent E. cutting herself(!)

(Apart from an unidentified illness in 1930, the following information was gleaned from the records of Doctors Urquhart, Borges and Veitch.)

1943. Dermatitis.

(This was due to the wearing of nickel-plated suspenders and, although serious, did not affect her eyes.)

1944. Parotitis epidemica.

(Besides inflaming and swelling the parotid gland, it also caused painful swelling and hardening of the breasts.)

1951. Influenza.

1960. Dysmenorrhea.

(Dr Borges also diagnosed paresthesia which affected her face at night prior to sleep and which he deduced as narcolepsy. Both he associated with a birth-control pill which E. had begun to take. He records that he advised her against this form of contraception.)

1962. Anxiety/cancer of womb.

(Dr Borges recalls that the patient refused examination and he referred her to P.G.H. for a cervical smear. He received no communication from either P.H.G. or the patient that this had been carried out.)

Also recorded in Dr Borges's notes is his conclusion that the subject E. suffered from acute agoraphobia which he evidenced by her obsessional use of curtaining material to cover her windows, tacking it securely onto the window frame (1963-64). Dr Gunter Veitch, with whom Dr Borges conferred, disagreed with this diagnosis, believing it was an attempt by E. to efface her sex completely. In a letter to Dr Borges, Veitch points out that he (Dr Borges) had overlooked the significance of the small opening E. had left in the curtaining and which he thought was evidence of her attempt to seal off her sex while leaving a small opening through which she might urinate.

Dr Borges did not pursue this correspondence but drew at the bottom of his letter a question mark enclosed within a circle.

In conclusion, examination of the stomach contents revealed that toast, marmalade and coffee were eaten prior to death, the manner of which is known to you.

COLLECT (7. iv.1964)

"Woe to him that is alone when he falleth; for he hath not another to help him up."
Ecclesiastes, Chapter 4, verse 10.

Leaning heavily on the chauffeur's rigid arm, Gloria Sansum, obscured beneath veils of mourning, stepped from the hired limousine. The chauffeur, his measured step matching her unwilling feet, his cap tucked respectfully beneath his arm, his leggings and boots brightly polished for the occasion, led the widowed woman dressed all in black towards the Norman gate.

Black? Gloria in black? She told me she would rather be dead than seen dressed in black — and Erowina made mention in her diary of a present of black underwear which Gloria had returned, underlining Gloria's aversion with thick strokes of her pen.

(I will romanticise the brief but telling entry — imagining pale Gloria stood on Erowina's familiar, tatty bedside rug, her naked chalk-white blotting up a spreading blush:

"I can't."

To which Erowina might have replied, "But you look delicious, dressed like that."

And poor Gloria, weeping to please in shaming, snappy black knickers and tight-bunching, satin-black bra, answering, "Nothing would induce me to wear such a shaming colour," while she palmed her sex and breasted her crooked arm.

"Don't be so silly, Gloria. Turn round," Erowina might have insisted. And Gloria would have turned — the black-laced frill ballerinaring, revealing the double crutch gusset and the diaphanous wisp ghosting her bum which would have looked pretty, but dead, like two slabs of putty.

"I'm sorry, darling, but I can't possibly wear them. I just can't." Sob. Sniff. And sniffing back real tears. "What must you think of me? I'm so ashamed. Especially as you went out of your way to buy them."

The clothes, I imagine, would have slid, whispering, and tumbled into an apologetic bundle round her pretty little feet. Naked, Gloria would have had tears running from her nose to her toes while she stood shivering.

"It was very sweet of you." Sniff. "But BLACK!" Sniff. "I should have told you." Sniff. "You see, dressed in black," sniff, "I feel like a dead tart!" And she would have burst into tears while she struggled back into her still warm clothes.)

THE PRIEST AND THE CLERKS MEETING THE CORPSE AT THE ENTRANCE OF THE CHURCHYARD, AND GOING BEFORE IT, EITHER INTO THE CHURCH, OR TOWARDS THE GRAVE, SHALL SAY OR SING, St. John X.I. 25, 26. Job XIX. 25, 26, 27. 1 Tim. VI. Job 1, 21.

Gloria, her pumice-stoned body shaved raw and tear-salted, mummied in sheer raven stockings with black gartered tops, fashionably knickered, bra'd and silk-slipped in black and dressed in a belted, ash-black frock and elbow-gloved in ash, tottered on her shiny, black patent courts and went clattering up the hollow aisle, the fresh pink of her fleshiness gloomed under a long veil of mourning. Sadly, the only gleam from the cringing woman was the slim gold cross stamped on the Bible-black Book of Common Prayer, its uncracked, thickly-glued spine wilting in her warm, crying palm: and a crush of white blooms.

AFTER THEY ARE COME INTO THE CHURCH, SHALL BE READ ONE OR BOTH OF PSALM XC. Domine, refugium, OR PSALM XXXIX, Dixi, custodiam.

Gloria, within her napped, shrouded gloom, pearled tears which dropped, splashing diamonds onto the white posy of flowers she kept tightly clutched to her soft, expiring bosom.

THEN SHALL FOLLOW THE LESSON TAKEN FROM THE FIFTEENTH CHAPTER OF THE FORMER EPISTLE OF SAINT PAUL TO THE CORINTHIANS.

Gloria, knuckling the puff of her red-rimmed eyes, wept while mucous strung her gaping mouth and her dull blocked nose exuded a swallowed thickness into her restricted throat.

"Come," I heard the chauffeur say when he drew the blind, widowed woman into the grey morning to stand knee-deep in mist. "Best get it over with."

WHEN THEY COME TO THE GRAVE, WHILE THE CORPSE IS MADE READY TO BE LAID IN THE EARTH, THE PRIEST SHALL SAY, OR THE PRIEST AND CLERKS SHALL SING: Man that is born of woman has but a short time to live and is full of misery.

Her manly crutch discreetly withdrawn and stood beneath a dripping tree, Gloria groped the air when the coffin settled uneasily into the bowels of the earth amongst the worms.

THEN, WHILE THE EARTH SHALL BE CAST UPON THE BODY BY SOME STANDING BY, THE PRIEST SHALL INTONE: Forasmuch as it has pleased almighty God of His great mercy to take unto Himself the soul of our dear sister here departed . . .

Gloria, her cheeks smeared and rubbed black with dribbled mascara, pitched forward into the gaping hole below her, mouthing a silent grief.

Even as her cobwebbed veil streamed in the dampening wind, the red-raw hands of the startled clerks pinched into her trembling flesh and re-strained her. "We therefore commit her body to the ground; earth to earth, ashes to ashes, dust to dust; in the sure and certain hope of the resurrection to eternal life, through our Lord Jesus Christ."

THEN SHALL BE SAID OR SUNG: I heard a voice from heaven, saying unto me, Write, From henceforth blessed are the dead which die in the Lord.

The goose-fleshed priest, his chilblained finger warmly book-marking the heart-learned litany clasped to his chest, turned his watery eyes to heaven.

"Lord, have mercy upon us."

The ramrod clerks, awkwardly grasping the groaning widow, stared in alarm at the breaking earth beneath their Sunday shoes; earth which crumbled and fell drumming onto the coffin lid, deep in the damp clay pit.

"Christ, have mercy upon us," they repeated in unison, almost forget-ting.

Gormun and I lit up a fag each. The chauffeur refused with a shake of his head and a disapproving frown.

"Lord, have mercy upon us. Our Father."

And the clerks heaved on the limp, wailing, grieving, weeping widowed blonde wilting between them (pleasurably alarmed by her soft plumpness, I hoped).

"And lead us not into temptation; but deliver us from evil. Amen."

"Amen."

"Almighty God, with whom do live the spirits of them that depart hence in the Lord . . ."

The mad widow, grieved beyond endurance, made one last effort and jumped into a scream, dragging the clerks with her — and they disap-peared.

The priest, helpless and entangled in ceremony, forgot the Collect — God forgive him — and finished at a gallop.

"The grace of our Lord JesusChristandtheloveofGodandthefellow-shipoftheHolyGhostbewithusallevermoreAmen," and offered his open hand to the grave.

From deep within the black hole came a single, muffled response.

"Amen."

And the clay-streaked clerks, tumbled from their dignity, tried to heave out the mad widow between them.

The chauffeur, settling his cap, picked his way through the clay lumps. Self-assured, muscular and masterful, he gripped the widow and pulled.

The gravedigger, picking at his dirt-filled nails, watched from his discreet vantage point behind the mildewed tree. He saw, and heard, as did we all, the black material of the widow's dress slowly rent and a gleaming, naked thigh, thistle-downed with golden hair, slap wide as, screaming and kicking, the widow was dragged from the collapsing grave.

And we watched in silence while the pinioned widow was led to the limousine, heard the door clunk shut and stared while the car rolled noiselessly away from the kerb; in the back an occupant oblivious of the world and the all-seeing, mirrored eyes of a chauffeur scheming a lecherous comfort for the mad widow Gormun and I knew as Gloria Sansum.

Our fags trodden out, we caught on the slight breeze the whispered conversation of the priest and grimed clerks who were stood beneath the silent bell tower.

"Are you sure you weren't mistaken? She was hardly in control of her faculties."

"I'm only repeating what Gordon and I heard her say, minister."

"In that case, I will have to make enquiries."

HERE IT IS TO BE NOTED, THAT THE OFFICE PRECEDING IS NOT TO BE USED FOR ANY THAT DIE UNBAPTISED, OR EXCOMMUNICATE, OR WHO HAVE LAID VIOLENT HANDS UPON THEMSELVES.

Gormun and I, the pubs not yet open, hung back and watched the gravedigger, his task of filling the grave almost completed, accidentally step onto the small bunch of white flowers which the blonde, hysterical woman dressed in black had dropped. He examined the crushed posy and threw it into the grave, covering it with earth.

The mound finally raised, and the lumps of clay tidied, the gravedigger picked up a wreath of flowers from a grave nearby and laid it with reverence on Erowina's grave.

When he walked away, trailing his spade, Gormun and I approached to pay our respects to the woman we both loved.

The inscription on the wreath which had been laid on her grave read: "To Fred. A Captain straight and true. From his fellow team mates at the Chepstow Black Bull Darts Club." It was signed Tim Fitch, Harry Willis, Allen Allen, Alf Coe, Marshy, Jumbo and A. E. Backler.

"The joke is lost on her."

"It always was," said I, meaning life was one long, grim joke, not that Erowina lacked a sense of humour.

And I thought of her lying in the coffin embedded in sawdust to absorb an excessive discharge. I tried to imagine what she looked like with the top of her cranium taped to her cheeks and her brain cavity stuffed with newspaper. It would be ironic if Doctor Carter had used Sunday newspapers to fill the cavity, and I reminded myself to ask him. He told me he had put her brain and what was left of her womb into her jumbled intestines, after his post-mortem examination, and closed the crude incision with loops of coarse cat gut. He could have spared me the details but as I had asked him for others, he no doubt thought I had the stomach for it, myself having been a sawbones, once.

"I wish I'd glimpsed her before she was screwed in," sniffed Gorm.

"Better it is you contemplate the headstone we propose setting up," says I. "And he'll have begun."

He had. In a cluttered yard two miles from the church, a humming stonemason had already bent to his task with chisel and mallet. The inscription he had been commissioned to carve upon a fine white marble headstone lay at his feet. Written in longhand on a piece of paper torn from an exercise book and weighted with a chip of marble to prevent it being blown away, it read:

<pre>
                 E R O W I N A
                    ICAME
                    AMONG
                    YOUAS
                    ASTRA
 1927   NGERA   1964
                    NDYOU
                    DIDNO
                    TMAKE
       MEWELCOMEBUTCASTSTONESATMYHEADICAME
       AMONGYOUASASTRANGERSEEKINGHELPBUTYO
       UTURNEDMEFROMYOURDOORICAMEAMONGYOUA
                    SASTR
                    ANGER
                    ANDFI
                    NDING
                    NOONE
                    ITURN
                    EDTOO
                    THERS
                    TRANG
                    ERSWH
                    OWERE
                    KNOCK
                    INGAT
                    YOURD
                    OORSA
                    NDWEP
                    ASSED
                    THROU
                    GHYOU
                    RCITY
                    CURSI
                    NGFOR
                    GIVEU
                    SEACH
                    ANDEV
                    ERYON
                    EOFYO
                    UAMEN
</pre>

THE BLACK SWAN WAKE (*7.iv.64*) *or* THE TEMPTATIONS OF ST. GORMUN

> "... and the women they* seduced shall become sirens."
> *The First Book of Enoch*

* Angels who laid with women and whose spirits, assuming various forms, defiled man and led them astray.

— God rest her soul, says I.

— Not forgetting the dear ones.

— Their grieving.

— So young.

— And for why? WHY? (I am given to questioning.)

— Don't fret so, Tammy, says he. Another?

Tam(me) drains my thimble glass.

— She couldn't have cast herself off Leucas, could she? Eh? And dragged that wretched Gongyla with her. (Which was proof I'd dipped her diaries, but not that I despised the blonde Gloria. Which I didn't.)

— Charity, Tam.

— Why couldn't she have mingled her blood with Sappho's on some God-forsaken shore, eh? But did she? No. She went and did it wid an owd pin!

Gormun looks inside his empty pint pot, up-ends it and sucks out the last little dribble.

— WID AN OWD PIN POKED IN HER EAR! I screams.

Gormun rises.

— Same again, Quirk, and he lays an unnecessary, sympathetic, comforting hand on my shoulder. (Or was it between my blades he sank the dagger?)

— A pint, Mister O'Connor?

Gormun fingers his red neck.

— From the barrel. And yourself?

— That's kindness, Mister O'Connor. A bobsworth it is, then.

Mr Quirk, the tenant landlord of the Black Swan these past three and twenty years, helps hisself to two fingers of cold tea from a Jamieson bottle. And turns round.

— One and two and two. Three and two. And, one shilling. Four and two.

Ting.

The cash register crashes open. Change taken. And is pushed shut, rattling ting.

— What's grieving Tammy? says he, as if I was nowhere to be seen.

I spy a conspiring finger raised to Gormun's hushing lips and watch the gathering of loose change.

— Bad news, is it? Quirk asks, absentmindedly shining the mahogany with his damp tea towel.

— Aye, says Gormun, watching the polishing.

— I noticed the parsley set in the brim and wondered why you chose the form. Close, is it?

A slow blinked nod.

— Sad. Very sad Tammy's a man who could do with the luck a lump of coal would bring.

— Misfortune comes in threes.

— So they say.

— Pity he couldn't get the feel of a red-haired donkey's prick.

— A phallus charm would do.

— Aye.

— It's sad, though.

— 'Tis.

— Your health, Mister Quirk.

— Good health to you, Mister O'Connor. To that warm heart of yours.

A cold tea toast, a lip-smacked mime and: It's times like these, Mister O'Connor. In times of need.

— I know my duty, Mister Quirk.

— It's easy to recognise a friend in you, Mister O'Connor.

— Happen I'm the only one.

— That you are. I cannot recollect the wake bench so bare.

— Aye, just the two of us to skull the skiff.

Gormun carries the two glasses to the long bench, places them between us and, sitting, draws his mac close about him.

— Happen you know how long it is? says I.

— Since when?

— Since I bloody lived with her!

Gormun shrugs his shoulders.

— Eight years, it is.

— Eight! That's a long time, Tam.

— It seems like only yesterday.

Gormun winds his watch, downs a copious draught and proffers his open packet of Sweet Afton.

— Ta. I loved her, Gormun.

— After eight years, loving pales. (Says he, lusting still these fifteen years.)

Gormun's match flares at the second strike.

— Two thousand. Eternity. What does it matter? I loved her. And do.

To my lasting shame, I begin to weep and have to resort to my handkerchief for a good owd blow.

Honk.

— I'm sure you did.

— I did! And does. No one knows better than I. (I trumpet again.) And shall, till I die. (Accompanying m'self on double nose flute. Sniff. Sniff. And cornet. Honk.)

Mick MacCoym, settled in the corner, lifts his watery eyes to heaven and his mouth drops open.

Honk. Honk.

Quirk, glass polishing, glances up at the tinkling chandelier. From the look in his eye, an inappropriate, over sentimentalised lamentation, he thinks. The sod.

Honk.

Patrick — Polly to some — MacDonald, a concussed light heavyweight, corkscrews slowly on his own owd chair, dribbling.

— It came from under the door, Guv'nor, says Mick, pointing. I felt it. (Raising his eyebrows and nodding.) That's what did it. That's what set it tinkling, says he, leaning backwards and looking upwards.

— I hope you're right, Mister MacCoym. The brewery wouldn't take kindly to having it come down because of a sneeze or a good owd blow (glancing at me and polishing.)

— I know'd it was a draught. It cut right across here. Mick chops his left leg off just below the knee. Come in sharp, it did. Like it was whistled up. And then. Up it went. That's what set it janglingling.

— Very odd. At a wake, too.

— Queer. Never know'd it afore — 'cepting when Old Ma Mead's ghosted daughter haunted Perseverance cellar.

— Not you too!

— I know'd what I seen with me own eyes, Mister Quirk. I sin her. Marina. Like she was flesh and blood. Naked as the day she was born, with a cleft you could finger.

— And the rope round her neck, I suppose.

— Did I say? But I tell you this. There was the same howling draught. Like a knife it was. Like just then. It's omnious. I say it's omnious, Mister Quirk.

Sniff.

— GOR!

Gormun, listening with his other ear, turns.

— Sorry, Tam. I was far away. Journeying. What was you saying? And with his little finger he pokes about in his right ear, removes some wax and studies it before wiping it along the bench.

— That's unwise, says I.

— There was a draught, Tam. Like a whisper.

— The wise voyager retains his deafening wax, it helps him resist temptation. And memories can tempt just as assuredly as sireens. (And I pause for the warning to permeate into his noggin.) It's a likeness I haven't, says I, changing the subject, thinking his noggin permeated.

— What are you on about? says he.

— I meant, says I, to have stolen a likeness from her bureau. (Erowina's body removed from the flat, I had burgled her room of a tin trunk containing, I thought, all of her diaries.)

— Is it criminal you've become of a sudden?

— It is not, but my visual recollections are distorted, Gormun. Vague . . . The edges blurred. If I had something to refer to. Something to strait-jacket my fanciful memories. To sharpen them.

— Eh?

— A snapshot.

— O.

And Gormun is reminded of

What?

EROWINA, WHO, BEING WITHOUT SHAME, DID TEMPT AND INFLAME HIS DESIRES BY ALLOWING HERSELF TO BE EXHIBITED IN INDECENT POS-TURES?

(Soft Gormun tells me everything.)

— Where did you go grubbing for this? says he, holding between his sweaty palms the cheeks of a female arse.

— I took them.

— This!

(A 10 x 8 inch print with a matt finish, taken on H.P.S, film with an aperture of f/16 and a shutter speed of 1/100, it is the rear presentation of a female, wearing only gartered stockings, lying prone on a candlewick bedspread, her face turned away from the camera.)

— I didn't know you were interested in — well, photography, says he, his eyes glued to:

No. 2. A rear presentation of a naked female; kneeling.

— I thought I might take it up seriously at one time.

— Whose . . . erm? says he, boggling at:

No. 3. The same presentation as No. 2 but of anal interest only.

— Can't you guess?

— No, says he, unable to think who'd. As in:

No. 4, in which the female model was reclining on her back with her legs apart, but with her face obscured by a raised arm.

— I don't know any women who'd willingly . . .

— Look at the next one.

In No. 5, the naked female model, her stockings rolled down to her knees, lay on her back. Using her fingers she was exposing her sex to the camera lens and looking straight at him — the viewer.

— EROWINA!

Disbelief. And another look.

IT WAS!

— But, says he, his heart thundering madly while he gazes and is carried into the realms of erotic disbelief by photograph number six. And number seven. And eight.

— But what?

And he shuffles them against his chest, not daring further.

— I'd never have thought that . . .

— Erowina? She's no different from the rest of them. They jump at the chance, he said, poking Gormun in the chest with his finger. Can't wait for them to be developed so's they can have a good butchers at themselves. Now. What about it? A quid the set.

But the images were already implanted and the terror had started.

— Ten bob, then?

— You're a pig, Pazzeroni, says he, tearing them in half. Into quarters. Into eighths and letting them fall. There's your erotic confetti for the two you've just wedded into shame. And God help you!

Miss Alice Ketyler, born Kilkenny, baptised Canice but from Galmpton and Dittisham, pokes her head round the door marked PUBLIC. She spies me (Tam).

— How's me owd Robin? she hisses.

— O. Firm and frisky, Kitty, says I, wiping a moist eye, but fattening and plumping under me idle celibacy these long years. She gives a toothless smile, does old Kitty. And.

Quirk pretends not to see or hear while she shuffles in.

— Tam, me love, says she, humping her willow basket onto her creaking hip and leaning on her ferulled blackthorn. I'm still vestal. (Giving her gold finger a good suck and holding it out towards me.) Look. Now'er ring, Tam. And, in a piping, childish, pleading voice, with her head to one side and an impish look in her old eye, A pin for your button?

She holds up a tiny flower from her basket.

— Goodness. A vinca minor!

— A pretty periwinkle, kind Tam?

— Not one, Kitty, nor two, but a garland, madam, if you please. A blue necklace to wear while I mount the scaffold of my misery and to hide the burns of my punishment. (Sniff.) But am I not reprieved since I chanced to meet thee, Kitty vestal? Mmm? No matter. Memory still pains because I set the very same posies 'bout the joyless river, my love and I furrowed upon our bleak mattress those eight years ago. And all to no avail.

— At five shillings. And. Leaning closer to gain the privacy of my ear. If it's gone she is, more than these three months — there's little I can do.

— Do?

— I saw the abortificent set in the brim. . . .

— Eh? Oh, putting my hand up to my fanny hat. Ha-Ha. A misunderstanding. Differing crafts, my dear. I am bereaved these several days. But what have we here? says I, poking about in her basket.

— Nowt but what the itchy spouse won't brew to belay the watchfulness of her suspicious mate. Hey? (Giggling and nudging me.)

— So I see. Sarothamnus scoparius. Good. Mercurialis perennis; frangula alnus; ranunculus ficaria; arum maculatum; convallaria majalis; hyoscyamus niger. Atropa belladonna! Ye gods! Solanum dulcamara; colchicumautumnale — pretty verbals that; conium maculatum; datura stramonium; ranunculus bulbosus; daphne mezereum; euphorbia lathyrus — no Christ-thorn? Tut, tut. Laburnum anagyroides; helleborus viridis; AND foetidus! Phew! A veritable willow of poisons old Kitty.

— And who let you in, Petronilla?

— Meadowsweet, Mister Quirk, or a celandine for your button? Pick and choose, turning to him pretending not to have heard the insult.

— Off with you, Cowslip, and take your dried charmings back to Dittiglamptonbury where they still basket their babies.

— Fie on you, Quirky. FIE! says she, cursing and gesturing with her physician finger.

— Don't you come the dirty. Shoo! cries Quirk.

Kitty holds out a limp bunch of budding curly doddies.

— A shilling.

— Be off with you. Pest some other shuvly-kouse!

— Sixpence, then?

— Out!

— What about some butterbur, Mister Quirk? Or a posy of field penny cress? I've got dwale, throat wort, Bear's-foot or St Anthony's turnip. What about a twist of tamarisk; or setterwort? No? Black Bryony then, or earth-nut. I've got goose-grass, spurge olive. Naked ladies? Or wind flower? A tansy nosegay? What about a chaplet of loose strife, Mister Quirk?

— Off with you, Miss Kitty, before I call the police!

— Meadowsweet for a bright new shilling?

— Will — you — get — out! You old witch!

Stretching out my arm, I tug the flapping rags covering her brittle arm.

— Here, says I, in a moment of generosity.

— Yow're me owd Cock Robin, Tam Tiddly, says she, kissing the coin and hawking up her creaking basket onto her old hard hip. You're me Robin, Tam, bless yu.

Putting a tiny nosegay aside my booze, she hobbles towards the door marked PUBLIC and eases herself and her basket out into the street.

— You're cursed, Quirk, says Gormun with wilding eyes. Pointing downwards.

Quirk shrugs.

— She throwed it down deliberate.

— Scrophularia nodosa, says I.

— Someone'll heel that into yow flur and yow'll stink f'weeks.

Another shrug.

Sniff. S-N-I-F-F.

— A-sa-foetida, says I, finding my nose prickling again.

Sniff. Sniff.

— I can't smell nothin'. And Quirk picks up a glass.

The unlovely publican of the Mourning Swan, before he huffs, spies the idiot mute pawing the bottom of the unpolished pint pot. He lowers his singular binocular and looks across. From Polly MacDonald's open, dribbling mouth come silent screams.

— Ecod! says Quirk aloud, plonking down the glass. Polly! Deuce take you! What is it you're getting yourself into? (Flipping up part of the mahogany against its rubber stop. Pointing.) Just what is it you think you're doing? Eh? (Still pointing.) There'll be no more Tuesdays for you. (Wagging his pointer as he walks.) No more boozedays.

Quirk eases MacDonald round in his chair and wipes his nose for him. Looking into his dull, bruised eyes, it is paternal Quirk who says:

— 'Bout time you could blow it like owd Tam-Tam, ain't it? Mmm? pushing the untouched drink nearer. Now, stay put. Don't go dashing about again. Or. (Tap.) Or else. (Tap. Tap.) Elsie. Understand? (Tap, tap.) I won't let her bring you again. (Sniff. Nod.)

— Good.

As he walks back to the bar he hears Gormun say:

— Pretty.

I answer with an: Aye. (Sniff.) A lovely. (Sniff.) Woman. (Sniff.) Beautiful.

— She was that.

— And dignified. Full of dignity.

— O. Aye.

But Gormun remembers.

What?

EROWINA WHO, UPON NEARING THE END OF HER JOURNEY, DID TEMPT HIM BY HER UNASHAMEDNESS?

She had turned blood-red in the tail light. Her thighs fat while she squatted, baring her warm arse over the damp grassed verge of Phelim Rumball's parsley garden.

Couched in the nodding, knowing eyes of the unblinking, kissing briar roses, erotically garlanding her stretching bum, she'd spoke:

— Never seen a woman about her business?

— You might have had the goodness . . . a little further off . . .

— I don't mind you gawping. And a liddle giggle. Gawping Gormun.

The sounds of a leaking hose and, staring into the thundered darkness, bound to his masted urge waiting for the last littlelittle-widdledrip to drop. And yes. But!

Another car went hushing past on the glistening macadam; lights bright; and seeing.

— Hurry!

— O, let them see. Then. Tucking up cumfy. Fingering elastic. Snap. And, shrugging down her voluminous skirt, Start the barque, Gorprude.

— It's not that.

— Doesn't Penelopee? Ever?

— Never.

The windscreen-wipers polished the crystal image of his iquatting desire, flicking the pearling, glittering drizzle.

— Never?

— Never ever.

— O. Well. Now you know. Home.

O, Fionnghuala, my faithless Me-O-My.

— Mmm?

Gormun shakes his head and Pan, his son, the fleshly sperm of Penny's six suitors, screams his presence while Cilla yelps — snapping at the tyres.

Gormun, remembering, wipes his mouth with the back of his hairy hand. And sups.

— And educated. She'd had education. Grm.

— She was not ignorant.

— Came from a good family.

— Not wishing to give offence, but she spoke with a plum in her mouth.

— She did that. But she was an innocent, despite her breeding. I said, she'd a child's innocence.

— She was sweetness itself.

— A more shy and retiring woman I never knew. (Sniff.) An innocent. (Sniff. Sniff.) Chaste, she was. AND decorous.

— Modest?

— O, decidedly.

— Yes.

But Gormun, his mind full of the past, remembers.

What?

EROWINA WHO, AT THE ENDING OF A PARTICULAR NIGHT, DID TEMPT HIM BY HER LICENTIOUSNESS?

Pazzeroni told me when.

Safe from the cold, black, Monday night; kitchened and boozily elbowed and sat fat; dog-end doodling yesterday's breakfasted-sauce and crunching brittled gammon rind. And. Occasionally belching John J. Tollemache and Cobbald light gasiness and drinking quantities more. And laughing. And hysterical. And with imagination unlimited and daring.

— Cummun. Fur O'g, then?

— Barney — you old goose you, the white, red-eared hound sets up a howl under the table, alerting the Gabriel Ratches, who knock on the ceiling.

— Down, beast! Even he wants to see it, and he kicks. The knocking stops.

— I must be going.

— You stay where you are. You're going to see something, the likes of which . . .

— Gorm doesn't want to see.

— 'Course he does. Cummun, Erowina. Show O'Gorm your O'Quim.

— No, really. But the chair is scraped back.

— Cummun.

Then:

— Only a don't touch look. And.

Hem to her chin she. Jeeeesus. Down with her panties and. Out with her small little, black little, fluffy little, tight-clammed, mole-holed skin purse.

A lid blinked gawp and:

— An owd bum for owd Gorm . . .

— For you, you mean. So.

Two facefuls of juddering pink-white flush.

— How's that for an owd Gorbum, eh? And he slaps it.

Cilia yelps.

She turns. And.

Going going.

She ups with her pants and drops her hem, sits on it; spilling her drink.

— Satisfied now, you two?

— How's that compare with Penelope's Boy-O?

O, Fionnghuala, my faithless, Me-O-My.

— Leave him be, Giacopo.

But he couldn't tell if she'd understood his humiliation.

Gormun drains his glass, glances up at me and swallows down a memory. (I read him like a book.)

— I know I romanticise, says he.

— That you do, says I.

— Some consider it a weakness.

— Some is too hard of heart.

— Aye.

— Not me, says I.

— You are an illusionist, Tam, says he.

Pleased with himself, he thumbs the arm-holes of his wescott; not daring to thumb his nose.

Quirk, a teacloth over his shoulder, walks over to pat me on the hack. Gently.

— My condolences, Tammy-O.

— Thank you, Mister Quirk, says I. Thank you very much. But a correction, if I may be allowed. Your Church tells me it is the dead herself who will be wanting our sympathy.

— It's my prayers she has.

— Then direct them to the seventh level, Mister Quirk, wherein she has taken root and become a gnarled and twisted tree with branching limbs whereon brute harpies nest.

— That's scribbler's talk, says Quirk, raising an admonishing finger. It ill becomes a man to misuse God's gift. Shame on you, Tam.

— Would you have her tormented by eternally falling flakes of flame, Mister Quirk?

— I'd have her rest in peace. God rest her soul.

— And have it speed on sandy wings?

— To what are you alluding?

— The Culcus Canorus — according to Linnaeus. Mopsus, I mean.

— What blasphemy's this?

— Of the family Cuculidae. Pardon. Family Caenus. Or was it (Caenis? No matter. I am become brilliant all of a sudden. (Narrowly avoiding knocking my glass to the floor.)

Gormun, apprehensive, starts to wash his hands with a:

— We'll be obligated, Mister Quirk. At your convenience. No hurry, you understand.

Quirk bends uncommonly low.

— On the house, Mister O'Connor.

— That's kindness.

— Think nothing of it. In times like these . . .

My thimble glass drained, Quirk proceeds to the far side of the mahogany with dignified solemnity.

Says I to Gormun: And do you know what awaits us, Norman O'Gorman? Eh?

No response.

— We will be condemned to swim perpetually — in a river of blood . . .

— I'll be content to leave me empty boots on the banks of the river Lethe, Tam-Tam.

— . . . watched over by centaurs armed with arrows. That's what awaits us, Gurnom.

— Why should we be damned? Weren't we always kindness and love? Filled with respect for her? Weren't we? I was.

— We clayed her to death. Ajaxed her, we did.

— Balls.

— Not with them, O'G. We did not a-sex her. It was with bloodless words, Gormun O'Gormo. Bloodless words did for her, long ago. Like clay wedges thrown onto captive kings, they left no scars but killed her as assuredly as a thrusting sword. And that we did, Grunmo. With words.

— Not me.

— No. You did it with bloodhound eyes and knotted tongue.

— I respected her!

— So did I! So did I. But I should have sheathed my words, Gumron, not used them to fence and parry. It was I who worked that pin into her gristle.

— You shouldn't be blaming yourself, Tammy-O, says Gormun, rubbing his stubbled chin.

— Oh, but I do.

— Your mouth knows not an unkind word, Tam-Tam. And, poor soul, she heard none. Not from you.

— Your ignorance is your charm, Gomrun. And best it is you remain untutored, my faithful, likeable, loveable, innocent friend. Gormun inspects his nails and stands.

— I must go piddle.

— Then I shall accompany you, Grumon, for my back teeth are awash with the drowning of my sorrows in so much grain. Let us descend. Back for part two in a moment Quirk, says I.

Quirk acknowledges our departure with a nod and tops up his glass with cold tea.

Confronted with a row of empty, evil-smelling stalls in the damp, subterranean urinal, I command Gormun to: Choose, Onmurg, and gesture regally.

Gormun acknowledges my patronage with a bow.

— Right of centre pleases. And, advancing, reads: WOY LIK HER ARSE.

— Ah, anagraman.

— A nagaram?

Nodding and looking.

— Are you with me, Mr O'Gun? says I.

— An anagram.

— Exactly. In a in year of war after the setting gun of Ramanag Cairo, a hungry sergeant rat writ the legend, KILROY WAS HERE.

— O.

— And thus established, for some unknown and obscure reason, a universal fat frogi.

— Fat? O! Graffito.

— Exactly. Gif farto.

— Done. Wherewerewe-wee? Oh, yes. Speaking of fat frogs. I see the lounge lizards have been using this vivarium to slough their skins.

— So I observe. But middle-class men have always equated spawning with pissing. They speak of off-loading their dirty water into the house-wife of their choice.

— Married to a urinal.

— Unfortunately. Does old blind bob know where he is in this dark hell hole?

— He does. Under an exhortation to follow a line of arrows up. And up. And up to. Unbuttoning. To a brief Joe Miller in 3b which informs me that having followed these directions I should, by now, be venting into my footwear.

— I am more fortunate, says I, standing left of centre and confronting the green, mildewed wall. O'er my piscina, a legend in modern ball-point assures me I will contract a carnal obligation with one Jaqueline — in brackets (Pussy) — Regalo. Regalo? Galore, surely.

— Undoubtedly.

— Of three hundred and ten, Sunderland Place, Slough, any Friday night after the hour of six. And, mark you, not for Peter's pence or peppercorn rental, but free, gratis and without obligation.

— A female heart which gold despises?

— It's up to us to nail that lie, Gonrum.

— Fridays, you say?

— After six on Fishday.

— I will keep Fryday free.

— Hark, tho'. Her attraction, so the legend would have us believe — and confirmed by several signatories — is her capability of engorging and retaining within her gunny-sack the mythical yard and a half!

— Perhaps the two of us . . . together?

— A baker's dozen would barely satisfy this faggot's heated oven. Apparently, she likes being bottled and only melts when her muff is dived or when she's tittie oggied.

— Divine.

— According to one Able Seaman Sammy King — who has sketched an enlightening but unskilful portrayal of his extraordinary weapon — he has already urged upon the said Jaqueline his monstrous tool but she failed to accommodate it in its entirety. Which does not surprise me. However. This said Jack Tar refuses to be thwarted and advertises in no uncertain manner for a companion — of either sex — who will undertake the Herculean task of accommodating his elephantine meat engine.

— Behind the behind.

— Dogways, Yes. He is also willing, is our verbose Tar, to grease the palm of anyone who can provide him with a satisfactory telephonic numeral which would. But here it seems his plumbago broke, was wore wooden or else, importuned, he was no longer rudderless.

— Possibly by my fair Esra.

— Palindromically speaking?

— No, no. Her likeness accompanies an indelible pot-hooked and hangered text.

— Describe.

— Well, this purple Esra, with the surname Isaacs . . .

— Has been cross cut.

— Pardon?

— Has had the little boy in her boat topped. — Don't interrupt.

— Proceed.

— Her form graces and illuminates a minimum multum parvo.

— Excellent. Describe.

— She has deformed legs, a grinning death's head and remarkable upstanding, lying down diddies and a veritable playing field of short and curly invested with purpureal gleams which . . .

— Sticks to facts, Grm. Leave the poetry to me.

— I pass then.

— I am. Have. Did. Almost.

— The last littlediddle.

— There's the dif-fic-cul-ty.

— A knocking post, perhaps?

— Brrrrrrrr! says I, shuddering while I button. Winter is icumen in. A pencil please. (No response.) Gormun. A pen-cil. IF you please.

— Never.

— That is why I will. A pencil. The muse is upon me.

— I will not lend myself, says he.

— Damn it, Gormun! I've waited a lifetime! A pencil!

— No.

— I should have a stub about me. Somewhere. In one of my poc-ket-me-nots. HA. Ah-ha! The very one when saw I the trimmed-oak death of the denuded King and gleed with Cerridwen on a ghosted, moon-lit page. Perhaps again. Perhaps. (I turn and search the wall for space.) Blodeuwedd, dear heart, from the look of things, I fear we are crowded from this far bank o'er the trilling stream by innumerable un-niceties. Turning. Stand aside, Norgum swine. Behind you is space enough for the eye of the turning buttoner. Thank you. Now. Sniff. Sniff. Phew! These mephitic fumes could well induce an appropriate, paranoiac trance and be substitute for an acorn munch. Aside, swine.

— Tammy!

— Huish. Observe genius at work.

And I write the following on the wall of the lavatory while Gormun overlooks my shoulder.

> This is an open lecher to Piss Onawhoresnipple and Moist Whore-shitful Nare of Basewhoresdaughter and to the Allhercum and Cuntslitwhores of the Copulation and fur the atitshewn of Mr Quirk (Master Bates' son) Handwhored of the Bollock Swung Pubic Louse, and anybugger wrinkle-testicled Genitalcum.

I then drew a line. So.

It arse been broad to my notits that squirmtongue nateworthy shittybums of this cumonhertitty have taken tit upin theirarseholes to pricktickly cover the hole of the balls of our Pubic Comeventyourarses with vulvar whiporkissbums, nude cockcondums and prickchewers of inthiscrapwhoreshole underherscentedtittys. Knock yoni are these scrublingams both feelthigh and whorerubaball — cuntsquirming all mammae of suckyouranal pertwhorestittys, but they also incest that hairyarsed, thisquimlicked peepull will, if cuntshagtit, fartinhisnate in semenlar acts of cunnygamornibble breastlyness. Dames and Oddarses, as smell as Toolorhorn Numbarse, are gammhim of these insuckpricktongue, quimmyscent peppill. In so fuck as their arse a sorequim a-mount of trussfullness in the prodaballlightly that a myrawtitty of squityzones may, for horn wee know, cuntduct thumbelles likevice in the privvy of their homos, slit kiss not, acockhardening to our pisscent whores, laygirl to oddvirginties in suckaway on the balls of our Comeventyourarses. Bott, this navel not be so in the fuckher. In the mantime, propaps wee cum circumcise these whores. Tits only a gash in the park, butt nif the haveashag ferkin man toolinhernates it, why snot the upher-arse genitalcum? I keep foreskin myself. Lick it or thump it, tits very niffycunt to rape an abreast or to prostitute these suspenders — so why bugger? Crotch pongs me to the point of my lickher — bitch kiss, a comesuckhernipple rudenudeview cod be gammed from these muchchewedturdinherarse oddvicebums which arse at proscent titssplayed in our Cuntsold Labiahairies and in the hairyarse Pubic Louse Lesbianfairies. Under the horsepisses of the Carnal, a discharge could be maid of freeponce a turd or sexslottingles and whorepence a paragraffitti. I tossamate that, by this pimple pissinhis-lick puporshiton, the pisscent thigh nates could, much to the shagherquim of some members of the Corkhermotion no doubt, be cuntslitinherbelly real-juiced. I kink, in fucked I'm whore, that these cuntdriplotions would become bugger and frigher arse time pisses. A Bawd of Cuntsores or an ajuicyclitor is not ascenttool for the sucksexual organinhisbum of this motion; although it would be french letter to knobinnate a rubponcesnipple man for the toss off orgasmiscoming and fornicating a workaball plan — becoarse there are bound to be harlot of wangers on. Funanally, I fartwhore propuss that I be arsesinged to the knob of undertickling this wank of pubic bummyfuckedwhore.

Written this Seevent of Aprick, Nudeteenagers and Sexy-whore. Tummy.

Having written, I turn to Gormun.

— How say, Numrog?

— You've dated it wrongly. Should be May. I'd have thought you would have twigged. It's Ascension Day.

— God speed the flight of her soul! I was forgetting, says I.

— You're drunk, says he. And fancy putting your name to a work of dirt. We'll have Quirk nosying for the worry of us if we delay longer. Come on.

We emerge into the light of the Public Bar.

— I was beginning to wonder 'bout you two.

— Don't, says I. Your pencil, Gumron.

— Not mine, says he.

— Have you been scribbling filthies on my walls again?

— Again? says I, hurt to the quick by Quirk.

— Again.

— Don't pretend annoyance, Quirky.

— But I've got to buy the whitewash!

— One day, Quirky, you'll preserve that wall and create a legend from the fact that, once upon a time I, Mace Lamlin, scribbler extraordinary, was, like Kilroy — here. (Finger pointing to the quarry tiles to emphasise.) Charge a bob a knob. You'll make a fortune. Think of it, Quirky. Rich beyond your imaginings — all because you were too mean to buy a bucket of whitewash. HA!

— Ha, nothing, Here's your drinks.

And Quirk, carrying a red tin tray on which, after I and Gormun have seated ourselves.

— With respects, Tammy,

a glass of whisky.

— Gratefully accepted.

— And your health, Mister O'Connor.

a pint of porter

— To your respectable house, Mister Quirk.

and a tot of salubrious amber tanin were once balanced.

The beer drips off the round tray tucked under Mr Quirk's arm. He raises his glass of Jamieson amber tea.

— My condolences, Mister Lamlin. And downs it with a lip-smacked, screwed-eyed swallow; Quirk's Command Performance. And: Don't hesitate, Tammy. After all these years . . .

A raised hand, a lowered head and:

— You're very kind.

— When a friend . . .

— Say no more.

The least said.

— True, Mister O'Connor. Very true. What the ear never hears . . . (And he smells his nails.) The heart never misses.

— True.

— Well, now, and Quirk slaps his stomach. That's warmed me.

— It has?

— Wards off the cold, does whisky. And cold it is. Bin a terrible winter.

— Don't remind me.

— Winter doesn't suit you, Mister O'Connor?

— One particular winter didn't. I aged that winter.

— Did you, now?

— I did.

And Gormun recalls a momentous occasion when ("and you'll not believe me, Tammy")

EROWINA WHO, WITHOUT SHAME, DID, AT HER LEAVE TAKING, TEMPT HIM BY HER LASCIVIOUSNESS.

The glittering stars crowded themselves into the black gaps left by the hurrying clouds.

Erowina, standing in the lighted doorway of the Perseverance, the gap between her legs — right up to her wide crutch — visible through her crocheted dress, gasped and stepped out into the freezing darkness. The door slammed shut behind her and she made her invisible way to his side, searched out his hand and held it in hers.

— By hevun, that's wind.

Her words went scudding with the leaves — gambolling and blown away upon a sudden northeasterly. (A terrible blackthorn winter wind, whistled up on triple blasts from blizzard wastes.)

— By Christ, I've had a belly full t'night.

— That we hey.

— Brrrrrr. Cummun.

And she snuggled up.

— Hey on.

— Well . . .

He put his arm about her shoulder.

— Gis a snuk.

— Tak it, and she put her face up to his.

When they'd kissed, she nuzzled him and whispered: Yow cummi back?

— Eh?

— Back.

— Wi yow?

— Aye.

— Nair — git on wid ye, yow owd tease.

— I ain't teasen, and she stroked his back and hugged him.

— Me t'yewrs?

— Aye, cummun.

— Whut fur?

— Day yer want?

— Stoo bloddy cole. I slep on yow flur afore an ner froze.

— I' wi me, daft. And she squeezed him,

— Wi yow?

— Yow'll be werm.

— Werm? I'll be too bloddy werm.

— Yew kin see me blank't.

— Aye?

— Me blank't. Snew. Ids or ow fow skins wert an tik as a wully bugga boo.

— Git on wid yer.

— Snay an owd Ermy. San oran Widney. Tik as tat. Nay heri boot squirmy suft. Suft. Re suft. She screwed him gently, whispering her fingers over his bottom. It's owl oran. Breet oran. An tik and widdly wum.

— Yow widdle?

She giggled.

— Yow si owd bugga-yum you, and she pushed him. Why dow yow cum udder't wid me, eh?

— Huisha.

— I n'ver sin yow owd nooky-doo, and she scrootched down onto his thigh.

— Yow will fyow don stopt.

Gormun gripped her and looked into her teasing eyes — filled, he imagined, with the reflections of the brittle, glittering stars.

— By the Christ. Gis anowa snitch, ya yummy slit-slot yow. Erowina strained herself against him; grinding her pelvic bones into his lap.

— Tik an oran, an re-al suft.

— Damn yow blankt!

— Doo noo wana snug a boo wid me thn? Hum? Er durst yow crank yern girt nurdle i me dinky dooz?

— I'm fur creen for't, dammt.

He reached for her crutch but she held his hand.

— Unner me oran blankt, and she bellied up to him.

— He-ar.

— Nay, she brought his hand up and slid it under her arm.

— Boot . . .

— Nay, he-ar.

— Yow en git a widdly wim.

—Hayn't? Yow gis nowa yum then.

And they embraced and kissed.

Mmmmmmmmm mm, yum. Yum. Tung. Tungiyum, yum. Umm. Yum-mytunnng. Mmm.

— By the . . .

— Weel . . . ?

Erowina breathed into his ear. And licked it. And poked her tongue into it. And whispered: Snug unt m'oran blankt and appen yow ktung yum me owd quirm. Mmm? And, raising her forefinger, she tapped him lightly on the nose with it. Un toneat. Nay a nairy neat. Now. Toneat.

— Aw, Ee-o. Gi oer. Appen wun too mur fur yow wid erm. And he nodded towards the shadows where Giacopo stood sicking-up in groaning abundance.

— Appen I lik yow up'n or. She grinned wickedly and whispered into his ear: Atayowls, dayn't know.

Gormun sucked the freezing air between his aching teeth.

— Ee-o!

— Fowr creen owt, Gorm . . .

She slid her hands over his buttocks again.

— Nay. Nay. Offt.

Aware of his uncomfortable erection and frightened by the violence of his shuddering, Gormun pushed against her: Na neat boot a tiklen squirm, Ee-o.

— Nay, Gorm, and she dragged him to her. Aw gis anowa sook. Gis anowa . . . And they bumped against each other like furies.

— Sook me!

Mouth to mouth, they kissed until spittle ran off their chins. Gasping for air, Gormun freed himself at last.

— OH, EE-O. Git love. Git. Erowina tried to draw him to her again. Nay, Ee-o, nay, love. Please — git wa. And he picked her hands from his shoulders. Please . . . wa'r drunk. Jest drunk. S'drink doon us bed. S'drink. His eyes filled with tears.

— Nay. Ist Penn. Ist Penn?

— Aye.

— Aye, well. Erowina kissed his cheek and squeezed his hand. G'hum, Gorm. G'hum t'Penn. And she trailed her fingers over his trouser front as she turned away. Yow'll do better'n stay wi me.

— Nay.

Erowina turned, hunched her shoulders and pocketed her hands.

— Nay?

— Nay. Yow'm all. An as bin. Allus.

— Tha's nice. Re-al nicen yow. G'nye. And she kissed the darkness before she turned and was gone.

— Gormun squirms uneasily on the long bench, trying to obliterate the image, fearing I will sense his guilt and shame. Having risen, I bang the mahogany. I have just realised a dreadful truth, says I. Gormun starts, blinks rapidly and chews his lip.

Quirk frowns.

— I've been blind these past years. I've had a revelation. One which fills me with sorry.

— What?

— I have been betrayed!

Gormun changes the letter E he had been tracing in a beer puddle to the letter B.

— A judgement is at hand.

Gormun fumbles for a reassuring cigarette.

— Come, landlord. Drinks all round.

Quirk, having drawn a pint of porter, clunks down the overflowing pot on the mahogany. After a moment he turns round with:

—Two Jjs.

— Angimmeapackedofwhiffs.

— Whiffs? Turning and reaching while I conjur.

— There. Now. Four and two and three and six. Seven and eight.

The register crashes. Ting.

Quirk slaps in the note and scrapes out the change. Shutting ting the drawer with his hip.

— Seven and eight. Eleven. Eight. And two. Ten.

— Your health, Mister Quirk.

Hands on mahogany and a glass of amber between, smirking Quirk, his head on one side, reaches for his glass.

— Deepest respects, Tammy.

— Cheers.

Quirk raises his glass with a steady hand, takes a deep breath and, throwing his head back for a Command Performance . . .

— Aaaaaaaaaaaaagh!

The glass goes POCK on the quarry tiles and shatters; tinkling.

— Yastupidfatheadedtwat!

— Mister Quirk! Pl-ease.

— Don't you Quirk me, you longhaired scribbler! and he misses with the bottle of Jamieson tea which breaks on the beer engine pump handle.

— Mother of Mary! he cries as it shatters.

Mick, half risen, is watching with popping eyes but Polly daresn't move in case.

— Restrain him, Gormun, he's gone besquirk! says I.

His tongue hanging out, Quirk holds his neck with one hand and grips the shattered bottle in the other. He points the fragmented bottle. I'll embroider your bloody mug one day, Tammy Lamlin!

Giving my impression of a Cheshire cat, I leans across the mahogany and, with a flourish, drinks down Quirk's glass of tea.

— Hush your hullabaloo, Quirky. Or. I holds up a finger and taps the side of my nose. Or else the turrible truth will out.

Then, turning. Gormun, pour our dear friend and landlord Mister Quirk a Jamieson. He's bin taken horrible queer.

— Don't you take a step this side of the bar or I'll . . .

— Take no notice, Gormun.

Quirk slams down the flap.

— I'll do my own honours!

— Bravo. We'll all have one. Poured from the same under my very eye.

— I'll do for you one day, Tam.

— Pour.

It is done with a shaking hand while a puzzled Gormun watches.

— Your health, Mister Quirk. To your remarkable recovery.

Mr Quirk glowers over his own raised glass.

— An nay owd cowd tay agin mind, says I.

Quirky growls and drinks.

The door marked PUBLIC breezes open and through it come two wobbling, jiggling, giggling Fulham Virgins in all their finery; and slippers.

— God help me if it isn't Perimedes and Eurylochus!

— Lena! Darling! (Advancing.)

— Tammyrandy! (Squeezed and hugged.)

— Len O'Gorm! (A sucking kiss like an eased-out cork.)

— Well, well. Bubulaha! (Pronounced BUB-OOL-LA-HA.) Looking and taking a handful.

— Gammy! Encircling. Comforted by the slack fat.

— And 'ow's Lena love?

— Fair drained, says she, taking a deep breath so that her bubs swell and rise up. A dozen edible bivalvular moluscular wouldn't lubricate me right now.

— A quart of spotted amanti muscaria you mean, says I with a wicked smile.

— Faint, not spent, says Lena, poking me with her finger. Eh? Weary Willy.

— Don't be trying to bring that up, says I, remembering when she didn't.

— Patience wasn't rewarded last time, was it? Hey? Ha!

Gormun gazes into the chasm between her large breasts.

— Hold your horses, Curtius M., says she. And Gormun blushes to the roots of his hair. Drinks first.

— I was admiring your maiden hair.

— A-HA HA HA HA. O, and she pats her rose. You dirty bugger.

— Whatlidbe, girls?

We all turn and face the patient Quirk.

— A small and large, Quirky, please. The small to tickle, the large to fill. Eh? Hey? Ha. HA HA HA. Ha. Ah, ah. O. Dear-hear.

— Gammy?

— A short and strong but not too long! AH-HA HA HA HA. O-HA. Oh ha. Ha ha. Han-han-hand double quick. . . .

— If if-if-if if it's not too thick! HA HA HA HA!

— An not go'n back'n forn fur fowf owd nour ! HA HA HA HA! HA. Ha. Ho ha. Ho dear. Deary me.

Both fat women cough and their eyes fill with tears.

— What yer bin doin' wi yerself, Tammo? Owt what we couldn' a done better, eh? Heh? A-HA HA HA HA! Ha. Oh. Ho. O Ho. Oh. O me 'airy palms! HA HA HA HA HA! Hey, Gorm?

And Gormun turns, remembering.

What?

EROWINA WHO, DURING THE RESTLESS HOURS OF NIGHT, DID TEMPT AND INFLAME HIS DESIRE BY HER INSATIABLE NYMPHOLEPSY?

Lying on a pillowed dream she stirred the fitful sleeper with the slow, gentle convolutions of her dreaming.

Alerted into blackness, couched and lodged in unfamiliarity, his seeing ear quickly tuned to the quoit springing her timid rhythm, an arm's length away.

Could she be? No. Not with him only an arm's length near. Listening, blind, not breathing, time ticked on; matching her unhurried rub-a-dub.

Because of the insistent, persistent repetition — an impossible prolongation, he began to imagine it a call to witness. Never! NO.

He stretched himself noiselessly on his night-loaned, lumpy sofa, wedged into the corner, only an arm's length away, and allowed the sound to enter through his open mouth; not daring to breathe.

But the mechanical squeak jangled his tingling ears and comets burst before his eyes as his banded chest burst and a sigh escaped him and went whistling, unnoticed. Unable to endure more, he thought to cough. Instead he prayed for a quick deliverance.

But on it went, trudgingly; bent on spending.

Again, he ridged himself and lay taut under the dome of his incredulity; an impotent attestor to her necessity: only a hand's stretch away.

But slowly, inevitably, imperceptibly, her fingering imagination spread softly and wetly in the slack darkness, jockeying her desperation on the Devil's invocation, and she began ruthlessly to enervate the yawning vessel of her desire with a maddening animality.

An arm's length away, his separate barque shuddered from stem to stern as her groaning wake slapped the sides and she filled his great sails with the breath of her lipsticked haste, and the waves of her lubricity swept over him and bore him in imagination onto the rocks of his infatuation: only an arm's stretch away.

And Tammy slept dead on their tossing barque with his voluptuary close beside him being swept into her Sea of Sweetness while he, listening to the stillness, watched sleep, wreathed in smiles, bypass and go dusting all but him, before he dared to reach across.

— You look droopy, Tammy-hee.

— HA HA HA. A-HA. Ah ha. How, 'ow would you-hoo know, hey? HA HA! HA.

— 'Cause I felt it soon's I saw-rim.

— You wa-hot? You . . ? A-HA HA HA HA! AH! HA. Ha ha ha.

— Ged on wid yer. What's wrong, Tam?

— He's in mourning. — Is hehehe? Oh deara.

— That's sad, Tammy love.

The tenants in Dower look away; sipping their drinks in silence and holding down belches which lie uncomfortably filling.

— Not your owd mother, were it, Tam?

— No no, Cantatrice. My mother has not yet joined the majority.

— Who were it, then?

Gormun raises a warning finger to his lips and, shaking his head, frowns at Gammy.

A slow dawning of comprehension lightens her face. Her plump, violent mouth shapes the letter O and her tiny, dull eyes widen.

— Not the little dear what used. Not that lovely gal. The one with the pretty name. What was it? Worked as barmaid in The Perseverance before Marina hung herself. (She bites her lip.) You know, and she pokes Ivy with her finger.

Gormun grimaces and shakes his head.

— Yes, you know her.

— Erowina.

— Yes! Erowina. That's her. Oh, no. No. Not her. She weren't n'more'n thirty. You don't mean her, do you, Tam?

I nod and Gormun turns away, grinding his teeth together.

— Her! says Quirk, surprised.

— Oh, I AM sorry, Tam. Truly.

— So am I. What a shame — and her so young.

— Poor old Gor. You must miss her too.

— I grieve as for a very dear friend.

— Aye? Oh. Yes. You an' Tam t'gether. But fancy. Her.

— What she die of?

— She committed suicide, says I, defiantly.

— Kilt herself! Quirk says, quickly crossing himself. Good grief!

— What a way to go.

— Poor soul, and the two women cross themselves and kiss their thumbs.

— No wonder the bench is bare.

— We were not the only mourners. There was another.

— Kin?

— All dead.

— How sad.

— She'll be missed.

— I know she will. Poor owd Tam-Tam. Patting his arm. You mustn't take it hard. It's not like you to go frettin'. She didn' treat you proper, that girl. And, pulling in her chin, Doin' away with herself indeed. It isn't decent.

— I take a deep breath and look up at the ceiling, hoping it will soon be over.

— Weren't she queer?

— Must have been to do herself in, says her sister in sin.

— No, QUEER.

Gormun, his back turned, bites into his knuckles and licks the blood from the broken skin.

— Was she, Tam?

— 'Course she was. A real Leslie, weren't she, Tam? Patting my shoulder. A lesbian man.

— A real camp perv.

— Saw coupling snakes . . .

— And caught the disease.

— A tribad Lemian, says I.

— That's what I said. A kinky sucks.

— Woad died and stinking. . . .

— AND a good deal more, I shouldn't wonder. Raving she was. A proper bull-dike queer.

— . . . she intermarried desperation, and, stained, she died. An outcast. (But they wouldn't listen.)

— Oh, drink up, Tam. You mustn't take it hard.

— Yes. You a man an' all. What you want with flat fucks, eh?

— Fricatio mutua coniunctorum genitalium muliebrium, says I.

— You say what you like, but the lover under her lap made no bones, I'll be bound. Little darling indeed.

And once again Gormun's mind is flooded by.

What?

The memory of.

EROWINA WHO, TOGETHER WITH HER FRIEND GLORIA, DID TEMPT HIM TO MADNESS BY HER VOLUPTUOUSNESS ONE EVENING WHEN THEY WERE CLOSETED TOGETHER.

He sees their entwined fingers squeeze lovingly beneath the upturned edges of their intermingled wraps when Erowina sits close to her darling Gloria on the vast counterpane of their bed.

His embarrassment is tinged with an uncomfortable sensuality. Or was it jealousy? Probably.

— Of course we don't mind you coming late. Do we, Gloria darling? Milk?

Darling Gloria, with her free hand as pale and cool and as fragile as alabaster, silently turns the pages of her pin-up magazine. Coming across a photograph of a particularly busty girl, she glances up to see if he is looking.

He wasn't. He had no intention of playing a game from which he knew he would emerge the loser.

— A little, please.

Another page is turned and her eyes search out his embarrassment.

He looks away. Away from her eyes, her fondling hand, her bared thigh and legs, past her painted toes and searches the patterned carpet for distraction.

Had Erowina spoken to Gloria about him? Evidently. Her instant recognition of him as a contender for Erowina's affections could not have been intuitive. Or was she so confident she could afford the luxury of teasing him? Of humiliating him? Man that he was.

— How's Fionnghuala?

— Don't you think she's nice? Mmm?

Gloria shows them a young girl who is all bust and bottom and who is biting the tip of her extruded tongue. She is sitting astride a bicycle which has a perspex saddle.

He ignores the deliberate diversion.

— Penny's very well.

— She's very pretty, darling. And the page is turned. And Peter Pan?

— Oh, he's growing rapidly and just like his mother.

He groaned inwardly. Why hadn't he been content to say the boy looked well and left it at that? Erowina might not have told her darling everything. Or was he being too sensitive? "Just like his mother" was a statement of fact. It was true. It hadn't necessarily revealed his overwhelming relief that Pan did not resemble any of his mother's many lovers. He ventured a quick glance at Gloria but her head was bent over the magazine and her long, blonde, falling hair obscured her face.

— Is she more your type, Gormun?

The page is wrapped round and the magazine thrust towards him. Over the top, darling's clear mauve eyes search his face.

Two girls, as pink as their nipples, gambol together in an unlikely setting.

He sets his face and glances uninterestedly at the glossy page, and then away.

He couldn't ignore Gloria completely, but if — as he suspected — she was overtly emotional, he might, by his deliberate indifference, so infuriate her that she would be tempted into an indiscretion and so lay herself open to his domination. However, if she were more capable than he supposed and turned the situation to her advantage, he would have to count on Erowina coming to his defence. Either way, it seemed a wedge could be driven between them.

— Gloria! Stop embarrassing Gormun. Put that away. Did you say milk?

Was Erowina also embarrassed by the book? If she was, and her darling didn't slide it back under the cushion, it could be used as a fulcrum to lever them apart.

He found his eyes attracted to the warm, brown hollow between Erowina's swollen breasts which caverned when she leant forward to pour the milk.

— Yes?

— Yes. Please.

— I haven't seen Penny for ages.

Darling's head is jerked up and her look is penetrating.

— I understand she suffers with terrible depressions.

— My wife?

He spies a warning toe pressing up against another.

— You're thinking of Joan, darling.

Was she warning her darling to prevent the confusion of a half-told truth or had she shielded him with a lie and wished the lie to continue? For his sake.

— Oh. Am I? I thought SHE was frigid. Or have I got the two mixed?

He sat perfectly still. Gloria's subtle mockery had revealed the extent of her knowledge. It couldn't have been chance which made her choose to go directly to his wound. So, Erowina had told her; everything. And her darling had remembered.

He takes the cup, rattling on its saucer, and looks up to see Erowina's brown nipple sliding back into the concealing folds of her scented wrap as she sat up straight.

If Gloria suspected he was on the defensive, she might quickly carry the impetus of her attack to its logical conclusion — his humiliation. On the other hand, if she was unaware, her next sortie would find him securely entrenched and prepared to resist — which might make her think him stronger than she supposed and might dissuade her from further action. He didn't imagine she would retire gracefully, but he was determined she would have to be content to score with sly innuendoes only.

Erowina raises her arm and, with nimble fingers, tidies the damp circlets of hair in the nape of her neck. Her smile is relaxed and reassuring.

— We've just had a bath together. His tea slops into the saucer.

Erowina had presented him with an image so startling he was momentarily confounded. He saw that Gloria would be quick to seize upon this opportunity.

— The sisters D'Estrees, don't you know.

And darling Gloria forms her thumb and first forefinger into a delicate, obscene O.

— Je suis Gabrielle, she says, revelling in the rolling tongued diction of an exaggerated pronunciation. And she smirks.

He sips his scalding tea.

However ignorant Erowina might appear to be of her darling's brazenness, surely she couldn't be so innocent as not to recognise Gloria's defiance of his masculinity? Perhaps she approved? It was a thought which had not occurred to him before and one which disturbed. He had presumed her relationship with Gloria, however bizarre, was only temporary. Now he was faced with the possibility — and worse, the reality — of having to accept that Erowina was living her new life with the confidence of one born to her situation and intended it to be permanent.

He searches her face for clues but finds none.

— Does Penny still go to see Tuldorfy? It was Tuldorfy, wasn't it?

He could see in her darling's eyes the puzzlement of ignorance. He would not enlighten her.

— Yes.

— That's the man Joan ought to have put herself under.

Gloria's questioning eyebrows exact a response before he can impose himself between them.

— He's a psychiatrist.

— O.

He sees Gloria's illuminated mind absorb this information while she pretends interest in her magazine.

He must, and rapidly, particularise the antagonism between Gloria and himself. Was it her instinctive dislike of him as a man, or the man Gormun, or as a contender — of whatever sex — for Erowina's affections? If the two had consolidated their intimacy it couldn't be the latter unless there were doubts. Doubts? Of Erowina's committal? Her dislike of him as a man? More than likely. As Gormun? Possible; but of no consequence. Of the three possibilities, her lack of confidence in the total commitment of Erowina's affections would be the most likely. Therefore, being uncertain, she would be more aggressive because it was her own relationship which was being threatened. Yes, that was it.

— Can you honestly say he helped Penny?

Darling snorts down her beautiful nose.

It told him all he needed to know.

He returns his cup to the saucer and sees his reflection giddying round in the depths of the dark tea.

How strange he looked. And alien.

And then his other self withdrew and hovered above him, so that he was able to observe the scene below. The warm, intimate room; subduedly lit. The two, fresh-faced young women; pink and scented from their bath. And, sat apart, hunched in his dirty macintosh, a small, ageing man of no significance whatsoever.

— Did it?

— Mmm?

— Did it help her?

How should he answer? With the truth? He had always been honest with Erowina.

— Yes. I mean, no. No. No, the effect has been to sever the very tenuous bond which held us together. The darling smiles.

Smug satisfaction or triumph? His pride had suffered before, and would again; many times, but he was still not used to the pain.

— No doubt Tuldorfy expected this and views the result with infinite satisfaction.

Was he being too cynical?

— Of course, it's made her more independent. Self-sufficient. And, naturally, now that she has confidence in herself. . . . He hesitates.

Could he say it? Would either of them understand how painful it would be? Erowina might; Gloria, unless she knew his difficulties, would not understand.

— . . . and in what she does. I mean she knows why; now; why she does it. Why she sleeps around. And that's strained our relationship to. . . . More than ever.

Were the mauve eyes mocking him? They looked down to the magazine on her lap, so he couldn't be sure. But he was certain of one thing — he had Erowina's attention and, from the tilt of her head and the look of compassion in her eyes, her sympathy.

— The new alienation seems to have been imposed by the analysis. I'm certain Tuldorfy would expect me to blame him.

I can accept this. As I could Penny's crush on him. In the beginning. But of course that's finished with. Now.

Gloria bulges one cheek with her tongue and, moving her head from side to side, admires a photograph. Certain that Gormun is looking, she glances up at him, narrows her eyes to slits and sucks in her cheeks.

Had she understood nothing or was she willing his tongue to outstrip his better judgement? Or was she poised with a snide remark? He couldn't tell. For the moment it didn't matter because his compulsive honesty was directed to Erowina; to draw her closer to him.

— Oddly enough, since her self-realisation — if that's what you can term it, I find her more attractive; and — exciting. Unfortunately, the affection I lavish upon her is falling on to even stonier ground than before.

He could not fail to detect Erowina's look of commiseration, and it pleased him; greatly. He was very satisfied.

— Do you use real pubic hair?

Erowina twists and scowls.

The darling knew his profession!

— Oh, really, Gloria. . . .

He had to be quick with his reply to show he was alert, but more important, that he couldn't be thrown.

— No.

—O.

— Superfluous detail — warts and such, or blemishes, they are not required on medical models. They are for tuition — not titillation.

— I just wondered.

Was she trying to alter the pace of the conversation, divert it or, and which was probably nearer the truth, being devious in order to confuse him? He couldn't connect in his mind what he had said before the interruption which could have initiated her peculiar attack with what might follow. Perhaps it was her intention to prevent his anticipation?

— You're not over-dramatising the emotional return of affection which all of us experience, are you?

— Pardon?

— The imbalance. You know. The do-you-love-me-as-much-as-I-love-you?

Was she disbelieving him?

— This is a Swedish magazine.

— O, do be quiet, Gloria darling.

— But perhaps he's never seen one.

— Gormun's not interested. Put it away.

He waited. As a listening spectator there was more chance of him spotting a breach into which he could drive his wedge. That is, if Gloria wasn't deliberately luring him.

Gloria, bright and innocent, turns towards him. Full face.

— It was an association of ideas.

Erowina frowns.

It would be in her unnecessary explanation that the clue to her attack would be found. This she was making clear to him. He must be on his guard against the unexpected.

— Oh?

He giggles.

It had occurred to him that a man who has been shewn a sixpence in the gutter does not bend down to pick it up without first taking the precaution of putting his hand over the pound in his back pocket in case he is robbed of the pound and is left holding sixpence.

He giggles again.

Gloria frowns.

Was it really so funny, or was it his nervousness? He hoped Gloria would think him a fool.

— This unsightly, if not unhygienic, pubic hair . . . and knowing Gormun's interest. . . .

Interest? Why interest? Why not "job" or "the work he does" — why "interest"? And could she know?

Darling avoids his eyes and opens the magazine at the pages between which her finger had lain.

So, she had made ready for this moment, had she? Had enough confidence to lay her plans in advance. Odd, then, that she took so little care to conceal her preparations.

— Of course, a lot are shaved.

Very slowly she opens out the magazine and holds it out towards him.

— And because it's a Swedish publication, it makes no attempt to hide the fact.

Their eyes meet.

He knows he must look — is expected to look; it is all part of the elaborate game she has staged, but he holds her gaze.

For a fraction of a second, perhaps less, he dares to admire the beauty of her eyes and to be dazzled by their mauve clarity. But the thinking beyond the look brings him back to the unreality of the situation.

Is what she holds before him the opening gambit of an intricate, but well planned, preconceived game of destruction or does she imagine she is already hammering on the darkest door of his last defence? If the latter, and if she knew, then he was already defeated.

So, he looks.

A wet nymph rises full-chested from the bath, a gleaming drip poised to drop from the pizzle of her pubic hair; and another, the arch of her nymphae clearly discernible within the exaggerated posture of her tonsured sex, ludicrously spread-eagled for the ravages of the myopic lens.

— O, really, Gloria! Give it here.

Erowina snatches the magazine and rolls it.

— Here. Take it with you. She presses it into his hands.

Her darling smirks.

— Go on. Put it in your pocket.

He stuffs the magazine into the pocket of his macintosh.

Gloria smiles.

Was it a smile to conceal her contempt or was it one of triumph? Triumph? At what? Knowing that he would look at it later? That was a hollow victory. Did she consider herself the instrument of his libidinous perusal, hoping her action contributed to his feeling of guilt? He didn't know women well enough to answer that. Perhaps she felt a perverse titillation at the possibility that she was, by default, arousing his desire which would be spent needlessly? No. It was too remote. She would want to watch over her victory. There must be another explanation — one he had overlooked; unless her aim had been to puzzle his mind and thus divert his attention.

— Won't it distress your wife to find a girlie magazine in your pocket?

So that was it!

— Penny? Good heavens no!

Gloria turns to Erowina.

— How fortunate to have a wife who is so understanding about nakedness.

Had Erowina told her? And everything? She was deliberately avoiding his eyes. Did that mean her sally had been exploratory? Or that she had guessed?

Darling would only turn and face him when she was certain. She would want to watch him die in full view of his Erowina.

The faintest of smiles dimples the left side of darling's soft cheek.

She was letting him know she knew his weakest point. If he were a strategist, now would be the moment for a show of strength to avoid a rout and give him time and space in which to manoeuvre. He knew he wouldn't emerge unscathed but the extent to which he was humiliated depended on how Erowina deployed herself. Being sympathetic, she might well hinder him.

— Shut up, darling. PLEASE.

Even darling shows surprise.

— I — want — to — talk — to — Gormun — S-E-R-I-O-U-S-L-Y.

She turns to Gormun and shows her concern with an earnest look.

Gloria waits — patiently. Her eyes downcast.

— Now then, Gormun. Erowina leans forward; elbows on knees, hands clasped in front of her, concentrating her attention. You said things were worse. She holds up her hand in anticipation of his interruption.

He hadn't intended replying. He was done with talking.

— You know I never presume to give advice — to anyone; even when asked. Erowina presses her lips to the back of her hand. Therefore you must forgive me for what I am about to say. She places the palms of her hands together and puts the tips of her fingers against her lips. My advice to you is — leave. Leave her. For your own good.

Leaning back, she takes the weight of her body on her hands. I honestly believe you should.

Gloria shifts but keeps her eyes downcast.

— If you don't — or soon — Penny will reduce you to a shadow.

She leans forward and again raises a cautionary hand. I have never concealed the fact from you that I sympathise with her — I do, but that doesn't mean I condone her behaviour. I don't. I think she has behaved disgracefully. I know you love her, and you say deeply, but aren't you perhaps exaggerating the quality of your love?

Quality? He didn't understand. Did she doubt his sincerity?

— It is not for me to ask — even suggest why, in view of what you have had to put up with — why it is you still love her, but have you ever thought that you may so overwhelm her with love that she is being drowned? Erowina notices his gathering frown. And not only her. Others, too. In a flood of emotion which either they haven't warranted, or with which they can't cope.

She hesitates and then continues with a rising, thinning inflexion in her voice. And in return, ask too much?

Gloria snuggles up to Erowina and blows gently into her ear before placing the tiniest of kisses upon her neck.

It seemed like a sign of approbation; a symbolic sealing of her neophyte's success. He saw it as revenge, too, and the affirmation of her domination.

Goosing, Erowina smiles and hunches her shoulder against her darling's bussing.

He hadn't thought, when summoning up his courage earlier in the evening before he dared to knock on Erowina's door, exactly lion. He only wanted to be near her; to see her again. She was the first he would have liked to have turned to in his misery; but she had been the last. Unlike the others, who had treated him almost too casually, Erowina had whipped him like a cur. He felt himself whimpering.

— I don't think you're being fair, Eo.

Darling pronounced it Ee-o, not E-o like Gormun.

— Gormun's been under a tremendous strain and all you have done is to scold him for being too emotional. That's hardly comforting. You've destroyed his basic pride.

Her astute fraternisation, in order to be able to shift the guilt of her victimisation onto Erowina's shoulders, was the final indignity. There seemed no need to contain himself any longer.

— What the hell do you know about it? You've got the best of both bloody worlds. What about YOUR husband? You stupid cow.

For a moment only there is a profound silence and then Erowina's voice, firm and clear:

— You will apologise, Gormun. At once.

Gloria, deliberately avoiding his eyes, shakes her head.

— No-no. No Erowina. It was said in anger.

But Erowina shook her head. Gormun. You have offended ME. Do you understand? ME!

He did; only too well. He would have to apologise immediately or else hump his shame about indefinitely. He would purge himself.

— I beg your pardon. Yours, too, Gloria. I'm sorry. I can offer neither of you an adequate excuse. Please forgive me.

— Thank you, Gormun, and Erowina touches his knee.

He was now ready for the sacrifice.

Gloria turns her eyes on Gormun and looks him full in the face.

He heard his breath whistling from him like a stuck pig's.

Gloria speaks.

— I know very little of the personalities involved in either your past or present difficulties, Gormun. Erowina has told me little. She has been very discreet. I mention this so as to put your mind at rest in case you should think that you had been betrayed. I am a perceptive woman — you may prefer to call me intuitive. I am also intelligent. This does not mean I am lacking the range of emotions which overwhelm other people, but that I am the more able to rationalise them. To you, the refusal of your wife to return the affection you lavish upon her, is illogical. Am I right?

He remains silent.

One does not interrupt the judge's summing up. There would be time enough after the sentence had been passed.

Erowina lays her hand on her darling's thigh. It is a gesture encouraging restraint; not one of complicity or approval.

— Many women will not comply with their husband's particular wishes: to expose themselves to scrutiny; to be kissed in what they consider an indecent manner. There are many things a woman may not grant the man she loves. A spurned man, if his wife takes herself a lover, will imagine the very things she denied him, she grants her lover. Next, that she requests it of her lover and, the final insult to his imagination, shows herself to be enjoying it. The illogicality shewn by the husband is the assumption that, by renewed, overt attempts to woo and win back his wife's affection, he will, if successful, become her lover and participate in what before had been forbidden. (She paused.) That this will not happen may lead to murder.

Stunned, he was only vaguely aware of what she was saying. An hour before — or had it been yesterday? the week previous? — he had attacked Penny with the bread-knife, cutting her about the face and chest; trying to stab her, to saw off her smile. He may have killed her. He may have. He had wanted to. Oh yes, he had. HAD. Had. But now? The deed done? No.

Self-pity welled up, obscuring his senses; obliterating.

— Gormun. Gormun!

— Mmm?

— Gormun! Oh, my God. This is your fault, Gloria. Gormun! He felt his knee being shaken.

— Gormun, where are you staying? Gormun!

Suddenly he was where he had been. Erowina was leaning towards him, her hand on his knee.

— Pardon?

Should he stand for his sentence to be passed? Was it now?

— Are you staying with Tammy?

He shakes his head.

— Well, where?

Where? Where what? He could feel his skull slowly filling. With what? It flowed up his spine like warm blood and flooded into the enormous cavity of what had been his head.

— Are you back on the streets again? Tell me.

In a moment he would be able to answer.

— Oh, he is. Gormun, dear, look. You're going to stay here. You're to stay here with us. Do you understand?

The mauve eyes narrowed to slits and below them the nostrils slowly flared.

Darling draws up her legs beneath her.

Exposing.

Even as he ran from the room, he was convinced he heard her laugh and imagined them embracing.

Once in the street with the hard pavement beneath his feet he again began to summon up courage to go and see Erowina. She was the only friend he had.

— Wipe yu eye, owd Tam, says Ivy, taking a ruffed-up, squeezed-out, banged-about old concertina from her leather shopping-bag. Quirk! A rip-roaring revivalry for owd Tam. Was say?

Quirk shrugs and looks away.

— Afore yow start, yells Yammy Gammy, slapping the mahogany with the flat of her fat, ringed hand, let's have a small and large, Quirky-O. A short and pale. That's Ivy's ale. And Tammy? Gormless?

— Whisky I, says me.

— And a pinta porta, daughta.

— Did you get that, Quirky? A porter's daughter. A James. And your-self?

— No, no, indicating his vested stomick.

— QUIRK! I boom.

— Enough to wet the end, then.

And Quirk, smouldering, deads me with a look.

Ivy Hodge, bastard daughter of Jack John Ketch — a nasty coincidence, that — settles her great fat backside onto a high wooden stool, belches, spreads her knees, hooks her heels onto the bar of the stool below and fills her concertina with a warm west wind. (Good old Nik-Nik.)

Lena Sawney (Gammy to some but Bubulaha or Haha to most and Bubs to very few but Yum-Yum to every male client) leans her monstrous, milk-smelling breasts into the mahogany, burps into her fist clamped round a damp pound note and, having done so, much to her relief, turns a smile on Ivy.

— Don't strangle it, Ivy-O. Nice fingerin' now.

— A tune it is then. Who'll say?

— Mider's call to Befind, says Gorm.

— Let Tammy choose.

— The Voyage of Bran.

— I said, Tammy.

I give Ivy a wink. Ivy nods and begins.

While I sing to the assembled company, Quirk clears away the bottles and wipes the mahogany with his cloth.

Finished, he stands listening to my ending.

— She has left me here alone.

With my chin on my chest to sustain the C.,

— All alone.

Another breath and, throwing back my head, I force my lungs open for,

— That sometimes did lead with herself,

pause,

— and me loved

pause, then, with feeling,

— as

and held. Another breath and the assembled join me in singing,

— her own.

Clap. Clap. Clappity-clap clip clap. Clap. Clap. Clip. Pat. Clop.

— You've still got your voice, Tammy-O.

— You near squeezed the tears that time Boy-O.

— He did too! Sniff.

— How about the Wooing of Etain?

I decline, modestly, and leave the singing of it to Mick.

Bubulaha, sitting next to Gormun on the Wake bench, bites into a fat pork pie. Noticing, he pulls a face and, putting his hand to his mouth, shouts: You've come down, Quirko — selling them! He indicates the pie. Faggots 'n' peas was the days. He turns to Bubulaha. He was caught out, though. Weren't yu? Hey? Tried to turn us into hippophagists, dayn't yer. He git fined n'all.

Bubulaha pushes the pie into her face and bites. Gormun, devil'd by her greediness, nudges her. Would yer be as 'ungry fur meat 'n' two veg, Yum-Yum?

She manages to say: I don't smoke, before she almost chokes.

— Bloody liar, and he leans into her lavender scented ear to whisper.

Miss Sawney pulls a face and munches on.

— How's Mamsy's owd charity box, Bubba? I ask, knowing she'd caught the clap.

— Chamst psfont qwive snpuffway but mwery buch metter. Much better. And she takes another bite. Pfwaruppin herowninger an, pswont is mwellingly nwore nown. Dit dontich so.

— Glad to hear it. I must pay her a visit.

— Myewm do.

Quirk, bustling and querulous, shoulders his way through the drinkers.

— Who's the Tom-fool who give Polly a whisky?

— Doloroso com. Hum. Ah-hum. HUM, coughs I, clearing my throat in preparation for a song.

— WHO WAS IT?

— More drink, Quirky. DRINK!

— I want to know who give Polly this?

— S'mine, says I. Give.

— Liar! says he.

— It is too, says Grom.

— I wouldn't trust you alone with our dog, Mister O'Connor.

— Now, now, Quirky — it's not a let's be beastly to Ormun Gorm day, says I, with emphasis. It's kind words he needs in time of stress.

And Gormun remembered.
EROWINA WHO, WHEN NIGHT FELL, DID SORELY TEMPT HIM WITH HON-EYED WORDS.

She told me.

In the light of the glowing bar pulsing heat into the chill gloom of our dark room, she stretched luxuriantly on the floor. Her woolly pulled over, crackling and sparkling with each stroked rub and tug, she rolled on her side and her upper haunch bulged and went slack.

— You've got lovely eyes, Gormun.

She squirmed and ground down onto her compressed buttock.

— And such beautiful teeth.

She drew her silk washed legs up and curled herself like a puss-pussy cat on the lazy hearth.

— You're damned attractive.

Propped on her elbow, she played with the zip at her hip and teased it open; and shut.

Her smile went on waves to her toes, negligeed in their silken sheaths; worming to the fire's heat.

— I'd have thought few girls would have been able to resist you. She surrendered her full length to the voluptuous rug and the room became stifling under the quilt of her vaporous scent.

— You're very good-looking, you know.

Arching her back, she quivered like a strung bow.

— Penelope is very, very lucky. If I were her. . . .

But the outer door slammed shut, way below them in the empty, hollow house.

— That's Tammy come hame.

And Gormun sat tight in the disembowelled chair listening to my footsteps on the stairs.

Cupping her enormous breasts in both her red-chapped hands, as if to relieve their pendulous weight, Yum-Yum belches. Fortissimo.

— That pie's going to be trouble.

Ivy plays on. Her fingers, like squabbling sparrows, force a rapid jig from her concertina.

— For God's sake, someone, give us a hand with this coring mush. Come on, Mick. MICK! Help me set Polly straight.

Mick MacCoym is dancing on his steel-tipped boots and striking sparks from the tiles. He catches his toe on his heel and nearly trips.

— Slower, Miss Kitty. Me talent's no match for me breathin'. Gone's the days when I used t'exhibit Bumpin' her Belly on cellar flap.

He makes a saut mineur.

— Sit, says Quirk, forcing him down onto his chair. And stay sat, you owd fewl. He pushes Mick's half-finished drink in front of him. Sup that.

And while you do — keep an eye on Polly there and see he don't slip under the table again.

    — What about singing "With my finger in her muff", Tam?

    — All twenty-four verses.

    — I'll not have indecorum, bellows Quirk.

    — Go pull your pump, Quirk, says I. And the same all round. Quirk slinks behind his bar.

    — I'll not have that song.

    — Sing it, Tam.

    — Not in here, says the landlord Quirk.

    — All right, then. To The Perseverance everybody!

    THE PERSEVERANCE. That took him back a bit! (I saw the look in his eyes.)

    And Gormun remembers.

    What?

MISS IVY HODGE AND MRS LENA SAWNEY WHO, WHEN CLOSETED IN 4A EBURY PLACE, DID TEMPT AND INFLAME HIM WITH THEIR CEASELESS, SHRILL CHATTER ABOUT EROWINA?

(The scene is the back bedroom. Yum-Yum and Nik-Nik, dressed only in their slips, are sprawled on the bed. Their only customer, Mr O'Connor, sits on the edge, his back towards them, a bottle in his hand. He is wearing a shirt, tie, socks, but no trousers.)

YUM-YUM: It was when we worked The Perseverance we got to know her — didn't we, Nik-Nik?

NIK-NIK: She was all tits and teeth.

YUM-YUM: Holdin' herself so tight she could crack nuts with her tail.

O'CONNOR: Erowina?

YUM-YUM: No, daft. Old Ma Mead. The landlady.

O'CONNOR: Oh. The one with all the corsetting?

NIK-NIK: She was allus ploughin' inta me and Yum-Yum.

O'CONNOR: Who? Erowina?

NIK-NIK: NO. MA MEAD! Miss Hodge, she'd say. Miss Hodge, a word in your ear.

YUM-YUM: She'd say it JUST like that! (Nudging NIK-NIK.) A word in your ear, Miss Hodge.

NIK-NIK: Wrinkling her nose like she'd walked into a silent fart.

YUM-YUM: With her elbow on the mahogany and her hand limp as a wet fish.

NIK-NIK: And creaking all the while.

YUM-YUM: Queening it and flashing all that paste she had on.

NIK-NIK : Some of my regular customers, Miss Hodge, she'd say, some of my customers have been complaining about your carryings on in the tap room.

YUM-YUM: Her customers, mind you!

NIK-NIK: I don't wish to bar you altogether, you understand, but I DO have a business to consider. I can't have you interfering with my customers . . .

YUM-YUM: Interfering! They sat about with eyes like marbles and their mickies standing up like rhubarb!

NIK-NIK: With thoughts as dirty as cows' tails.

YUM-YUM: We'd be black and blue from their pinches.

NIK-NIK: And their language!

YUM-YUM: Always trying to creep up behind you and ticklin' with their free hand.

NIK-NIK: Not just ticklin' either!

YUM-YUM: No!

NIK-NIK: We'd be standin' sippin' our stout all nice and relaxed when — THUMP, a dirty great stiff thumb. . . .

YUM-YUM: I don't want my daughter getting wrong ideas. . . .

NIK-NIK : So you'd grab it and let them breathe down your neck.

YUM-YUM: HER daughter! Marina was allus in the puddin' club!

NIK-NIK: And it didn't stop at that.

YUM-YUM: They'd elbow your bub. Oh, I'm SO sorry, they'd say. Did I? Raisin' their hats and bowing to get an eyeful.

NIK-NIK: She said THEY complained! Lucky WE didn't!

YUM-YUM: She'd 'ave lost her licence.

NIK-NIK: Fur keepin' a broddel!

YUM-YUM: Her respectable customers, indeed.

NIK-NIK (Sitting up): They queued most Saturdays. QUEUED. And shot their load right here. (Patting the coverlet.)

YUM-YUM: Every man-jack.

NIK-NIK: Oh, we could tell you a thing or two. (Lying down.)

YUM-YUM: That we could.

NIK-NIK: Respectable indeed!

YUM-YUM: Dirty buggers.

NIK-NIK: What they didn't dare ask their wives. . . .

YUM-YUM: . . . was all right for us.

NIK-NIK: Expected us to like it.

YUM-YUM: Dirty beasts.

NIK-NIK: If wives thought their old men. . . .

YUM-YUM: You'd never believe the tricks they get up to.

NIK-NIK: . . . their dear little, quiet little, be home by ten little. . . .

YUM-YUM: Out with the boys.

NIK-NIK: Well! They'd have heart failure.

YUM-YUM: Never natural.

NIK-NIK: Never.

YUM-YUM: There it was — and they weren't interested.

NIK-NIK: Never.

YUM-YUM: It made you wonder all right.

NIK-NIK: Filthy — the lot of them.

YUM-YUM: And there was old Ma Mead saying they complained about me and Nik here.

NIK-NIK: Wouldn't wonder she put the police on us.

O'CONNOR: Shift over. (YUM-YUM makes room on the bed for O'CONNOR. He lights a cigarette, throws the matchstick on the carpet and lies on his back.) And that's when she told you?

YUM-YUM: Eh?

O'CONNOR: Erowina.

YUM-YUM: No. no. It wasn't her.

O'CONNOR: You said. . . .

YUM-YUM: I said — that's when we got to know her.

O'CONNOR: Oh. When was that?

YUM-YUM: Now you've asked. (Turning to NIK-NIK.)

NIK-NIK: Wasn't it about the same time that fellow got put away for indecency?

YUM-YUM: Mister Scamel — of course!

NIK-NIK: And his samples.

YUM-YUM: In his little suitcase. Very regular, he was. Once a month. Six
o'clock on the dot.

NIK-NIK: He gave me the shivers.

YUM-YUM: A proper gentleman.

NIK-NIK: Too quiet. Liked wearing our knickers.

YUM-YUM: Poor sod.

O'CONNOR: What's this got to do with Erowina? (Groping under the bed to
find his bottle of beer.)

YUM-YUM: Tammy had turned up earlier in the afternoon. . . .

O'CONNOR: TAMMY HERE? (Propping himself on his elbow.)

NIK-NIK: And why not?

YUM-YUM: Think we're not good enough for him?

O'CONNOR: No. No, of course not. It's just that. . . .

YUM-YUM: I know what you're thinking. Well, you're wrong, see. (She
struggles into a sitting position.) Tammy's bin good to us.

NIK-NIK: None of this dirty nonsense.

YUM-YUM: And he never come here when he had that girl.

O'CONNOR: You mean Erowina?

YUM-YUM: Who else.

O'CONNOR: But he's still with her.

YUM-YUM: (Rolling her eyes and looking at NIK-NIK.) But he don't have
her do he? Or didn't you know?

O'CONNOR : No, I didn't.

YUM-YUM: Not since her babby was born so he says.

(NIK-NIK leans out of bed and picks up a packet of cigarettes. She lights two cigarettes and hands one to YUM-YUM.)

NIK-NIK : Gorm? (O'CONNOR shakes his head.)

O'CONNOR: I think he might have told me. A word to the wise from you two wouldn't have come amiss.

YUM-YUM: What are you babblin' about?

O'CONNOR: Told me. Here I have been playing the friend. Respecting his wife.

NIK-NIK: She's not his wife.

O'CONNOR: I — KNOW — THAT! But all the while he's been coming here.

YUM-YUM: You too! And YOU'RE married. So? Why the long face?

O'CONNOR: It's deceitful, that's what. He ought to have more respect for her.

YUM-YUM: Respect? My arse! (And she makes a playful grab at him, but NIK-NIK sits up and, swinging her arm, catches YUM-YUM a resounding smack on the bottom with the flat of her hand.)

NIK-NIK: Give over, greedy. (And she turns to O'CONNOR but he has lost interest.)

The four of them sup in silence.

Quirk, barrel rolling, stops and straightens his back. He looks at me, then at Miss Sawney and raises his eyebrows.

Gormun looks at me.

Ivy looks at me.

I regard my boots.

— 'Appen the joy's gone from him, sighs Ivy.

— 'Appen we'll bring it back. She stands and walks up to Mr Quirk. Let me pre-zume, Quirky dear. And she stands the barrel upright. Placing one foot on top of the barrel — exposing a stockingless leg bulging with varicose, she turns. Well, help us up, yu mangy priest you. Quirk obliges. Now pass me virgin's vingal. She takes the broom from him After ten, Ivy dear, mix in with three-eight and three-four time.

Ten times she strikes the tub with the end of her broom; ten times she groans her ecstasy and Ivy rushes into a fandango while Bubulaha dances on top of the barrel.

— Madness! groans Quirk.

Sweat pours from Bubulaha and her bubs bob.

The rest clap in quick time. All except me.

Gammy takes hold of her skirt by the hem. And raises it.

Everyone laughs and shouts — except Quirk.

— You'll take a fall! and he looks away, disgusted. (Which is my cue.) I claps my hands together and jumps to my feet.

—AMATERASU! squeals Bubulaha, as I makes towards her. AMATER-ASU! And she drops her skirt over my head.

— Me lode star! says I, muffled in a familiar smelling darkness.

But all good fun comes to an end.

Giggling, Yammy is helped down and I places a fraternal kiss upon her mother o'pearl brooch.

— I've come through me gloom. And am ready, says I.

Quirk rolls his barrel away.

Yum-Yum, Nik-Nik, Gormun and I form a circle and put our arms round each other's shoulders. We begin to dance. Stamping our feet we revolve with the sun, chanting: DET es jan mol. DET es tau mol. DET es seben mol.

And we changed direction every fourth beat.

Mick slips into the circle with an empty beer bottle and stands in the centre.

The circle contracts until.

— YOU DIRTY BUGGER, MICK! yells a laughing Yammy.

We all laugh. And laugh. Oh, yes. And the circle begins to weave a different pattern.

— What the devil are you doing? enquires an alarmed Quirk, breasting the mahogany.

The circle scatters — Bubulaha chased by Mick's phallic bottle, and the rest of us jumping out of the way.

— MICK MacCOYM! Shame on you!

Mick jabs the bottle into Gammy's retreating buttocks, turns and plonks the bottle on the mahogany.

— Get bottled, Quirk. Fun's fun.

— And indecorum is indecorum. So you watch it, Mick MacCoym, or you'll be out on your ear.

Mick blows a raspberry, turns up his backside (pour chasser le moin chrétiens), and walks away.

— Tam, says Gorm, tapping me on the backside while I am climbing onto a table. Tam, am awa. Am awa t'Pen.

— Gis a leg up, Bubulaha, says I. I'm going to sing.

— Am owd asimpahee wi ma se, Tam, addressing my backside. I canna bur t'lose anower tear fr hr. TAM!

— Bugger off then, says I, standing on the table.

— B'Tam! says Gorm, his Greco eyes turned appealingly up a t me while he tugs m'trouser leg. Tam . . . TAM!

— Ivy-Nik. Let's have, The Muff. The tune, now. Doloroso, mind.

Ivy fingers the melancholy opening refrain. I throws back my head to sing, but. Surprise, surprise.

Mrs Gloria Sansum enters the public bar and walks unsteadily up to the mahogany counter.

There is a hush and Ivy's note expires.

Mrs Sansum, her long, blonde hair cascading like a waterfall, is elegantly sheathed in skin-tight, yellow silk; and bra-less. (Knickerless, too, by the look.)

We stand agog, staring, while her clouded perfume engulfs us all.

— Scotch, please, landlord. A double.

— Certainly, madam. Water or soda? says Quirk, his eyes spinning like Catherine wheels.

— I will drink it neat, thank you.

Quirk had met his Waterloo-loo and his firework was beginning to sparkle.

— You must excuse the, er. It's a Wake. There's a little. At the back, says he, remembering when Mavis abetted his snuggery. For ladies only, it is. And private.

— Thank you, no. These are my friends. And. (Effectively dampening Quirk's squib.) Hello, Tammy darling.

— Mrs San-sum! shouts I. Glorious Gloria. Good . . . (Gammy's busy fingers had tied my bootlaces together so that I bowed on "morning", took a step forward on "God" and fell with an "Aaaaou, sod!")

C-R-A-S-H.

A table splinters, a chair breaks and two glasses shatter.

— Ohhhhhhhh . . . ME . . . Holding her backside, Mary, Mother of Jesus! Right up me bleedin' arse. Get it out, someone. QUIRK! The chair leg!

Quirk, flapping like a bat, excuses himself and ducks under the mahogany. Pushing aside the fallen table, he leaps me and bends over Mac-Donald. Polly? POL-LY?

Ivy takes a swing at Gormun with her concertina. Fat head!

— Who — me?

— GORMUN! Stop belly-aching and give us a hand with Polly. He's croaked.

— He's what?

— O, me elbow! Me drinkin' arm! Then, spying my boots: Who's the Tom-Tit did that? YAMMY, YOU OLD COW! You could 'ave kilt me!

— He's not breathin'.

— Lay his head back.

— What about me?

— Bugger you. It's Polly.

— Someone ought to try giving him the kiss of life.

— Well, go on then, Yammy.

— Me? I ain't doin' it.

— You've kissed worse in your time.

— I couldn't. Not that. You do it.

— Not me. Gormun?

— Tammy's the doctor. (But who was sat on the floor having difficulty unlacing his boots.)

— Out of the way. And Mrs Gloria Sansum, dressed to kill, kneels down to save the old man.

With varnished forefinger and thumb, she pinches Polly's water bonce and looks into his gob. His swollen, white-coated tongue lolls in a mouthful of rotting teeth while he gargles with the last of his breath.

As Gloria bends over him, we all try to squint up her dress to verify the probable. (We are all of us human and, being human, inquisitive.) And she didn't.

— Are you going to. . . .

Of course.

And she does.

But.

— AGH! She recoils. HE'S — NOT — DEAD! and she spits and wipes her mouth.

—He's not? Not? HA HA HA HA. Ha, ha, ha, ha. Ha. HA.

— HO, dear dear dear, dear. HAHAHAHA. HA. Ha. Ho deara. Deardear.

— Was it 'orrible, eh? HEY? HA-HA.

— Did 'e kiss yer, eh? EH?

— The crafty old bugger. And Gloria rises.

Quirk, the spectator, turns to his offended customer and bows. Well help, Mrs. Brandy's. It was for, he nods to the giggling Polly. It's highly medicinal. A disinfectant.

She accepts with a smile, forcing Quirk's rhubarb.

— I take my hat off to you, Gloria, says I, still sat on the floor. It was a Nightingale gesture you just made.

— I came to apologise, says she, looking down.

Explanations are not needed. Quirk! More drinks. (Quirk eyes the distinguished and sexy widow.) Grief is an odd emotion, my dear. It is so rare one cannot be expected to conform to a pattern. Help me up. Perhaps I should have said, per-form an unaccustomed ritual without embarrassment. Her death has affected us all. And differently. Poor old Gormun's taken it badly. As if . . . well. Never mind. Poor sod.

— He loved her.

— We all did, says I, standing.

— But it was I who forced her hand, she says demurely.

—No. I was at fault, says I. It was myself I loved. Loved love. The idea of love.

— But it was I who unbalanced her with no thought for the consequences, says she, sincerely.

— No.

— Yes.

— Who knows?

The landlord Quirk, spying Mick about to pinch Yammy's bum, points.

— None of that. Go look after Polly. Get him back up on his chair afore Elsie comes looking. And drink up. Time!

Yum-Yum and Nik-Nik help MacCoym set Polly straight.

Gormun swaggers up to the glorious Gloria Sansum.

She smiles.

He spits.

Quirk stops wiping.

The two tarts crane forward.

I intervene and put my glass of whisky into Gormun's hand.

— This was bought you, says I.

— Says you, and lets it fall.

The glass smashes and the lovely widow's pretty little shoes are splashed.

Is it any good my apologising to you, Gormun? says she with her voice.

— Apologise? For what? FOR-WHAT! (And I saw he had a mind to put his knee into her maidenly crutch.)

— Now, now, Gormun, says I. Don't spoil the wake for want of love.

— LOVE? What do you know about love, you bleedin' scribbler! Or you! And he jabs a stiff finger into the softness of Mrs Sansum's jelly and bra-less boobies.

— WHAT DO YOU KNOW ABOUT LOVE, YOU BLEEDIN' FREAK! says he, addressing her nose.

But suddenly, the world for Mr O'Connor is no longer real.

— What d'YOU, any of you, know about love?

He stands with tears streaming down both cheeks; crying like a great big babby.

And he no longer hears us.

For him, the wake is over.

For us, too.

Quirk had called time.

Gormun went, he said, and told me later, back with the Fulham Virgins, to their soft bed and maternal hugs. I have no reason to disbelieve him.

Whereas I, with a bottle in my left pocket, Gloria's hand in my right (pocket), turned left, the other way — the left-handed way, back to my room with a lock, where we took it in turns. Any widow in a storm, thought I. Yes, yes, says she. But it was the drink which made her vomit, not the sight of me in vest and pants.

Come the morning, she used my comb to part her hair.

— I'm not so ashamed, I'll not see you again, says she to me, holding me close, like a sister may. It was you who gave her what he wanted. A baby.

— Which died.

Gloria began to comb my beard.

— You only did what a man may.

— Not last night.

— But you could have. Why didn't you?

— It was the dead herself I had a respect for, says I.

— Says you. Where was your respect for her when she was alive? Eh? And her only gone round the corner shopping. Or when she stood waiting for your coming, while it was with me you were; on your knees in my car — all condensation and mouthing.

— A case of mistaken identity. And why the Irish?

— To learn to speak the language of a foreigner is to understand him.

— Then why didn't you swot up Erowina's prose?

— I knew her like the back of my hand.

— Really? Then you know she was christened Emily, and that Erowina was not her real name. Nor Erica, Eunice, Esmeralda; ad infinitum.

— What?

— That her birth was unusual. That she cried out inside, I repeat, IN-SIDE her mother's womb. It's termed vagitus uterinus. Erowina — Emily — thought it significant and summed up her whole life with the words, "vox et praeterea nihil". A voice and nothing more. But, of course, you knew this.

— I did not.

— Not? Then you didn't know she was relatively wealthy. That her father was a recluse and an eccentric. That she was brought up by a de-generate cook. That she left home at eighteen but later in life went back regularly to pick up her allowance and play with her dolls — up until her death.

— Who? Erowina? I don't believe you.

— Then you won't believe me when I tell you she was a practising witch.

— Rubbish.

— True. Did you know she was allergic to roses?

— What nonsense is this?

— The only two times she worked in her life was as a telephonist at St Veronica's hospital and as a barmaid in the Perseverance — just to help pass the time.

— How do you know?

— I stole all her diaries.

— DIARIES! Gloria sat down on the bed as if struck by a bolt.

— In that tin trunk. They are not all diaries. Erowina wrote essays, short stories — plays even. They're all there. I lie. The years fifty-two to fifty-six are missing.

— Fifty-two, fifty. . . . That was when you. . . .

— Yes.

— Convenient.

— I watched her burn them.

Gloria was recovered, and recovered, became kittenish.

— What does she say about me? Does she mention the years when — we were great friends?

— Oh, yes. In mouth-watering detail.

— Let me see.

— And the newspapers? Gloria frowned. On the day Erowina died, she ringed various headlines in the Sunday newspapers and made marginal comments.

— So?

— Aren't you interested in Erowina?

— Yes, but I want to know what she wrote about me. Is that so odd? Hand them over.

— No.

— I'll stay until you do.

— On one condition, then.

— What?

— Marry me.

— You?

— Me.

— And if I refuse?

— Erowina despised me because I didn't dominate her. Couldn't. Didn't want to. As a man, I haven't changed.

— Open the trunk, I said. . . .

I obliged, and it was a smiling Gloria who settled on her knee beside me and folded back the lid.

— It'll have to be you who 'phones Martin, not me, says she to me.

And as we began to sort through and read Erowina's papers, I wondered if I would. Could. As it turned out, I didn't.

FATHER'S SKIN (1931)

In the darkness, hanging limply from a rusty nail hammered into the back of the door, was my father's skin.

Standing on tiptoe in the gloomy corridor, I reached up and lifted down the warm, tobacco-smelling skin and, bundling it under my arm, raced up the thickly carpeted stairs to my room and closed the door.

Victorious, I spread the skin on the floor and smoothed away the creases with the palm of my hand. The skin was much hairier than I remembered and was covered in tiny brown moles.

Undressing, I pulled it on and went cautiously towards the full-length mirror.

My disappointment was overwhelming.

The skin hung in folds; sagging and wrinkled. The arms were too long and hung limp whilst the legs crumpled around my ankles like fallen stockings. The stomach, a deflated, wrinkled bladder, aproned my knees and the navel protruded like a teat on a baby's bottle to which the cat's hair adhered.

Turning my back on the mirror, I let the skin slip from my shoulders and drop to the floor.

Stepping out of it with a show of temper, I kicked it across the room and threw myself down onto the bed.

As I lay sulking, I spied the black-handled scissors and was off the bed in a bound.

Kneeling to the skin, my tears forgotten, I snipped and cut, reducing the size. This done, I sewed up the seams; experiencing great difficulty in forcing the slim needle through the glutinous skin.

To my great delight, when I had finished, I found that the skin lilted perfectly.

I admired my muscular figure in the mirror and spoke gruffly to my strutting image.

Full of confidence now, I opened my door and walked boldly over to my mother's bedroom door and knocked.

But it was Miss Nancy Sedoloid who lay in bed wearing my mother's nightdress.

UNDER SAINT DYMPNA'S PATRONAGE
(1934)

— Could we go to the Zoo afterwards?

— O, hush, child. You're forever chattering. And stop scuffing your shoes.

Nancy Sedoloid, dressed in her best Sunday satin, which revealed all the mysterious bumps and lumps of the rigid corset which held in her stomach and buttocks, bustled ahead. Her feet, buckled in her best patent blacks, clunked on the stone steps as she puffed her way up to the imposing entrance in the sooty Victorian façade of what she termed the "Academy".

Emily noticed Nancy's stocking was wrinkled and saw the bulging varicose vein which was exposed each time Nancy stepped upward onto her left foot.

— Oh, come on, child. And, turning, she stretched out her gloved hand. Stop dawdling.

— You've got a hole in your glove.

— What?

— A hole.

— Where?

— There.

— Damn and botheration. Peering into the fork of her fingers. That would happen, wouldn't it? I'm sure it means something.

— It what?

— Like dropping a fork or falling upstairs.

— If you spill salt you're meant to throw it over your shoulder so that whatever was going to happen won't.

— I can't go throwing my glove over my shoulder, silly.

— What does the hole mean, then?

— How do I know? A gentleman visitor, perhaps. Or death.

— It doesn't mean we can't go to the Zoo afterwards, does it?

— I don't remember them being holed when I put them on. Thank goodness your Uncle Harry won't notice. Mildred will.

Nancy peeled the offending glove from her plump, puffy fingers and inspected the glove as if it were a kipper she were buying; turning it over and over.

— You haven't been dressing up again, have you?

— No.

— I'll carry it. And she looked approvingly at the limp glove held in her gloved fist.

Settling her large patent handbag under her arm so the diamanté clip in the shape of a boat in full sail was visible, she said: Come to think of it, I was talking to your father when I came to put on my gloves. I didn't notice the hole then nor when I came to pay the taxi fare. I hope no one saw. And then: Come on.

— And we can look at the monkeys before we go home?

— Shush. Keep close to me if you don't want to get lost. Putting her hand on the polished brass finger plate, she pushed. And remember. Don't gawp.

Emily followed Nancy into the gloom of the large cool building and down the shiny corridors. The noise of Nancy's feet clattered from wall to wall whilst Emily's tipped and pattered a few paces behind. The black line which separated the glossy cream and green paint on the walls was just above the level of Emily's head. She could not resist it.

— What d'you think you're doing? Just look at your fingers!

Nancy gave Emily a push from behind. Now, just you walk where I can see what you're up to, you naughty girl. And don't hunch up your shoulders like that. Stand up straight or you'll turn into a hunchback and be touched for luck. I don't think!

The corridor down which they walked terminated in a large hall where rows of wooden benches were ranged.

— Go and sit on the bench and wait for me. And mind you behave yourself.

Emily sat down gingerly on the edge of the nearest slatted bench while Nancy clattered away to her left, towards a small door with the word "Reception" printed in gold upon it. Emily squinted sideways at a bird-like woman who was sitting on the bench next to her. The woman was clutching a pudding bowl in her lap over the top of which was tied a piece of muslin. Emily glanced at the pudding basin and then up at the vacant face of the woman who, gazing into space, had allowed the upper plate of her false teeth to drop down.

Nancy punched Emily's shoulder when she returned and said under her breath: I thought I told you not to gawp!

In the silence which followed, Emily heard the birdlike woman click her teeth back into place and swallow. Emily, for want of something better to do, began to swing her feet backwards and forwards.

— Stop that.

She stopped.

An elderly gentleman with a distinguished bearing entered the hall, paused while he removed his gloves and glanced round before going to the door marked "Reception" and knocking on it with one of his bare knuckles. Twice and lightly.

— I said, stop it! What's wrong with you? Do you want to go to the W.C.? Emily shook her head.

— Well, behave yourself, then. Jigging about like that.

Emily slid forward on the bench seat so that her feet were flat on the stone floor.

— Apparently Mildred's not here yet. It's not like her to miss a visit.

A door was unlocked and a man dressed in white trousers and a white jacket entered the hall. He locked the door behind him and walked over towards the elderly gentleman with his hand outstretched.

— Mr Quinton?

They shook hands and the man with the white jacket said something, which Emily could not hear.

—I wonder who he is? Came in after us, too.

The man in the white jacket unlocked a door and both men passed through. The door was closed behind them and Emily heard the key turn, locking it.

IN THE CONFINEMENT WING FOR BLOCK "B" MALE INMATES, MR JAMES ORDINANCE, BALDING, AGED FORTY-THREE, LAY IN BED 170 WITH HIS CANVAS GLOVED HANDS STRAPPED TO HIS CHEST, STRAINING TO REACH HIS ERECTION.

— I told Mildred I thought Henrietta — I mean Harry, ought to have gone to a private sanatorium so there wouldn't be all this hanging about. But Mildred's as nutty as her daughter. Went queer when she lost her brother on the water, she did.

— I like Uncle Harry.

—You would. Just look at that split. Thank goodness I'm not family, that's all I can say. They said it was congenital. His, her condition. They SAID.

— What's congenital?

— I wish it had been my right glove. Mildred's bound to notice I'm wearing Elfreda's ring. I really must get it altered, but I don't like the idea of having it cut off.

— Having what cut off?

— How else are they going to get your mother's ring off my finger?

Emily, her eyes wide, stared at Nancy's hand.

— Stop swinging your legs like that. It's not ladylike.

— I wasn't.

— Don't argue. I know what you were doing. I can see, can't I?

— You were jigging about again. Stop it. You'll get into bad ways and goodness knows where you'll end up.

— I'm bored.

— That's when it happens.

— Who's going to die?

— Who said anything about dying?

— You said that if you had a hole in your glove. . . .

— Oh, shut up, do.

IN THE DAY ROOM OF BLOCK "C" FOR FEMALE INMATES, MISS GLADYS FAIRLEY PUT HER HAND BEHIND THE RADIATOR, FEELING FOR WHERE THEY HAD HIDDEN HER BABY.

— Is Uncle Harry married?

— Now, what made you ask a silly question like that? Who'd? . . . Oh, never mind. Is Uncle Harry married! and she sniggered. Now, who would believe that! Look.

An attractive young woman with red hair, dressed in a bright green, cotton print dress walked into the hall on white, high-heeled court shoes. She tip-tapped her way up to the reception door, opened it and, holding onto the door jamb, leant into the small office.

Nancy snorted down her nose.

— Hugh! You can see what she is. And. Crossing her hands over her handbag, she pulled it up against her ample front.

The young, redhaired woman turned away from the reception office with a wide smile and pulled the door quietly shut behind her. Nancy and Emily watched her progress across the hall.

— She hasn't even the common decency to wear a girdle. She's all bottom. Disgusting. Wouldn't surprise me if she wasn't wearing any as-is.

Emily wondered what as-is were and watched the retreating figure of the girl whom she envied.

— You can always tell, you know. Those sort of women give themselves away. They never keep their tails tucked in. They flaunt their backsides. No sensible man takes any notice of a girl like her. You remember that.

IN THE CONFINEMENT WING FOR BLOCK "A" FEMALES, MRS JUDITH CHARM LAY QUIETLY IN HER BOXED COT LOOKING AT THE SCRATCHED WOODWORK.

A young man wearing a short-sleeved white jacket and dark blue trousers with very wide bottoms suddenly appeared in the hall and with a jaunty step walked over towards the benches. When he drew near, Emily saw that his arms were covered in long black hairs and round his wrist was a gold watch attached to a very wide black leather strap.

The young man rattled some keys in the palm of his hand, moistened his lower lip with a bright red tongue and, flicking back his curly quiff, looked over the occupants on the benches.

— Who's for Hambuck?

— That's us, said Nancy, rising. Come.

In front of the locked door all three stood in silence while the attendant selected the correct key.

Nancy tugged at her holed glove.

— I've come as a friend, you know, she said, leaning towards him when he bent to insert the key.

The attendant, stooping, with his head level with Emily's face, gave an exaggerated wink.

While he continued to fiddle the key in the hole, Emily stared at his long sideburns and into his ear, which was stuffed full with black hairs.

When the attendant smirked, Emily stepped nearer to Nancy.

— Look what you're doing! and Nancy patted her plumpness and smoothed away imaginary creases in her satin dress. Children! Who'd have them?

The attendant smirked again, but at Nancy.

Emily was aware of a sudden change of smell which began to emanate from Nancy, and she wrinkled her nose, as the attendant opened the door and stood aside.

— Thank you. Come along, Emily.

Emily avoided the attendant's hand which was too low down in the small of her back and, stiffening herself, entered the corridor sideways.

He locked the door, leaving them on their own in a grim, short passage at the other end of which was a swing door. Nancy walked up and pushed it open to reveal a large, dirty hall. Emily hesitated but Nancy's firm hand forced her into the hall.

The dining room, which was also for the use of visitors, was large and gloomy. It smelled of tea-leaves, condensed milk and damp, mildewed bread. The walls were painted in the same green and cream paint as elsewhere but were dusty and grimed above where the arm of a slovenly cleaner could not reach. The floor had no covering and the boards were worn and had large gaps between the planking, filled with dust which even the light tread of Emily's small feet raised, while the hollowness of each step was carried up to the high, dark ceiling. Facing Emily when she was pushed through the door was a row of windows high up in the wall through which she could see the sooty leaves of a tree and the monotonous brickwork of a black, surrounding wall. There were streaks running down the wall where the rain, falling from a sky which she could not see, had dribbled down, carrying with it a black soot. The bars on the windows were so close together they prevented the windowpanes from being washed, so that the small amount of light which managed to filter into the hall was tinged with a sulphurous yellow.

— What a nasty smell of cabbage. And Nancy pushed past Emily.

Only a few humpbacked people were in the room; sat in small, silent groups, gazing at each other across some of the many trestled tables which were arranged in orderly ranks down the length. Drooped on their wooden benches they sat unmoving, vacant, hardly breathing while an atmosphere of despondency shrouded them. None of the visitors had removed their hats or coats, and scattered between them on the tables was an odd selection of parcels wrapped in newspaper and tied with coarse string. A few of the men were smoking and the smell from their cigarettes was strong and peppery. Emily was reminded of the old men who stood all day outside the public lavatory on Gate Hill and of the few times she had persuaded Nancy to take her up on to the top deck of a bus.

Emily tried to catch hold of Nancy's hand but Nancy deliberately held it up and away from her, across her bosom. Emily felt tempted to snatch at Nancy's skirt, but checked herself and coveted the little confidence she gained by staying close to the bulky, powdered sourness of Nancy's haunches.

Trailing after Nancy down the length of the hall, Emily caught the eyes of one or two of the seated people who either gazed at her unconcernedly or grinned idiotically.

Frightened, she tripped on Nancy's heel. Nancy turned round. Irritated, and with a sharp reprimand of "Leave off, child", she bustled ahead, fuming.

— Harry! How nice to see you. How are you? You're looking well. Ever so well.

A white-coated attendant nodded and withdrew from Harry's side. Nancy fluttered the attendant a too sweet "Thank you", with a silly sideways tilt of her head and a flickering of her sparsely eye-lashed lids.

Emily recognised the sudden warm surge of smell which blossomed from Nancy, and tried to hold her breath. Glancing round Nancy's satin skirt, she looked up at Uncle Harry who was stood on the far side of the bare table.

Harry was smiling with one side of her mouth and looking at a point somewhere in between herself and the pale green and pink satin rose which Nancy had pinned onto her dress where her giant milk breasts were crushed together in the V of her neckline.

Emily looked away from the flower and shuddered.

Nancy scraped back the wooden bench which almost toppled over.

— Drat the damned thing. You'd think they'd give us chairs.

Carefully, she shuffled in between the bench and the table until she was opposite Harry, then sat down. Emily, relieved, quickly scrambled onto it, next to her.

— I've brought Emily with me. Say hello to your Uncle Harry. Emily smiled but found she could not speak.

— What's up? Cat got your tongue? She's a funny girl, and no mistake. Been chattering non-stop all the way here, she has.

Harry was still smiling with the side of her mouth; her left eyelid lowered.

— Sit down, Harry. I'm sure she's pleased to see you. Aren't you, Emily? Now. Tell us how you're keeping. What have you been doing with yourself?

Harry thought for a while and then, cocking her leg over the wooden form, sat down with her hands together in front of her; her shoulders hunched.

— Emily brought you a present. Didn't you, dear? Give Uncle Harry the present you brought.

Emily opened her tiny handbag and took out a small screw of paper in which were some toffees.

— Give them to your Uncle Harry.

Emily put them gingerly on the scrubbed wooden table top in front of Uncle Harry. When he didn't attempt to take them, Emily pushed them towards him until the little crumpled packet almost touched his folded hands.

— You'd better take one out for him, dear.

Emily, on tiptoe, reached over and dragged the packet of sweets back towards her. Fumbling inside, she took out a toffee and pushed it towards her Uncle Harry.

— Why don't you unwrap it for your uncle? said Nancy, because Harry sat contemplating the toffee on the table in front of her.

Emily retrieved the single toffee and twisted off the crinkly, bright red cellophane and held out the sweet for him to take.

— A toffee, Uncle.

— Better put it in his mouth, dear.

Emily turned towards her stepmother, her eyes wide with alarm.

— Go round to him, and put it in his mouth.

Nancy forced Emily off the bench and pushed her towards the end of the table.

— Go on. He won't bite!

Emily ventured round the table and approached him nervously. —Go on!

Emily held the sweet up to her uncle's cheek where the smile stayed fixed on his face.

— Put it in his mouth, then.

Emily pressed the sweet into her uncle's crooked smile and watched the skin dimple. When she thought it wedged, she snatched her hand away and scampered back to her place beside Nancy who leant across the table and pushed it into her sideways smile, saying, I thought you liked toffees? Harry, with the tip of her white, furred tongue, licked the toffee into her mouth.

The movement was so quick, Emily imagined it a trick and beamed at her uncle in admiration.

Harry, closing her right eye, looked at Emily from under the permanently hooded lid of her left; and blew a raspberry.

— It was Mother who said I liked toffees. I never told you I liked them.

Harry, I know I'm not family, but. Well! I think you ought to show a little more courtesy to Emily. After all, she bought and paid for them herself.

Harry looked away and Nancy sighed.

— Well, we won't argue. We don't want to be at loggerheads when your mother arrives. We've come to cheer you up. I don't expect you get much decent company in here, she said, looking about her.

— She won't be coming.

— Not?

— No.

— Oh.

IN THE DAY ROOM FOR BLOCK "C" FEMALE INMATES, MISS JENNY GREY, AGED FIFTY-ONE, SAT ON THE FLOOR IN THE CORNER OF THE ROOM UN-PICKING THREADS OF COTTON FROM THE BUTTONS ON HER CLOSELY PATTERNED FROCK BECAUSE THE STITCHES CROSSED OVER EACH OTHER INSTEAD OF BEING PARALLEL.

Emily looked round at a man pushing a rattling tea trolley on which was balanced a giant silver tea urn. He was passing out mugs of steaming tea and slabs of dense, yellow cake.

— Do you want tea, Harry?

They waited in silence until the tea trolley came to their end of the table.

— All three?

— Please, said Nancy, smiling and shewing all her artificial teeth.

Three plain white plates were placed before them, each bearing a piece of cake which the attendant picked off the end of the long slab with his fingers. The tea, in thick white mugs, was already milked and sugared. Nancy passed Harry her tea and cake, attended to Emily and then pro-ceeded to break her slice of cake into small pieces. Emily concentrated on the cake but, finding it dry, took a mouthful of very hot tea to soften it. Then, breaking off another piece, she glanced at Nancy before dunking it in her mug and.

— Emily! Stop that. Really! Anyone would think you'd been brought up in the gutter.

When Nancy looked up to Harry, she saw she was glowering. Nancy smiled nervously. Harry looked away and took a deep breath.

— Eat up, Harry.

When Harry took a large bite into her cake, Emily saw the unchewed toffee lying on his coated tongue.

— Did your mother say why she isn't coming? She's always saying she's never missed a visit.

— Not once.

IN THE HOSPITAL WING DR OSBORNE, HANDS ON HIPS, WATCHED NURSE JACQUETTA FRINK USE THE STOMACH PUMP ON MR DOGHERTY, A SELF-MUTILATED CASTRATE WHO HALF AN HOUR PREVIOUSLY HAD BEEN FOUND UNCONSCIOUS IN THE PASSAGE LEADING TO BLOCK "C", HAVING SWALLOWED AN AS YET UNIDENTIFIED POISON.

Emily watched a man who was gnawing his toothless gums while he dunked the whole of his piece of cake into his mug of steaming hot tea. She watched enviously until the sodden cake broke off and plopped into the mug. She could not restrain a giggle and, hunching her small shoulders, tried to stifle it in the crossed palms of her two hands pressed against her mouth. But the suppressed snigger came snorting down her nose and Nancy turned on her. — For goodness sake, Emily, behave yourself! And she smacked Emily's bare thigh beneath the table. Any more of that and out you go.

Emily, out of the corner of her eye, saw the man fishing about in the mug with his fingers, trying to salvage the remains of his soggy cake. She bent down her head; bursting to snigger.

— Listen. If you don't behave yourself, I won't take you to feed the monkeys. Do you hear? Now, stop it.

— You're going to the Zoo?

— She keeps on pestering me to take her. I wouldn't have brought her only. . . .

— I was going to ask.

— . . . Sidney has got his neuralgia badly. In his neck, you know. And he has to stay wrapped up warm. Even in weather like this. He said he'd have written but he's been so busy of late.

Harry sniggered girlishly, poked her forefinger into her right ear; examined the end of it when she took it out and then looked up at the window.

— Truly.

Harry giggled again.

Emily looked up in surprise.

Harry shrugged her shoulders.

Nancy placed her handbag on the table and gave a tug to the front of her dress and patted out the satin leaves of her flower. Emily, with her half-finished mug of hot tea cupped in her hands, glanced round at the silent groups of men and women who, seemingly embarrassed by their companions, averted their eyes; deliberately avoiding the accidental glances from their friends and those about them. All of them looked depressed and there was an aura of hopelessness about them even in the varied yet similar attitudes of dejection they had taken on the wooden forms they sat upon. Their clothes, shabby and dull, accentuated the depression which emanated from them, reminding Emily of the crowds of men who congregated on the pavements, stood idly, doing absolutely nothing, who appeared lifeless except for the shiftless movement of their eyes and whose hands were forever buried deep in their trouser pockets while they leant against walls or stood in ranks toeing the kerb of the gutter. Idlers, Nancy had called them; dirty good-for-nothings who obstructed the pavements and made it difficult for honest citizens like herself to go about their lawful business. Unemployed, said her father, whose shares had dropped; but Emily had not understood.

Looking about her, Emily noticed that one of the men in the hall appeared to be asleep. One of his arms, on which his head rested, lay along the table top whilst the other was beneath it; in his lap somewhere. He was trembling and Emily imagined he was crying. When he turned his head and looked directly at her, she saw that his eyes were wide and staring and his face suffused with blood. It was as if he was trying to hold his breath while he out-stared her. Emily was disconcerted but not alarmed because she was sat close to Nancy.

Suddenly, from between his compressed lips, a strange sound began, like that of a heated vixen.

Nancy, attracted by the sound in the quiet hall, looked up to see the man jump to his feet and try to finish off what he had begun under the table.

Giving a cry of horror, Nancy seized Emily by the scruff of the neck and forced Emily's head beneath the table. Although Emily yelled, Nancy clung on. Emily tried to squirm out of her stepmother's grip but Nancy's fingers were buried into her scraggy neck, so she used her elbows. Failing, she kicked Nancy's shins.

— OUCH! and Nancy shook Emily, much as a dog might shake a rabbit it had caught hold of by the scruff of the neck. You horrible little thing!

— You were trying to kill me, sobbed Emily.

But she was hauled to her feet and given a resounding slap on her bare thigh.

— Don't talk nonsense. It was for your own good. Did you see anything? I said. . . . But her leg pained and she bent to feel it. Right on my vein, too. You could have burst it. You. . . And stop snivelling. Use your handkerchief.

Emily withdrew her handkerchief but Nancy snatched it.

— That's right. Spread the dirt about. And she spat on the handkerchief and rubbed Emily's face vigorously. Here. (And she gave back the hanky.) And sit up.

Emily sobbed quietly; her lips compressed.

— Oh, stop it, do.

Mr Cavanner having been removed, more attendants drifted into the hall to stand with their hands behind them and their backs to the wall; eyeing the huddled groups of men and women. Not a sound could be heard and everyone seemed suddenly concerned with the ends of their fingers.

Nancy coughed. I hardly thought . . . I mean. One hears things, or course. But. Well. And that a child should see. It's disgusting.

She gathered up her gloves and pulled at the empty fingers nervously. You'd have thought they wouldn't have let him have visitors. I mean, we should have been advised it might happen.

— In all probability it was the presence of Emily which gave rise to his action.

— Well, I think it's disgusting. It's quite upset me. People like that; they're a menace. They ought to be put down like the animals they are.

Silence.

Nancy drew her handbag towards her.

— I think we'd better go. I shall have to think twice about bringing Emily again.

— There's no need, Miss Sedoloid. I shall be out soon. She may visit me at her leisure, then.

— Yes. Well, we'll see.

— Within a month. I said — next month.

IN THE DAY ROOM FOR INMATES OF BLOCK "B", MR HARBEN, THIRTY, EMACIATED AND SMELLING STRONGLY OF URINE, AND WHO IS A CON-FIRMED "WALKER", PACED THE ROOM MUTTERING : "WOMEN. DISGUST-ING. DISEASE. WOMEN. DIRTY. VESSELS."

— You're not being very realistic, Harry. I know how much you must want to leave (she leant forward and patted Henrietta's folded hands), and I'm sure it won't be long now. We all hope it won't be long.

— I'm certain.

— But if the doctors haven't. Shall I have a word with one of them?

— There's no need. I know.

— Yes, well, if you say so, Harry.

— You don't believe me do you? and she looked at Nancy with her eyebrows raised but only one of her eyes fully opened.

— Of course I believe you.

Emily, fingering the inside of her mouth which brimmed with saliva, was turned round on her seat watching a woman sat very upright on the edge of her form who was breaking up cake with her thin, nervous fingers and scattering the resultant crumbs over the surface of the table as if she were feeding birds. Her companion, who sat opposite her facing Emily, was embarrassed by Emily's stare and, after failing to deter Emily with a fierce scowl began to brush the crumbs into a little pile with her hands and, leaning forward, whispered to her daughter who put out her tongue.

— They haven't told you, then? No one said anything to you when you went to reception?

— No.

— I thought you didn't know. As soon as I saw you walk through that door and saw your dress I said to myself, she doesn't know. No one has told her yet.

— Why don't you tell me, then?

— Shall I?

— If you want to.

— Oh, yes. I want to.

— If it won't upset you, you tell me. Nancy gave a smile to encourage Henrietta and to hide her mounting exasperation. Harry leant forward with her elbows on the table. She grinned and looked for a long while at Nancy.

Nancy kept the smile upon her face and gritted her teeth while Harry continued to stare.

— Mother's dead.

— Is what?

— Dead.

Nancy's smile evaporated and her face became slack. She straightened her back, tugged at her gloves and her mouth became a thin line.

— Finish your tea, dear, she said.

IN THE DAY ROOM FOR BLOCK "D" MALE INMATES, MR LUKE QUELCH, AGED TWENTY-ONE, PASTED ALL THE LEAVES OF ROBERT'S STAMP AL-BUM TOGETHER AND GIGGLED.

Emily watched Nancy pull on her left glove and spied the pink tip of one of her fingers through the hole in the fork as Nancy worked her hand into the glove.

— That's why she won't be coming today. Or any other day. I can leave now.

Nancy withdrew her hand from the glove, laid it on the other and, picking them both up, began to squeeze them.

— Harry. . . .

— It's true. Ask Dr Griffiths on your way out. He'll tell you. It happened last night. She had a stroke. She's dead.

Emily, realising that Nancy was not watching her, leant her head onto her hand and, shielding her actions with her right shoulder, began to dunk the remains of her cake into the cooling mug of tea, taking great care not to make it so soggy it would break off and fall into the mug.

— The superintendent came to see me first thing this morning. He said I could go out on parole to attend the funeral. Apparently Elspeth has taken on the job of seeing to everything. I thought she might have been in touch with you.

— No.

— You don't sound convinced.

— Henrietta, I'm going to be quite truthful. I'm not. After all, in the past. . . .

Harry rubbed the palms of her hands together vigorously and said, It's not very important you believe me, Miss Sedoloid.

— You mentioned it so casually. Even now you don't seem to be upset.

Emily began to blow bubbles in her tea.

— Shush, child, said Nancy, laying a restraining hand upon Emily's thigh. Let's suppose it is true, isn't it going to make things more difficult? Who's going to take on the responsibility of looking after you?

— You imagine I'm incapable of looking after myself?

— But, Harry. Even with your mother looking after you, you weren't . . . What will you do if you start getting your depressions when you're on your own?

— What makes you think I will?

— Who's going to cook for you?

— Dora.

— That was years ago. What makes you think that suddenly, out of the blue. . . .

— Because we've been writing to each other these last eighteen years.

Nancy pursed her lips. I didn't know.

— Why should you have known? Mother didn't.

— I still can't see it working out.

I shall sell the house and go down to Dorset. It may not be much of a job helping out in the post office. . . .

— You really think they'd accept you in a small village like that?

— How are they to know if no one tells them?

Nancy sniffed.

At heart you know, you're just like my bloody mother. She had the same way of sniffing to indicate her disapproval.

— Harry!

— And another bloody thing! I'm going to marry Dora Bollod!

IN THE W.C. FOR FEMALE INMATES OF BLOCK "A", MRS ELIZABETH SPALDING, AGED THIRTY-NINE, MOTHER OF TWO CHILDREN, SQUATTED DOWN IN THE CORNER TO MASTURBATE HURRIEDLY FOR THE TWELFTH TIME THAT DAY.

Emily, impersonating a grey-haired woman who was almost as small as herself, probed round the inside of her mouth with her tongue, making her cheeks bulge. Tiring. she bared her lower teeth and breathed through the cracks, making a sound of wind blowing through the tops of trees in a storm.

— Stop it, said Nancy, thumping her in the ribs with her sharp elbow. And face your front. People don't want you gawping at them.

Emily slewed round and, with a sigh, thumped her elbows on the table and supported her head in her hands.

— All right, we're going. And Nancy gathered up her gloves once again.

— To the Zoo? asked Emily brightly.

— I suppose so.

— Oh, good.

IN THE DAY ROOM FOR BLOCK "D" FEMALE INMATES, MRS RIDDLE, AGED THIRTY-TWO, ATTRACTIVE IN THE ASYLUM GOWN, STOOD BEFORE THE WINDOW CRYING WHILE MRS ALICE FAYE, PLUMP AND MOTHERLY, BUSILY DUSTED EVERYTHING TO GET RID OF THE GERMS.

— Well, Harry, I don't see any point in hanging on for the bell. I shall see Dr Griffiths on my way out. Whether I visit you again or not will depend on what he says. I'm not family, I'm just doing my duty. But I'll not come just to be insulted.

— As you please.

— Pick up your bag, child, and say goodbye.

— Goodbye, Uncle. I hope you get better soon.

— The transformation is complete, my dear. Have a nice time at the Zoo. She pushed the crumpled packet of toffees towards Emily. You'd better have these.

Emily looked back as she followed Nancy through the swing door and waved to Uncle Harry as an attendant took her arm.

Emily had to wait a long time in the outer hall while her stepmother talked to a man who was wearing thick pebble glasses and who stood with his hands on his hips, shaking his head.

When they eventually left the asylum, Emily asked brightly, Are we going to the Zoo?

But Nancy appeared lost in thought and did not answer.

— Are we going to the Zoo?

— Eh? Oh, yes. Yes, we'll go to the Zoo.

Emily jumped up and down excitedly, but Nancy, having pulled on her gloves, peered into the fork of her fingers and looked at the pink flesh of her hand which showed through.

In the Zoo Nancy let herself be pulled from cage to cage by an ebullient Emily. She heard little of what her stepdaughter said and didn't appear to see the people she bumped into from time to time. Only when they were in front of a cage containing male gibbons did she come to her senses, when the other spectators turned away from the cage and they were left standing alone watching the male gibbon nearest to them. Immediately Nancy seized Emily by the scruff of her neck and twisted her head away. Holding on to the protesting Emily she hurried down the path muttering: Oh, my God. My God.

Back home, sat in the basement kitchen, Emily looked up from her sardines on toast and said in a very clear voice, "Uncle Harry's got big bosoms, hasn't he?"

For her blasphemy, she got knocked clear across the room, and the cat pounced on her scattered sardines.

"The sooner your father sends you packing to boarding school, the better. Now, scrape up those sardines. I'm not opening another tin just for you."

FOR LADIES ONLY (1939-1943)

They had started by doing it on each other's thighs. When they became bolder, having found it was not painful, and more defiant, because in the gymnasium only the girls noticed and not Miss Gilpin, they took to cutting the backs of their hands with Mr Edgebank's discarded razorblades from which they first removed the hardened crust of soap and stubble hair.

At the beginning of this new phase, they had been content to incise their own and each other's initials; as they had done on their thighs. Two weeks later, they added entwined hearts and an elaborate crucifix. By the end of the third week, competing with each other, they began criss-crossing their flesh with a mesh-work of razor cuts. They covered not only the backs of their hands but carried on down to their fingernails and up the outsides of their arms as far as their elbows.

They revelled in the thick crusty scars which formed and spent hours teasing them open with their fingernails so as to enjoy the mouthwatering spectacle of the blood streaming out over their hands and down their arms.

Their bodies, protesting against this grotesque offence, swelled the indecent arms, puffing and inflaming the skin.

This pleased the girls even more and they swaggered about with their painful arms swollen tight in their woollen cardigans; glorying in their defiance of nature and man.

Discovering them, a bewildered headmistress ordered their parents to fetch them and justifiably argued that until both girls came to their senses, she, as both headmistress and school governor, could not accept them as pupils in a school which prided itself on turning out young ladies. But she was constrained, and a solution offered — which was, the two girls should be separated by being moved to different school houses and forbidden to see each other during recreational periods. The headmistress agreeing, but demanding they be punished, they were thwacked on their bottoms — not their sore hands which was school custom.

While the faint scars lasted, Daphne and Emily regarded them as fraternity badges and were content, although forbidden to walk about the school with their sleeves rolled up.

When the scars were hardly discernible and the two girls judged by the headmistress to have come to their senses, they were once again allowed to see each other outside classroom hours. When their school friends, no longer alarmed by their peculiar behaviour, drifted slowly back and re-formed the old, well established coterie, Daphne and Emily began taking aspirin tablets dissolved in Tizer lemonade.

Meeting in the quadrangle after breakfast, they would compare the sensations each had experienced. Because neither had suffered anything more than a mild headache and stomach upset, they were loath to admit to each other the failure of their experiment. However, for their disbelieving friends, they concocted bizarre hallucinations which they related with melodramatic breathlessness, even going so far as to simulate dizziness and slurred speech whilst in class to convince the Lower Third that they were drugged.

On the night Daphne was violently sick, and the house matron discovered tablets beneath Daphne's pillow and suspected a suicide attempt, Daphne was isolated in the school sanatorium until her parents came and wormed out of her the truth of the dangerous but childish jape in which she had indulged.

Released, and given a final warning about expulsion, Daphne rejoined Emily in the school library to giggle.

A week later, they bought themselves identical notebooks, and there followed a long period in which both girls wrote poems, kept diaries and composed long rambling essays.

Their diaries were written in a code they had invented themselves and which was intended to prevent anyone, especially the staff, from reading their most secret thoughts. The entries were mostly about themselves: how they had denied themselves or undertaken tasks to test their ability to subjugate their flesh, and their reactions to the way other girls talked and behaved — especially those who took a delight in boasting about their experiences with boys during the school holidays or who were forever pointing with grubby fingers to some atrocious incident in a well-thumbed, salacious book they had acquired.

Their poems and essays followed the same pattern as their diaries and, besides the contempt and scorn they revealed when attacking women's unenviable and disgusting destiny, they interwove their own esoteric religion which, although they would not have admitted it, was not far short of a monotonous death wish.

A typical poem of this time by Emily and entitled "Unfair" began, "O thoughtless God", and went on:

> Who dices erratic chance
> and fates us
> without a passing glance
> to a destiny
> unwished,
> unwanted;
> not to be undone.
>
> O ageing God
> whose imagery is moulded
> in dumb clay
> to be bronzed and soldered
> to a destiny
> unwished,
> unwanted;
> not to be undone.

And concluded after several closely-written pages and some thirty verses later:

O merciful God,
darken our life with sleep
and sleeping
deliver us who weep
to a destiny
wished for
wanted
and never to be undone.

Similarly, a poem by Daphne, although much shorter, expressed the same, hopeless frustration.

'Tis but the lot of the unhappy few like we
Who live their death each passing day in agony,
Not wishing to have been born yet afraid to die
And doomed to live on under the wandering eye
Of man made mad by his abominable lust.
Misunderstood; thought odd and queer, and cast out just
Because we are denied a chosen destiny
And forced to pass our days in female misery.

Unfortunately, during one school holiday, because of the long hours they spent closeted together in Emily's stuffy room and the fact that their copious writings were misunderstood by Nancy, who imagined the girls' closeness was unhealthy, she accused them of getting up to "dirty things". This unwarranted and thoughtless remark forced the two girls closer together and made them re-examine their friendship in the light of this puzzling accusation.

Although both girls were extremely fond of each other and could not bear to be parted, their embraces did not go beyond the linking of arms or lying on the bed side by side. That they got up to "dirty things" was most improper to their way of thinking. Although they exchanged ideas and discussed every subject known to them, imagining they delved far deeper and had a greater understanding than anyone living, although they developed a crush for the slim-hipped French mistress, Miss Sewell, who they thought "super", and loved their ponies with an unnatural enthusiasm, neither admitted to the other she had sexual feelings. And certainly not the feelings which some of the girls of the Upper Sixth had for Lower Third girls into whose dormitory beds they slipped after lights out. To Daphne and Emily, sex was disgusting; to be a woman, even worse. Told that their various and ludicrous physical protestations or the reams of paper which they covered in their curious back-sloping scrawl with exaggerated pot hooks were the suppressed awakenings of sexuality, they would have been convulsed with hysterical laughter. So, and without having to discuss it, it was only natural that Nancy displaced the headmistress and went to the top of their list of "Foul Females".

With several notebooks crammed, aware their writings were becoming repetitious and beginning to lack bite, they once again began subjecting their bodies to indecencies so as to sharpen their spirit. Many were tests of endurance which, the more complicated they became, they saw as martyrdom. The last of these took place when Daphne, as usual, spent the week after Christmas in Emily's house.

They had gone to the coal cellar and carefully selected lumps of coal which they stuffed into their knickers until they became knobbled and uncomfortably full. Curiously shaped and finding it difficult to climb the stairs, they trailed through the kitchen, went up to the vast drawing room and climbed yet again to the bedroom of Emily's father.

Sat on the huge counterpane, Emily slipped out of her blouse and settled herself on her back, while Daphne opened the cardboard box she had been carrying, took from it a large garden snail and laid it between Emily's developing breasts. She then laid herself down and, baring her chest, placed another snail on the tip of her right nipple.

Emily's father in Paris, Mathew in the mews garage cleaning the car and Nancy out shopping, the two girls could count on having the house to themselves for at least two hours.

Safe in an empty, silent house, they lay waiting; dreading the moment when the snails would emerge from their shells and begin crawling. While they waited, they held hands and, whispering encouragement to each other, watched for the slightest movement.

Eventually, the snail balanced between Emily's flattened and barely distinguishable breasts, either sensing there was no danger from the little heart fluttering below it or that the undulating surface did not present a hazard, emerged from its shell and peered out.

Emily gripped Daphne's hand and cried, "Look, look!" when the snail, erecting its horns, turned and began creeping; trailing over her chest towards her armpit.

Daphne's snail was still curled within its shell when, somewhere below, a door slammed shut.

Both girls scrambled to their feet in a panic, ran in circles buttoning their blouses and then made a mad dash for Emily's room upstairs. As they ran, Nancy yoo-hooed from the hall two floors below; but they weren't stopping — even though bits of coal fell from their knickers and the two abandoned snails wandered about a lawn mysteriously become carpet.

It wasn't this near discovery which led them to abandoning their experiments but the confusion which arose when their own dawning sexuality began to press their awareness with considerable urgency. Their bodies were undergoing alarming changes over which they had no control, and they found themselves blushing when meeting certain boys or could not rid themselves of thoughts about them.

For a while both girls were listless, continually sighing, and found time dragged because they were no longer interested either in their writings or in thinking up new ways of imposing their will over bodies which bled of their own accord.

Shortly after the regularity of her periods was established, Daphne became obsessed by the son of one of the school's groundsmen, Nicholas, who set about her initiation into questionable womanhood by his ignorance of the true nature of copulation. Fortunately for Daphne, his call-up papers arrived and he was posted to Colchester but left Daphne with several facts which she could lay before Emily who blushed at her friend's revelations.

Halfway through the same term, the school was evacuated. It was chance which had Daphne and Emily billetted together but providence which threw them into a small community rife with accessible boys who smoked, had slicked hair and up-and-down voices.

Daphne, all discipline relaxed, threw herself wholeheartedly into innumerable romances but Emily did not. However, spurred on and dragged unwillingly by Daphne to partner her current beau, Emily found herself forced into the company of boys. Unlike Daphne, she found none of them likeable and was frightened. So, while Daphne larked about and appeared to be thoroughly enjoying herself and in control of the situations she galloped into, Emily sat nervously by the side of some gawky lad who could not make head nor tail of a girl who neither talked, laughed or teased him into daring to kiss her.

Both girls had started to experiment with lipstick and cheap make-up. They shared what they considered to be outrageously daring underwear and giggled over the tiny pearl buttons. They spent hours adapting cast-off clothes to current fashions and believed the results alluring and seductive. On Saturday mornings they combed and set each other's hair in styles which varied with their moods but which nevertheless made them look more like nineteen than fifteen and, tarted up in their clothes with long dangling earrings which set off their constant giggling, steeled themselves to join the adult world.

Amongst the village girls, they were considered daring and were envied. The village boys, however, were either disarmed by their sudden transformation or else avidly curious; expecting them to behave according to the image of the film stars on whom the two girls had modelled their rather flimsy likenesses. The results of their various dates were often comical because the veneer of sophistication collapsed quickly whenever situations arose which were outside their experience — having never seen Norma Shearer or Carol Lombard cope with a man who had one hand cupping their breast and the other struggling to get under their knicker elastic.

Thus they entered into their adolescence and, like all other children, longed impatiently for the magical moment when they could be pronounced adult.

But Emily was still an introspective and quiet girl whose dreams could not be equated with the world in which she found herself. She envied other girls whom she thought managed their lives with confidence; envying their ability to emerge from disasters with cheerfulness and a carefree shrug which she was totally incapable of either feeling or simulating.

Daphne, on the other hand, positively split at the seams with the excitement of living and bounced back after every disaster; eager and relishing the next escapade.

It was natural, therefore, that there came a time when Daphne no longer needed Emily as a foil; having gained the necessary confidence in herself to be what she termed "a loner".

She had been sympathetic and more than patient with Emily but, realising she took up more and more of her time and that whatever advice she offered Emily turned down, Daphne was forced to the conclusion that Emily was naive, stupid and bloody childish; refusing to acknowledge the fact that Emily was excessively shy.

The break between them came one Sunday afternoon in London when both girls were lying on Emily's bed.

They had been talking quietly for some time — mostly about a girl called Cynthia who was currently causing a stir by announcing she was engaged to a man aged twenty-two and was trying to get a court dispensation which would allow her to marry him. During the silence which followed this discussion, Daphne felt the need to lie; partly to bolster her own ego and partly to shock Emily into the realisation of the gulf which was broadening between them.

Her boastful confession concerned a clergyman whom, she said, she had met in a railway compartment when she had been returning from Bristol after visiting an Aunt whose house had been bombed.

While she related the story of what had taken place in the carriage and the subsequent meetings in London, Emily was overwhelmed by sadness at her friend's necessity to lie. The moment Daphne had begun her tale, Emily knew she was lying, and the longer she went on, the worse the tension between them grew.

Daphne, unconvinced by her own invention, realised Emily knew she was lying, and therefore cast about in her imagination for situations which would have about them a ring of truth and with which she could smother the obvious falsity of the tale she was telling. But the more she endeavoured to weave plausibility into the plot, the more involved she became and, the more involved, the more inventive she had to become in order to extract herself from a situation which had got completely out of hand.

When the tale was finished, Emily wished her luck with her handsome clergyman and got up off the bed. Whereupon Daphne took the opportunity to pretend that time had simply flown and that she must be going because she had a date. Upon impulse, and finally setting the seal on the charade, she said her date was with "that divine clergyman". And then promptly wished she were dead.

The damage to their friendship was complete; Daphne being too self-willed to admit she had been lying and Emily too timid to challenge the truth of her friend's confession. And so their friendship trailed off into a dismal, tasteless ending.

In the autumn of 1943, Daphne moved from London to Wiltshire and, although they exchanged several letters, their childhood friendship was over. When they met later, as women, it was as strangers with experiences they dared not tell each other but at which they could only hint; and both found it necessary to lie to the other. Emily especially, who, calling herself Emma, had left home and was living with Raphael Arlington, a book illustrator, whom she referred to in her diaries as Adam, and to whom she never revealed the truth — which was a more sophisticated way of lying.

THE ROCKING CHAIR SANCTUARY
(2.ii.1948)

They'd gone arm in arm, hugging the one to the other, smiling with happiness; their cheeks red and stinging as they walked in the frosted air (she wrote).

Playfully, their excitement heightened by the treacherous surface of the road on which they walked, they huffed into each other's faces; sending their laughs and giggles on thick clouds of breath which steamed from their gaping mouths. If there had been snow quilting the road and softening their footsteps, they would have scooped it up in icy handfuls and sent the splattering balls plopping against the garden walls; just for the fun of it. Or, with woollen gloves encrusted with glittering droplets of freezing snow, struggled with each other and hunched their shoulders against the teasing handfuls forced between their collars to draw gasps of astonishment as it slid and fingered its way under their close, hot vests and, melting, trickled downwards. But the street was diamond-hard with frost as, on uncertain legs, they nosed their way through the brittle air — gasping as it stung, their smiles stretched tight — and arrived at the shop, eager to be out of the cold which had stiffened their clothes and numbed their club feet.

The shop bell jangled violently on its curled spring long after they had closed the rattling, glazed door. The warmth — a paraffin heated fug — blanketed their faces and they turned to look at each other to express their relief and surprise.

— Gosh, but it's cold!

— It's the coldest, said Mr Isaac Fox, advancing towards them, picking his way carefully between the stacked furniture. Too cold to snow, I shouldn't wonder.

Mr Fox wore his thickest, longest overcoat and a scarf wound several times round his mouth and neck. His red nose jutted out over the scarf like a beak. A greasy hat was pulled down to his ears, shadowing beady eyes.

A carrion crow, thought Emma: A scavenger of the wasi ready to fly to my shoulder and peck out my soft eyes.

She smiled brightly.

Isaac shuffled to the centre of his dirty shop and stood in the clutter warming his black mittened fingers over the blood-red paraffin stove while he eyed Emma suspiciously — from the top of her fur hatted head to the tips of her black patent boots; and sniffed up a dew drop.

— Well? What do you think of it? and Adam extended his arm.

Mr Fox didn't look at the young man whom he remembered from the previous day. It was the young woman on whom his eyes rested. She was the one who was going to make the decision. When the young man had said he would return the following day to look at the chair with his wife, Mr Fox hadn't believed him; imagining it was an excuse of the young man's to withdraw from the shop. He had been wrong.

The young man had returned with his fancy-bit who stood waiting and willing to please.

— I've had two offers since yesterday.

— But you haven't sold it.

— You said you'd come back.

— And here we are. Adam smiled down at Emma and hugged her to him with his eyes. Do you like it?

In the cluttered shop with its dusty, mahogany smell, reminding her of spiced snuff, Emma, amidst the confusion and in the half light, could not distinguish which chair it was that Adam had described and was so eager to buy. She was feeling so happy that she was quite willing to praise the qualities of any chair, just to please him. Because there were so many chairs, one on top of the other, fitting inextricably, she stood, a smile on her face and ready to say on an instant: "Oh, yes. YES. I DO like that. VERY MUCH."

— This is the one.

— American colonial. A very fine piece, and Mr Isaac Fox rubbed his hands together in nervous anticipation. Up you get, Freda.

Seated astride a very low rocking chair, which was shaped like a collapsing letter S, was a young girl with long, softly flowing hair. She sat facing the back of the chair with her head leant against the buttoned padding.

— What do you think?

The young girl was sucking her thumb while she rocked backwards and forwards; lost in a world of her own making.

— Well?

Emma hesitated before answering. She no longer smiled but stood staring at the child; struggling to remember.

— It's a bargain at four. In the West End you'd pay a tenner for that chair.

The chair was, if she could remember that far back, identical to the one she had straddled as a little girl and, like the child now rocking backwards and forwards, she too had found it to be the one safe refuge from the adult world which pressed confusingly and frighteningly about her.

— Get off the chair, Freda.

Turning, Mr Fox pulled down his scarf and smiled his crooked smile. His long, nicotine-stained teeth looked like bunches of loose firewood.

— S'good as new. Bin looked after. Not a sign of worm in it.

It was a chair which, when straddled and set gently rocking, conjured up the same delicious dream which could be lived through to its happy, mouthwateringly beautiful end.

— I said get off the chair, Freda. Let the lady 'ave a look atit. Emma remembered her father's large hand round her wrist. Her thumb sliding out of her mouth; chilling in the air. She remembered swallowing down the delicious taste of it when her father dragged her to her feet. She remembered standing dazed and uncertain in the sudden glare of reality; suspended between a dream world and that which existed about her. Floundering, unable to comprehend, she had stood shivering.

Freda's wail cut into Emma; piercing her heart.

— I'll give you a slap round the leg if you don't shut up! Now get back into the kitchen! Go on!

The chair disappeared shortly after that. Nothing was ever the same again. No other chair, however she tried to curl up in it, was the same as her small rocking chair. Her life became unbearable. There was nowhere she could isolate herself and live out the fantasies which were so essential to her life. There was no longer a place where she could thumb up dreams on the wet ridged roof of her mouth and smell the acid warmness while she tunnelled her nose in the palm of her hand and felt her breath alive and curling in her warm palm. She remembered the weeks of boredom and the feeling of helplessness after the chair had disappeared and how she had despised her father and the hateful Nancy who seemed both cosy and loving towards each other, but spiteful and short-tempered towards her as she wandered homeless through the house.

Outside the shop Adam shook his head in bewilderment and pulled his scarf up over his mouth — as much to hide the disappointment on his face as against the biting wind — and holding the cold, rigid arm of an Emma who had become gaunt and tense, trudged back towards the flat in silence, chairless.

— It was Nesta who suggested we buy it. What am I going to tell her? You couldn't afford it?

— Tell Miss Wilson, I please myself. And always have.

— She gave you those mirrors in the bathroom.

— And took what? Took what from me in exchange?

Adam shrugged off his coat and flung it on the bed. His scarf he held between his hands like a strangler's ligature.

— Do you want I should fling Pazzeroni in your face? Well?

— Go suck Miss Wilson's marbles, stupid.

— I might just do that.

— You do. And while you're about it, check if they're made of glass.

— You're no pearl to cast before swine.

— No, but I've a damn' good mind to pig it with Pazzeroni.

PAZZERONI. THE JEW (1950)

"Blessed art Thou, O Lord our God, who hast not made me a woman."

— Twist your arse towards me. That's better. Didn't you know? Did you never suspect?

— Is this how you want it?

— Yes. Now hold still. Well?

— It's come as a complete surprise.

— Haven't you ever wondered what became of my Gentile foreskin? Why my bishop lacked capped modesty?

— I never gave it a thought.

— You must have thought something. Did you imagine I was a proselyte exposing my knob at the gate to speed my acceptance or something?

— I tell you, I never gave it a thought. I accepted it as a fact. Adam was and he hadn't been done. He told me. I know that some Gentile mothers have their sons circumcised. It will be time to suspect women are asserting themselves over the male and taking their revenge when it becomes common practice for mothers to have their sons' foreskins cut off.

— But I'm a Jew.

— You call yourself a Yog.

— A Jew. Circumcised to denote the consecration of my body, and demonstrative of the subjugation of my passion.

(Eunice rolled her eyes up to heaven and coughed to hide a snigger.)

— It's a sacred covenant, sealed in flesh. Not totemism, mutilation or a hygienic, Gentile desire to be smegmaless. It is the enactment of the Law — and God delights in it.

— And the origin? Do your Tanna'im say? I'm sure they wouldn't have told you that kings were once castrated and that later — probably in deference to this humiliation — circumcision was substituted.

— It was the first Commandment that God gave to Abraham.

— That the child should be circumcised on the eighth day after birth? I know. Kings were first mutilated — or circumcised — before they began their eighth year of reign. To me, Abraham's sudden revelation suggests an attempt to identify the people with God. Or, if you like, kings with divine power. God.

— Stop fidgeting.

— Sorry.

— There must be unquestionable obedience. To argue is to rebel against God. An enactment of the Law husbands discipline, self-control and purification.

— You've been misled by an evil angel.

— Barnabas also mistakenly said there were two Laws. One, allegedly, was broken and the second — the true Decalogue, given to the Christians by the Lord Himself.

— Three. Moses broke one in a fit of temper. Are you going to take very long?

— Draw up your legs a bit more. That's better.

—You know, I'm surprised, Giacopo. Truly. You're the last person in the world I would have suspected of being a Jew.

— Suspect is an apt word in a Gentile's mouth. It's succinct. Precise. A word on which we Jews have been nourished.

— Even those who do not live by the Law?

— When a Jew is a Jew, he is always a Jew.

— No Jew can exist without the Word of the Law. The two are indivisible. If he turns his back upon it, he is no longer a Jew. And it is only the Word which has bound the Jews together; as Jews. The relapsed Jew who ostentatiously relishes the blood-soaked terephah fools no one — least of all himself, because he regales not the steak but the outward, symbolic gesture of casting off his Jewishness and is therefore constantly reminding himself that he is a Jew. He is like a man who is forced to walk with a crutch but who does not, by casting it away, convince himself that he has no need of it because he is constantly reminded of his need while he hops on one leg.

— I see we shall have to talk blood. Gentiles love their blood.

— Don't be so silly.

— Aye, yi, yi. Drink this in remembrance that Christ's blood was shed for thee and be thankful. Amen. The congregation will now join the choir in singing Cowper's "There's a fountain filled with blood, drawn from Emmanuel's veins". And your pious, bloody tomb at Walsingham.

— I don't give a dam.

— Or a kerse. Just so. We have come a long way.

— Except that your Talmud says if I am menstruating and walk between two men, one of them will surely die.

— We've advanced since then.

— Have you? You still insist your butchers draw the prohibited ischiatic nerve.

— A friend of Amalek was once entrusted with the sacrifice . . .

— SACRIFICE!. Tanhuma born Abba said: "He that is wise wins souls."

— Proverbs. Face the wall.

— How do you explain the contradiction?

— There is none. Your back was caved more than that.

— *Za'ar ba'al hayyim?*

— Are you less cruel in your abattoirs? Do you really care how your meat is brought to table? Have you made it your concern? No. You are quite willing for the animal to be slaughtered as long as you are reassured there is not too much suffering and that the abattoir is of a certain hygienic standard. You abhor the taking of life. So do we. Both of us might agree that all living things are a gift from God. But you, unlike us, would steal life without acknowledging Him who gave it.

— Can I scratch?

SILENCE.

— Your shoulders were a bit more rounded. Yes. Stay exactly like that.

— It's very odd to be drawn into an argument with a Jew whose activities and thoughts are in opposition to the Law yet who insists upon defending it so vigorously. Odd, because one very rarely hears of a Jew being brought to justice for moral or civil disobedience — rape, sodomy, that sort of thing; or murder. Yet your guilt complex is as tragic as a Christian's.

— That is very reassuring.

— It's true. The arguments you use to get me to let you . . . well. They are the arguments of a man trying to justify a perversion about which he feels guilty. You also paint — which is odd for a Jew. No doubt you'll say that because you are an abstract painter your imagery is purely intellectual and therefore entirely in keeping with Jewish tradition.

— There is the example of Soutine. Kokoshka. Chagall. And, many more.

— That's what I mean. None of you are REAL Jews. What did you do during the war, Giacopo? Jews were exempted from conscription at the time of Christ because they might have come into contact with idolatry in the Roman Legions. But in the last war?

— I allowed myself to be conscripted.

— But what did you do?

— Oh, much. I thought, too, which was far worse to bear than the fear. I also concealed my Jewishness.

— That was not very brave of you.

— As it turned out, my refuge was also my private Gehenna.

— How so?

— I was one of the first to enter Belsen.

— Oh, Giacopo, I am sorry. I can understand why you feel so ashamed.

— Can you?

— I think so. Don't forget that if the war had gone against us, I too might have dyed my hair blond and pretended I was an Aryan.

—YOU?

— Don't sound so incredulous. More Christians died in the concentration camps than Jews. So it's possible I too might have taken refuge behind a disavowal of my heritage.

— But you didn't. So? What DID you do? Let the Americans fuck the arse off you?

— Don't be silly. I wasn't more than a child.

— Were you evacuated?

— Yes, to Kent, where I saw dog fights.

— The battle of Britain.

— Yes. And then later, we used to watch the buzz bombs going over — towards London, while we larked about in the hop fields.

— We?

— Daphne and I. We LOATHED it. The woman we lodged with was a proper Gorgon. I remember one Sunday she mistakenly poured chocolate sauce over the roast beef and sprouts, and gravy over the tinned peaches. Daphne and I were far too scared of her to say anything, so we ate it down in silence. YAK.

— But you were never involved — directly, with the war.

— Goodness, yes. Our school was burnt down by incendiaries.

— Oh.

— But most of the time it seemed we just sat about and waited.

— Of course.

— Had I known then, the waiting might have been different.

— Why?

— Because death cannot be imagined, it becomes the greatest of our fears. Had I known what was happening in the concentration camps — what you witnessed — then this would have become my greatest fear.

— Torture.

—The utter degradation. Even now it is unimaginable that limn can behave like this.

— But the Germans?

— Are men amongst men. It just happened that they were Germans. This is the horror.

— You would forgive them?

— I find it difficult to forgive some and not all. But I must.

— St Augustine said that the good deeds of the nations are only brilliant vices.

— Oh, Giacopo. REALLY! My charity is not a boast and therefore not a sin. Don't be so silly. I suppose you, the Jew, would have it different.

— I wish I could get my tongue round the word Christian in the same way you Gentiles eject the word JEW — as if it were some phlegm being hawked up to be spat into the gutter. Somehow you've managed to adjectivise the word Christian into meaning ethically and religiously perfect, and the word Jewish as imperfect — belonging to an old, dead religion.

— You're too sensitive, Giacopo. However, your beauty clothes you in assurance. If it wasn't for what I know about you, I could worship you just for your beauty.

— Unless you want a damn good thumping, you'd better face the wall. I'm feeling horny as it is.

SILENCE.

— Do artists HAVE to get involved with their models?

— Picasso suggests they must. He satirises the academicians for regarding them as bloodless objects.

— It must be awfully tiring — for the artists.

— Ha-ha. Draw your knees up more.

SILENCE.

— How do the Jews regard Jesus Christ?

— Mmm?

— Jesus.

— The Jew Jesus was an Essene. He scrupulously observed the Jewish feasts, expounded Jewish doctrines; his ethics were those of a Jew; the expressions he used were Jewish. He was a Jew.

— A Rabbi?

— Yes. Being an Essene he wasn't allowed to teach until he was thirty years old.

— Who taught Jesus?

— Probably Hillel.

— A Pharisee?

— Yes. Saint Paul was, too. In all probability, Jesus studied at the Qumran monastery.

— The Pharisees reasoned out their religious philosophy, didn't they?

— They were religious thinkers.

— And the Essenes?

— Celibates who lived a very religious life in isolation.

— From whom the idea of a Christian God. . . .

— It was Abraham who bequeathed the idea of an invisible God.

— So what was Christ?

— Semitic languages lend themselves to verbal juggling. When this happens — and it did — a mystery cult is formed. Jesus was a magician; a necromancer — a zealot, if you like. He wasn't the founder, nor, indeed, the originator of Christianity, but an inspired teacher. It was the half blind, deformed Saul of Tarsus — who who incidentally and significantly took upon himself the Roman name of Paul — who founded the Christian Church. Had he been made an apostle and not quarrelled with Jesus's brother, it's possible there would have been no schism and no carrying of the Christian ideal to the pagans. A Christianity which, with time, became Pauline Christology.

— But Jesus . . .

— Was, as I said, an Essene Jew. Of a sect who lived a monastic life; overemphasising virginity and consumed by guilt. This is the Jew Jesus's background.

— And for that he was crucified.

— The Jew Jesus was a pacifist who announced he was the Messiah. To the Romans he was inimical with the other, self-appointed Messiahs who counselled armed rebellion against imperial authority. These other Messiahs are rarely mentioned. There was the Jew — Judas of Gallilee, who was crucified. The Egyptian Jew, Benjamin. The Jew Theudas. All crucified, as was the Jew — Jesus of Nazareth; by the Romans and for the same reason.

— But why did the Jews, his own kind, turn against Jesus?

— They didn't. In all probability they were trying to protect him.

— Oh, really, Giacopo!

— All the apocalyptic writing of that time was permeated with the expectation of the imminent coming of the Messiah. Tradition held that the Messiah would appear when the afflictions of the Jewish people had become unendurable. Under the Romans it had. Revolt was imminent when Jesus, the Essene pacifist, rode into Jerusalem — and in a manner which Jewish legend had prophesied.

— But Jesus didn't call himself the Messiah — I mean, he only acknowledged it later. And, being a pacifist, saw that if he presented himself to the people as the Messiah, he might be able to calm them.

— That's pure speculation. In any case, the overturning of the tables — especially when you realise that the city was ringed by legionnaires — was an unwise gesture. To the Romans it suggested he was militant.

— But he was only remonstrating with the Pharisees for not living up to the standards set out in their own teaching.

— Jesus's attempt to speed the reformation of the Temple cult — a reformation incidentally which the prophets had begun some eight hundred years earlier — cumulated in this gesture — yes. In consequence — and three DAYS later, mark you, according to the Gospels written nearly NINETY YEARS later, Jesus was arrested by the Jews! Isn't it more likely that the Jews arrested him to protect him from the Romans and to demonstrate to them they were still capable of containing civil disobedience? The suggestion that he was arrested at night, tried and condemned by the Great Sanhedrin, is nonsense. No one could be arrested at night, nor could court proceedings be instituted after sundown, nor on the eve or day of the Sabbath, NOR on the eve or day of a festival. Trials never took place in the Palace of the High Priest, nor in fact could the Sanhedrin initiate an arrest. Also, which is always overlooked, the fact that the procedures — for any trial — were laid down in the Talmud, and were strictly adhered to.

— But the Romans, not the Jews, crucified him.

— Of course.

— And Caiaphas?

— Was a pro-Roman Sadducee — which, to all intents and purposes, discredits him at once. In any case, is it probable that the Procurator would have delegated his own, supreme, Roman power to a Jew? Of course not. The Gospel writers, in their desperate attempt to blame the Jews for Jesus's plight, suggest that Pilate could find no fault with Jesus. As a Roman, as a legal-minded Procurator, Pilate could not possibly have said this. It is ludicrous. As are his letters in the so-called Lost Books of the Bible. Anyway, as if it wasn't enough for Pilate to say that he could find no fault, they suggest he turned to the crowd and, as if it was custom, asked of them, because it was the Passover, whom they wished to be freed — Jesus or Barabbas. Nowhere, absolutely nowhere in Jewish writings is there mention — or even suggestion — that it was customary to free a condemned criminal at Passover. The whole thing is absurd. Ridiculous.

— The notion that it was the Jews who were responsible for the death of Jesus was part of the Pauline doctrine. It was a deliberate attempt to widen and affirm the schism between Christian and Jew. And, I might add, at a time when many Christians were Jews but who believed the approach to God was through Christ and not the Word.

— Jewish, traditional vindictiveness was responsible, then?

— Christian love is Jewish love. There is no difference. Jesus the Jew rebuked the Scribes and Pharisees for their lack of love, not for their disrespect for the word of the Law. He contributed nothing new because already the greatest commandment in the Old Covenant is the love of God, and love for a neighbour as thyself. It is simply not true to insist it is the Christians alone who preach love. The Jews taught this long before Christ was born. If you want to argue this, then I shall, inevitably, be forced into the sad position of having to quote Matthew and John, and we shall spend a miserable afternoon to no avail.

— All of what you have just said is not much comfort to a Christian.

— No. But a Christian heretic, who was once an Essene Ebionite, said the Hebrews should not be condemned because of their ignorance of Jesus and for adhering to the Commandments of Moses if God saw fit to conceal Jesus from them. And, likewise, the Gentiles should not be condemned because of their ignorance of Moses and for following Jesus if God saw fit to conceal Moses from them.

— How cosy. How bloody cosy! GOD!

— Keep still!

— It's so damn' easy, isn't it?

— The communists — the politicians, here; America — anywhere; right down to the miserly council clerk with his mousey wife tucked safely away in some neat bungalow with her dog for company and her piano for dreams. . . .

— What ARE you ranting about?

— The manipulators of power — all of them, who distort, and twist like slippery eels to stay in office; who force the mad ideology of men onto man by devious and dishonest argument! Hats off to the Church — at least they've refined their argument down to a simple statement even though they have failed to paper over the cracks through which one can see the unheavenly construction of their Church. The politicians are still crude and convince only the maddest that their edifice is not built upon the bloody backs of their tortured opponents.

— What has this got to do with Moses? And turn round.

— I'm talking about "you know who". Of Abraham's encounter with him. And Paul's on the road to Damascus.

— God?

— Adonai. Lord. Elohim. Jehovah. The same vision the ageing, illiterate camel driver Mohammed saw. Doesn't the similarity of their inventiveness strike you as odd?

SILENCE.

— Moses, of course, was a Jew.

— Yes.

—Indeed? To which one are you referring? The Levite or the Midianite Moses?

— Are you going to give me that Freudian spiel?

— Why not? Why shouldn't Moses have been an Egyptian Prince? He wasn't circumcised and the name Moses is not a Hebrew word but an Egyptian one meaning child. And his stuttering? WAS it a defect or was it that he couldn't speak Hebrew and had to have an interpreter?

— Why don't you bring in the Golden Bough?

— The White Goddess would be more appropriate; after all, Moses' wife Zipporah circumcised him — to appease the God.

— Mythological twaddle.

— An exaggeration, perhaps — to you — but is it so fanciful to believe that the Jewish religion was really the Aton religion based on the all powerful, unseen, Sun God?

— Aye, yi, yi.

— You can aye-aye as much as you like, Giacopo — but by the same argument you used to discredit the events of Jesus's arrest by saying the Gospels weren't written until ninety years later, remember that the Pentateuch wasn't assembled until nearly SIXTEEN HUNDRED years after some of the events described in it! So, why shouldn't Jewish history be distorted too? Why the continuous duplication? Perhaps there were TWO chosen people. The Hebrews of Abraham and the Israelites of Moses — each with a different God. The Hebrews with their Jehovah and the Israelites with their Elohim? Mmm?

— Moses universalised the Jewish Godhead.

— Maybe his was the strongest faction.

— Hugh!

— Doesn't it strike you as odd that the manner of his death is unknown or that there is no record of where he was buried? And why the reference to — the chosen people? Isn't it possible that the Egyptian Moses, after the overthrow of Amenhotep and as a believer of Aton, knowing the Egyptians would not become adherents to this faith, chose instead the Israelites who were enslaved in Egypt?

— Chose?

— Yes. Chose. How much easier to encourage and convert a slave by telling him that he had been specially chosen by God and therefore his slavery could not last for ever. It would restore his dignity and give him a renewed will to fight his way out of slavery.

— I feel that the undercurrent of your argument is Spinozian in so much as you believe that the Jewish religion — ALL religion — is the product of man's imagination. Of man who tends to channel all his impulses towards piety.

— Of course! What could be more obvious than the convenient discovery of Deuteronomy in the time of Josiah, in order to weld together emotional nationalism to demonstrate the fraud men inflict upon man?

— ALL religion is man-made.

— Certain aspects of it are sensible — in so much as it is upon these principles man can base an acceptable, universal law so that he can live peaceably — not only with himself, but with his neighbours.

— Don't you think so?

SILENCE.

— Of course, there's all this involved sexuality. Virgin births, circumcision, guilt. . . . Have you finished? My bottom's going to sleep.

(Pazzeroni, his head bent, added the finishing details to his drawing with loving care.)

THE VOYEURING BUTTERFLY
(18.xi.1951)

G IACOPO (male, aged thirty, Anglo Italian Jew, surnamed Pazzeroni, a painter by profession who is rough-skinned, sensual, dyspeptic, quick-tempered, moody, vicious and suited in white linen): Siri, sit next to Jaro. Jaro. Ski Jorgensdatter. Siri. Jaro Svensen.

Siri (female, twenty-seven, Swedish, divorced, Captain De Lord Hun'gan Smollet's mistress, a sculptress by profession who is small, rotund, cosy, high-cheekboned, brown-eyed, fair-haired, eager and frocked in apricot gold) takes (enthusiastically, ardently, rapturously) and shakes (energetically) the hand (large, moist, manicured, cold, soft) of Jaro (male, thirty-two, Swedish, married, a gallery owner who is long legged, puffy-eyed, pasty-faced, an Anglomaniac, conceited, arrogant, affected, diamond-cuffed, immaculately dove-grey pin-stripe suited).

GIACOPO (thoughtful, deliberate): Sidony, sit next to Jaro. Conrad, next to Sidony.

Sidony (female, twenty-six, English, surnamcd Lovering, a lithographer by profession who is divorced, attractive, elfin-faced, long dark-haired, pliably-bodied, slim-waisted, scented, vivacious, spirited, ravishing, sexy, dressed in lurid scarlet velvet) sits (slowly, studiously, provocatively).

Conrad (male, forty-two, a Dutch Jew, surnamed Rossiter, who is a journalist, unmarried, large-framed, bulky, dark-skinned, hook-nosed, spectacled, thick-lipped, sensual, brooding, conspicuous, imperishable, suited in mottled-brown tweed) sits (clumsily, heavily, breathlessly) next to Sidony. He whispers (conspiratorially, suggestively, inaudibly) into

Sidony's ear (small, ovoid, clean, hidden). She smiles (sweetly, defensively) and laughs (girlishly, shrilly).

GIACOPO (authoritatively): Tammy. Sit on Siri's right.

TAMMY (perfunctory, supercilious, facetious): Right what?

Tammy (male, thirty-one, English, surnamed Lamlin, an ex-doctor turned writer who is unmarried, short-legged, sallow-skinned, thick-set, doleful-eyed, buffoon, mimic, argumentative, vulgar-tongued, cynical, garbed in raven black) scratches (deliberately, playfully) Siri's knee (taut, warm, silk-stockinged) with his finger (long, crooked, calloused) under the table (wooden, scrubbed, oblong, bare).

GIACOPO (relieved): Mariota, sit next to Tammy.

MARIOTA (disappointed, polite, unsure, sarcastic): There's nothing I'd like better.

Mariota (female, twenty-nine, American, surnamed Jaquier, an unemployed spinster of French extraction, an Anglomaniac, tall, green-eyed, cat-faced, impeccably groomed, smooth-skinned, odourless, sarcastic, vindictive, juvenile, dressed in a tightly fitting malachite green silk dress) sits down (decorously, gingerly). GIACOPO (personable, affectionate, scheming): Gormun. Sit next to Mariota. Erowina, sit there (pointing) and, Finola, dear, sit next to me.

Gormun (male, thirty-nine, Irish, surnamed O'Connor, who is by profession a maker of medical models, is married, broad-shouldered, barrel-chested, markedly stooped, black-haired, rotten-toothed, delicately-handed, aggressive, stubborn, sensitive, sentimental, suited in roan-coloured corduroy) sits (reluctantly, awkwardly, slovenly) next to Mariota.

Finola (female, twenty-seven, English, surnamed Foster-Butt, of private means, who is unmarried, aristocratic, thin, nervous, blonde, bony, censorious, perceptive, hypercritical, gowned in cerulean blue) sits (graciously, elegantly, squarely) on the chair (wooden, light brown, varnished, upright, hard, uncomfortable, greasy, one of thirty-two).

Erowina (female, twenty-four years of age, English, Giacopo's mistress, green-eyed, slender, healthily-complexioned, submissive, attractive, intense, frocked in saffron yellow) sits (hesitantly, decorously) down.

Giacopo (relieved) sits (unceremoniously).

GIACOPO (impatient, commanding): Christoforo! Food!

Christoforo (male, fifty-five, Greek, tallow-skinned, black-eyed, small, delicately-boned, vain, contemptuous, efficient, aproned) walks (mincingly, quickly, smilingly) from the restaurant (Theopolos, 48 Wardour Street, London, W.1) kitchen (small, square, steaming, busy, dirty, cluttered, hot, smelling).

GIACOPO (dictatorial, vainglorious, egotistical, patronising): Christoforo. Get this. No beans once. No beans and no potatoes once. Two steaks medium. One without beans. One steak overdone. Got that?

CHRISTOFORO (smiling, confident, professional): You're wanting six rare with chips, beans and salad. One medium, chips, beans and salad. One over, chips, beans and salad. One medium, no beans, chips and salad and one rare, no beans, no chips. O.K.?

GIACOPO (condescendingly): Correct. And hurry.

Christoforo (beaming, bustling) lays (quickly, automatically, obsequiously) the cloth (American-oil, washable, sticky, damp, chequered, red and white, worn, perished, cracked, greasy) and the knives (sharp, various, steel-handled, stainless, press-moulded, stolen, black-market, cheap, made in Chicago and Sheffield) and forks (four-pronged, bent, steel, electroplated, dissimilar, dull, dirty, ex W.D., made in Sheffield) and the glasses (half-pint, thick, plain, polished) and plates (two, large, decorated, chipped, made in Derby) of bread (sliced, thick, square, crusty, soft-centred, moist, free with the meal) and saucers (two, stained, diminutive, odd, white) of peppers (hot, red, wrinkled, pickled, small, free with the meal) and puts (reverently) the bottles (six, tall, green, labelled) of wine (Beaujolais, red, cheap) and a jug (glass, heavy, streaked) of water (cloudy, chalky) and a bottle (tall, bellied, stopperless) of vinegar (watered) and a bottle (screw-topped, greasy) of oil (yellow, rancid, thick, cooking), pepper (ground, white), salt (free-running, dusty) and mustard (hot, English, yellow, thick, old, crusted) on the table (laid). He (concerned) draws (carefully, approvingly, systematically) the corks (long, unstamped, squeaking, aromaed) from the bottles (wine).

CONRAD (forthright, loud, commanding): What do we drink to?

TAMMY (derisive): To whom, you mean.

EROWINA (quiet, informative): To Giacopo. It's his birthday.

TAMMY (brash, chummy): A happy birthday, me old mate. Up yours.

MARIOTA (eager, felicitous): A birthday party! Oh, lovely. Cheers. All the best, Giacopo.

FINOLA (sincere, direct): A happy birthday.

GORMUN (casual, diminutive): And many of them.

CONRAD (obsequious): Your very good health, Giacopo. AND in the years to come.

JARO (hesitant, laboured): A-a-a-a happy b-b-b-bir-bir-birthday.

SIRI (bright, clipped, clear): Skol!

EROWINA (sincere, intense): A very happy birthday, my dear.

SIDONY (deliberate, provocative): Bottoms up, you old bugger.

GIACOPO (unruffled, amused, explicit and smirking): Now, now, Sidony, darling. No need to let on we were once more than just good friends.

SILENCE (long, uncomfortable).

EROWINA (relieved, observant, informative): FOOD!

TAMMY (irreligious, boastful): Thank God. I could eat a horse.

SIRI (cautious, facetious): Shh! Not so loud. That's probably what it is.

They (hungry, peckish, ravenous, craving, pinched, starving, famished, open-mouthed, esurient and already gorged) set about (greedily, noisily, zealously, breathlessly, ravenously, genteelly, rowdily, daintily, euphemistically and regrettably) the food (steak, chips, peas, beans, cabbage, cucumber, tomatoes, bread) and ate (gorging and swallowing, pecking and nibbling, bolting and devouring, gobbling and gulping, picking and toying, hogging and crunching, cracking and cramming, stuffing and chewing, licking and gnawing, and masticating) drank (swilling, tippling, supping, sipping, gulping, guzzling, quaffing, lapping, swigging and tasting) and found the wine (lifting, edifying, fortifying, elevating, addling, embracing, fuddling, intoxicating, inebriating and mortifying).

While they ate and drank, they talked of friendship. 'Impossible with women'; of enmity: 'All too often founded on jealousy, envy or disgust'; of courtesy: 'A formal display of inbreeding'; of rudeness: 'An armour against deficiency' . . . 'Reveals the chink in offended pride'; of love: 'Purely chemical' . . . 'A much misused word which needs qualification' . . . 'Should denote sexual expectation'; of hate: 'Sustained objection to the audacity of another to hold up a mirror in which one's secret guilt is reflected'; of resentment: 'Rebuffed pride' . . . 'Forfeited ingenuousness'; of endearment: 'Lesbian homosexuality' . . . 'Nonsense. Platonic regard between either sex'; of marriage: 'Communal necessity engendering female security' . . . 'Masculine responsibility'; of divorce: 'A human activity brought about by human activity' . . . 'The natural severance of unnatural pairing'; of celibacy: 'Masturbatory idealism' . . . 'Inverted guilt' . . . 'A godless s-s-sac-sacrifice' . . . 'The pinnacle of male masochism'; of benevolence: 'Archaic socialism'; of philanthropy: 'A rich man's Heavenly insurance purchased with guilt' . . . 'Returning the poor man's stolen money profitably'; of pity: 'Displacing the conscience while experiencing total recall' . . . 'Self-pity is a flagellator's orgasm in perpetuo'; of ingratitude: 'The masculine attitude towards feminine submissiveness' . . . 'The price a rich man pays for his philanthropy' . . . 'Underwriting the godlessness of charity'; of forgiveness: 'An unctuous manifestation of grandeur and pride' . . . 'Which time transmutes effortlessly into limbo but which immediacy martyrs' . . . 'The sheathing of a wooden sword in the scabbard of complacency'; of revenge: 'Buggering the surprised lover before kicking him out' . . . . 'Private jurisdiction publicly commuted by legal jurisdiction' . . . 'Primitive mathematics'; of jealousy: 'Imaginative reconstruction of unfulfilled fantasies in which the wife is indulging freely with her lover'. . . 'A cornucopia of sexual frustrations'; of envy: 'Momentary inability to shout snap' . . . 'Suspension of credence and the substitution of impossibility'; of right: 'Instinctive p-p-p-pos-pos-positivism' . . . 'Succinct, shorthand conception of troublesome, subtle revelations' . . . 'Moral doctrine for convenient, social administration' . . . 'The urgent knocking of order appealing for archaic conformity'; of wrong: 'The courting of disrespect which is injurious' . . . 'Innocent outcast's social pigeon-hole' . . . 'A cloakroom of pegs for hanging inherited guilt'; of duty: 'Religious and secular concoction of guilt and power' . . . 'Masochistic discipline, discipling pride' . . . 'The motivation towards self-satisfaction' . . . 'The bastard daughter of ignoble work who was spawned by necessity' . . . 'Amouring persuasion in guilt'; of respect: 'The defence demanded to assuage the authoritarian's inability to discipline with love'; of contempt: 'Lawful guilt' . . . 'The satisfaction gained from being safely in one's own shoes' . . . 'The only time an unsightly, long nose comes in useful'; of flattery: 'The wish fulfilled by a recognisable untruth' . . . 'The multiple key for unlocking boxed affections' . . . 'The only chink in a woman's armour which, if pierced, immediately rusts' . . . 'Turning plumpness into voluptuousness, voluptuousness into desirability, desirability into love, and all the while smiling as you keep your eye fixed on her inflamed pimple'; of accusation: 'The pinning down of a probability' . . . 'Defending a position by attacking a proposition'; of vindication: 'Obsessive self-esteem' . . . 'Useless expenditure of effort to establish publicy that one is' . . . 'Trial by effort with a prejudged, negative verdict'; of selfishness: 'Feminine conception of masculine success after she has succumbed to flattery' . . . 'Experiencing an orgasm with a frigid woman'; of virtue: 'The acknowledgement of moral animality by the abnormal inanimate' . . . 'Prudently weighing the justice of chastity, easily lost, against the fortitude needed for faithfully preserving virginity in the hope that a charitable angel will reward such temperance' . . . 'A negative attitude accomplished in a positive manner'; of vice: 'Repetitious infantile regression' . . . 'Illusion of ultimate sexuality' . . . 'Unlike a monk's, which clothes his pure, outer form, it is a habit which cowls and blinkers a singular, evil intent' . . . 'Something which was nice, is nice, will be nice and could be nicer still'; of innocence: 'Ignorance made into a virtue' . . . 'A female allurement in civilisations where virginity rouses a male's lust' . . . 'The inability to match intuition with superstition'; of guilt: 'Imagining that you are the only one who does it' . . . 'The reawakening of one's father's or mother's revenge' . . . 'The shout of victory when implanted conscience triumphs over instinct' . . . 'The Church's fulcrum' . . . 'A built-in stabiliser' . . . 'A geographical and historical absolute which is inconsistent with time or place'; of good: 'The doing of which is a negation, unless one is' . . . 'An impenetrable front behind which real evil can flourish' . . . 'The advertising and practical denial of guilt' . . . 'Adjectival affirmative of nonconflicting wills'; of bad: 'Injurious intent' . . . 'A yardstick for the assessment of material objects or a belabouring stick for the chastisement of abject subjects' . . . 'The unnecessary handmaiden of wrong'; of penitence: 'The sadistic revelry of the self' . . . 'A hirsute conscience suitably macintoshed for weathering public opinion' . . . 'The mortification of the flesh for the satisfaction of the self' . . . 'The sadistic sentence of sententious adepts' . . . 'Is done in the open prisons of the Church'; of atonement: 'Reconciling the anatomy of God with the atomy of man'; of temperance: 'That which is countenanced by those whose natural capacity, inclination and temperament is less than in those beings who they wish to admonish by example' . . . 'The bookmark of humanism'; of the sensualist: 'He who dries himself on HER towel' . . . 'The infinite capacity for taking pain' . . . 'One who turns a minor motion into a major sensation' . . . 'Is the wearing of fur knickers' . . . 'Imagines the looking before he looks and finds the imagining better than the looking'; of purity: 'The deed before the thought' . . . 'The figment of man's lust and the gift men ask of a slut' . . . 'Believing that exposing it will frighten away the devil'; of drunkenness: 'An appropriate state for an English bedroom over the weekend'; of the libertine: 'Your sublimal self, dear Tammy'; of jurisdiction: 'The administration of human law which, being at variance with historical continuity, not only appears to be, but is seen to be unjust' . . . 'For the benefit and infinite satisfaction of the jugglers of jurisprudence when implementing their short-sighted conclusion'; of condemnation: 'The act of a responsible Christian sentencing an irresponsible Christian, in a Christian-like manner, to an un-Christian sentence, to be served in a Christian jail'; of punishment: 'Parents' outward expression of their inner conflict' . . . 'The inability of society to socialise the unable' . . .

'The majority excuse for the sadistic pleasure of tanning minor bums' . . . 'The installation of respect by the insulation of retrospect'; of penalty: 'Is always twofold. The judicial and, upon release, the civil; or the Church, as in suicide, and, after death, God's' . . . 'Because of the impossibility of administering law, it is always known and shewn to be unjust' . . . 'That it can be one thing, and then another, does not deter a changing society from altering it yet again. That this is possible, that this is acceptable, does not mean civilisation is advancing but that it is coming nearer to the time when prisons will be turned into schools for the compulsory education of those who we now term criminals' . . . 'Imprisonment is not in itself a punishment, but the outward and visible declaration of society's power to do so, supposing punishment is meant to be a corrective' . . . 'The end consequence of certain action, not the end action of certain consequences'; of reward: 'Sophisticated compliment in bad taste' . . . 'The beginning of the ending of endeavour if one has pride' . . . 'The thirteenth labour of Hercules' . . . 'Insurance against unfaithfulness' . . . 'The knobs of sugar the benevolent rattle in their pockets'; of Christianity: 'The overthrowing of the reigning goddess and the beginning of the war against the female as declared by Jesus Christ'; of deity: 'An abstract conception of a conceited attraction' . . . 'The father figure at whose feet is cast the doubts created by a father figure' . . . 'That there was a beginning is assumed; that there is an ending is known, but that the ending may be a beginning is a wild dream; so a totem is set in the soft sand to mark the beginning of the thinking of the ending'; of Satan: 'Sympathetic alternative' . . . 'A convenient whipping boy' . . . 'If a state of goodness were easily obtainable — without too much effort — he would be obsolete'; of heaven: 'Man was born neither good nor bad, but lazy, and therefore his dream is to be able, and finally, to live in a state of suspended animation' . . . 'That it is rarely described in detail, whereas hell is graphically and lovingly detailed, is significant' . . . 'A very un-un-un-undeveloped area'; of hell : 'All toast and crumpet' . . . 'Good enough for bad men but not bad enough for good men' . . . 'A scrap heap for God's continual and atrocious mistakes'; of theology: 'One of the bastard sciences' . . . 'The bigoted approach to the universal lie'; of worship: 'The final humiliation and degradation of man unable to look his maker in the eye' . . . 'An outward expression of an inner conflict' . . . 'An appeal to the supernatural by the appalling irrational'; of idolatry: 'An attempt by an uneducated man to match his instinct against spiritual etiquette' . . . 'A more realistic representation of a Christian cross' . . . 'A meagre affectation condemned by a Church groaning under a surplus proliferation of gazed at and kissed smooth paraphernalia'; of sorcery: 'An unscientific equation to an immoral persuasion' . . . 'A prick of comfort where the Church's conscience most hurts' . . . 'A thousand years of repression, liberated in a thousand seconds of repudiation' . . . 'A unique way of averting disciplined inversion' and the clergy: 'The bricks of the Church, mortared with smug piety' . . . 'Collared penguins, gathered and trapped upon an ice floe thawed from the ice cap of humanity'.

And they spoke (loudly, quickly, quietly, brusquely, slowly patiently, at length and briefly) with affection: 'Your shyness, my dear Erowina, and which you find so painful, is one of your attractions'; with feeling: 'That I am a Jew contributed a feeling of personal disgust and prickled my insularity, but what I saw as a man amongst men while we wandered through Belsen, so overwhelmed me, and still does, that words alone are entirely inadequate. Even the most copious of tears are insufficient'; with sensibility: 'It is wrong to suggest that example alone is sufficient to influence a child. Only their experience of the example set them will enable them to assess the advantages as it applies to their own personality'; with pleasure: 'I don't even care if it makes rats' tails of my hair or rusts my suspenders, the feeling of rain splashing on my face is delicious'; with pain: 'I'm well aware that when one's in love, we are supposed to accept the agony of the wounding penetration, but I'm damned if I can bear the masochism of childbirth'; with relief: 'Having realised I no longer needed the security of a father substitute, it wasn't difficult'; with regret: 'I suppose it is because the demands I make are excessive. Then I drink, become maudlin, and, in trying to turn a dream into a reality, bog down in my own immaturity. Anyway, that's what Penny thinks'; with aggravation: 'You term my outspokenness as vulgar, obsessively sexual and indicative of an underlying frustration. I would suggest that your objection stems from excessive prudery, frigidity and an inability to come to terms with your own sexuality, Miss Butt!'; with dejection: 'Introspection is all very well, but how do you cope when you find yourself and know yourself to be short, ageing, unattractive, with a Lilliputian sex and yet possessing a prodigious sexual appetite AND capacity which, by comparison, makes Don Migual Mafiara Vincentelo de Leca seem an impotent charlatan?'; with rejoicing: 'Don't worry, the meal is being paid for by the Hutchinson Bequest who bought a painting of mine from the Beaux Art Gallery. So. Here's more for Mrs Lessore!'; with lamentation: 'I didn't suffer the humiliation of failing. I was thrown out for drunkenness. So, what with one thing and another, what else could I do but illustrate medical textbooks and turn to the manufacture of teaching models for the use of sober students?'; with amusement: 'Elsie Gudroun was touching her toes when someone shouted "change". She stood up so suddenly that Heinrich, who had been sitting very close and behind her, drawing, nearly got the end of his enquiring nose pinched in the cheeks of her bare arse!'; with weariness: 'The arguments put forward to repudiate God are the same as those which are meant to confound the simple basis for any moral truth'; with dullness: 'The Social Government in Sweden has proven the necessity for planned equality; over and over again'; with wit: 'A woman's sense of humour is situated halfway between her navel and her knee and this is why it is impossible to look her in the face when she's telling a funny story'; with simplicity: 'As a child I never gave sex a thought and now that I am an adult I am equally unconcerned'; with taste: 'It would be truer to say that circumstances necessitate the relief and to bear in mind that in Japan it is considered to be one of the minor pleasures and as such, an activity from which no harm or guilt arises'; with vulgarity: 'And the girls purposely gathered round Nurd — I think that was his name; had myopic glasses and squinted through them all the time as if they weren't powerful enough. Anyway, instead of painting, the girls used to stare at his genitals because they discovered by doing so they could make him get an erection. That done they would stream out of the studio, twittering like excited sparrows, leaving poor Nurd mounted on his throne looking for all the world like a hat rack'; with praise: 'The gifts which you, Tammy, take so much for granted, are the very talents which the mass of civilisation, were they to possess them, would consider not only worthy of praise, but as a gift which set them apart'; with affection: 'None of us has a symphony of good looks. There is always a discord struck by one feature or another. Being mortals and not gods, this is to be expected. You have a just complement of good and bad, but you are more fortunate than most, in that your eyes, Erowina, are almost too beautiful to look into'; with hope: 'It is latent in all races, only Germany has deliberately cultivated it to manure the roots of their civilisation. It will take years of torrential rain to cleanse and wash it into the substrata of the unconscious and the severe pruning of the youngest plants who were unfortunate enough to have been mulched on the National dung-heap of an obscene Fascism, before it can be eradicated. The same may be true of Communism. Only time will tell'; with affection: 'Much as I detest deflating your ego, Giacopo, which, like all men's, has been buttressed by an inherent arrogance, I must destroy the delusion under which all you men suffer, which is, that the penis is essential to feminine pleasure. Setting aside the function of intercourse is for the begetting of children and assuming it is undertaken for the satisfying of sexual needs, then I do assure that very satisfactory orgasms can be obtained without the necessity of masculine participation'; with courage: 'I am aware that it is unfashionable to speak out against the modern trend towards lax moral behaviour and irreligious thinking, but because what has been said so far this evening disturbs me so much, I am forced to take up the defence of what you so eagerly wish to destroy and say I think that each of you, in one degree or another, represents all that is base, worthless and degenerate. Your ideas are unoriginal and are culled from instinct; your deliberate rejection of moral standards, pretentious and uncivilised, and the dignity which you, as part and representative of the race of man, exhibit, would disgrace the gibbon'; with fear: 'If not spiders, why not mice? There's not a person who thinks of them without picturing them scurrying into a hole. You'd panic if you were us'; with desire: 'To have exchanged places with Gyges when Candaules revealed to him his expansive, pneumatic, crapulous wife which Jacob Jordaens wished upon him and whose whole queenly bulk and gesture invites all and sundry to kneel and to'; with indifference: 'Sex becomes a concern when I am faced with the imminence of it happening; but between times, I neither think about it nor am occasioned to feel the necessity for it'; with dislike: 'Snails look delicious and smell particularly appetising because of the garlic butter, and I can imagine them tasting nice even while they're on my fork — but as soon as they're in my mouth, I want to vomit'; with wonder: 'A fully qualified doctor? I don't understand. It would explain your friendship with Gormun, but to abandon a career which took so long to achieve and to take up writing — especially so late in life — well, it's almost incomprehensible'; with boasting: 'Before he married Princess Margaret, Anthony took reams of pictures of me'; with insolence: 'You bloody Swedes are all the same. Your own aristocracy is depleted and mixes with the commoners so you stream over here in your hundreds and do your damnedest to rub up against our miserable upper class, hoping that something will come off on you and justify the arrogant attitudes you adopt. And, God knows, you pick up their worst habits. Did you know that at this moment you're slumming? Explain that'; with modesty: 'I write them under a pen name because I'm a little ashamed of admitting to be the perpetrator of such rubbish. But I thought you all knew that I was Iolo Flemminwyn?'; with knowledge: 'She was the seventh wife of Herod the Great and it was their son Phillip, the Tetrarch of Iturea and of the region of Trachonitis and Lysanias and Tetrarch of Abilene, who married Salome, his niece. Salome later married her first cousin Aristobulus and it was she who danced before her stepfather Herod Antipas and his niece Herodias to whom Antipas was married and who was Salome's mother. But that is digressing. We were originally talking about Cleopatra. Now, the Cleopatra to whom you were referring was not Herod's wife but the second wife of Mark Antony and it was the offspring of their daughter, Selene, who married King Juba the Second, who became known as King Ptolemy and who, incidentally, was murdered by

Caius Caligula'; with intellect: 'That is where you are wrong; or should I say where your Newtonian mechanics are at fault. Your recession would not be nought point seven five, although by adding nought point five — your OWN, to nought point two five, the rocket's speed, would appear to be a common sense answer, but, according to Einsteinian relativity, it would be nought point seven one'; with curiosity: 'You say they are all proteins — which is beside the point. What I want to be told is how you know that they are secreted as separate hormones from the pituitary?'; with evidence: 'I saw the face clearly — like in a photograph; the hands pierced by the nails; the whole length of the body and the nail holes in the feet dribbled with blood. ALL with the definition one would expect in a good photograph. Except that this was printed on the winding sheet. And I saw it with my own eyes'; with qualification: 'I assure you Bronzino's Allegory is. I saw it just after it had been cleaned and before they overpainted it again. Next time you're in the National, look at it closely and ask yourself what's really going on. Why the leaves and why the odd space to the left of Venus? The overpainting is less now than it was, perhaps in fifty years they'll clean it again and let us look at it in its entire obscenity — or else flog postcards in plain envelopes'; with probability: 'It is wrong to say that a man possesses instinct if you apply the same word to the inborn automatic behaviour of, say, bees. It is energy over which intelligence has no control whatsoever. If it is agreed that energy — or drive — in man, over which he exerts his intelligence and therefore modifies it, is sex and aggression — as Freud believes it is possible to argue that the bee's instinct derives its compulsive energy from sex and aggression'; with certainty: 'The crown of thorns placed on Christ's head was to discourage the use of hawthorn blossom in orgiastic rites, and for no other reason'; with reasoning: 'Puritanism is a reaction formation against strong sexual desires. Therefore, how can they condemn others when they haven't resolved their own problems? By sublimating them and turning the energy into a more useful and socially acceptable impulse would be the logical thing to do. After all, Gormun has successfully turned his obsession into a business; Giacopo his infant dirtiness into painting and Jaro his frustrated sexual curiosity of childhood into the amassing of a prodigious knowledge of micro-organisms — albeit esoteric. These three men's professions are ALL sociably acceptable'; with sophistry: 'To be rid of the natural pressure which builds up and which solitary alleviation only satiates in part, and not surrendering their pride and modesty to a domination achieved by flattery, they find adequate compensation amongst themselves. If this activity is properly concealed from society, nature is satisfied, respectability sustained, morality conserved and society, in its ignorance, commends the lesbian's acumen, her wisdom, which it believes such a state generates, and her virginity — being unable to accept that this latter state can be endangered by a game of tennis either'; with judgement: 'The knowledge of why such impulses arise does not alter or lessen the argument that it is immoral. The Greeks raised Venus Callipygea in much the same way as an analyst raises unconscious formations in order to alleviate the guilt. Supposedly it is Salmacis whom the heterosexual masses should blame for their dilemma. Mania, athletically sexual, when she submitted to Demetrius, as was required by other hetaerae, was not veiled in guilt when she so pleased him — but she was immoral on both counts, was she not?'; with confutation: 'I didn't know either — even after squeezing them. It was she who told me. Said she'd had a Cleopatra's needle work-out — and that's why her tits were so morbidly swollen; because they'd been pumped full of liquid silicone!'; and, sometimes, in opposition: 'To say that it is vicious and aesthetically unacceptable is wrong because you are unconsciously equating pleasurableness with aestheticism and vice with satisfaction'; and in submission: 'The mind controls the body. Various physical attitudes and activities can become associations which the mind will not tolerate. The unquiet person is rarely released from this imprisonment even after prolonged and conventional analysis, which may well have revealed the disquiet but afforded it no outlet. It becomes a frustration because the goal is unobtainable. It is the achievement of this goal or end-result through muscular attitudes or activities which the analyst will have to resort to in the future; not only because it overcomes resistance — in the psychological sense — but also affords, although clinically and yet in a very real sense, the very end-result which the patient had been denied. You and I might not, or cannot, visualise that the threshing about — the contortions, are anything other than what they appear to be: gymnastics. But can you, by the observation of a mental patient, see much beyond the very slight eccentric — perhaps abnormal — behaviour? I suggest not. The obsessive scratching won't tell you very much; neither will the patient who remains perfectly rigid and lost in thought. So it is muscular activities and attitudes these new patients will be encouraged to perform. What is also interesting is that part of the definition of "attitude" — in the psychological sense, but which I used as indicating a physical, muscular positioning and activity — is, that attitude involves expectancy of a certain kind of experience, and readiness with an appropriate response. It is the resistance to this, or rather these, which can be dealt with even though the method may appear to be both bizarre and distasteful. But I'm sure it will alleviate distress'; but mostly with ridicule: 'I suppose your theory that the world is flat explains why so many people disappear each year — because they get too near to the edge and accidently fall off'; and with belief: 'It's not credible that a hung man dies with an erection'; with ignorance: 'Don't be so silly. It wouldn't have made any difference whether they were Communists or not. Churchill didn't drop arms to them before the invasion for the simple reason that we hadn't got them'; with error: 'It isn't a felony to do it with your wife — if she agrees that is. Good God, if it were, half the population of England would be jailed for life!'; with absurdity: 'She's made of Latex foam rubber. And things. We're not married because she's underage. I call her Mandy, but her real name's Patience Pending. She's pregnant at the moment. We're hoping to produce enough rubber babies to be able to keep Woolworth's dolly counters continually supplied'; with truth: 'I'm a bastard. My stepsisters are quite amiable and my mother a very lovely, energetic woman who hasn't any misgivings. It's my real father who resents my presence. The thought of me being alive and kicking brings on such a guilt complex that he barely avoids having a heart attack whenever I confront him'; with maxim: 'Regardless of political doctrines or humanist idealism, equality is impossible. Vacher de Lapouge rightly re-garded it as an error for which Christianity was responsible. All that one can hope for is that inequality becomes less apparent'; with wisdom: 'To particularise an opinion is to suggest that it is true and has become fact. It would be far better not to discuss opinions but to reveal to each other the sequence of events and/or the reasoning which led up to their formation. Perhaps in this way one wouldn't be tempted to hang onto opinions which have not been reasoned or which have been dragged up from the uncon-scious'; with folly: 'H-hh-h-how in-inun-unn-interesting. Youhoo should have-have-have have told me you were er-a-a-a-a married t-to a-a-a nig-nig-nig-negro man'; with sanity: 'It is no good thumbing through history to find a pattern for our future conduct or to discover parallel circum-stances which will guide us. No other age possessed the bomb or the pos-sibility of destroying what would amount to the whole of the civilised world. All that can be expected and hoped for is that this generation will desist from using it until the generation born during the war grow to ma-turity and, because of their love for one another, make its use unthink-able'; with memory: 'Muriel and Sidney Box saw us do our act once and gave us an introduction to the Players Theatre. But we never went. Do you remember that, Tammy? I wonder what would have become of us if we had?'; with expectation: 'What else have you got in store for us, Giapoco? Anything exciting?'; with foresight: 'If he could have his way the men would visit a brothel and the girls a gymnasium. So, what's it going to be? A compromise? A visit to an indecent club to watch muscular strippers?'.

Exactly one hour and twenty minutes after the start of the meal, Pazzer-oni paid the bill, amounting to nine pounds seventeen shillings and six-pence, and the now merry company trailed out of the underground res-taurant and hung about outside the entrance smoking, chatting and laughing while they waited for Miss Finola Foster-Butt who was in the ladies lavatory and, unknown to them, injecting herself for the second time that day. Feeling the drug beginning to work, she left the lavatory and joined the now impatient group out on the street and together, they all made their way to a certain club; led by Pazzeroni.

They (Jaro — expectant, bouyant; Siri — curious, venturesome; Finola — relieved but despondent; Conrad — cautious, embarrassed; Gormun — wary, truculent; Sidony — excited, elated, flushed; Tammy — enthusiastic, lecherous, impatient; Erowina — frightened, reluctant, overawed; Giacopo — amused, impetuous, imprudent; Mariota — confused, hypercritical) pass (hurriedly, briskly, leisurely, hastily, brusquely, slowly, impatiently) photographs (large, glossy, cracked, dog-eared, wrinkled, fly-blown, coloured, retouched, enlarged, monochrome, faded, improper) of girls (nude, busty, coarse, slim, fat, gross, pretty, bony, tall, comely, dainty, haggard, well-endowed, bonny, short, dumpy, Asiatic, gaudy, dissipated, common, hippy, elegant, Negroid, smiling, bloated, leering, dowdy, naked, matronly, provincial) posturing (obscenely, suggestively, lewdly, artistically, melodramatically, classically, horrifically, captively, naughtily, slavishly, nakedly, erotically, amorously, bewitchingly, boringly, dotingly, seductively, winsomely, intriguingly, angelically, indecently, equivocally, shamelessly, immodestly, lasciviously, salaciously, wantonly, rudely) which are pinned (unimaginatively, securely, edge-to-edge) inside a box (large, glazed, fingermarked, scratched, locked) in a passageway (narrow, gloomy, long, uncarpeted, boarded, bare, brown, littered, dusty, dilapidated, musty) leading (down) to the Club (The Butterfly Club, Berwick Mews, London, W.1., private, members only, drinking, dancing, striptease). They look (casually, studiously, disapprovingly, admiringly, longingly, guiltily, stoically, sublimely, impartially, jealously, venially, magnanimously, secretly, suspiciously, indulgently, quickly and dispassionately) at them and, laughing (contemptuously, heartlessly, hysterically, boisterously, irrepressibly, unavoidably, tolerantly, lugubriously), go (pushing, dawdling, scuffing, elbowing, walking, jigging and pressing) down the stairs (narrow, uncarpeted, wooden, winding, tortuous, rickety, dusty, uneven, scuffed, steep, worn, dangerous, well-trodden, and unlighted).

In the Club room (low-ceilinged, overcrowded, smoke-filled, noisy, dimly lit, cavernous, oppressive, stifling, concrete-floored, sparsely furnished, tatty, dank, subterranean, satanic) Giacopo (conceited, obstreperous) shows (ostentatiously) a Membership Card (soiled, frayed, folded, creased, out-of-date, borrowed) to the man (West African, muscled, broken-nosed, garlic-mouthed, red-eyed, white-tongued, gold-toothed, cauliflower-eared, suspicious, stubborn, corrupt) at the door (barred, bolted, spy-holed, low-lintelled, thick, wooden, zinc-faced).

They (alarmed, embarrassed, shy, confident, indifferent, scornful, jaundiced, plebeian, exultant and perturbed) make their way (grunting, giggling, guffawing, sniggering, chaffing, whistling, grinning, snuffling, bantering, wheezing, twittering, quipping, scoffing, laughing, coughing and sniffing) to a table (small, wooden, wobbly, cluttered, unoccupied) and order (hesitantly, brashly, timorously, pompously, coyly, demurely, ceremonially and formally) drinks (Imperial vodka and Bolger's lime, Prince Charles Edward's drambuie, Old Bushmill's Irish whisky and corporation water, Coates Plymouth gin and Schweppes tonic water, Smernoff vodka and Schweppes tomato juice, Carlin's lager and Bolger's lime, Guinness, Bell's Standfast Scotch whisky, Charrington's bottled pale ale and Beaufoy's number two pale dry South African sherry.

In between drinks (singles, half-pints, pints, doubles and bottles) they (squiffy, canned, blotto, sloshed, half-keeled-over, tanked-up, pie-eyed, stiff, pissed) dance (weaving, rambling and staggering, thumping, jogging and elbowing, straying, trotting and skeltering, rebounding, jolting and shouldering, roving, bounding and buffeting, banging, bumping and butting, jostling, shunting and springing, bending, rebuffing and hustling, slouching, cheek-to-cheek and wheeling, accelerating, at arm's length and drifting, dashing, striking and hurtling, shuffling, prodding and shoving, recoiling, thwacking and swerving, roving, cornering and veering, twisting, dodging and edging, tripping, backing and falling) to the music (modern, orchestral, medley, jukebox, deafening, ragtime, jazz, waltz-time, syncopated, instrumental, vocal, blatant) or talk (loudly, drunkenly, sentimentally, foolishly, outspokenly, rudely, jokingly, boastfully, untruthfully and salaciously).

So it came about that Siri danced with Jaro while Tammy danced with Mariota; Conrad with Sidony; Giacopo with Finola and Gormun with Erowina. Then Jaro danced with Finola; Siri with Tammy; Mariota with Conrad; Sidony with Giacopo and Gormun with Erowina. Then Sidony danced with Tammy; Mariota with Jaro; Conrad with Siri; Giacopo with Finola while Gormun and Erowina watched. Then Tammy danced with Sidony; Mariota with Jaro; Giacopo with Finola while Siri, Conrad, Gormun and Erowina sat at the table talking. Then Tammy danced with Erowina while the rest sat and discussed. Just as Giacopo and Finola rise to dance.

Aristotle Chabas (male, forty-eight, Maltese, obese, pencil-moustached, bejewelled, suited in purple with a thin black stripe) rises to his feet (flat) and shouts (loudly): QUIET! Quiet there, please. QUIET! Let's have a bit of hush.

The dancers (Negro, American, French, English, Welsh, Polish, Czechoslovakian, Swedish, Irish, Dutch, Canadian) sit (expectantly), breathlessly) down (quickly).

— Miss Marienne, tonight's star — better known to you as Thunder Hips — is about to dance an exotic number she calls

Madras Velvet. Gentlemen — and, ladies — for your titillation, our very own — yours and mine — MISS MARIENNE! Give her a big hand now.

He (bored) inserts (absentmindedly) a coin (one shilling, English) into the jukebox (American, chrome, squat, gleaming, sleek, gaudy, hired, profitable).

Miss Marienne (female, twenty-three, Welsh, baptised Avril Garonwy, short, stocky, platinum blonde, vague, inane, satined in black) enters (unexpectedly) from behind a curtain (blue, spangled, torn, dusty) carrying (nonchalantly) a carpet (stair, small, fragment, rolled) and lays (carefully, neatly) it (coloured, two feet square, patterned, hessian-backed, red, blue, green, flowered) on the floor (cold, concrete, dusty, rough, grey) and stands (squarely) on it. The music (rhythmic, pulsating, voluptuous, throbbing, sensual) commences (slowly) and Marienne (bored, expressionless) begins (half-heartedly, reluctantly) to dance (swaying, gyrating). She removes (leisurely) her gloves (black, lace, cuff-buttoned, split, darned) unzips (awkwardly, with difficulty, scowling) her dress (black, satin, mended, tight, low-backed, slit-skirted, sleeveless, unbecoming) and steps (demurely, carefully, delicately) out of it (crumpled, discarded). She (wriggling, expressionless) undoes (without looking, hastily) her suspenders (black, stretched, old nickel-tabbed) and belt (suspender, black, brief, skimpy, lacy, elastic, tasselled) and drops (nonchalantly) it (shrivelled, diminutive). She (teasing, cheeky, over-acting) turns (deliberately) her back (broad, white, plump) and asks (coyly, hamming) Tammy (surprised) to undo (speedily) her brassiere (black, nylon, transparent). This done (efficiently, unhurriedly) she shows (exposing, lifting, weighing, squeezing, bouncing, juddering, creaming, lathering, stroking, spreading, compressing, pointing, flipping, massaging) her breasts (white, veined, pendulous, milky, pneumatic, firm, twin, full, matronly, goose-pimpled, amazon, aromatic, motherly, wholesome) and nipples (erect, brown, pimpled, spreading, haloed). Still dancing (twirling, bending, stretching) she (smiling) begins (immediately) to remove (erotically) her knickers (black, semi-transparent, moist) when the music (climactic, deafening) stops (suddenly).

MARIENNE (gum-chewing, shivering, truthful) to Tammy (amused): — Talk about freezin'. I'm ice from me bum to me toes. An American (male, twenty-one, soldier, Chick Bolan, 14046911, had been indiscreet and that it was only a joke, but that Tammy private, 89th Marine Corps, decorated, slim-buttocked, button-booted, uniformed in khaki) puts (hastily) a coin (one shilling, English) into the jukebox (illuminated, silent).

When (later) the music (urgent, pulsing) begins, Marienne (relieved) starts (immediately) to dance (diligently, strenuously, earnestly, monotonously) and removes (lasciviously, slothfully, drowzily, indolently) her knickers (lace-edged, double-gusseted, frilled, scanty, tight, silk). Afterwards (immediately) she (provocatively) holds (closely, securely) them (screwed, balled) over (obscuring) her sex (unseen) and turning (slowly, skilfully) displays (proudly, pertly, ceremoniously, jubilantly, boastfully, saucily, imperiously, affectionately, sisterly, sociably, impolitely, precociously, perversely, amorously) her bottom (plump, pink, aromatic, personable, resplendent, shapely, symmetrical, glowing, spacious, aesthetic, paintable, spotless, elastic, refreshing, misused, enhancing, bracing, impeccable, cardinal, adequate, memorable, copious, liberal, turgid, solid, restive, wobbly, tenacious, irresistible, pleasurable, sculptural, porcelain. moulded, demonstrative, dense, cumbersome, compressible, vaporous, pneumatic, steaming, oleaginous, humid, capacious, rigid, taut, ingratiating, familiar, tart, affable, gregarious, cosy, enchanting, luxurious, erotic, kissable). She (frantic, wide-eyed, open-mouthed, malevolent) turns (undulating, quivering) and exposes (bit by bit, suggestively, inching, wantonly, salaciously, lickerously) her pubes (plump, puffed, hairy, mysterious, shadowed, fluffed) and her sex (closed, neat, small, pink, compact, dry). Dressed (erotically) in only her shoes (black, court, standard, high-heeled, stained, scuffed, metal-tipped) and stockings (black, net, nylon, laddered, darned, seamed) she (professional, underpaid, unmarried, prostitute) dances (voluptuously, suggestively, shamelessly, erotically, obscenely), making (enjoyable) movements (rapid, undulating, coital) with her hips (broad, feminine, pungent), until (two minutes later) the music (vibrant, climactic) stops (suddenly). She (disenchanting, poker faced) picks up (scooping, gathering, snatching) her clothes (dress, bra, pants) and the mat (rolled) and disappears (magically, swiftly) behind the curtain (swaying, obscuring).

Everyone (hilarious, excited, inebriated, quarrelsome, frustrated, jovial, reflective, maudlin, aggressive, lecherous, satisfied) applauds (clapping, whistling, stamping, shouting, encoring, hollering, jeering, cat-calling, booing).

Ten minutes later the club closed (officially).

It was two-thirty when the party of ten who had dined, wined, talked, danced and laughed together all evening went home. Jaro took Mariota in a taxi back to her mews apartment where she wished him goodnight and shut the door firmly against him. She was in bed and asleep within ten minutes. Jaro, walking, reached home an hour and ten minutes later and, undressing, woke his wife when he knocked a silver backed brush off the dressing room table.

Tammy walked Sidony back to her flat where she gave him coffee, refused to share her bed but allowed him to sleep on the sofa. Stood in his underwear before turning off the light, Tammy asked Sidony if she thought Erowina was unhappy. She replied that Erowina was and asked if he fancied her. Not answering, Tammy turned off the light and settled himself on the sofa.

Long before that, Conrad had taken Siri back to her studio in a taxi and used the same taxi to get himself home.

Giacopo had seen Finola back to her flat, drunk three more whiskies sat on the floor and, having become maudlin because Finola turned aside his advances, allowed himself to be driven home in her Jaguar. Seated behind the steering wheel in her nightdress, she had allowed Giapoco to kiss her and then hurriedly driven home in great pain.

Gormun, meanwhile, had escorted Erowina back to her flat; commiserated with her and had hung about waiting for Giacopo to return. Finally, at three-thirty, Erowina persuaded Gormun to return home to his wife Penelope. He did and a bitter quarrel ensued which lasted until dawn.

Erowina went to bed at a quarter to four and was awakened by Giapoco at six who was unable to account for the time between when Finola had set him down and when he found himself on the landing outside Erowina's flat door.

Undressing and climbing in beside Erowina, Giacopo remarked the party hadn't been such a success but that he felt damned sexy.

Erowina asked Giacopo if he had known Tammy Lamlin long; to which Giacopo replied, two years, adding, Tammy was a quack turned writer. Asked if Tammy was married, Giacopo did not answer. He had fallen asleep.

When Giacopo woke midday, Erowina, dressed, lay in a dead faint. The door was ajar and a large bouquet of cellophaned roses lay on the floor beside her. The card attached to the flowers read: TO EMILY H. FROM HER FATHER CONFESSOR, TAMMY LAMLIN.

Revived, asked who was Emily H. and why Tammy should be sending her roses, Erowina replied she had been drunk at the party, was kindness itself and would Giacopo please, please put the flowers in the dustbin.

ALLERGY

"L'Homme passe (la nature) à
travers des fôrets de symboles,
 Qui l'observent avec des regards
familiers."
— Baudelaire.

(1932)

She'd gone lopping as she marched. In strict rhythm at first while the nodding buds were within reach of her energetic switch. Then later, amidst the blooms on her well-dug island surrounded by a billiard green sea of grass, Emily slashed and flicked; making confetti of her joy. Whooping and lopping, she decimated the surrounding brilliance and carpeted her island with petals.

— You little devil you! and Father drew her trailing scream into the brown, back, book-lined study.

Bent to his hard knee,

— It's time,

her skirt dragged up

— time you were taught a lesson!

he pulled at her knickers,

The unsmelt buds lay in the sun.

and exposed her.

— That!

The scattered petals stirred.

— That! and the smacking palm imprinted each pain upon her tiny buttocks, raising a rose red blush; petalling the fragrant orbs with slaps.

— That!

The sweet aroma of the crushed, bruised roses, wilting in the sunlight, was gently dissipated by the warm wind.

— And that!

The violated roses, nosing the earth, cringed before the breeze and tumbled scattering:

— And that, and that!

shrivelling.

Emily bore the final blow upon a scream and was flung into the brambles of her humiliation with the thorn of her father's guilt embedded in her innocence.

From this incestuous union

(But the entry is incomplete.)

(1934)

A good, solid book weighting the knees, and sat cosy in the ageing settle blistered by the winter's crackling fire.

— In those days we seemed to have more time.

The big book split; grinning yellow pages.

— Your great-aunt pressed each and every listed in Reverend Lang's *English Hedgerows*.

Between the wedges, buttercups cracked and shivered into fragments.

— All we girls did.

Colourless pansies breathed like tremulous butterflies newly emerged from their chrysalis. And sedge. Dry as ash. Powdering into dust.

— Don't go blowing them. It took patience.

And there. Was it? Yellowed to tissue and stuck; absorbing the spreading, haloed linseed print. A petal. Delicately brittle. And dead. Yet.

The ghosted rose breathed.

— Mind, child!

But the Good Book cannoned shut and fell; tenting on its mashed corners.

And so did I.

(1940)

Don't you know? It's what they make itching powder from. Maurice took the red, polished hip and pressed his thumb nail into the hard, juicy skin. Splitting it down its length, he laid bare the fluffy, yellow pith.

— Do you really mean to tell me you didn't know? And he showed her: what you do — is . . . .

He seized Erowina and, with snuff pinch thumb and forefinger, struggled the pith down the back of her collar.

— Stop it! and she pushed him away and stood feeling the back of her neck.

— Well?

— Well, what? It doesn't itch.

— Doesn't it? Well, this will! And he threw himself upon her rolling her and forcing his hand beyond the elastic of her knickers

— You horrible boy. How dare you! And she scrambled to her feet and ran a short way off, shrugging down her skirt.

— It was only in fun. Catch!

She caught.

— What is it exactly?

— I told you, silly. It's what they manufacture itching powder from.

— But what is it?

— Good grief! Are all the girls at your school so dim? It's a hip. A com-mon-or-garden hip. A ROSE hip.

Emily stood off and began to scream while her knickers became alive and she could feel herself being bitten by a million, red-hot tiny jaws which slowly converged.

(1946)

(Erowina and Raphael Arlington had intended visiting the cinema but were stopped in the street.)

— A rose for the lady, sir? and Adam took the monstrous bud and pinned the obscenity onto Emma's falling shadow.

Patted into awareness, she weighted the crooked and helpful arm while a passing boot squashed, dragged and irritably scraped the offending bud of excrement into the dusty gutter.

(1950)

I caught it up in a hastily snatched handkerchief and looked staring past the spreading transparency to the finely embroidered rose. Startled, I stayed my hand and passed out (backwards, I think).

(1951)

Unlike the upward, joyous rush on the spongy stairs of dreams, or floating upon an effortless gossamer whim, or wallowing and churning in the syrupy liquid of an amorous lake, but like the rattling, clattering, iron-clad train, fixed and grooved to the dead straight track which plunges into the diminishing mouth of a Gulliver tunnel or the slow unwinding snake gobbing dribbled venom, the single budded rose, bedevilled on its shaft by barbarous thorns, is the outrage of my nightmares.

It comes erect on its stem. Its bud packed tight, retaining the pungency of its acrid aromatic sourness and the stem heckled with rapacious barbs.

At such times, I fill with lead and am nailed fast to my fear for the bud is cast in iron and clad in ice.

Entering, it fills and, enlarging, blooms into a cancerous growth. And then the stem breaks clean and I retain the enormity whilst the broken shaft saws into my other gut; tearing. And I start up, to pass the night waiting for the morning.

(1951)

Energised by a loathsome but dutiful activity, the swollen bud, shiny and purple skinned — at bursting like a squeaking balloon, pulsed a single tear of dew. Eunice, fearing the association, sought to draw the sepal up and hood the myopic eye, but her stretching drew forth the searing sun and the bud blossomed as she fell away, retching up her dinner of minced meat and mashed potatoes.

(1952)

— Oppenheim's fur cup and saucer always dries out and shrivels my mouth whenever the image comes to mind.

— Really? I find handling coke more disturbing. Or a blackboard duster. That raises the hair on the back of my neck.

— I turn inside out when a piece of chalk squeals a long, sliding line.

— Having to pick out the long and nauseous threads of slime from the waste-hole of a kitchen sink bugs me.

— It's no more nauseous than drawing fistfuls of yak from a chicken.

— Try disembowelling a hare which has hung for a week!

— Eunice. What about you? What makes you squirm?

She tries to fight down the remembrance of a cloth rose. Bleached mushroom pink and satin furred; downed like a velvet spider, it sat soft and hairy, gross and alive, rising and falling in the powered, smelling cleavage of Nancy Sedoloid's best dress.

The memory parts her lips; the hair steals up her spine and, while her bowels drain, she slips through the membrane of a stifling, soundless insanity.

It was Tammy who told Esmeralda she had fainted. Later.

(1953)

— For you. Guess, and (Tammy) the magician conjured from behind his back a bunch of cellophaned screams and thrust them at Esmeralda. To celebrate your pregnancy, stupid.

But Esmeralda turned and ran into the door's edge, and into unconsciousness.

Drawn into awareness by (my) concern and tenderness, the fallen, forgotten, red celebration posy scratched at the corner of Esmeralda's eyeball; attracting her repulsion, and the shuddering began all over again.

(1956)

She had rewrapped the nightdress and hidden it in the bottom drawer.

— Why? Doesn't it fit? It's what you wanted. A white, cotton nightdress with long sleeves, a high neck and smocking on the chest.

— You haven't looked.

— It's exactly as I have described.

— And the tag?

He looked. The significance of the rose-bud symbol was all too apparent.

— Couldn't you cut it off?

She shook her head.

— Shall I return it? But she was not answering. I'll return it.

When he returned, she was feeding sheets of paper onto the fire.

— Why didn't you hit me, Tammy? Another man would. He would have lost his temper and struck me.

— What are you burning?

— But you never demand. Never tell me what to do. Never assert yourself. Never try to dominate me. You are not good for me, Tammy. You are weak.

She tore the last few sheets of paper in two and laid them on the fire.

— My diaries — dating from May fifty-two.

— Is it memories you burn, or me?

— These you may destroy yourself, and she handed him a thickness of foolscap. They were part of his book.

— If I don't? Won't?

She waited, stood by the fire.

— Who'll know it's you I've written about?

— I will, she said.

He dropped the manuscript onto the fire and Esmeralda gathered him up in a huge hug. When they rolled apart, the manuscript was still smouldering.

They had made vigorous love; a triumphant but humiliating coupling; Esmeralda prone, superimposed.

— I'll not hurry you, Tammy, but I think the sooner you find yourself a room, the better.

It was then he saw the look in her eye was not one of love.

Esmeralda despised him.

— I need to be dominated, Tammy. Told. Not written about.

— Will you promise?

He promised and stirred the ashes with the toe of his boot.

— May I be permitted a tear?

— For yourself, yes. For me, no.

— I had it in mind to cry for the both of us. But I'll find a room.

It would be ironic if it had roses on the wallpaper.

In passing, Esmeralda ruffled his hair.

— It will be a reasonable excuse for me not to come calling. But I shall miss you.

(1959)

Straining to look, on tiptoe; nosing the sheen of waltzing heads. Palming the cool wall. Flower? Not unless he . . . Please God, let him come. Make him come.

The band soldiered on. The heads vortexed like bobbing corks while the fat saxophones unisoned their cackling three-four drone.

One dark head, bouyed atop the swirl, was static. Motionless. It was!

Cinderella pressed towards her Prince while the band's drum thumped and bumped. The watery dancers parted for her mad, breasting rush and the cymbals splashed.

Suddenly, across the distance of a reaching hand, Evelyn faced him.

But, courteous and smiling, he lent his arm to his rightful spouse who, in sequinned splendour, clung, queening her possession with a spiteful smile. Imprisoned on her putty bosom, broached securely, a touching, thoughtful gesture, sincerely given and graciously accepted, was the wild-est of love's roses; nipped in the enormity of her maternal breasts.

Betrayed, Evelyn turned with the waltzers and corkscrewed slowly into the thundering boards.

(1962)

The inhibitions shrank like noon-day shadows when, hoofed and hairy, Ribaldry, his erect phallus cleaved to a bulbous stomach, mounted his glorious throne.

The laughter came cackling, coated in phlegm; and the drinks kept coming.

— Hairy pie, said the blindfolded vicar!

Veins fattened in the reddening necks and the drinks kept coming.

— Vot's a blind man vont vid a pair of testicles anyhow, he say!

The knees hardened to the slapping and the drinks kept coming.

— The Bishop's a long time coming, said the actress, stirring her tea with her other hand.

The bottoms quietly blushed under the lecherous nips and the drinks kept coming.

— I said, use the butt of your fid-pin to wedge in the futtock cried the Admiral!

And the bladders strained at each compressing funniment.

But.

— Look what you're doing!

— Duck! as the publican's daily-dusted flowers went tumbling over shoulders and the plastic rose fell into Evelyn's slack lap. To be covered in vomit.

(1964)

The Harpic tin, read, was returned. The pristine roll scratched from its wrapper. And. Waiting. Two squares purred off and held. Waiting. For the moment when. Then. Reaching behind when. The discarded wrapper blinked its print. PETAL SOFT.

The limp, clammy cabbage rosy blossomed under my warm rump and I fell, knicker-hobbled, into the side of the bath, bruising my shin. Badly. (She adds she was drunk at the time and, having no identity, was suscept-ible. "There must be a solution but, try as I may, I have not found one.")

FEMALES ON ALTERNATE DAYS
(June 1956)

No one had told her she would not have to pay on entry. This surprise made her falter and she felt her courage drain while she stood, her handbag wide open, her hand inside and her smiling, enquiring face bent down to the small opening in the glass window. When she stood up, the bored face of the seated female cashier disappeared from view; only her busy hands continued to knit. Tomorrow, it would be a man; doing what — rolling fags?

Without further embarrassment, Erica was shown to her cubicle and was able to lock the door on a retreating attendant.

The odour inside the warm cubicle was a mixture of rotting, damp wood and discarded face flannels. Glad she could not detect the smell of unwashed bodies or carbolic disinfectant, Erica hung up her coat and began to undress.

Her clothes, the intimate garments she had carefully chosen to cover herself with that morning, seemed strangely impersonal as she discarded them, one by one.

Finally, standing naked on the warm, marble floor, she fluffed her pubic hair before slipping into the thin wrap provided.

The wrap was white and had been washed and ironed so many times the shiny ironed seams appeared fused and held together by starch. There were no buttons and, although she searched, she could not find a tie-belt with which to keep the gown closed. Patting her hair into place, she gathered the robe about her and opened the door; feeling vulnerable.

After locking the cubicle door and rolling an elastic band from which hung the numbered key onto her right wrist, Erica walked towards the heat.

The room was a hall, large and warm. In the centre was a shallow pool. Golden carp, garishly contrasted against the bright green tiles, swam in circles; occasionally rising to breast the myriads of tiny, cooling bubbles which aerated the pool at either end. Circling the pool, discreetly clustered round low tables on which were scattered newspapers and magazines, were wooden framed chairs with green canvas bottoms and backs. Against the walls and reflected in the mirrored arches potted palms and wild grasses grew in such profusion they turned the baths into a Victorian jungle. As she walked, Erica half expected the thin sound of a "tea orchestra" — piano, cello and violin, to come strained and intense from an imaginary dais at the far end of the palmed court.

Choosing a chair away from the rest, Erica sat down, keeping the edges of her gown discreetly together.

Up until that moment, although she had been aware of other women in the hall, she had been far too embarrassed to seek them out individually. Seated, unable to turn the damp pages of a magazine she had picked up to shield behind, she began to scrutinise her fellow bathers.

There were about twenty women, mostly elderly, a majority carrying on a discreet and whispered conversation with their neighbour. Between nods or disagreements in undertone, they sipped lemon tea or drank aerated water from slim glasses. Most sat sprawled in their chairs, legs apart, utterly relaxed. Erica observed there were only three younger than herself and these girls stood giggling round a weighing machine. But there was a fourth, judged by Erica to be the same age as herself, who sat apart and stared. Erica avoided her gaze; jealous of the woman's good looks, her long, blonde hair and her extraordinary mauve eyes.

Grown bored with trying to make sense of the jigsawed, patterned blue, red, cream and green tiled floor, Erica rose to her feet and padded across the floor towards the entrance of the tepidarium. Overtaken by the three younger girls who, despite the objecting frowns of the older women, were running and shrieking, she followed at a more leisurely pace and with what she hoped looked like an air of confidence.

As she walked, Erica delighted in the sensation the warm tiles made on the soles of her feet. The mild heat was sensuous, reminding her of all the Eastern palaces she had, in her imagination, drifted through since her early childhood. She smiled to herself and wondered how many others shared her exotic dreams or came to the baths to indulge them.

Pushing the green canvas curtain aside, she entered the tepidarium. A wave of heat buffetted her in the face and she stood gasping. Had she mis-understood Pat's directions? This was a hell hole.

Several women, sat in green canvas deckchairs with their eyes closed, perspired gently; blowing occasionally and patting themselves with tow-els. Erica chose a deck chair and sat down.

Fifteen minutes later, unable to perspire, she began to wonder if there was something wrong with her. Her forehead was cool.

A woman with cropped hair, broad shoulders and a hard athletic figure with only a suggestion of a bosom, strode into the tepidarium. She wore a blue bathing costume and carried a folded towel over her arm. Giving a hearty smile, the woman marched towards Erica.

"You forgot your towel."

Erica folded under the woman's eyes which had the texture of splintered glass. However, she managed a "thank you" when she caught the thrown towel.

"Can I book you for massage?"

Erica, tongue-tied, hesitated before answering.

"It's an extra, you understand. But if you can't afford it . . . ."

"Of course I can afford it!"

The woman with the shattered eyes approached, smiling. and took Erica's wrist to look at her tagged key.

"Two-o-five. Good." And she squeezed. "Just sit in the forecourt when you're through."

The attendant gone, Erica dabbed her face with the towel, crossed her legs and, closing her eyes, tried to relax. Minutes later, without having to open them, she knew someone was looking at her. She resisted the temptation to see who, until the feeling had passed. When she did, Erica was disconcerted.

Standing opposite to her was the attendant in the blue bathing costume, her head cocked to one side and a lemon-sweet smile on her face. She held out a long pink ribbon.

"I couldn't find you a cap. Have this," and Erica was forced to accept the ribbon.

Even as the attendant ducked under the canvas curtain, Erica was aware of the disapproving frowns of the women who had turned to stare. Her embarrassment turned to fury, Erica looped the ribbon about her hair.

Fumbling to tie the bow, she saw the beautiful woman with the long blonde hair and the curious mauve eyes regard her with flared nostrils and turn her head away with a proud flick of her long blonde tresses.

Damn you all, thought Erica and, struggling up, walked purposefully into the Caldarium. (Or was it the Laconicum?).

The dry heat hit her like a flat iron.

Walking through the mazed room, determined to escape the tut-tutting women in the tepidarium, Erica glimpsed motionless bodies lying on slabs or stood in alcoves. One tiny miscalculation with the heat regulator, she thought, and they would all turn into roast pork.

Ducking out of the room, Erica crossed a corridor and entered a heated room moist with steam. Instinctively, she paced to and fro while the sweat began to pearl on her forehead and flood from the small of her back. Feeling her robe grow heavier as it absorbed the steam and her perspiration, she stood aside when the three slim girls she had seen standing by the weighing-machine, ran stark naked and giggling past her. She wished she had their energy and was not so inhibited.

Panting, and her heart thundering in her ribcage, she was forced to stop. With the sweat dripping off her nose and glistening between her breasts, she laid out her damp towel on one of the stone slabs recessed into the wall and, wrapping the wet robes about her, swung up her feet and lay flat on her back.

The hard shelf bore into her body while she lay blowing and sweating. She was battling with her will. Alone and unobserved, except for the occasional passing, misty figure, she could lie absolutely still and will her body to endure what it so palpably found unacceptable.

Why? Why should she punish herself? True she endured minor discomfort for the sake of appearances, but what she was subjecting her body to now was ludicrous. She had been told the baths would be hot and uncomfortable but Pat had not warned her the rooms would be so devilishly subterranean and satanic.

She rolled her head from side to side when another wave of suffocation surged over her.

Seeing a block of wood, evidently a head rest, she put it under her neck.

Now, she was truly being racked.

Streaming the air through her nostrils like some dragon, she imagined herself imprisoned in the palace of her dreams, chained in a dungeon. She knew she would have to endure more if the Prince were to be persuaded to look at her, so she must stick it out.

She had come, partly to relax — in this hell hole?— partly to overcome her loneliness now that Tammy had moved away. To overcome both and begin afresh, will had to be exercised and that was precisely what she was doing. Action engenders reaction, Tammy had said. She had agreed.

Suddenly, feeling faint, she sat up and, swinging her legs off the shelf, forced her head in between her legs till the giddiness passed.

Rising, she began to walk about, enjoying the perspiration which poured from her. In the catacombed room, she saw only two other women who were lying apart on stone slabs. The loneliness encouraged her to go peering into other vapoured rooms in search of, what? Adventure?

The fourth room was spacious and warm. Along one wall was a row of showers with slippery duck boards ranged beneath; in the centre, several slatted wooden benches back to back; to her right yet another steam room but this had glass windows and a solid door.

As she was making her way cautiously over the slippery wet floor towards it, the door opened and a woman of ample proportions, carrying her robe and towel, was borne out on a billowing cloud of steam. The woman stood panting and grinned. Her breasts hung down to her waist and blue veins, swollen and ridged, converged on nipples stretched to the size of saucers. Erica turned away; nauseated. But the woman came from behind and walked into Erica's line of vision. And she glimpsed the woman's pocked and wobbling buttocks which hung yellow and huge and saw that her legs were not bruised but lumpy with veins. To try and erase the image, Erica repeated to herself, grass is green, grass is green, before seizing hold of the door knob and flinging herself into the fifth and final room.

With the door slammed shut behind her, she immediately felt trapped.

The steam was so dense, she couldn't see her outstretched hand. But worse, there was no oxygen in the hot vapour for her to gulp.

She wrenched open the door, and stood mouthing in air like a goldfish.

Facing her, stood under the showers, all naked and all exceedingly gross, were several women. The sight of them made Erica want to vomit. Each had their eyes screwed tight, their faces turned up to the tiny jets of water and all of them revealed a kind of ecstasy on their faces while they stood gently patting or massaging their gross, bloated shapes. Like a frieze of monstrous, blue-veined jelly-babies, larding their bulbous, feminine prolapses, thought Erica.

In her haste to escape from the steam room, Erica nearly slipped on the floor but saved herself by grabbing the window sill. Having heard a cry of alarm, all the women under the showers opened their eyes and looked. Embarrassed, her way blocked by a group of animated women entering the shower room, Erica had no alternative but to fumble with the brass handle of the steam room door and breast the suffocating steam again.

Burying her face in the wet towel for a moment and then turning, Erica began to pace up and down. When she was passing the door for the fifth time with her teeth gritted, she dropped her towel onto the stone shelf and, pulling off her robe, threw it on top. Naked and feeling defiant she continued her pacing in the obscuring steam.

The steam was so dense that it always surprised her to come across her clothes or to see the wall towards which she was pacing, suddenly within a foot of her face. Blowing and occasionally wiping the back of her hand across her face to remove the perspiration, she counted the seventeen steps which took her from wall to wall.

While she walked, she tried to rid her mind of the images of the women smoothing and larding the fatness from their bodies. The words of Joyce kept reiterating with each step, the yellow mellow, smellow . . . and she became exasperated. She must never, never never let herself go so completely that she came to resemble the women outside. It was bad enough coping with her birthmark but to have the added disadvantage of a disgusting obesity as well would be unendurable.

Turning at the wall Erica reflected, somewhat reluctantly, that the gross women under the showers were, in all probability, loved by someone as much as others of more attractive proportions. But the possibility that they aroused desire was almost too much to imagine. Although she could visualise an encircling, comforting and perhaps loving arm round their shoulders, by no stretch of her imagination could she believe in the possibility of a lecherous eye, slowly licking the bulging forms when the soft sour-smelling flesh was eased in perspiring handfuls out of a constraining, outsized frilled girdle, in the warm intimacy of a bedroom. Her mind sickened at the thought. Yet she knew it must happen. But what spurred them to sport in front of their loved ones with the reckless immodesty of passion? Love? Or desperation? Their lumbering ungracefulness and smiling passivity seemed repellent.

She groaned and stood leaning against the wall; her legs lost in the mist below her. Feeling the sweat oozing out of her skin and watching it run down between her breasts, she thought that it must be doing her good, however much it exhausted her body.

Had it been a silly idea to come to the baths and hope to emerge cleansed; able to face the world minus her hump of discontent? The bodily effusion draining out of her would quickly be replaced and the temporary buoyancy evaporate, leaving her sullen and weighted once again. Her inner lethargic spirit would remain untouched. Nothing would alter that. What was, would always be. Tammy and the rest of them would go on adding to the dull heap that was her. To have come to the baths was to escape as she always did, only this time, in a palace inhabited by grey ghosts who loomed out of the mists; a tactile dream of which she was part, rather than lying in her white-enamelled tub at home, sucking her warm flannel and tracing her desires along the meandering cracks of the bathroom ceiling. Did others come to escape? To lie curled and robed in some hidden corner and, while the mists of steam closed round them, imagine themselves to be no longer part of any world but that of their own making? Erica doubted it. She was the only oddity; the adult child looking for an eternal teddy bear to hug. Even in this vaporous underworld of drifting souls, aimlessly wandering from room to room, wrapped and towelled or strangely naked while they endured the torments of the sulphurous steam and heat, she was still the odd one out. An outsider.

Erica leant her head against the wall and, surprised, drew back. On the wall was a drawing of a prick. What woman would go to all the trouble of secreting a pen in her pocket and, in the farthest room, obscured and hidden, draw a man's erection? Then she remembered. On alternate days, men wandered through these very rooms, naked and wrapped in towels, just as she had been doing. And one had gone to extremes to make his mark. It might have been a woman of course. Women did. She had been into lavatories which were covered in graffiti. Poor, confused souls. They wanted love, attention; excitement. It was only because they were bored, unfulfilled, thinking themselves unloved and unlovely they sat on the pan and vented their wrath. Who could blame them? She too must have love. Be loved. Rejoice in the confidence which only love could make blossom. She refused to die before she had conjoined with someone who loved her as she loved them; for the same reasons, with the same intensity and with an understanding. She wanted to be able to turn a slow smile on the world around her; an admixture of pride and supreme self-confidence that came with fulfilment. She knew that within her, somewhere, a dormant bud lay ready and waiting to be stroked into blossom. She imagined it to be like a Chinese water flower which would magically unfurl and remain suspended in a dazzling show of glory. It would expand; lapping, filling and intoxicating her whole being so that she would radiate love and confidence and it would shine from her like a brilliant, flowering sun. It would be abundant, luxuriant; final and overwhelmingly fulfilling. Yes. It was love she wanted; love on her own terms. A love without agony, recriminations or doubt. A love which would give life meaning.

She stroked the sweat from her arms and continued her pacing. Four more times and she would be through. Four more times and she would emerge from the steaming hell; her flesh cleansed as never before. Four more times and, when she opened the door and stepped out, back into the real world, she would try to be stiffened by resolution; not cowed by the looks or the cruel remarks which whipped her spirit, and made her cringe. She would exercise self-control over her sensitivity. She would ride remarks as easily as a bobbing cork. She would become impregnable. Not hard, but have the capacity to be able to wrench out the barbs before they festered the wound. She would create round her an aura of confidence and purposefulness which would deter anyone storming her defences. This she would do.

Only three more times, she told herself when she reached the wall; blowing and gasping.

She'd buy herself a swimming costume. That was it. Yes. She'd do that. Right after she left the baths. A swimming costume. Let them see her birthmark. If they thought it was shit, that was their embarrassment. Anyway, she was certain there must be a shop somewhere which specialised in a make-up for such things. She'd ask about. Deliberately. She wasn't going to be embarrassed. If she couldn't get any that would be too bad, but she was going to buy a swimming costume. Not one with a frill in a half-hearted attempt to cover up. No. A high-legged costume, She would show as much as she could. Nothing would put her off.

She wiped her face with the palm of her hand and turned when she came face to face with the wall. Feeling her legs weak beneath her, she turned and when she drew level with her sodden towel sat down. She would count to a hundred and then go. Leaning backwards with her eyes closed, she began to count.

At eighty-eight, pulling at the soft flesh on the inside of her leg, she endeavoured to stretch her birthmark into view. After straining the skin and opening her legs wider, she could just see the tip of it. Standing, having counted up to ninety-three, she twisted the top half of her body round in an effort to see from the rear. At that very moment at ninety-six, Erica saw the blonde woman, her gown removed, lying motionless.

Even while she was falling, before her head struck the edge of the stone slab on which she had been sitting, Erica knew the woman had been there all the time, watching.

For a fleeting, agonising moment when her head exploded on the stone slab, it filled with bright, flashing lights, and she thought she was dead. But a painful thunder rushed into the vacuum of what had been her mind.

Letting out a long, low moan, she stayed crouched on the wet floor, rocking backwards and forwards, cradling her head. How could pain be so intense?

She did not shrink when a gentle arm went round her shoulders and someone tried to lift her. She accepted the help and was relieved to find she could stand and, although her head swam, she seemed to be in command of her senses.

"Are you all right?"

"Yes. I think."

The blonde woman removed her encircling arm and held Erica's hand.

"I'll walk you back to reception, if you like. You went down with an awful bump."

"No, no. I'll be all right. Thank you."

"You've a nasty graze on your arm."

"I slipped."

"This floor's treacherous."

"Yes."

"Yes."

Erica turned and gathered up her robe and towel.

"Thank you."

Stood outside, Erica looked at the graze on her arm. It was raw but it was her elbow which hurt. And her head. Fingering through her hair, she found that a large, hot swelling had already formed. Rubbing her temples to rid herself of an ache at the back of her eyes, she became aware of the blonde woman stood in the open doorway behind her.

Pretending unconcern, Erica walked away; but the blonde woman followed.

Erica began to panic. She was carrying her robe and towel which left her bottom exposed and shamingly bare. She imagined it being closely scrutinised by the following blonde who watched, in disgusted fascination, her birthmark flashing brown between her legs, appearing and disappearing like a fast moving weaver's shuttle. She would have to put her robe on while she walked; casually; unhurried. But the green canvas curtain was a long time coming and she died with each step while she struggled to get her hand into an inside-out sleeve.

Moving past the canvas curtaining, Erica made to turn right but stood rooted to the spot — unable to go further in case she fell. She had walked in the wrong direction and stood facing a small swimming pool.

The cold plunge! Friends had joked about it. She knew from their forced laughter that even if one had found the steam rooms uncomfortable, the cold plunge was the final indignity to which few people dared surrender their tender and warmed bodies.

The ceiling above the pool was arched and strangely low. It and the walls were painted a deep cobalt blue and the colour carried down under the water and across the bottom on similarly coloured, glazed tiles. The effect was impressive and Erica imagined she had wandered into a subterranean grotto. The water shimmered its reflection on the walls and the arch of the ceiling, adding to the illusion. But it was a fantasy from which there was no escape because the walls ran straight down into the water on all three sides and the ledge on which she stood was the only place from which she could dive in or scramble onto out of the pool. The only way to reach the steps of the small dribbling fountain at the far end was to swim.

Erica turned to see the blonde woman walking towards her and wondered whether the smile on the woman's face was one of amusement — perhaps supercilious mirth at Erica's ridiculous behaviour — or whether it was one of anticipation of a shared plunge into the icy water.

Erica looked away from the woman's mauve eyes and gazed unseeing into the pool. She was flustered. A blush was beginning its slow, warm climb up her neck and suffusing her cheeks. She stood petrified; covered with shame. She was both trapped and painfully exposed. But why was she blushing? Why was she trembling all over at the thought of the blonde, naked woman walking purposefully towards her?

The woman was about the same height as herself and probably the same age; although she looked younger. Her skin was golden, maybe through lying in the sun, but there were no bands of white skin where the flesh had been cupped or covered by a swimsuit. She had large pink nipples, smooth and eatable, which contrasted with her own which were dark brown, nearly black; the colour of figs. She had already noted that the blonde woman had a much better figure than her own; it looked as if it were constantly exercised. It was obvious she took great pride and lavished a deal of attention and care on it as was evidenced by her carefully shaved sex. This disturbed her because she felt such frankness revealed a morbid and shameless concern for that particular part of the body. She herself had been shaved when about to give birth, but when she had seen herself in a mirror thought "it" looked obscene.

With the woman drawing steadily nearer and closer, she thought her only hope of escape would be if the blonde dived into the water and, while floundering about, she could flee to the main hall.

Erica didn't know whether it was the woman's hand which brushed against her or the woman's thigh, but she dropped her towel and robe; made an inaudible cry of alarm and dived in head first. Before the water clapped her into a freezing grip, she realised how silly she had been. The woman could not have got past her without accidentally brushing against her because she had stood blocking the doorway.

The icy water cracked when she broke into its sharp splintered coldness. She died instantly and shrivelled. While she struggled to the surface, her body clamped tight in the surrounding watery vice, the bubbles trailed past her like cubes of ice, bruising her skin. Shocked, unable to fill her lungs sufficiently when her chest heaved in protest, she turned her body in the stiff water and started to swim back to the edge of the pool. Relieved to see the blonde woman had disappeared. she puffed at her breast stroke, praying her limbs wouldn't seize into an immovable and frozen mass. Her breasts felt shrivelled to the size of small hard apples and glowed painfully in the water but three more strokes would carry her to the side of the bath and safety.

When her fingers gripped the edge and she had drawn herself to the side, she heard the sound of someone behind her surging to the surface after a long underwater swim. Turning, she saw the blonde woman rolling in the water to face her; her hair streamed like floating seaweed. Their eyes met across the surface. Erica looked away. The cold pain in her shrunken breasts and the terrible ache in her body made her fear a sudden attack of cramp. She'd got to get out.

Gripping the rough stone sill, she put first one arm then the other flat on the concrete above her. Straining, she pulled the top half of her body out of the water and pushed herself up on the palms of her hands. The rough concrete edge cut sharply into her flesh, just below her breasts. She glanced down. Her nipples were shrivelled like dried prunes and the whole of each breast covered in hard blanched goose pimples, under the diamond droplets of water which ran helter skelter, repelled by her skin. She strained to draw the lower part of her body out of the water and summoned up her strength to get her right knee onto the ribbed concrete. At any moment her birthmark would come dripping, up, out of the water and the blonde woman would see it. But if she could get herself out of the water sufficiently to be able to turn sideways and sit side-saddle on the edge of the pool, there was a good chance, in that position, with the inside of her left leg away from the woman, she could keep her birthmark concealed. She hoped she wouldn't look too silly sat in that position and would be able to stay long enough for the woman to get out of the swimming pool, gather her clothes and leave. When her bottom came dripping up out of the water and she struggled to get her knee onto the side, she glanced over her shoulder and saw the blonde woman's head, half submerged; her watery mauve eyes fixed, unblinking, on her back. At the very moment when she should have gracefully side-saddled the edge of the pool, her arms gave way and her weight took her slowly forward onto her face so that inevitably, and with the utmost indignity possible, her bottom rose slowly into the air, exposing between her straddled legs, her long brown birthmark.

She collapsed sideways onto the side of the pool. She wanted to scream, to die, anything but have to get to her feet and, with her back turned, gather up her robe.

Slowly, and beginning to sob, she got to her knees, and made to stand up. Behind her, the water in the pool swirled and she heard a wet hand slap down onto the concrete and the dull thud of a knee humping the blonde woman's body up, out of the pool, sending water splashing over the tiled floor. Erica ran blindly towards her towel.

Scooping it up, she realised with horror that in her hurry to get into the pool she must have accidentally dropped or kicked her robe into the water. She could see it wrinkled and spreading on the blue tiles at the bottom of the pool.

Erica burst into tears, and tried to wrap the towel round her. With tears blinding her eyes she turned and fled, but ran into the side of the open doorway.

Reeling from the shock, she buried her face in her towel and stood, her shoulders shaking with grief.

She was so overcome that she didn't realise a robe was being put round her shoulders, her hands taken and pushed into the sleeves.

With tears in her eyes, Erica turned to the blonde woman who ordered her to stay where she was and dived back into the pool.

A moment later, Erica's wet robe sloshed onto the side of the bath and the blonde Venus humped herself out of the water.

Having wrung the robe, the blonde woman slipped into it and smiled.

"Do you want to cry more?"

Erica shook her head, but could not stifle her sobs.

"Let's sit in the shower room until you're completely composed, then."

She allowed herself to be guided to a slatted bench and sat down.

The shower room was empty.

When two chattering women entered to shower, Erica was grateful when the blonde woman deliberately shielded her from their gaze.

Minutes passed. (Or was it hours? Several women milled about whom she had not seen enter.) The blonde woman still stood in front of her smiling down.

She's holding my hand!

Erica withdrew it but not before she had glimpsed the blonde's bare pubes and felt herself blushing.

The blonde woman drew the robe together and seated herself next to Erica.

"Do you smoke? My cigarettes and lighter are in the pocket of my gown." She had to add, "You are wearing it."

The case opened, there was seen to be only one cigarette left.

"You have it."

And Erica had her cigarette lit for her.

Neither spoke and, as if on a given signal, both stood when she threw what was left of her cigarette onto the wet floor.

"Yes. Well. If you're feeling better . . ."

She stood so close, Erica could see the individual blonde lashes round her startling mauve eyes.

"I am."

"Good."

Was it for want of something better to do she pressed herself into Erica, caught hold of the hanging belt, tide a loose bow in front and gathered the folds of her robe to hang gracefully?

"By the way. My name's Gloria."

(What had she said? Gongyla?)

"I am . . ."

Who should she be?

It was the anticipated kiss which compelled her to be truthful.

"I am Erowina."

"E-row-ina. A pretty name. And what beautiful green eyes you have."

Her name repeated again, her arm touched, the girl with the beautiful green eyes was disappointed when Gongyla walked away without a backward glance.

"Thank you," she called. "Thank you, for — "

But Gongyla had gone.

With her head bowed, the girl with the beautiful green eyes followed Gongyla's damp footprints but turned right when they bore left towards the Laconicum.

Hurrying through the palmed court towards the safety of her cubicle, a heavy hand arrested her flight.

"I'm ready for you now, my dear. Come."

The athletic attendant in the blue swimming costume steered her towards the massage room.

"I timed it nicely, didn't I?"

The attendant's smile was keen and the girl with the green eyes was about to say she had changed her mind, when the attendant asked her what had become of the ribbon.

"Lost it? Never mind."

Ranged along one wall in the massage room were showers, opposite a row of cubicles and in the centre four slab tables constructed of grey marble. Lying naked on one of them was a woman. Standing next to her, an elderly female attendant running to fat and dressed in a black bathing costume looked up and frowned. "I've asked Elsie to clean out the cubicles, Miss Lebus."

Miss Lebus gripped two-o-five's arm.

"But two-o-five has been booked, Miss Fowler," and two-o-five was forcibly guided towards a curtained cubicle.

"Two-o-five will have to use the centre table."

Two-o-five fumbled at the plastic curtain and tried to find a way in.

"Miss Lebus! I must insist that two-o-five be massaged on the centre table!"

And the arm of the green-eyed girl was taken.

"Do you mind," hissed Miss Lebus, knocking away Miss Fowler's arm. "This lady particularly asked for me."

But her personality was not strong and she relented under the older woman's frowning stare.

Lain on the slab and looked up and down by a fuming Miss Lebus, two-o-five tensed herself; waiting the dread moment when Miss Lebus would dig her greedy fingers into her flesh.

Miss Lebus began with the green-eyed girl's neck; leaning with a veiled, suggestive smile as she manipulated the muscles.

Next came her arms which were thoroughly pulled, shaken and pawed; even her fingers, which were manipulated individually.

The girl with the beautiful green eyes, pleasantly dazed and her arms feeling weightless, gulped when water was sluiced over her from an enamel bowl.

Her breasts were the next to receive Miss Lebus's attention; but it was Miss Lebus's kneading which betrayed her, not her face which was passive because she was being watched by Miss Fowler.

Titillated sufficiently, another bowl of water douched her body and she relaxed.

"Now our tummy."

Miss Lebus's hands were insistent and the girl with the beautiful green eyes thought of herself as curdling when, under the continued stroking and plumping, she seemed to open and soften and her mouth fill with saliva.

It was a tell-tale swallow which Miss Lebus had watched for and chose to go directly, massaging deeply with slow, circular movements the inside of the shy green-eyed girl's sensitive thighs.

As the massaging continued, working into her softening flesh, the girl with green eyes began to suspect she was abandoning herself to the ecstasy she felt curdling her will. Worse, as she teetered on the brink of enjoyment, was the sudden realisation that, if Miss Lebus didn't stop, she would inadvertently empty her bladder. At the very moment she thought she would have to sit up and protest, Miss Lebus lifted the green-eyed girl's foot and, placing it between her own breasts, began flipping it; trilling the length with quick flicks.

Pummelled, feeling limp, douched yet again, the girl with green eyes was asked to turn.

"On our tummy."

She turned and flopped.

On the table next to her, also lying on her stomach and looking directly into her eyes was Gongyla.

They both smiled.

It was then Miss Lebus attacked.

Using both hands, she began drubbing up and down with such rapidity and firmness, the green eyes of the girl popped and she pulled a face, mimicing horror.

Gongyla laughed, her breath coming in low staccatoed grunts as Miss Fowler meted out the same punishment.

"Arm out sideways. Good. But we must open our hand."

The girl with the beautiful green eyes saw the look of alarm on Gongyla's face.

"Come on, now. Open."

Lifting herself so that her breasts tipped the table top, Gongyla transferred what she had been holding in her clenched fist in to her right and laid down again, her face turned away from the girl with the beautiful green eyes, her arm thrust out, her hand open, but empty.

"Good girl. But your head turned the other way."

And Gongyla was forced to endure the gaze of the girl with the beautiful green eyes who had seen her transfer from one hand to the other the pink ribbon she had stolen.

Trying to look away from each other but continually returning to gaze, the two women endured the scouring of their backs with curry brushes while the one puzzled the theft and the other, frankly adoring, treasured the ribbon which she held crushed to her flattened breast.

Miss Lebus, confronted by the green eyed girl's buttocks, treated them separately before seizing her left leg.

"What have we here?"

"My birthmark."

"You should have it removed. A thing like that."

The girl with the beautiful green eyes winced. How could she explain it wasn't the sort that could be removed by surgery?

"Have you nearly finished?"

"Won't be long, dear. Just a little more flexing."

Flexing was an understatement. Her heels were repeatedly tapped against her buttocks and the muscles on the front of her thighs were stretched until she thought they would tear.

The girl with the beautiful green eyes grimaced and appealed to Gongyla. Gongyla just grinned. She was receiving similar treatment.

After warm water had been repeatedly swilled over the green-eyed girl, lulling her, Miss Lebus patted her bottom.

"Up we get, dear. Sorry it's all over."

The girl with the beautiful green eyes rolled onto her back, received a wash of water on her front and struggled to sit up. As she swung her legs off the table and walked her bottom to the edge so she could reach the floor with her feet, she felt decidedly weak.

"Let me help you."

Guided to the shower and stood facing into the room, she clutched the chrome handles when Miss Lebus reached to turn on the taps.

"Tell me if it's too hot, won't you?"

The girl with the beautiful green eyes shook her head, smiled and managed a drowsy, "Lovely. Thank you."

Stood, shrouded in a fine mist of warmed water, it was the most delicious experience she could remember. Through half-closed eyes and the falling spray, she watched Gongyla rise off her table and pick her way delicately, like a shy deer, towards the cubicle where she stood.

"After you."

As she stepped out, she noticed Gongyla tense and draw in a slight breath, as if desirous of drawing attention to her breasts.

Before she could reflect further on Gongyla's pink nipples, Miss Lebus had enclosed the girl with the beautiful green eyes in an enormous towel and had begun to drub her dry. Hardly able to stand up straight, the green-eyed girl nevertheless managed to turn and saw Gongyla step under the still falling shower and breast the falling spray with a sensuousness of one gowning herself in her lover's clothes. Arching her back, Gongyla threw back her head and, opening her mouth, gulped the water.

The girl with the green eyes watched fascinated but at the very moment Gongyla turned, Miss Lebus bent down and, with one hand behind her knees and the other in the small of her back, lifted the girl with the beautiful green eyes off her feet and carried her like a small child out of the shower room and into another where tightly-packed beds ranged round the room, each curtained from the other.

The girl with the beautiful green eyes allowed herself to be laid on the bed. She felt the damp hair at the back of her neck and turned her head on the soft pillow to look at the flowered curtains. She was home. Miss Lebus, smiling and motherly, drew the bedclothes up and tucked in the side.

Tensing herself against the comforting hand which never came, she glared at Miss Lebus who frowned and backed away unable to understand what lay behind the green eyes which followed and bored into her with a silent hatred. The curtains closed, sealing her privacy and, Miss Lebus gone, the beautiful girl closed her green eyes and felt the hot eyelids slide over her eyeballs and meet in the sore line of her lashes. She was home and tired. Home with the tiled blue-green, red and cream floor of the bathroom. Bath-time. Bedtime. Slow sleepy rub-a-dub-dub-time in deliciously smelling talcumed warminess.

Exhausted, grasping at cobwebbed memories, the girl with the beautiful green eyes fell into a deep sleep.

"Four o'clock, dearie."

A tiny, toothless, gnome of a woman, overalled and capped, shook me awake and waited for me to take the rattling cup and saucer.

The tea was aromatic and I enjoyed every hot, tear-making mouthful I swallowed down.

Surprised I felt weak when I stood and aware of a slight headache gathering at the back of my eyes, I slid aside the flowered curtain hung on clicking brass rings and paused. At my feet was the pink ribbon; pushed through the curtain to fall on the bed, it lay on the floor.

In the cubicle, I dressed slowly, marvelling at the cleanliness of my feet. Managing my unruly hair as well as I could, I used the pink ribbon to tie it up. Checking the seams in my nylons were straight, I glanced round the cubicle to make certain nothing had been forgotten and unlocked the door.

Stooping to the cashier's glazed window, I handed in my tagged key and was given my bill. It came to more than I expected. A little angry at having to pay so much, I gathered my change and stood up straight.

In the mock Gothic entrance hall which made me think I was just leaving Church after an exceptionally wearing confession, I noticed a slim and elegant woman stood waiting by the glass doors. The woman was about twenty-five, dressed in a simple pink sheath with a thin gold belt at her waist. She wore gold, strapless sandals and from her shoulder hung a simple, square, golden handbag. The woman was very blonde and her hair was drawn back from her forehead and hung straight. Envious of the elegant woman's looks and her confidence and coveting her gold bag, I approached to pass. Given half the good looks this woman so obviously had, my problems could have been solved in an instant.

My hesitation was like a trip when I realised with alarm the elegant woman I was walking towards was none other than Gloria.

And I had that damned ribbon round my hair!

I intended to hurry past without raising my head but when Gloria's golden sandals and her tiny toes varnished pink came into my vision I risked a quick glance only to find I was exchanging looks of admiration with eyes that were mauve in colour, and worshipping.

Feeling the tatty ribbon tied round my hair had caught fire and the bow three feet wide, I hurried down the steps leaving a blush, hung and warming the air while the tips of my ears turned bright red.

The walk down the crowded High Street, through the park and in the quiet roads leading back to my flat should have been leisurely, but I took them at a brisk stride and arrived home out of breath.

The kettle on, and untying the pink ribbon, I stood at the window gazing down into the street. On the opposite side of the road and under a tree stood Gloria.

Seen, we both drew back in surprise and waited.

It was I, in panic, who made the first move, when the rising, thin shrill of the boiling kettle screamed its attention behind me.

Pouring the chuckling water into the teapot, I glanced towards the door waiting for it to open. It did not. Not immediately. Not until two months later when we had become friends and Gloria, her marriage to Martin an unhappy one, left her daughter, Leslie, with her mother-in-law and tapped on my door late one afternoon in November.

ALTER EGO (12.xi.1956)

I recall the day easing itself out over the windowsill, withdrawing; pale. And the twilight, gloomed in muslin, busily spinning a cobwebbed greyness — and then night.

I remember the yellow nicotine-stained fingers of a street lamp shyly fingering the uncurtained windowpanes; the scuff and click of heels below; the dropping metal latch of a shuddering garden gate and the drone of cars busily passing. And after the mac darned hush, nothing.

Silence clung by its fingernails that night and walled us in with its clouding breath, muffling the night which pressed chill black palms against the windowpanes, isolating and shrouding the house in solitude.

I recall my lovely's blurring edges dissolving into blackness; wrapping a cloak of confidence round her faltering tongue.

And me; with wide-eyed blindness, staring into the troubled stream of her breathless confession.

With strained ears crackling, I remember waiting in the long silences while her inadequacy of words matched my tumbling heart. Apprehensive, lest across the silence there crept the sound of sliding silk, bringing the lipsticked breath to the nape of my prickling neck. I swallowed mouthfuls of black silence while I ached to hear.

I remember straining lids blinked sore into the black eye of sound; the dull drum and pulsing thump of my heart booming my swollen breath from wall to wall; the acid burning, turning in my bladder, and the slow, painful softening of my bowels.

I remember — oh, how I remember — clenching my palmed thumbs in damp, hotly sticking fingers against the coming moment. Gnawing my shredded lips in smarting agonies of disbelief. Glad there was no bright lit light.

Glad her mauve eyes brushed the darkness.

Glad the rising blush bloomed black upon my cheek.

Glad I could cower under the humpbacked night and cosy my agonies unseen.

I recollect being stricken rigid. Like a plank I lay. The burning coverlets searing my back while my sweat-soaked clothes sawed and chafed; absorbing my perspiring fear.

I recollect the nervousness which gristled my caving stomach, swirling the juices in monstrous circuits and in meandering, bubbled, inconsequential spurts.

I remember marshalling excuses against the moment. Forming defences of unassailable emotional outbursts and objections. Dredging my timid imagination for a palisade against an unforeseen assault which my inexperience had left soft and vulnerable to her amassed and plundering demands.

I cast about for attitudes; imagining my praying hands and cowed back would exhaust her intentions which rolled over me like thundering surf, and that my thin cry would be heard above her storming. I remember praying, like a drowning mariner mouthing spume, for a miracle to pluck me from the maelstrom which sucked greedily at my languishing innocence like a milking Charybdis.

But I did nothing, and lay tensed while a hesitant guilt pearled upon my forehead.

And the talking.

I remember my whispered answers, thinly breathed, expiring in the velvet blackness; or, on a cough repeated, clattering about the room. And my silent responses — unwinding like spools of cotton through the needle eye of my imagination, to be stitched and sewn into a nightmare quilt of an impossible experience.

I remember the swallowed questions which shame nervously asphyxiated, and nasal affirmations grunted in a vigorously nodding head.

I recall nonsensical detours, falsely trilled, which skipped gaily into the gaping mouth of silence and were swallowed up.

And all the while I clicked and picked at the nervous rosary of my finger tips and strained my twisting ring against a swollen knuckle; feeding my guilt with the pleasure of a searing pain.

And I remember the beginning when she sat springbok-kneed in the cosy chair, snuggled warmly in the confidence of the cloaking darkness.

I remember her recalling the moment when certainty had illuminated her yawning weariness and the sharp, wet knife of yearning slashed into her reason. How she had stumbled amongst the sidelong glances, cradling her bewildering stigmata. How obsession had energised her fingering imagination but how the releasing climax brought, swilling into her overburdened conscience, only further doubt and grievous disgust. How, curbed and emotionally hobbled, she had cast herself into a desert of purgation; her fleshly desires rough shirted and her face turned blindly towards an absolving intent. But how, upon returning from the wilderness, expiated, repentant and stiffly resolved, her cloying flesh became so insistent and demanding again that she had succumbed and overrode her jockeying imagination on an even wilder abandonment of prolonged joyousness. Of long, sad nights, frigid and void, knuckling the livid frustration of her humpbacked, bewildered Martin. Of meekly accepting her obligations and the partnered embrace which, reaching deep inside her, awakened the loathing as she lay quietly shuddering. Of tears, hotly spilled for her hopeless inadequacy and unintentional nettling indifference. Of her betrayal and her dereliction to homologated immorality.

And I remember the whirl and twirl of the flailing bullroarer while she gyrated with unrelenting condemnation of herself.

I remember the pitiful cry which groaned up from the nadir of her destruction where she lay abandoned, humiliated and utterly debauched; luscious carrion for an eager, lemon-tongued moralist.

And then I remember — God, how I remember — my inadequate stumbling, mumbling; as I reached out a hesitant watery solace and demurely stroked her crying heart. Feebly I probed the the hopeless gloom, dribbling prosey comfort, until her wretchedness drove an iron cleat through my dry emotion, and there bubbled forth, first a trickle, then a torrent of unrestrained concomitant confession.

Eagerly, with adolescent naivete, I remember tumbling the jumbled admiration, whipped and creamed with curdling fervour, which my racing heart enthusiastically misjudged as matching her infatuation; until one appetising, indulgent silence cleaved my mad, glad whirl and shattered into my comprehension.

Doomed; foresworn by my own binding innocence, I sat amidst the chains of my own forging, fingering the new-found realisation with incredulity and disbelief.

It was then, I remember, fear laid and straddled my experience; filling my being until I was overflowing — apprehensively discharging a rheum of fear and glimmering, satanic delight.

It was then, I recall, I emptied of all previous knowledge and felt its long drawn mucous string, unravelling; being slowly pulled from my softening bowels.

While I drained of substance, the darkness became transparent and her seeing ear, stretching the membrane of tension between us, applied a tourniquet of guilt on the avalanche of my disclosure.

It was then.

Then I remember.

Oh, how I remember the soft silk sliding on the perilous edge of a lip chewed silence. The sudden torrent when the rustling silk, ridged and squeaking, crackled and burst about me in a monstrous embrace, born on a saffron cloud-burst of jasmine scent. The sudden other warmth; the colliding breaths; the tumbling hearts and, amassed between my rising breasts, a shock of golden hair.

Betrayed by my racing heart, I strained against the enveloping hug and ridged my emotion in a deluded comfort.

I remember time.

A clear glass Clepsydra brimmed with tears, softly weeping.

Tremulous and dropping, the drip splashed time lulled and calmed; soothing the hour until the aching grasp relaxed and there flowed between us a mutual, lapping warmth of trust and composure.

But the magic stirred and, rolling in its tortured sleep, struck sparks from the embered flints. And the lipsticked breath butterflied my throat and stole secretly up my prickling awareness. I gasped into the succulent flower which blossomed on my mouth and felt the soft, honeyed probe; delve, moistening my resistance.

Turned away, my desperate cry was blocked on a dissolving scented breath and pierced repeatedly by a thrusting desire.

Unhurried, the exploration turned slowly, juicing; whetting a gruesome appetite until desperate reason slid guiltily, breathing apologies, into my goose-fleshed ear.

But instinct, born of desire, made me seek out the comfort of her flowering mouth. It was the limit of my indulgence; the climactic solace of my compassionate heart. And I remember this as the end and the final gesture; the goal of my indiscretion.

I remember, while the sudden spring blossomed magically on my experimental offering, the frightening realisation that the turmoil sweetly sucking at my inexperience was a beginning and not the oddly comforting end. My generosity blanched; my awareness illuminated the carnality and, petrified, comprehension stormed my disbelieving barricade.

Me, I remember thinking, me! Timid me embroiled in an odorous carnality which affronted sensibility and reason. Me! with generosity mothering the wilful milking of my emotional dugs, surrendering with a frightening and eager submissiveness!

I struggled and, with pursed, muscled lips, snorted my contempt down flaring nostrils while I pawed away the sliding silk.

But darkness bound us, weaving a cocoon of insidious, undetectable criminality which satanic perversion goaded into daring. And I succumbed — to myself.

I remember I forgot all thought of coming light and dawning morrows veiled in guilt and harrowed by disgust when I would have to face the clear mauve eyes, but drifted, muslined, into limbo. I forgot all thought of tongued scents and tactile smells, unwashable from the soiled imagination where they squatted, ballooning memory: all thoughts of accusing recrimination, darting on bitter, snake-forked tongues: of all thought of habitual corruption, wallowing upon the spike of satisfaction; all thoughts of the veiled, knowing eyes and the chattering gossipers, gnawing at the bone of insidious contempt. To all these I gave not a passing thought and temporarily blinded by consequential surrender with tissues of immediacy to the black, confident darkness.

Not all at once I remember. Slowly. Relinquishing to tenderness and fraternal disclosures. Warm and somnambulent in the solitude of superficial exchanges; brushing lightly the strung emotions, harmonising melodic lullabies which dusted the sanded innocence in peace; or chirping like hopping sparrows between the titbits of pecking kisses and breathing mouthfuls of childish happiness.

But sadness I remember — or was it the exhausted silence, tiptoeing on delusion — warmed the desperation so that the tiny, merry birds scattered when a crow-black passion squatted upon our childish preamble, attracted by the morsel of tongued joyousness.

I remember it happening.

I remember the long, long sliding under the washing spume; jawing into the squirming delirium and drowning in the rivulets of juicily squashed excess.

Then the happening began, I remember.

It began when it had already started. But I was not to know this.

I remember the cradling cupping, massaging my swelling pride, and from which I did not shrink but rose and pointed my thrusting passion — buttoned, like flat brown coppers into the restricting purses, and ached for a beginning. But patience gripped and squeezed my haste, acknowledging my desire, and I was forced, fumbling blindly, awkwardly, to return my lassitude in an embarrassing patting complicity; hastening the urgency of my private ending.

But I was altogether naive.

What stopped short was only the slow unfolding of the beginning. And I remember I experienced the curling, cool blown air caressing my hurriedly unbuttoned shame which lay expiring, shrivelling with shock exposure, while I died a sensual embarrassment at such an indignant outrage.

Shrinking, I remember, no longer proudly breasting my desire, I dared to hope it was sufficient and that all other unseemliness was done with. But, as under other busy plumping hands, the swelling blood extruded and betrayed my tingling recognition which rose beneath the insistent, gentle fingering.

Endurance, camouflaged by immobility, was, in retrospect, my only hold upon a receding reality, and one which I mutely adhered to throughout the terrifying silence. But I recall shock and disbelief crumbling my expiring fortitude when guiding hands fumblingly unbloused her own desperation and I was stiffly drawn to palm her sighing warmness.

Dismayed, a limpet of her sensuousness, I clung in disbelief to her desire; slowly warming to my other self.

I remember I lay remembering my previous doubts, recalling dismal failures to recreate under my own imaginative fingering the knowledge of another's caressing hand. Of trying to find, while I teased my flesh in desperation, how it felt for them. But I perceived it not as it was to others but as it was for myself. This dimly narcissistic confusion existed because of my depression at not being able to reflect the languorous passivity of my flesh under the enticement and impetuosity of an erected masculine demand, and so I had floundered in limbo waiting, unknowingly, to be recreated under a contemplative feminine love. For I lay sucking the breasts of my other self, knowing myself; neither victorious nor submissive, neither the object nor the aggressive sovereign but enjoying a mutuality made known through the secret preferences indicated in my own body; so long denuded and rendered as an instrument.

And I remember that was my real beginning.

I recollect fear expired upon an exhaled breath and there was no longer a hesitant exploring while I lay palming my other self. I was filled with knowledge and understanding because the way was known to me.

The images I retain are confusing but I remember sufficient to recall the rapture of the simple embrace. That my timidity would be replaced by familiar boldness, my trepidation by wholesome, languorous combinations, could not be imagined, because the innocent, in the beginning, and however willing, are trussed upon their inexperience, and innovation rolls out before them, carpeted with apprehension and incredulity.

And so it was.

I remember the faultless simplicity while we breasted each other's quickening desire and imagined my own, sweet, secret coming as a concluding manifestation and dared to think my other's ecstasy was equally concealed in blushing shyness.

Contented, I expired with a humming breast which dancing lips continued to buss with joyous fullness. Contented, I returned each kissing kiss and, to show the completeness of my adoration, added fondling assurances; each of which, unsuspectingly, posted the long slow climb to come.

I remember the sudden beginning with a beating heart. Against the imminent disaster, clamping my secret in columned tension, I violently sought to withdraw the groping, trembling extension up to my willing breast. Pleading contentment and riding my startled disbelief, I strained against her intention, willing God to intervene.

But my pleading failed so that inevitably, slowly, against my constraining embarrassment, as if willing the exposure of my humiliation, I softened and, giving, submitted to the lewd embrace. Mortified, trembling under my resignation, I hesitated upon the deplorable experience and died with disgrace and shame.

Yet imperceptibly I remember, my tension sagged and pillowed my relief until I was content to flower thus, my secret swathed and, resisting the guiding mutuality tugging at my unwillingness, I allowed her mastery undisturbed.

But my timid acquiescence was abruptly and rudely revoked and, upon a sudden start, my rising, tumbling heart thundered out its disillusion when the fumbled desire, scrabbling, made its blind groping attempt to lay bare my warming passion.

I remember my drawn-out frantic tussle, wrestling the jungled silk, and, jackknifed, sought to restrain the unthinkable intent.

Vanquished, activated by frustration, there was a scrabbling rustle and the jasmine scent rode on billowing waves while the silk squealed and the rubber slapped the pedalling legs and down beside me, flopping from out of the agitated darkness, a reckless love entered my mouth, extruding sweet delirium.

Calmed, cradled safely, I was softly lulled and, hoping by example to stimulate my acceptance, was drawn gently onto her naked wish. Inch by inch I was forced to trace the familiarity of the yielding plains, approaching my burning shame with quickening heart beats, until, the inevitability of my lasting humiliation seeming as nothing, I steeled my nerve to act out the crude drama, and I went directly, unaided: swooning.

Upon arriving I can distinctly remember a mantle of comprehension warming my shuddering aversion when, unmistakably, I recognised the other me, palmed within my reluctant affection. Suddenly; illuminated, the fear, all guilt, slid from me. I had, at last, arrived. I was complete.

Perhaps it was the similarity which assured an inevitable pleasure; for, delighting in the known secrets and the preference of my desires, I would not have to battle. It was as if after all the years consumed by unsatisfying submission and countless desperate hours spent trying to exhaust the boned male desire, my burden had fallen and, with it, the reason for all my discontent.

I remember the lightness of my heart as I hummed with revelation and turned to my love; my other self.

I remember my quick submissiveness, helped and denuded in breathless haste amidst the jungled clothes, exposing the minimum of desire as the heat of our flesh smacked against the other in a grinding embrace and then falling into the slow unwinding, when our freed intentions, no longer confined, stretched on infinity before us.

Nestling my blushing girlishness into the enfolding mothering, I waited in shame for the exploring restfulness to stroke into my unbecoming precociousness. Apprehensive but content and preening under the wandering, gently brushing love, I ached for the uncovering of my premature excess; to have done with the imprudent short coming and to lend proof of my desire. But my love's caressing stretched the longing on waves of enticement, washing the buds of my exaltation under the dalliance of amorous fondling.

Eventually, slowly, delirium whirlpooled her intention and she went directly — but gently; exposing, so that, smilingly ashamed, I settled my disgrace into her comforting and was willingly guided into complicity; into a detailed exploration.

I remember the expectation of a dividing difference to add to my childish embarrassment; expecting within the tonsured severity a commending maturity. But as I fondled my other self, fingering the idealistic beauty, my apprehension evaporated as, in a reverent reunion, I felt the blossoming of my mirrored reflection.

How else should it have been? For I to her was but herself in me, so that in our reflecting images we were the same.

I recall we flowered upon each other's lips, as one; knowing the other to be ourself: twining, identical flowers, identifying each in the other on slowly rising aromatic scents; twinning our pulsing buds in an identical confrontation. Languorously we blossomed under the complicity of our indulgence and were slow to hasten the other. Each was the other, and the self languished in the generous drawn-out voluptuousness of the other, knowing herself and able to string the threads of rapture in the pearling coral of the other.

So our duality mirrored each minute inflection of the other; each minimal preference was covetously rewarded; each trembling longing assuaged and each rapturous hesitation prolonged with understanding until we held each other's own full blossomed glory within the assuring certainty of extending satisfaction in an incontestable finality. Such was the perfection of our intuitive understanding.

And within the opening tumescence of our revelation, quietly flooding, each found in the other self a comprehension of one's own desirability and the guilty perturbation became tranquil on the fingering enlightenment. Each recognised in the other the quintessence of her own uniqueness because the other was one's self. In step, timed by the very slowness of the drawing out, we reached our unison and understanding of ourselves through the other self.

I remember the unhurried complications while the spreading flowers of our desire, gently assisting the trembling senses, eased their complex preference in groaning satisfaction. Expressive contractions, directing the prolongation of some delicious foible, flourished under the other's understanding tenderness or, gasping, involuntary rhythmic dilations sweetly engorged the compassionate, rewarding loving. But within the tumescent confusion the slow dawdling, exhilarated by the intoxication which extended the succulence of the surging sweetness, gently prolonged the final coming.

I remember time washed over us, its madly ticking haste drowning in the surf of our unconcern, and expiring, superfluous to our needs. And I remember, upon looking back, the dawning of another time. Time without tightly wound divisions, or lengths; which had no beginning and no ending and no middle to hasten the watching eye. Cocooned within this infinity, we stretched our lives and yawed the vessel of our desire over the endless churning sea, bound for no destination and content with the slowness of our arrival.

But, I remember, the extension of our abilities diverged upon desire and I was compelled to show my unwillingness against the gentle forcing. Not believing that the existing, almost unendurable ecstasy could be prolonged or heightened beyond the extremes of my experience and imagination, and the memory of grovellings suffered with dismay. I was loath to surrender my embrace to the distasteful satisfying of so bizarre a whim.

Desperately I clung to my passive, mothering desire and begged with silent clamouring to be excused. But an outgrown passion, wild and urgent, galloped, undulating convulsively; akimbo and distorted, its strained, mouthing eye, gaping into the satanic blackness; yearning. Aghast at the gristled passion, outpaced and unbelieving, I cowered in shame, unable. But feverish hands were my forceful guide when, unwillingly, I complied and, with sinking heart and aching with regret and shame, I buried my columned blush.

I cannot remember my thoughts at that moment. Perhaps shock blanketed my reeling senses. I can only recall a nauseous disgust, a breath-held hesitation and my refusal and inability to act out her desire. Perhaps I cried. Perhaps. There was the sadness of standing of a demoniacal resistance to sovereign her gross desire. losing my other self; of being cut off and isolated from my under-Daring drained from my bowels and I was incapable. Even assisted, prompted and patiently waited upon, I shrank and died.

Released, unchained from her intent, I gladly reclaimed my other self with a joyous rush of forgiving and, safely nestled, prepared to dream again.

But it was short-lived, for my other self unwound and a turbulent jasmine cloud cooled in my empty grasp and went sliding. Then shame spread, parting my gentleness as I tensed against the sundering; dying at my exposure. Ensnared, over-ridden by determination, I struggled to sandwich the aggressiveness in shrinking revulsion; only to be mastered and pinioned under a frantic domination. Obliged, I submissively endured the revelling liquidation of my subjugation in an onerous complicity.

Tensed and arched as I was, waiting for it to be done with, imperceptibly, upon the tiniest tracery, was writ an understanding. Slowly I expired, became all soft and limp and fused with willingness. Warming to the extension of my understanding, I snuggled down, into my selfishness, with lips curled in ecstasy, desiring, and nearly oblivious.

And then was the beginning.

For, jigsawing upon our haste, interlocking our intentions in a breathless confusion of elbows and knees, we settled our desire in a geometric configuration and, in unity, articulating our wedlock, bridged our emotional completeness.

And that was our beginning.

What had gone before was also the beginning; but this too.

That each had found within the other her own self and in the finding resolved an understanding of her individuality — only to become part of the other — was now perfected. We were one.

I remember I did not shrink but cautiously savoured the finality of my arrival, rolling the sensations upon the palate of my inexperience and tongueing the desired lipped smile tentatively until I had dredged up from my subconscious and recognised the me I had always desired to be. And so it was. On the relief of recognition I expired and was borne away, and up, into the illuminated senses; to the very gates of Heaven.

And I remember the lapping swell which broke against my willingness until the pooling hollows brimmed and flooded; awash with a languishing passivity. How, exposed, the wanting, inadequately expressed, bulged, ballooning the ruptured darkness; fastening upon an impossible contortion to expose the innermost content to a rapturous, obliterating sweetness. How, carried on the groaning intimacy, ecstasy fattened upon the distillation of the thickening extrusion and a heated madness sought asylum in delirious incomprehension.

And I remember clearly, while the viscous threads of my being were being sucked into the waves of a prolonged bliss, an agonising cumulation of sweetness while I tried desperately to straddle eternity.

In my coming I was not alone for, hastened by my quickening imminence, spurred by the grinding aggression of my sundered yearning, my lovely, fulfilled by the expectation, rode her relief, so that, as one, we arrived at the drawn out coming in groaning sweetness.

Quivering I remember, our reflexes uncontrolled, we bucked and, breaking, bucked again, unable to grapple the individuality of our conclusion and in a mess of contortions, collapsed and lay quivering; puppets of our exhaustion. Consumed, we withdrew slowly into a vacuum of inactivity and floated upon the woolliness of our spent carnality; drifting into a somnambulant release.

Having been transported, the tiptoes of our reason only slowly grounded upon our awareness and only for long enough for us to reassure each other of our nearness in a fingertip embrace.

Later, now snuggled, I remember exhaustion gliding on silent wings, drawing the blinds of my consciousness and, drifting, I tunnelled into oblivion; smiling and so, oh, so happy.

Then I remember the disturbing happenings tugging at my lax perception; ruffling a confusion into my passivity — attempting to stir and energise me from an eternal peace. Sleepily intoxicated, I became a willing subject, readily extending the warmness of my happiness and making ready in a dream for a delirium of prolonged repetition. But in my bleariness, while I groped armfuls of disjointed blackness, seemingly surrounded by tumbling forms which evaporated in my embrace, I gradually became conditioned to the guiding intention and accepted with languorous innocence the role of aggressor to appease a tormenting frustration. But there broke through my membraned dreaming while endeavouring to assuage her erecting voluptuousness, a gross viciousness which punctured the illusion; draughting in a cooling realisation upon my stunned awareness.

Steeled to please, I was carried upon the hysteria of her demands and, with frightening facility, hurriedly complied to the outrageous directing. Filled with disgusted awe, yet fascinated by the revolting aggressiveness, I was exerted into the realms of questionable fancy by her breathless ordering and so slaved to master the incomprehensible whim which odorously defiled my reasoning. But even my delirious devotion seemed of no avail and with the coming of my exhaustion, to bring about the ending, I reluctantly, and with distaste, directed my finality with aching conscience and, buried deep in the insanity of a mystic revelation, wept with longing for the ending while I probed her groaning perversion.

It came quicker and more mysteriously than I had anticipated, on waves of contracting delirium, relieving my conscience and enabling me to relax upon my sadness with relief.

Willingly, to obliterate the memory of my complicity, I succumbed to her tender mothering and, together, drifted unconcerned into the deepness of oblivion.

Later, dancing in and out of sleep while dawn gently fingered our tousled heads in the discreet gloom pressed snub-nosed against the uncurtained windowpanes, my love stirred an awareness into my fragility on cumulating waves of voluptuous sweetness. Brushed by her mauve eyes, I watched myself succumb and offered up my awakening to her sensuousness. I watched, with gratitude curling my smiling lips; adoring the understanding sovereignty and revelling at my blatant eroticism. And watching fascinated, I marvelled at the crudity of my yearning and at my vulgar willingness. Softening, I exposed the insidious longing without shame or thought of guilt, until that moment when, posed and prepared, I shut out the offending moment behind my fluttering lids. But a moment later, upon the first delicious groan, I peeped and saw the hazy image of my disgrace as an extension of my desirability, and was able, without shame, to discredit my morality with a lewdness I had not thought possible.

Yet it was only the beginning.

I remember being convulsed by the possibility of overwhelming disaster which hovered on the edge of probability but which constraining hands repulsed with a quickening assurance until a dissolving sweetness splayed my dissolution in an agonising carnality. I marvelled at my coming which reason repulsed in disgust but which divinity had implanted with cunning hindsight, and my whole being shuddered with extreme pleasure.

So guilt was displaced by knowledge and in that knowledge was my final comprehension.

Groaning, I remember, groaning and puffing up from my long journey, I gazed unashamed upon my lewdness and proffered the nearness of my contentment in a joyous satisfaction. But dawn, swathed in impatience, sat polishing the window panes; streaming in the light. Naked and exposed, we shrank under the thin cover of darkness and embraced the remaining time.

So, our day had a beginning and our night an ending.

Tousled, wrinkled, shockingly unashamed at our nudity, the day began upon a languorous stretch and relaxed, contented smiles.

The scattered, gold triangled sunlight was not sufficient to infuse my face with blushes so I was able and content to gaze, and in gazing, scrutinise the self I had become. The self which lay within kissing distance; the mysterious self which I could eye with the curiosity of knowledge and from the vantage point of revelation. Idling quizzically and revelling under the compulsive attraction, I knew I was no longer inhibited by my femininity and under my adhering gaze was able, with loving detachment, to scrutinise and satisfy my adolescent aversion with an ambivalence so long nurtured in ignorant imagination.

My curiosity assuaged, I hungered for the beauty in which my love lay embedded, for my other self who had so confounded my inhibitions, and was able to glory in her perfection. From the pink-tipped toes, up through the rising thigh, beyond the tremulous weight of her buttocks and out of the denuded fold, across the bellied swell to the rise of the blushing teats and beyond — to the smiling face, the mauve eyes and the spreading, never ending, golden hair. Breathless to behold, I saw reflected in her mauve and loving eyes, a similar, passionate searching so that I knew my beloved saw herself in me just as I found myself in her.

But perceptibly, the shadows shrank, revealing our hopeless entanglement as day climbed brashly into the room, brandishing its rousing, glittering sword; scattering and chopping up the gloom.

We struggled from our jungled bed and gathered together the discarded remnants of our inhibitions. Keeping close, I remember, warming with the other's love, we smoothed away, between hasty kisses, the wrinkled night and girdled ourselves with the new day's freshness.

It was a happy time, I remember.

So, too, was the drawn-out, cleansing coffee, lipped from each other's cup and, encircled, the slow perambulations through the dreaming rooms.

And the long farewell.

Carried on a hundred sighs; kissing and parting to kiss again. Kissing through the diminishing crack of time until at last, inevitably, the closing door of ending separated our desperate love.

And then I remember listening to the hurried tap of her quickening heels below, drowned in the bustling urgency of a day beginning; of cars starting and grinding up the road; the shuddering garden gate; the swing of her golden hair as she turned the corner; and then the aching silence.

I remember the languorous morning passed in smiling sleep; waiting. Alert but drowned by my content, listening; inhaling the scented memory of her jasmine, tingeing the crumpled sheet. Reliving the intenseness of the past night in an undisturbed repetition. Dying while I waited.

But it came. Suddenly, shrilly. On a bound, with a heart booming from wall to wall, I seized and snuggled the soft drone of her whispered love into my goosing ear and, attentive, listened; marvelling at her breathless planning.

Swooning, I spreadeagled my excitement upon the giving bed and while the sun, armoured in gold, went crashing about my room, I planned our unhurried life while my mouth and being watered in anticipation of a Paradise to come.

And it did. I glimpsed it off and on for nearly three years until slowly, inevitably, the recurring dream of the King of Siam alerted that part of me which had been dormant.

THE KING OF SIAM (12.xi.1956)

The first indication is when I hear them whispering outside the door.

Knowing it is the invaders, I get down from my nanny's shoulders.

Under the pressure from the soldiers outside, who are battering on it with their spears, the door gives way and falls to the ground with a clatter.

Nancy, terrified of being discovered, wants to throw herself upon the mercy of the invaders and tell them she is my mother and has every right to be in the room with her daughter. But, realising she is wearing her uniform, she turns and, running to the cot, climbs onto it and burrows feverishly under the bedclothes from the wrong end.

I am overjoyed to see Nancy has wet herself. This unique event is heightened by the odd fact she has left one of her stockinged legs sticking out from under the coverlets for all to see.

By the time the cot has stopped rocking, Nancy is fast asleep.

I turn to face the soldiers.

They are barbarians who have come down from the hills.

They are large, black men.

Very black. All of them.

With their armour rattling, they hustle over the fallen door and the room trembles. Clouded breath steams out of their dilated nostrils and their large, white eyes roll like skinned onions in the terrible blackness of their faces.

Each soldier is wearing a golden helmet with large earflaps which hang down unequally on either side of their faces. The flaps are edged with pearls, pendant and tremulous; like milky-white tears, clinging tenaciously to the deep blackness of their skin. To prevent the metal helmets from chaffing their flesh, each helmet is lined with a luxurious, soft red velvet which protrudes in places like the wattles on a turkey. Embossed designs which carbuncle and pimple the surface of the helmets, for some obscure reason, fill me with foreboding: as do the unequal ear flaps.

Extending down and over each of the soldier's noses, hiding the raised, fat veins pulsating down their length, are brightly burnished visors which extend to and almost cover the soldiers' thick, dark lips. Pinnacling each helmet is a long, fountained plume of vivid yellow hair which, spurting from a golden knob, drops cascading round their shoulders; each strand alive and snaking.

The soldiers carry large silver shields which they hold in front of themselves to protect their entire body. Each shield is embossed and ribbed in concentric, deepening grooves which catch and mirror the soldiers' red mantles; seemingly liquefying the silver and turning it hotly molten.

The soldiers also carry long, thick spears made from ebony which are tipped with very dangerous-looking but bulbous points.

I have never seen such monstrous spears before and, never imagining such length, am surprised when the soldiers, having squeezed through the narrow doorway, are able to hold them erect without damaging the ceiling.

While the soldiers struggle to get into the room and are forced to trail their shields behind them, I see the protective golden plates which, fitting together as neatly as fish scales, encase their legs and bodies.

Round each soldier's waist is a wide, goat-skin belt. Looped through it and attached by golden studs are tufts of coarse black hair which, because the leg pieces and the body of the armour do not meet, are arranged so as to hide the soldiers' sexual organs.

When one of the Negroes turns round, I am surprised by his naked bottom; not imagining the red cloak which hangs down his back would be split in two. When the same Negro bends down to pick up his spear and the skin tautens over his shiny ebony bottom, I looked away in embarrassment; especially as I recall Nancy would have good reason for smacking me if I looked.

The soldiers laugh when they see me blush, and begin to push one another like excited schoolboys. One or two deliberately turn to expose their buttocks, whilst others pinch their noses and point. My further embarrassment causes renewed and hilarious laughter.

A shouted command, in a tongue which I cannot understand, brings the soldiers into some sort of order, and they press closely round me, sniggering; waiting for me to undress.

I have been told many times by Nancy exactly what the soldiers would do to me and how best I might accept my fate.

While I undress I am aware of the soldiers' alarming maleness. Aware too of their male smell which is an admixture of the acidity of sour sweat and the odour of hot, peppery dung. I am very frightened, not of what they might do to me, but by their overwhelming size.

Feeling very small and fragile, I slip out of my clothes.

When I am denuded and my flimsy clothes lie in a small, impersonal pile at my feet, the soldiers, bending their heads this way and that, assess the shape, weight and colour of my naked body, but I am surprised when, turning away and ambling through the door, they make a sign for me to follow them. I had been expecting them to touch me and I am very disappointed.

On reaching the doorway, I see the soldiers have already formed themselves into line in preparation for the long march back to the capital. They have their backs towards me; presenting me with a view of a long row of black, bare bottoms.

I am about to step through the doorway when a pit opens up at my feet and I only just save myself from falling into it by clinging on to the door frame with my left hand.

The soldiers, hearing me cry out, turn round and, seeing me hesitate to jump such a small hole, begin to laugh and slap each other on the back as if it is the funniest thing they have ever seen.

I know that somehow I must hide my fear and try to jump the pit un-aided.

But I hesitate for such a long time that the soldiers, jeering and cat-calling, begin to throw their spears.

The spears fall short and disappear into the hole.

Meanwhile, unknown to me, Nancy has crept up behind and, having cut off my retreat, begins to paddle my bare bottom with a wooden pudding spoon; trying to force me into the hole.

I can bear the pain of her drubbing but when she reverses the mixing spoon and prods my buttocks with the wooden handle, I become confused.

The choice, between jumping into the pit which contains terrors of which I have no knowledge or of accepting the paddling spoon whose inflicted pain I know, is denied me when the ground beneath my feet crumbles and I go sliding into the great hole.

I stay crouched at the bottom, not daring to touch the sides; apprehensive lest something equally dreadful might happen to me.

Nothing does.

Greatly disappointed, fear is replaced by the puzzlement of ignorance.

The soldiers, peering down at me over the edge, thrust their spears into the hole hoping I will take hold of one of them so that I can be hauled out of my amusing predicament.

Eventually, realising what is expected of me, I clasp both hands round one of the proffered spears. It is not as thick as I had imagined and, to my great delight, I discover it is hollow.

While I am gripping tightly onto the spear and am being drawn slowly out of the pit, I manage, successfully, to spit straight up the spear's hollow shaft.

There is a jubilant shout and much innocent bantering from the soldiers when I am safely out of the pit and able to stand on level ground again.

I am surprised by the ease with which I am able to resume my former dignity and face the soldiers without blushing.

The soldier, upon whose spear I had been hauled to the surface and up which I had successfully gobbed while dangling below it, thanks me and offers his spear as a present. The other soldiers become angry at their comrade's indecent suggestion and threaten me with their own spears.

When the guard commander orders the soldiers to put up their spears and to accept their comrade's behaviour as natural, the soldiers reverse their spears and plunge the points into the ground.

The guard commander shrugs his shoulders and, refusing to argue, points to the soldier who has helped me out of the pit and now stands, his head bowed in shame, because he is pregnant.

From beneath their red mantles, where they had been hidden, the soldiers draw short stabbing swords and, as one, fall upon their unfortunate comrade. Screaming insults, they hack him to pieces and throw his dripping remains into the hole until it is completely filled and overflows with blood.

This done, they seize hold of my hand and, running with me between them, race down the hill.

When we reach the road, the soldiers form themselves into a column and, with me in their centre, march towards the capital.

On the way to the city, we are joined by more naked women and other soldiers who have been scouring the countryside looking for beautiful virgins. What had begun as a small column of twenty men soon swells to a horde of several thousand; over half of whom are women.

I know the soldiers have selected only the most beautiful women and am therefore surprised by the naked woman walking in front of me.

This woman, although very beautiful and desirable to men, has, on her left leg and to the rear, close to her bottom, a brown mark which looks like shit.

I am disgusted and draw the attention of a guard to it. The soldier looks, screws up his nose and calls to another man. Whilst the second soldier looks at the revolting smudge, the unfortunate girl, entirely unaware of the sensation she is causing behind her, swings along, unconcerned. By the time a great many soldiers have come up and looked — some even bending down to sniff the brown mark — the girl becomes conscious she is the centre of attraction and turns round.

There is a loud moan when everyone sees her face. She is not only very old, but exceptionally ugly.

Immediately, everyone starts to jeer, and the soldiers, striking the woman with the palms of their hands, force her off the road.

I feel sorry for the old woman who is forced to sit on the grass verge and who weeps as the column passes her by.

When we are over the brow of a hill and I can no longer see the old woman, I promptly forget all about her.

Before long, the white, marble towers of the city are discernible in the far distance and all the women become excited at the prospect of being shewn into the presence of the King.

The barbarians' King had taken over the palace of the defeated Sovereign and it is in this palace the women will parade before him. He will choose for himself only one woman from amongst the thousands. The rest, he will hand over to his troops for their common amusement. The woman the King chooses will be the most beautiful and desirable of all women.

There is great commotion amongst the civil populace when the barbarian army and we naked women wend our way through the gleaming, white city.

The sweating troops have to keep back shouting crowds and push against them with their spears held horizontally across their chests.

Amongst the crowd I recognise several people, one of whom is my father. He deliberately turns away and, taking advantage of the milling crowd, interferes with the clothing of a woman standing next to him. The woman smiles and aides his outrageous behaviour. I am surprised to see the woman is Nancy.

Nearing the palace, the populace, crowding the steps where they are assured of a better view of the naked women, roar their approval; clapping and shouting every time one passes who excites their lust: often catcalling and whistling in a most lewd and suggestive manner. Some women are fingered and stroked by groping hands pushed between the soldiers lining the street. Some men in the crowd try to crawl through the legs of the soldiers, in a desperate attempt to get at the women. I am disgusted by their behaviour and prudently walk in the centre of a group of women, keeping my eyes cast modestly to the ground in the hope I will not be noticed.

It is not long before all the women are assembled at the bottom of the long white stairway which leads up to the ornate entrance of the palace. The soldiers, yelling commands and pushing, marshall us into a single column which, having been given the order to proceed, slowly snakes its way in an orderly fashion up the hundreds of steps which lead to the door of the palace.

Feeling the smooth, warm marble steps beneath my bare feet, I am strangely reassured and my confidence returns.

Ahead of me, one or two women have sunk to their knees and are crawling up the steps, moaning.

Another woman, with dark, passionate eyes, turns her back upon the palace and sits down on one of the steps; refusing to go either up or down.

Yet another woman, whom I think I recognise and who is very beautiful, turns and walks up the steps backwards. I cannot understand why she should consider this a safer approach because, being so beautiful, she has nothing to fear.

One or two of the younger girls, giggling and overeager, try to race ahead — but are scolded by the older guards and are pushed, sulking, back into their rightful places in the column.

Perhaps the strangest sight of all is two women, entirely naked like the rest, who are determined to ascend the staircase in their own fashion. No one laughs at them although some of the men look knowingly at each other and dig each other in the ribs with their elbows; but most of the onlookers pretend not to see the two women making their way slowly up the steps. The first woman, walking on her hands, is held up by the woman behind her who walks between her partner's opened legs; holding them by the ankles as if they were the handles of a wheelbarrow. I am strangely fascinated, but repelled by their immodesty, and look away.

While I trudge up the endless warm steps, a young girl immediately in front of me falters and drops to one knee, as if exhausted. I feel sorry for her and put my hand beneath her arm to help her to her feet, but, made aware of the girl's warm, shaven armpit, which gives under my lifting fingers like the soft crust of a pie, and sensing the blood rushing to my face, I hurry on up the steps with my head averted, hoping the crowds have not seen.

Fortunately their attention is diverted by a tall, athletic girl who has sidestepped the line and is gracefully bounding up the steps with the stride and sure-footedness of a young gazelle.

At first I think the crowd's roar of disapproval is because the girl has deliberately jumped the queue and is racing on ahead, but when two guards seize and try to force her off the steps, I see, trembling between the woman's legs, a tiny protuberance.

Although it is not agreed by everyone, especially the women on the steps, that the girl is obviously a man and cannot therefore be presented to the King, there is an uneasiness regarding proof, and many of the women openly express their doubts and try to argue with the guard before they remove the unfortunate girl from the steps. Several women leave the stairway voluntarily because when they remove their hands from in front of their pubes, they reveal that they too have a tiny penis. Some women remonstrate and try to urge the rest not to take notice of such a natural phenomenon; but others argue that by the same token each and every one of them should be declared a male. There is confusion after this and all the women begin talking at once.

Eventually the guards lose their patience and begin prodding the seated women with their spears; urging them on up the stairway. When the column reforms and begins moving slowly upwards once more, there are small patches of blood on the white marble steps where the women had sat who had circumcised themselves with combs.

Although my heart is beating wildly with excitement as I draw nearer to the audience chamber, I too have doubts but hope the King will not notice.

On reaching the last step and standing on the patio outside the entrance to the palace, I am glad I am forced to wait because I am out of breath and want time to compose myself before being ushered into the King's presence.

Standing in the crush outside the door, I become alarmed when I am seized with an overwhelming desire to urinate. I know that if I lose my place in the queue, I will forfeit forever the privilege of an audience with the King. All I can do is to jiggle up and down, hoping it will be taken for enthusiasm, and pray my turn will come quickly.

From where I am standing I can see the dim figures of women passing down the length of the gloomy audience chamber, showing off their charms when they pass before the King I cannot see.

When the queue moves forward I find it difficult to walk because I have to keep my thighs pressed tightly together to keep in my water.

An exciting, overwhelming smell of incense, just as I had imagined, begins to drift out of the audience chamber. This stimulates the feeling in my bladder and a slight sweat breaks out on my forehead.

When I draw closer to the door, I can hear the low murmur of voices inside the audience chamber. I crane my neck, hoping to glimpse the King; and imagine I do, but the excitement increases my desire to urinate. So much so, I cast about in desperation for someone behind me in the queue with whom I can exchange places so I can slip away for a moment. But, before I can make up my mind whom to approach, I realise with alarm it is my turn to enter.

With bowed head and quaking from head to toe, I walk gracefully into the vast audience chamber. The warm, scented air enfolds my entire body and I feel I will suffocate. Suddenly, I am standing before the King and, to prevent myself urinating involuntarily, press my left hand hard up against my pubes, hoping my action will be interpreted by the King as a gesture of modesty.

The King of Siam pays little, if any, attention to me and seems far more interested in some State papers he is reading. Without looking up, he dismisses me with a wave of his hand but manages to convey at the same time that he has chosen me.

I leave the audience chamber through a door at the far end, and close it quietly behind me.

When I recall the King's handsome face, his beautiful hands, his white teeth and slow smile, his sumptuous, exotic clothing and the way he had sat with his elegant legs crossed, I can no longer contain myself and urinate between my fingers.

Unashamed by the hot water running down my legs and knowing I am alone in the tiny, dark room, I sink to the floor while my bowels move exquisitely and my body begins, deliciously, to drain of all its sweetness.

It is always at this precise moment I awake, have done with the desire or else pass the day irritably in argument.

A DISSAUSIVE (EASTER SUNDAY, 1959)

"Your Church, arrogant in the assumption that it is in exclusive possession of the truth, asserts that I — whether an Anglican or a
member of the Eastern Orthodox communion — am in error. Submitting
that the error is schismatic rather than heretical does not mean that I am
without error but that it is more clearly defined. This is a totalitarian attitude; and it is this which dissuades me."

"I think that's being unduly dogmatic. Rome has become far more tolerant."

"I would have thought you would have realised the fact that, like the
communists, the Catholic's definition of toleration is a perversion in order to maintain the security of their authority. It always strikes me as odd
that, while we are constantly being told about the lack of freedom of
thought and action behind the Iron Curtain, we are not reminded of the
Catholic suppression in Ireland. There, the Catholic hierarchy controls
the Government, approving or disapproving of its submitted constitution
and policy; the children skip in step to the hierarchical educational in-
junctions; the dominated Board of Censors wields its scissors, snipping
with a religious enthusiasm, devoid of literary judgement, and the priests
remain unprosecuted for infractions of civil law whilst devoutly adhering
to the Law of the Church; surely this is totalitarian rule and, as such, the
perverse definition of religious toleration? It is only understandable if
complete obedience to Rome is a prerequisite for its faithful; which it is,
so I don't see how you can say that they are tolerant."

"What are you trying to prove?"

"That if Rome assumes to be the true religion; if Rome demands complete obedience to its authority, then it is totalitarian. If it is, then the means by which it retains its power must be suspect."

"Implying?"

"That Rome connives. That the end justifies the means."

"Really, Erica, that is absurd."

"Is it? What about Croatia? Spain? Italy? France? Canada? All within our lifetime. Modern history of which Rome should be ashamed."

"You mean Monsignor Tiso and other priests whom the Devil . . ."

"I mean the Church of Rome; the so-called Church of Christ. The Pope, through whom God . . ."

"When governments become hysterically anti-clerical . . ."

"Don't you dare use that argument. Others — soldiers, civilians — are confronted by the same dilemma and their excuses fail to convince so they are put to the wall by the community in which they share, and shot. Not so the Church. As long as the Vatican can rally support and gain privileges, it will condone evils so that, in the long run, its position remains secure and its fanatical lust for power is, in part, satisfied."

"I can't sit here, Erica, and listen to this rubbish. You're talking nonsense! This is the twentieth century, not the fifteenth!"

"I hope for your sake, Gloria, that you speak as an innocent and are one of the docile flock whom Pope Pius the Tenth referred to in his 'Vehementor nos', and that you are another fearful but willing upholder of the Ne Temere decree, who does not see it as complicity, as a furthering of Rome's despotism."

"Would you not have Christ's teaching passed on to them?"

"Gloria, darling, all I'm trying to say is that your Church is despotic and retains its authority by questionable means. This very fact suggests that its omnicompetence is questionable even to itself; bringing about a feeling of insecurity and thus precipitating a totalitarian aggressiveness and unquestionable — I was going to say loyalty; an unquestionable obedience."

"I don't see how you can imagine that Christ's Church could possibly feel insecure. You forget that the Pope is infallible. God would hardly speak through one who . . ."

"Come off it, Gloria, what makes you think he is? In any case, although it might be imprudent or blasphemous to decry some statements, you must realise that very few carry the significant label of infallible. As to the insecurity — I don't like that expression, rather the determination to remain secure — infallible — makes it unable to deal effectively with such problems that arise from modern science."

"Really, Erica! What rubbish. You agnostics are all the same. It's not a basis for any argument to say science knows better or that a thing can't be true unless proved scientifically."

"You miss my point. I would have thought that the new Christian theology in regard to the Bible was based on a scientific criticism; and Rome, to save face and to retain the illusion of infallibility by issuing an encyclical emphasising the divine inspiration of the Bible, excluded the possibilities of error. Admittedly, this was nearly a hundred years ago, but since then it can hardly be admitted in argument that things have changed unless you believe that their renewed, complex and devious defence is sincere. To me, their antics show the tyrant unable to alter his tyrannical dogma because of the inevitable loss of face when it is shown that his infallibility is zigzagged with cracks."

"Erica, I can't see what you intend by this, unless it is your intention to hurt me by turning it into a personal attack. You will never alter my faith. I believe in it far too strongly to have it undermined by your destructive criticism."

"I've no wish to subtract your faith, Gloria, and I certainly wouldn't attempt to convert you to another. Rather I would wish it to burn more fiercely and not be blinkered, confined and narrowed by a tyranny which counts souls as profitable power. You should not resent or be afraid of arguments against your Church or God, otherwise your faith is untested."

"Don't you think it's been tested sufficiently already? Wouldn't a lack of faith have aired my spacious conscience rather than suffocated it with an overwhelming guilt? Wouldn't my faith have expired long ago under the strain imposed upon it? I have faith. An unwavering belief. But I lack strength. It is my will which is weak."

"Please, Gloria, no."

"Why not? Basically, that's what it comes down to whenever we talk, isn't it? My mortal sin. Correction. Sins."

"Gloria. Please. I'm not attacking you, honestly."

"No? It's difficult to believe you in the light of our previous arguments. God! I sometimes wish I was a miserable psychopath."

"Why should you want to be that?"

"Then perhaps I wouldn't feel it to be so wrong."

"Perhaps. But what of the one who feels it to be wrong yet believes it not to be wrong?"

"You should know."

"You mean that the knowledge of sin without the feeling of sin is not guilt."

"Not theological guilt. They must be concomitant."

"That's not convincing."

"Isn't it? Well, it helps to separate pathological guilt, or neurotic anxieties soured into guilt, from the theological sins . . ."

"Do you really believe that? Can you imagine Rome issuing an encyclical evolved from a psychological science?"

"No, I suppose not. Even if it was a true science."

"Is that your naive, unthinking orthodoxy?"

"Probably."

"Timid docility, perhaps?"

"Oh, for God's sake, shut up, will you? You know I'm obsessed with guilt. Can't you see the ashes of the apostate greying my hair? And why? Why? You should know!"

"Only too well. But I can't help you. If you believe in redemption then there is only one course for you to take. Take it. But don't make me part of your guilt in an emotional attempt to force an obligation. Also, enquire of yourself whether or not you understand the limitations of your ability to avoid sin. Then ask yourself if it is not this limitation which loads you with guilt and not the sin itself. You know I feel it to be wrong but believe it isn't. I have no feeling of guilt or shame in my inability to resist. But I'm sure that part of your guilt, perhaps all of it, is because you do. Isn't that so?"

"Maybe. I avoid Mass. I shrink from Holy Communion. I can't bring myself to confess. I have failed to observe the calendar, and I have wallowed in mortal sin. So, how else should I feel?"

"The priest will understand your weakness and advise you. I'm sure he'll point out the one emissary of the devil who ensnared you."

"It's got nothing to do with you. The guilt is mine, so also is the sin. The devil was already coiled beneath the stone of my heart."

"Hibernating under a damp, moist soul?"

"Be funny if you like, but it only proves how shallow your own moral values are."

"I'm sorry, Gloria, sorry that you think my moral values are worthless. Man's conceit is remarkable."

"You mean his faith."

"That, too, but I was thinking of the paraphernalia; the accoutrements which man requires in his endeavour to participate in or experience an eschatological climax."

"You want to make fun of the way man sets about . . ."

"Of course I don't want to make fun of it. No. I'm lying. Yes, I do want to make fun of his absurd, magical apparatus."

"You'd dismiss ceremonial, just like that?"

"Yes. I think it shows up man's weakness and tries to turn it into a strength."

"That's silly. What about the sacrament?"

"Especially that."

"Because it intensifies the Spirit?"

"You say that. You, of course, understand Latin?"

"I don't regard that as a trap so I can say without fear that I do not know Latin."

"Then how can you . . . ?"

"I only have a vague understanding of what is being said, but sufficient to know my way."

"So, in fact, most of it is mumbo-jumbo?"

"Of course it isn't mumbo-jumbo. Anyway, you miss the whole point of the necessity of having a common language and form of service. It binds the scattered Churches together so that in, say, Hong Kong, I can attend a service and receive the sacrament as I would anywhere else in the world."

"But you said that you didn't fully understand the words of the service? Anyway, it doesn't matter. It only proves to me that it is an effective way of keeping the ignorant dutifully respectful towards those who understand the magic formula. A bit out-of-date nowadays when learning isn't awe-inspiring or mystical, I would have thought, but it still works."

"Erica, if I said to you in defence of the sacrament, because you obviously think it impossible to express holiness through matter, that for us, the Word became Flesh; would you understand what it implied?"

"Yes, and I believe that you believe it. But at the same time what I can't understand is that you also believe in the assumption of the blessed Virgin Mary."

"Or the miracle of the fishes? Or the turning of the wine . . ."

"No, no, no. The assumption of the blessed Virgin."

"Of course I do."

"Even though it was four hundred years after her death before evidence had to be manufactured for the credulous believers?"

"I don't know about that, but I suppose you're going to scoff at the resurrection?"

"I don't believe it, but I accept that for the Church it is an historical fact on which their doctrine is based and through which your salvation is assured."

"Well, it's comforting to know that you believe in something."

"You're mistaken. I believe that Jesus Christ did live and that He was crucified, but I do not believe that He was resurrected. And if you want me to, I'll tell you why I don't think He was resurrected."

"Well, go on then."

"Because He never died."

"Erica, you're impossible! What sort of nonsense is that? You just said that you believed that He was crucified."

"Oh, yes, He was. But He didn't die upon the cross. He fainted."

"But His side was pierced."

"Exactly! And blood flowed out. If He was dead it wouldn't have done."

"You horrify me, Erica, you really do. And you expect me to believe it?"

"No, of course not. But I believe it. I think He was taken down from the cross in a coma and thought to be dead. When He was laid down, consciousness slowly returned to Him. In all probability He suffered from cerebral anoxia and this, plus the fact that His physical condition must have been appalling after such an ordeal, makes it understandable that, at first, His disciples did not recognise Him and, because of the anoxia, failed to see in His mumbled words the clarity and inspired wisdom of their former glorious teacher. However, what intrigues me is whether or not His followers, who must have known that recovery after crucifixion was possible, acted promptly, as soon as Jesus slumped on the cross, to get a centurion to deliver the coup-de-grace; and remember, His legs weren't broken which would have meant certain death; so that they had time enough to get Him to a place of safety and pray that He would revive. And, secondly, a far more intriguing question is, what happened to Jesus after that? When the disciples and Mary finally recognised Him, did they hide Him? And for how long did He live on afterwards? Or, again, was His mentality so impaired that for the sake of the followers He was spirited away? When He did eventually die, where was He buried? If His mentality wasn't impaired, is it possible that some of the Bible was written by Him? The possibilities are endless. It would even account for the legends that He came to England. Perhaps He died here and, unknowingly, we have on some fair upland the world's most revered grave."

"I think you're mad."

"No, not me. The idea is not mine, but it is one in which I believe. But quite honestly, Gloria, if you find that the resurrection essential to your belief, I think you are sadly mistaken. It implies a greater attachment to physical myths, rather than to the miracles of the spirit."

"But an idea like that would turn everything inside out! Everything would crumble."

"It would certainly throw things out, but these are the very things which, to my way of thinking, clutter up the most profound truth. You would gain by the simplicity. The one thing that stands out above all else is the simplicity of Christ's teaching. The profound simplicity. But what have we got now? What has your Church done to spread the inspired teaching? It's concocted a totalitarian . . ."

"Oh, don't start that again."

"As you wish. Close your eyes. Bury your head in the sand."

"I'm sorry, but I'm so confused. The funny thing is, though, listening to you I get the feeling that you do believe in something."

"I do, in an odd way. I believe that Jesus was the son of God if you mean that we are all children of God, and that He died for our sins, if you believe each one of us can, by example, help others towards a good life. But there is no eternity; either below stairs or with the angels up above."

"I shall pray for you, then."

"Thank you."

"I mean it."

"Of course you do."

"Well, don't be cynical, then."

"I'm not. I'm truly grateful to you. I don't think your prayers will do the slightest bit of good, but the willingness you have just expressed, and the intention, has added to your own sweetness and possibly, because of it, sown a minute grain of goodness in me."

"I just don't understand you, Erica."

"Equally, I do not understand your acceptance of a faith wrapped in so much stupidity and ignorance."

"Ignorance!"

"I think that's a fitting word. There's a ring to it. Better than mistaken doctrinal tradition; not a wanting of knowledge but a wanting in the acceptance of knowledge; truth; facts."

"Oh, back to facts again!"

"Gloria, darling, for your own sake; to sharpen your faith; to make sense of what you believe, please, I beg of you : open your mind. Think for yourself. Do not be frightened of discarding those things which your conscience or reason dictate as being wrong. You will suffocate, just as will your religion. I mean it. I'm urging you on to purity, to go forward with a sword which shines brightly, whose cutting edge will be far sharper than the one you wave so blindly now."

"And just how am I supposed to hone up this sword I'm meant to be carrying? Sit down with a pile of books or listen to you?"

"Don't be silly. Stand back from your faith and reappraise those things which you take so much for granted."

"What, for instance?"

"Why do you wear a headscarf or hat?"

"You mean in church?"

"Yes."

"Because . . ."

"Because of the angels?"

"Yes."

"You are far wiser than Saint Paul, it seems."

"The very act of covering the head . . ."

"Do you despise and hate the Jews?"

"Of course not."

"'Cepting Good Fridays."

"The Jews bent their knees to Christ in mockery . . ."

"But the whole congregation is asked to bend its knees for named individuals on Good Friday. Am I right?"

"Yes. It's called Flectamus genus."

"Yet you refuse to kneel in prayer for the whole of a race which has suffered collectively more than any other. What sort of Church is it that should instruct its members so? By now you should be sporting hardened callouses on your ritualistic knees for the race you so readily condemn and whom you refuse to free from responsibility for Christ's death!"

"It's an historical . . ."

"Hysterical popery!"

"Erica!"

"Have I scratched the scab of a conscience which does battle with slav-ish directives and perhaps uncovered an irritation, sore with the friction of a dilemma? No? No matter. Tell me, I think it was in Japan that a youth was taken to hospital, and from his lung was removed a fully developed embryo, sufficiently formed to be recognised as human; his twin. Would your Church have baptised it?"

"I don't know."

"They do baptise the oddest bits and pieces; even embryos, in order to ensure eternal life, you know."

"I am aware of that."

"And you agree?"

"I can find no objection to it."

"Yet you leave the problem of the unbaptised Neanderthal man to God?"

"How else would you have it?"

"Let us suppose — coming back to this child within a child — let us suppose that the embryo curled within his brother's lung could have lived, had the youth sacrificed his life like a pregnant mother who jock-eyed for life with her unborn child; would you think it right and proper for the youth to have given his life?"

"This is absurd."

"It is. Quite distasteful. Tell me. What are your views on contraception?"

"You know very well."

"And you don't question it?"

"No."

"But you practise contraception?"

"Do you want me to slap your face? Because you're going the right way about it."

"I didn't mean you, silly, I meant the Catholic Church. Stop imagining I'm attacking you as an individual all the time. Now, you do practise contraception?"

"Not in the sense of using a mechanical means to prevent conception."

"But what is the difference between using natural rhythm . . . ?"

"And exercising self-control; isn't it obvious?"

"No. Quite frankly, I can't see the difference between copulating with confidence by taking adequate precautions, or copulating with only a certain amount of confidence and relying upon the accuracy of a natural rhythm technique. And as for the restraint or the exercising of self control, such self-imposed abstemiousness is not brought about by the striving for a rigorous purity, but through a fear of conception. Fear's hardly concomitant with self-control or, for that matter, with a sound, moral truth."

"You can't argue on assumptions. And in any case, because you obviously know your argument is weak, you are cloaking yourself with arrogance and hoping your blustering attitude will force the effectiveness of your attack and disguise the cardboard struts of your paper folly."

"Well, if you want to gather the whole brood of Catholic believers behind you and in their defence pretend that they are other than a mass of weak, inarticulate, bewildered, easily corrupted humans, do so. But if I were to ask you to choose the Catholics from amongst a beaded string of anonymous souls, and should you make a mistake or show that they be different, you would not have condemned yourself through your mistake, but merely shown that, like me, you too are part of the same bewildered humanity. The ascetics you champion are the clasps of the beaded humanity who unite the necklace, but they are not the necklace. It is they who endeavour to practise idealism and, by their example, encourage the surging masses to do likewise. But I will never be convinced that a majority are sufficiently controlled to exercise restraint through motives other than fear. In any case, I'm sure that the strengths of the various urges which are meant to be controlled vary so much from one extreme to the other that those who are lucky enough to have weak or nonexistent impulses only have the appearance of being ascetic. Whereas those who are endowed with overwhelming impulses and who successfully manage to control them are, in actual fact, far more ascetic than their more undisturbed brothers or sisters. Wouldn't you think?"

"Possibly."

"Did you know you were allowed to masturbate?"

"Don't be ridiculous!"

"It's true. The good fathers say that a woman is allowed to manipulate herself in order to bring about a state of tumescence which would be conducive to sexual intercourse."

"So?"

"You don't find that ruling odd?"

"I think it quaint. I should have thought that you, too, would find it amusing. However, if it is a ruling, then I imagine it was drawn up at a time when physiological knowledge was very slight and it was believed that a woman's tumescence a necessary state for conception."

"I hadn't thought of that. Perhaps you are right."

"What other Aunt Sally am I meant to knock down?"

"Saints."

"It's only another way of approaching God."

"Through humans? What was the Incarnation for, then?"

"Saints . . ."

"Can gain the confidence of God's ear; being not so terrifying to approach. By what authority is a human translated into a saint? By what sign must they be known? And why was it so difficult to recognise the incarnation of Jesus and yet so easy to discern a saint? God bless Saint Philomena, Virgin and Martyr . . ."

"Her name has not yet been added to Roman martyrology."

"Mass is celebrated in her honour."

"Not with the approval of Rome."

"Hail Mary, Mother of Christendom! Must the Church only allow approved cultus? If so, why don't they disapprove of Eugenia, who robed herself in male clothes and became an Abbot; strike out Expeditus; expose Wilgeforits, the bearded virgin martyr who hangs from the cross, confusing hermaphrodites; repress Odilia, the blind Abbess who leads the blind; discount the life of the abused Rita of Cascia; disregard the eccentric Simeon Salus and his devotion to harlots and the wretched; rout or decimate Saint Ursula and her Eleven Thousand virgin sisters in Christ; doom to oblivion Bibiana; disallow Marina, the monkish woman; suppress the disgorged Margaret; abandon Gildas's De excidio; and equate Margaret Raparata's monkish seduction of a nun with an anonymous death which would allay the suspicion of a Christian mythology?"

"Other churches have their saints and the same accusation could be levelled against them. Anyway, why the emphasis on female saints?"

"Men make saints. Mark, I said men not man. As men they require their female saints to be either virgins pure and simple; women who have defended their virginity; or women who have repented of their sins — venial of course. Cecily, and Thecla Iconium, preserved it in marriage, as presumably did the Abbess Etheldreda, a liturgical virgin, during her two marriages. Dympna, Cecily and the Pelagias of Tarsus and Antioch successfully defended their honour, whilst two Katherines and others repented of its loss. Irene, Flora, Mary and Lucy, although exposed in brothels, went to their deaths intact — which speaks well of popular morality. And so on and so on, not forgetting Ursula's Eleven Thousand."

"You're becoming ridiculous, Erica."

"I think not. The importance — the stress — given to virginity as to celibacy, is a creation of men. Men who have the audacity to speak for man. Why haven't there been saints who either fathered great broods of happy Christian children, or from whose womb sprang energetic bundles of effervescent, healthy, bouncing sons and daughters? Why do the ecclesiastical calendars not contain the names of the good man and woman who lived a good Christian life and multiplied their kind in abundance? Why must it always be the sickly, the celibate or the virgin, or those who have suffered untold misery? Or those who caused the happening of dubious miracles?"

"You obviously don't understand the derivation and history of the honoured and respected title bestowed for devotedness to Christ."

"Perhaps not, but I object strongly to the inclusion of the names of men and women who are as suspect as Philomena . . ."

"Pope Gregory the Sixteenth . . ."

"Pope Joan . . ."

"On September the nineteenth . . ."

"A feast day."

"There have been miracles through her intercession."

"You said Rome excluded her."

"Nevertheless there have been miracles."

"You'll be telling me next that you believe in Katherine, the high-born maiden of Alexandria who was fed by doves and whose veins pulsed milk."

"She died on the wheel, hence the symbol of a . . ."

"The Catherine wheel? Rubbish! There never was a Katherine as told in that fabled romance. That's another feast day which Rome should repress."

"You'd have them all done away with."

"That I would not. There have been men and women — take Perpetua and Felicity, who as catechumens at the time of their arrest transcended their novicatur and faced their martyrdom with fanatic devotion to Christ. I do not doubt that these good people existed, but are they any nearer to God's right hand because we, mankind, have elevated them to the position of holiness? It's ridiculous. And that you should need them to intercede for you is disgusting. Your church is cluttered with such aberrations and with dignitaries whose very names should be struck from human record."

"I believe . . ."

"Pope Alexander the Sixth. To which particular corner of hell . . ."

"I believe . . ."

"...and most of the Popes in the second half of the fifteenth century?"

"I believe..."

"...and the poor, ignorant, Neanderthal man, condemned to eternal limbo, you won't save him, will you?"

"Will you let me get a word in edgeways? How do you expect me to answer you if you won't let me speak? Now, you expect me to be able to answer all the questions and know the anomalies and be able to justify my religion. I can't, I don't know enough. So the whole sham argument is a screen behind which you can attack me personally."

"Darling..."

"You're trying to back me up against a wall and get me into a position from which you know damn well I won't be able to extricate myself. Aren't you? "

"Gloria, darling..."

"You're determined to get me so positioned that the only way out for me is to agree to a compromise or to confess to something which is against my faith, aren't you? You're goading me to turn against you to satisfy some curious perversion which will delight in seeing and hearing me degrade myself..."

"Oh, for goodness sake, shut up! The only thing I would ever ask a Catholic to confess to is the historic barbarity of their Church."

"Just that?"

"Yes. Because insomuch as the present is the outcome of the past, so the present can only exist because of the past. If this is true, and I think it is, then your church cannot deny that its present power must, even in part, be the result of past conduct."

"Well, our history..."

"Rivalled the very hell which you are taught is the ultimate punishment for your sins. Yet it lived the very sins..."

"Are we going to have a little piece about the lewdness of monks and nuns?"

"You are. Starting with the gluttony of the priests; their carnality and abominable living; the unholy alliances and the vicious living in nunneries and the sins daily committed in abbeys, priories and other religious houses belonging to monks, cannons and nuns and which were more disgusting than the immorality practised by the corrupted peasants in the poorest hovels . . ."

"Yet you're the one who eulogises over such abbey ruins as Tintern, Glastonbury, Battle, Kirkstall . . ."

"Much to my shame."

"It's always predictable that when anyone mounts an attack against the Catholic Church they will show that monks and nuns cohabited in sin and imagine that they are certain of winning their argument by flashing past sins in front of the credulous listener."

"There are many other sins which deserve equal prominence. Is it not a sin to exhibit a vial purporting to contain Christ's blood?"

"I don't believe it!"

"It's true. It was duck's blood and it was renewed every week."

"Where?"

"In the Abbey of Hales. And in Bury St Edmunds they used to exhibit the coals which roasted Saint Laurence; the parings of Saint Edmund's toenails; Thomas Becket's penknife and boots; and pieces of the original cross which, had they all been glued together, were sufficient to have completed the whole. Thus making false the claims of thousands of other churches to be the possessor of fragments of the true and original cross. And in Maiden Bradley Priory in Somerset, they exhibited the Virgin's smock and, believe it or not, part of the bread left over from the Lord's last supper. In Bruton Priory they exhibited the Virgin's red silk girdle and in Farley Abbey her white girdle. All over the world, wherever a sculptor carved a madonna, he gouged out the Virgin's eye sockets and inserted a knot of resinous pine so that long after the eyes had been set in, gessoed and painted, some supplicant believer, upon looking into the compassionate eyes of her carved and gilded madonna, would behold in wonderment and awe, resinous tears oozing from the sockets and a miracle was pronounced.

"Ask Siri. Ask her about the store room in the Vatican which contains millions of carefully filed and indexed fragments of bone; splinters from long-dead saints; replacements for those lost or pilfered. Ask her how many shinbones Saint . . ."

"You hate the idea of saintliness, don't you?"

"You know I don't. But just as your saints were made, so too did you make our martyrs."

"What do you mean?"

"John Rogers. Bishop Hooper. Rowland Taylor. Bishop Latimer. John Bradford. Bishop Ridley; and three hundred others. English reformers burnt by Rome."

"Heretics. You can't compare them to saints."

"Jesus, Gloria. That is exactly the same attitude which has prevented your damnable Church from repenting of their treatment of the Vaudois and the Albigenses; the Spanish Inquisition or the massacre of Saint Bartholomew! And you've got the damned nerve and cheek to say that the martyrs you created can't be compared to your saints! Why, Hooper, Bishop Hooper, for his belief, stood and bore the flames of three fires with a bundle of faggots under each arm and strung about with bladders of gunpowder. With his hair singed, his clothes half-burned and his backside a mass of flames, he called out for dry faggots to speed the burning of the green wood about him and all the while praying to the Lord. Even when he was black within his mouth and his tongue so swollen that he could not speak, his lips moved in prayer until they shrank and stuck to his gums. Yet he still knocked his breast with his hands, to emphasise his belief, until one of his arms fell off. And then with the other, while the fat, water and blood poured out of the finger ends until it stuck to the chain that bound him and he fell forward in a faint. Only when his bowels erupted and fell free did he die. Wasn't he a saint? Wasn't he deserving of being raised to sainthood? Is there a God who would deny him? One who would turn him from the celestial heaven? Tell me, is there?"

(Gloria, her hand clapped to her mouth, mumbles a prayer and gropes blindly for the door handle and, having let herself out onto the landing, vomits onto the linoleum.

Erica invokes a yawn, summoning the Devil to her aid; to Esbial's aid.)

NEVOC 69

The basement room of "The Willows", 5 Ackland Avenue, London, W.11, is the present meeting place of Nevoc No. 69.

As early as 1743 the Almanac lists it as being "convened beyond Nottinghill, close to the Gate where water is natural sprung"; but it was in 1756 that the Nevoc was officially formed and registered in the Grand Master's copy of "The Lists of Regular Nevocs according to their Seniority and Constitution" as Nevoc No. 234. The entry is dated the 7th of December, 1756, and there is a small, engraved representation of a Well from which appears the head of The Lion.

In 1781 it was given the number 69, but which didn't necessarily denote it was constituted of female members, because this ruling does not appear in the Constitution until 1881, even though such Nevocs were known to exist — as is evidenced from Printed Ritual. However, there is considerable doubt as to the true reason for this Nevoc's rise to Seniority although Amalgamation is now widely accepted as the reason. Some argue it was due to the influence of Sister Madelene who, in 1779, successfully performed an Ipssimus and thus drew the attention of the M.H. to the Nevoc and who subsequently upgraded it. Whatever the reason for the Nevoc's startling rise to Seniority, there can be no doubt that it was most beneficial because, in the following ten years, no less than seventy-two Grand Opus were successfully performed and one hundred and seventy-one Adepts un-frocked.

The name of Sister Madelene does not appear in Printed Ritual after 1783, although the Works of Nevoc 69 continued to flourish. In all probability she died and did not become, as is often suggested, M.R. to the Reincarnated, Evranaeus Philaletha. The only other explanation would be that, being an Adept, she took an hermetic pseudonym and became a Daughter of Hermes. Whatever the true reason for her disappearance, there can be no doubt that, with the rise of Nevoc 69, their exceptional Works, and the blossoming of new Adepts, a rash of new Nevocs appeared in the late seventeen-eighties. Research does not show that Adepts raised by Nevoc 69 left to start Nevocs of Instruction, although it could account for the startling rise in the number of new Nevocs recorded in the Lists and all having one Adept within the Temple. Welcome as this activity may have been, their strength was dissipated and, because they were content with O.L. and F.B., they went into decline. Only one, Nevoc 505, is still extant and meets once a year with Nevoc 69 for the Feast of the Five Ways. (If, as some believe, Nevoc 69 is the Matrix of 505, then this annual Meeting of the Five Ways augurs Irrefutable Blooms.)

Although 1756 is always presumed to be the year in which Nevoc 69 was formed (as No. 234) and the Almanac date of 1743 accepted as proof of the Nevoc's previous convening, there are several references to other Nevocs which, because of the similarity of title, could be descriptions of Nevoc 69.

An entry in a chapbook entitled A Detection of Damnable Driftes, practised by Three Witches arraigned at Essex, dated 1576 and printed at "the little north dore of paules "refers to statements made by a Sir Gilbert Southcote, under the heading, "Witches of the West Gate Well", in connection with the trial of three Sisters — Anne, Mary and Elizabeth Dudding. An even earlier reference to a possible Nevoc under the protection of a Well symbol was in 1462 in the famous Book of Quarters. In it, mention is made of two Adepts, originally of the so-called "heretical" sect of the Vaudois. Jacques du Clercq, the chronicler, describes in great detail how these two Adepts fled Northern France and sought refuge in England — lodging in London, close to the West Gate Well, to await the arrival of Deniselle Greniere before continuing their journey onto Glastonbury and there to meet with ROBIN. Unknown to them, Deniselle Greniere had been arrested in France and accused of OVRAMMU. She was found guilty by the inquisitor, Pierre le Broussart, and her body burnt alive. That was in May 1462. In November, the two Adepts, namely Sister Jeanne de Beclier and Sister Clair de Marigny, fearing the worst may have befallen their Sister Deniselle, performed an Ipssimus — "when Seven were Saluted in the Presence of Sister Deniselle II!" Jacques du Clercq goes on to recount how "in fear of discovery, they cast the Furniture into a Well". (Although du Clercq makes no mention as to where the Ipssimus took place, it can be assumed that, lodged as they were near to the West Gate, the two French Sisters would convene at the nearest Well.) Du Clercq goes on to relate how, some six months later, "the Cloth being so remarkably preserved as was the Furniture, they did re-convene immediately, there being the number present for a Work of Nine". This tells us that the two French Adepts had gathered round them a minimum of five (Sister) Witnesses and suggests that, having found a favourable place (the "preserved Furniture "would augur this), and no longer fearing discovery, they intended to convene at the Well until, upon their Casting Over the White Cloth, they were instructed to move elsewhere. If it were not purely conjecture, the setting up of a Temple by the Sisters Marigny and Beclier on this spot would make Nevoc 69 the oldest — bar I and IX which have existed in "continuo"— and would account for the Sisters Dudding convening there in 1576.

In 1881, when the Nevoc was upgraded to Seniority and given the number 69, it convened at various Temples throughout the City of London. It wasn't until 1904 a permanent residence was allowed it. This came about by a discovery made in 1900.

Then a Novice of S.L.A., Sister Catherine, by diligent research, established the site of the original Well described in 1756 as being "set close by the West Gate". She placed her evidence before the M.H. who, after nearly a year's stay, deliberated in favour of Sister Catherine's findings. Subsequently, three years later, Sir William McFane, M.R., ordered the purchasing of 5 Ackland Avenue; the house Sister Catherine judged to be built over the site of the Well. After several months of laborious work, Christian workmen found and uncovered the Well. When it had been ascertained that the Well was not coveted by Saint Brigit, the M.H. immediately ordered the basement to be turned into a Grand Temple for the exclusive use of Nevoc 69. Furniture, including the altar from St Germain which was consecrated by incestuous relationships to avoid the Black Death in 1350, was moved into the proposed Grand Temple and Tracings arranged to allow for Ten Degrees. After the Ceremony of Dedication, Sister Catherine, in acknowledgement of her important discovery, was Raised and Passed into the Seventh Degree, whereafter the basement became Nevoc 69, and a Grand Temple. The rest of the house was given over to family living and two Adepts, Sister Secretain and Sister Sybille, were lodged there with their children.

This proved to be an unwise decision for on the fourteenth of June, nineteen hundred and twenty-seven, an Ipssimus failed — with dire consequences. It may have been that the Ritual was lax or incomplete or that the children were allowed an unsupervised and separate Five Ways. Whatever the reason, it was purported — and later substantiated — that Jesus of Nazareth, in the form of a large black dog, gained access through an insufficiently sealed Outer Ring. Before an enquiry could be held, indiscriminate attempts of Ritual Beatifux only added to the confusion and True Chaos — irregularly channelled, got astride the Nevoc which quickly filled with Adversaries.

In December of the same year, after Ritual Cleansing — performed by the M.R. himself in conjunction with The Chosen M.R., in a Ceremony last performed in 1818 — the Nevoc was reconstituted with seven Novices and two Adepts. Needless to say, little was accomplished and during the years following, up until 1939, the Nevoc went into decline.

During the Second World War, Nevoc 69 revived sufficiently to raise seven Adepts and Initiate and Pass Up one hundred and seventeen Novices. Several Five Ways were initiated with partial success. However, after the death of Hitler, the Nevoc again went into decline.

Over the last nineteen years, although Listed, it has convened fewer than eighteen times; other than to perform the Five Ways, the Annual

Purification and Dedication of the Mystic Rose and the Initiation and Passing Up of Novices. It has the minimum membership and composition required for the retention of nomenclature — the Adepts, both M.R. thro' M.R., are Sister Clitolde C.S. and Sister Justine F.B. However, neither aspire to Ipssimus and rarely accomplish a Tenth Degree Ritual; being content to Dedication.

This same slackness is apparent in their acceptance of new members who are Proposed, Initiated and Passed into the Seventh Degree; all in the same evening.

As was the case on the 6th of June, 1958, when they took the unprecedented step of Raising and Passing into the Tenth Degree one Sister ESBIAL.

> NOTE: Having established the former by research, I was curious to know in what surrounds "Esbial" conducted her magick and confess I broke into the basement room of No. 5 Auckland Avenue and was taken aback by the mysteries which confronted me and as seen in the light of a flickering candle I was bold enough to steal.

In the middle of the damp, uneven, flagstoned floor were the faint traces of a chalk drawn circle ringing the remains of a hexagram. Imposed upon this was a pentacle which had become smeared and rubbed as if by the milling and turning of countless bare feet. The Cabalistic Symbols which had represented Universal Matter — the Fixed and the Volatile; the Three Essential Principles and the Four Elements — were no longer distinguishable one from the other and looked like the scribblings of an epileptic.

Against the wall to the right of the door and placed in the centre was the Saint Germain altar devoid of Furniture save for a Funerary Flint, lying on a faded and rotting altar cloth, and a mummified Madragora grown from the sperm of hanged men. (Legend had it that this particular Madragora root had been found growing beneath the gallows at Tyburn where it was plucked during the burning, in a barrel of tar, of Joan Peterson. Fortunately the screams of Sister Joan drowned the shriek of the plant as it was torn out of the ground, so that the priests, standing and attending to the duties they performed out of ignorance, were unaware of the theft.)

Above the altar and extending over the mildewed walls on either side were three frescoes which, in the poor light and because of the lime which had bubbled up through the surface of the damp plaster, looked pockmarked ghosts of a former, and what must have been a brilliantly coloured, triptych.

At the top of the centre fresco was a representation of an open eye surrounded by an igneous halo in the form of a stylised, radiant, sol niger. Below this was a small, painted scutcheon on which were drawn The Two Crossed Keys with the carefully printed inscription A U M below. Round the scutcheon were three symbols pertaining to Creation, Conservation and Transformation. Underneath, in a standard, geometrical configuration, were the triangles of the Four Elements; each carrying and containing their appropriate symbol. Immediately below this the complicated, but almost unreadable, Universal Secret from the Book of Sacred Law was written in a Malachin text and flanked by the Four Columns of the Universal Temple, which were both round and square in conformation to the symbolism of Femininity. Below this was the Ansate Cross surrounded by symbols depicting The Universal Conjunction of Matter by the permutated copulation of the Four Elements.

The fresco to the left of this central panel had, at its apex, a representation of The Green Lion devouring The Light of The World, whilst immediately below it was suspended The Ninth Key to the Workings bisecting The Broken Ladder, behind which were two figures depicting The Union of The Red Man and The White Woman. Beneath this were the Four Lead Coffins of the Four Crowned Ones laid upon a griddle. In the centre of the panel was a painting of The Hollow Tree in which The Seven Conjunctions gazed outwards whilst above them and to the left, Asmodeus, The Great Architect, fecundated them with His Divine Breath. Below. and reaching almost to the floor, was a painting of The Temple of Participation with The Seven Steps leading up to it; each appropriately labelled. Mortification, Putrefaction, Sublimation, Regeneration, Coagulation and Fixation, Volatilisation, Reconciliation and Unification. On the Second and Seventh Step were the two, dead, waylaying tylers — initialled for identification and Instruction. On either side of this representation of The Temple and below it was The Serene Landscape through which flowed The Source of Water and by the side of which grew a Willow Tree whose roots erupted and disfigured The Serene Landscape.

The right-hand panel of the fresco triptych had, at the top, a painting of the Moon and, below it, also in crescent, seven Stars with the letters Z A B 0 printed between the central five Stars. Beneath were the broken fragments of The Tools of Alignment and the shattered remains of the rough and smooth hewn stones standing against The Cube divided into twenty-seven; and the whole contained within a circle and the legend K I N O S sealing it. Underneath were two figures representing The Union in Bap-hornet and therefore were neither male nor female but androgynous. Both were gesturing obscenely; inviting participation. Bearing letters, they could be used as Tracing Boards for the accomplishment of The Five Ways.

The wall facing this triptych was also decorated but, because of the damp which glistened like dew on the surface and the soft plaster which had fallen away in several places exposing the red brickwork beneath, the magical graphiti were rendered incomprehensible. Instead, nailed to the wall or hung upon crude hooks were myriad wax and clay images in confusion. Many of the clay figurines were missing heads and limbs which had fallen onto the flagstones below and lay in profusion where they had dropped amongst the sodden lumps of plaster or rolled into the circles of soot and pools of black wax and burnt out stumps of hundreds of candles. Also nailed onto the wall were sheep's hearts which were either shrivelled hard and covered with a bright, iridescent green mould or else putrid — reeking with rottenness and turgid with wriggling white maggots. All were pierced by blackthorn and all had their sympathetic clay or wax image above them. One or two of the hearts were bound with osier; out of respect rather than for magical purposes. Also hanging on the wall, wry and damp, were two amnia and one wax and wool crown. Standing in the left-hand corner was a collapsing wicker basket, covered in mildew and filled with discarded, disintegrating clay images which were slowly coagulating into a solid lump of dank clay.

The wall opposite the door was entirely covered by a white curtain hanging from a metal runner secured to the ceiling. Although new, the lower edge of the curtain was stained yellow and brown for a depth of about two feet along the bottom where the cloth had sucked up the damp from the sweating floor.

Across the other wall, and extending as far as the door, was a similar curtain but which was so old and rotten that it was tearing under its own weight, and gaping rents had appeared in it, exposing the Tracings on the wall behind. Through these irregularly shaped rents could be seen all, or part of, The Great Mystery; a section of the dominating figure of Lilith masquerading as The Eternal Magick Rood and Mystic Rose and therefore of necessity adrogynous and in the attitude of The Five Ways; part of the head of Sister Anne of the Nativity, who was presumably in the attitude of Mortification and delivering the Osculum Obscaenum; the lower half of Natas, for enclosed within a symbolic Matrix could be seen the Golden Rood, the phallus tip of Set the red-haired ass, entwined by the Kissing Serpents and above that the lower teats of his pendulous, female breasts; a Hand of Glory which in reality was a Tracing for the Fixing of His Mark; a serpent embracing the Phoenician Cross; part of the Cabalistic Metamorphosis as divined by Jean de Nynauld; and, also visible, some of the Sixty-Nine Acts of Obscenity for Novices — and other Instructional Tracings.

Painted on the back of the door was a faded and blistered representation of Harpocrates attended by gesturing Enariae. She held The Great Mirror of The World in her right hand and The Book of The Twelve Gates in her left. To signify her Divine Marriage, she wore a brilliantly coloured, obscene girdle about her waist, inscribed Sponsus et Sponsa, with the appropriate configurations detailed below.

Finally, attached to the centre of the ceiling was a Tracing Board from which the paint had flaked off long ago, leaving only the spongy gesso visible. Presumably, as in other Nevocs, it was used — when the Tracings were discernible — for a Tenth Degree Ritual of The Five Heavenly Ways, which had not been attempted for very many years; not since "Esbial", one day in May 1960, had undertaken The Five Heavenly Ways in order to bewitch Stanley Bowden. And it is in this bizarre setting "Esbial" writes in detail of the ritual she undertook.

MAY DAY (1960)

GROTTO DELLA MAGA

is the legend carved into the lintel above the door.

Glancing up at the familiar words she folded her hand into the form of an obscene fig and rapped her blanched knuckles on the door. Nine times.

— O Natas, it is Esbial, Daughter of Asmodeus, begetter of Gadon. She seeks Rosier, Second in the Great Order of Dominions; Adversary of Basil.

And Esbial made the sign of the Horned Hand.

— It is Esbial, begotten of Belphegor and Astaroth. She seeks Rosier of the Second Hierarchy, O Master of the Five Ways. She is messenger of Iuvart, Prince of Angels; Olivier, Prince of Archangels; and of Belias, Prince of the Order of Virtues. It is Esbial who craves admittance to the Great Temple of Abaddon.

And she slid the bolt from its mouldy housing.

— In the name of Carreau, Prince of Powers and of Carivean, Prince of Powers; of Oeillet, Prince of Dominions; of Verrier, Prince of Principalities and of Uriel and Achas, Esbial begs a Revelation of Rosier.

Again, she knocked upon the door.

— It is Esbial who stands without seeking admittance in the names of Easas, Celsus, Acaos, Cedon, Zabulon, Naphthalim, Cham and Sabulon.

Esbial started, as if pricked, and pushed against the door with her right hand.

— In the name of Baphomet, I command the Adversaries Martin, John the Evangelist, Bernard, Vincent and Vincent Ferrer — she kissed her thumb in acknowledgement of his Brothel Code — Peter the Apostle, Barnabas, Bartholomew, Stephen, Basil, Francis de Paul and Lawrence to resist their entreaties forthwith lest they might peril John the Baptist to Eternity.

The door, groaning, swung slowly inwards; opening. An overwhelming stench streamed out of the room and into the passage; enveloping Esbial in a fetid draught. Inhaling the stench through her dilated nostrils, Esbial filled her lungs and made the Sign of Invocation.

— O Beelzebub, Prince of Seraphim and Second only to Natas; O Leviathan and Asmodeus. O Balberith, Prince of Cherubim. O Astaroth, Prince of Thrones, Esbial, Foremost Concubine of Natas, enters Thy Holy Temple to perform Thy Will.

So saying, she entered the darkened room; taking great care not to trip over the raised step. With great difficulty, she closed the door behind her; bolting it from the inside.

Standing perfectly still in the damp blackness of the Temple she rummaged about in her leather sling bag until she found a box of matches. Fumbling out a match, she scratched it against the side of the box, holding it away from her when it suddenly flared, and, in its flickering light, peered down at the stone floor. Seeing a stub of yellow candle near to her right foot, she bent down and lit it with the almost spent match. The wick of the candle, bent and glowing, crackled and turned blood-red before it burst into flame and sent, streaming from its wavering tip, a thin wisp of black smoke. Giving a pained cry, Esbial dropped the match, rubbed the tips of her burnt fingers and looked about her in the flickering gloom. Making the obscene fig with her folded hand, she showed it to the room and charmed away the latent spells which might have been lurking in the darkness of the Temple.

Standing in the gloom, shivering from head to toe as the icy damp chill of the Temple needled its way through her clothes, Esbial, wriggling her shoulders in an attempt to create some warmth about her, cast her eyes over the familiar scene and shuddered; raising pimples on her goosed flesh.

She must hurry.

Removing her earrings, her watch and ring, she dropped them into the side-pocket of her leather sling bag. Stooping and lifting the hem of her skirt, she released the buttons of her suspenders and, rolling down her stockings, kicked off her shoes and drew off her stockings. Curling her toes on the damp flagstones and tensing them against the sudden chill striking into the soles of her bare feet, she gathered up the hem of her woollen dress in her hands and drew her frock off, over her head. After she had folded it carefully and placed it near the door, she laid her stockings on top of it. Puffing and blowing and giving involuntary shudders, Esbial removed her suspender belt, brassiere and knickers and placed them neatly on top of her dress and stockings. Completely naked, shuddering and her flesh covered in goose pimples and blanched, she rubbed herself all over vigorously before squatting down by her leather bag.

By the poor light of the candle, which was still flickering uncertainly in the draught streaming in under the door, Esbial loosened the tie-strings of her leather bag and began to take out the paraphernalia she had brought with her for her Magnum Opus.

Taking out a very small apple wrapped in a soiled handkerchief, she looked down at her fattened thigh and scratched what looked like the inflamed impression left by a tight garter on her right leg. Then, with care, removing them one by one and placing them to one side on the stone floor, she took out of her bag six small cakes which were still warm and moist and which contained the finely chopped hair from under her left armpit. Next to these she laid a bent penny wrapped in a small piece of bright blue cloth sealed with wax. Onto the material Esbial had sewn a long piece of green ribbon, forming a loop through which she could pass her head. Straining open the bag, she manoeuvred out a clear, plastic luncheon box in which two live toads regarded her with large, yellow eyes through the driblets of condensation clinging to the inside of the plastic box, while the soft underside of their throats puffed feverishly as they struggled to breathe. Esbial held the box up to her face and made little chucking sounds with her tongue and tapped the box with her nails as if the toads were pets who understood her show of affection. Placing them on the floor, she drew from the bag a twist of newspaper which she carefully unfolded, revealing a tiny shrivelled thing, the size and colour of a small mushroom. It was a swallow's heart onto which Esbial had sewn an elastic band.

Rubbing her purple haunches with her bright red hands, she glanced down at her erect nipples. She shuddered and her body hairs rose; pinnacling the hillocks of her goosed flesh. Sniffing, she delved into the bag and carefully withdrew a fragile clay image loosely wrapped in cloth, which she removed before laying the image alongside the swallow's heart. Taking a small newspaper package from her bag, she quickly stripped off the layers of paper and revealed a tin. Turning her head aside and pulling a face, she struggled off the lid. Inside was an image in such a state of putrefaction that the wriggling maggots were already beginning to destroy its shape. Pushing the tin away from her as far as possible, Esbial fanned her hand in front of her pinched nostrils to dispel the objectionable odour. Her eyes watering, she put her hand back into the bag and withdrew the neatly folded cloth of her Regalia. After placing it on the floor, she rummaged about the inside of the bag and grunting, removed from it a small length of loosely woven flax rope and a tiny tin, labelled Imp Cough Drops. Having satisfied herself the bag was empty, she struggled to her feet and, having painfully straightened her legs, began to rub her white knees. Relieved to feel the glow of warmth returning into them, she stood up and knuckled the sides of her body.

Still rubbing herself, she walked over to the remains of the pentacle chalked on the floor in the centre of the Temple and, with her bare feet, scuffed out the unreadable symbols. Seeing a lump of pure chalk about the size of her fist lying against the altar, she picked it up and went back to the centre of the Temple.

Seemingly lost in thought, Esbial stood for a moment, her fingertips pressed against her nostrils, and then, stooping, drew a pantagram on the floor. Round this, when she had finished, she drew a circle. Then, beginning from the Fifth triangle, she laboriously began to write anti-clockwise round the outside of the circle the following Mystery of Mysteries:

4 6 3 8 A B K 2 4 A L G M O R 3 Y X 2 4 8 9 R P S T O V A L

She inscribed another circle round this and began to describe the pentagram. By using the appropriate Ritual Symbols, as laid out in The Book of Law, she reduced four of the triangles to The Elements by division and identified each one with a symbol pertaining to her intended Opus — all of which were contained in the Gnostic Book of Foundations of 666. Having done this, Esbial identified and described the same four, plus the remaining one, as Universal Matter. Finally, and satisfied she had not made a mistake, she transfigured the completed pentagram, using a Theban alphabet; set up the Corner Stone and designated her Opus accordingly.

Crouched over her Tracings, still shivering and her gristled knees glowing stark white and contrasting with her blue and purple legs, Esbial related her Magnum Opus to the day — it being the Nineteenth Year of the Aeon of Horus, the Sun being in Twelve Degrees of Aries and the Moon in Seven Degrees of Libra, and underneath inscribed the legend

E R A   V U L G A R I

The pentacle completed, she stood with difficulty and spent a whole minute rubbing and slapping her body.

Warmer, but constantly sniffing back a thin, streaming mucous which threatened to drip from her nose, Esbial got down on her knees again and drew two more pentagrams behind the main one and enclosed them within Circles of Mystery. Because they were so much smaller and were sympathetic to the main pentacle, she described them briefly. Even so, it took a long time and when she struggled to her feet she grimaced with pain when she tried to straighten her numbed legs.

Rubbing and pinching her flesh, she wandered about the Temple gathering up off the floor the variously-sized black candles which were still long enough to be used again. When she had sufficient, she placed a candle on each of the points of the three pentagrams she had drawn. Having no Sacred Light from which to light the candles, she walked over to her Regalia, unfolded it carefully, and revealed a new, long, black candle. This she placed within the Main hermetic Pentagram.

Determined to get warm, Esbial slapped her arms round her body and pummelled her flesh with her knuckles, so furiously that her loose flesh trembled and her breasts juddered. Blowing and puffing, she continued for several minutes. Giving a last determined rub to her painful, hardened breasts, she stooped over her Regalia and picked it up.

Her Regalia was in the form of a small apron. She tied it round her waist and adjusted it in front of her. It was made from a square of light blue, watered silk and was lined with white velvet. There was a lozenge-shaped opening in the front, representing The Residual of Virtue, which was heavily embroidered round the edge in Gold, Silver and Red. From it were five similarly embroidered igneous radiations. The two sides of the apron, which did not extend round the flanks, and the bottom edge, which reached down to midway on her thighs, were heavily encrusted with embroidery but contained within a free-running margin, beginning on the right and finishing on the left, the symbols of The Mystery of Mysteries. Esbial, being of The Tenth Degree and an Adept, had the Seven Sisterly Symbols pinned or sewn to her apron: the prime orgiastic, wry-necked bird with spread wings; The Mystic Rose and Magickal Rood; The Divine Clasp; The Golden Rood entwined by The Two Kissing Serpents; The Lion; The Igneous Eye and her Craft Badge — which was 69 but had only one Black Bar. Having secured the bow behind, Esbial gave her apron a final pat and turning, picked up the small, yellow candle.

With her hand cupped round the flickering flame, she carried it to the Main Pentagram and set it on the floor, as her giant shadow followed her; sliding over the ceiling.

Having to kindle her own Source of Light, Esbial was obliged to pick up the new, shiny black candle and, leaning forward with her legs apart whilst still standing within the pentagram, insert the end of the candle into her anus. She pulled a face as she worked in the end but when she was certain it was secure, she put her left hand through the opening of The Residual of Virtue in her apron and grasped the protruding candle firmly. Still stooping, she picked up the stub of yellow candle and, holding the lighted flame in front of her face, closed her eyes. Lacking a bone dice rosary, she recited to herself the appropriate gnostic psalm, silently dedicated The Source of Light to Rosier in the name of Asmodeus, and lit the protruding black candle. Turning and making sure it was alight, she cast the small, yellow stub of candle out of the pentagram where it rolled over and instantly spluttered out. Holding onto The Source of Light securely, Esbial withdrew it from her anus then, widening her stance, pulled the candle in a smooth, unwavering, continuous motion between her legs and out through The Residual of Virtue. Pleased with herself, she proceeded to light the fifteen candles.

Soon the Temple was bright with flickering light, casting myriad trembling shadows upon the walls and ceiling.

Rubbing her thighs and bottom — for the faint warmth from the candles, instead of dispelling and heating the icy atmosphere, made her feel more chilled — Esbial went over to the scattered charms she had taken from her bag and picked up the short length of soft rope.

Returning to the pentagram, she stood within it and tied three knots in the aiguillette; making sure each knot was tied tightly and, by holding it away from her, each correctly positioned for the particular Ligature she wished to Work. Appraising it, she stepped out of the Main Pentagram and, going to the smaller, right-hand pentagram, placed the aiguillette in the centre of it in the form of a circle; making sure both ends were touching.

Collecting the small tin labelled Imp Cough Drops, she squatted down by the pentagram containing the Ligature. Carefully prising off the lid of the tiny tin, she took out a long, grey hair. Holding it very carefully between her finger and thumb, she placed it in the centre of the circled aiguillette and, keeping one finger on it, looked about for something to hold it secure. Picking up a lump of loose plaster, she placed it on the hair to prevent it blowing away while she fetched the clay image.

Kneeling once again by the pentagram, she tied the grey hair round the neck of the image and placed it within the looped aiguillette.

The image, unlike many nailed onto the wall facing her, was very detailed and Esbial had coloured it in an attempt to make the likeness more striking. It represented an elderly female with sagging breasts, a slight stoop and grey hair. There was only a slight cleft between the legs to denote the sex but great attention had been lavished upon the face and it was undoubtedly a very good likeness of Mrs Bowden.

Stretching with her left hand, Esbial reached over to a discarded clay figure and dragged it across the floor towards her. From it, she took nine pieces of blackthorn and threw the image back up against the wall. Shewing as much concern as if she were threading a needle, Esbial pressed the thorns into the newly painted image of Mrs Bowden. One she stabbed into the back of the figure where the anus would be; one in each ear; one in each nostril; one in the mouth; one in the heart and two she pressed into the genitals. Having placed the image back in the looped aiguillette, she looked down at the assembled pentagram and sighed, drooping her shoulders.

Sucking her teeth, she got to her feet and, rubbing her body, walked to her leather bag. Before she picked up the swallow's heart, she blew long and hard into her purple, cupped hands. Holding the swallow's heart by the elastic band, Esbial cast about by the wall amongst the broken images lying in the soggy plaster; raking over the mess with her fingers. Finding what she was looking for, she straightened her back and carried her find over to the Main Pentagram. It was a clay phallus, in a state of erection; some nine inches long. Standing within the pentagram, she passed it between her legs from behind and out through The Residual of Virtue opening in front of her apron. Almost absentmindedly, she wandered out of the pentagram, trying to roll the rubber band down over the bulbous end of the clay phallus. When she had worked it over the exaggerated rim, she quickly slid the swallow's heart to the centre and kneeling, this time in front of the small left-hand pentagram, stood it upright in the very centre.

Collecting up the six small, freshly-baked cakes, she knelt in front of the erect phallus and, still holding the cakes, leant forward to blow away the dust surrounding it. She let out a sudden and pained exclamation as one of the candles over which she was leaning burnt her hanging breast. She dropped the cakes and, squatting back onto her heels, held her hand over the burn. After a moment, she examined her breast, rubbed her nipple furiously and, still holding her breast, contented herself by cleaning the floor with the palm of her other hand. Giving a tentative blow to remove the last trace of dust and taking great care not to burn herself again, she blew the dust off the cakes and arranged them in a circle round the clay phallus.

Still kneading her burnt breast, she carried the small apple and soiled handkerchief to the Main Pentagram and set them down within it. Picking up the bent penny secreted inside its blue cloth, she slipped the loop of ribbon over her head and settled the charm between her breasts. With her toe, she prodded and slid the tin containing the putrid image across the uneven floor and manoeuvred it into the pentagram containing the phallus.

The image was made from the paste of the Six Bodily Exhalations which had been collected secretly by Esbial over a period of three weeks. But it did not contain any wax from her beloved's ear, nor his tears, although it did contain — as well as the Six Body Exhalations — some of his pubic hair, his nail clippings and some fibres from his tweed jacket. The image, which had been made nearly a month ago, had been buried in the Churchyard of St Peter and St Paul at the appropriate waning of the moon. When she had covered it with soil, Esbial urinated over the spot whilst reciting the gnostic Psalm: "Lord here is my beloved." The image lay buried in the churchyard for three weeks before it was dug up the previous evening. Now it lay in its tin putrid and reeking, alive with maggots; a messy image of a man with an exaggerated phallus.

Turning aside from the rising smell, Esbial rubbed the tip of her red nose with the palm of her hand and, walking to the plastic luncheon box, knelt beside it. Disentangling her earrings and watch, she took from the side pocket of her leather sling bag a pair of gentleman's jockey Y-front underpants. Spreading them on the floor, she smoothed away the creases, unpinned two large safety pins which had been attached to the under-pants and very carefully put the opened pins between her lips. Gingerly, she opened the lid of the luncheon box to take out the toads. After nearly losing one of them twice when it wriggled out of her hand, she finally held them securely — one in each hand. Taking a deep, deep breath, she offered the toads her breasts. The toads, their throats pulsing, turned their great eyes on her and sucked in the much needed air. Bringing her hands together, Esbial manoeuvred the toads so that their hind legs were together and then, holding them securely in one hand, took a pin from between her moist lips and ran it through the fattest part of the toads' hind legs. Hurriedly, by means of the same pin, she attached the toads to the crutch of the underpants. As a precaution, she used the second pin in much the same way.

Relieved, she squatted back on her haunches watching the squirming toads; secure in the knowledge that, however much they struggled, they could not wriggle free.

Picking them up on the underpants, she carried them to the Main Pen-tagram and set them down within it. Looking round her, Esbial realised that all her preparations were complete and that she was ready to begin her Opus.

Nervously, she paced backwards and forwards, up and down and across the Temple floor, carefully avoiding the pentagrams. She crossed and uncrossed her arms over her naked breasts and flapped her hands against her thighs, making the sounds of great waves slapping the side of a boat bellying the waves; and all the while taking into her lungs great gulps of air until her head reeled.

While she paced, her Regalia flapped noiselessly against her bleak thighs and glittered when the encrusted embroidery reflected the flicker-ing candles; sparkling as the apron tossed noiselessly and restlessly. As she strode up and down, so her crutch seemingly became liquid as the pale, watered silk rippled, agitating the eyes and creating an optical illu-sion of movement and wetness. And as she stalked backwards and for-wards, her bare, thick-soled feet padded the flagstones while her accompanying shadows, looming and diminishing over the walls and low, sagging ceiling, looked for all the world like a host of unrecognisable phantoms, rushing hither and thither, escorting her.

She stopped suddenly when a spluttering candle crackled loudly in the tomb-like silence, riveting her attention.

Going to the door, Esbial drew the bolt across more securely and leant an old ash and birch twigged besom against it.

Picking up the lump of chalk she drew a circle round the three pentagrams and thus enclosed herself. Unable to step out of it until her Great Work was completed, she set to and sealed the circle in a Malachin Text; making the circle impenetrable. This done, Esbial placed herself at equidistance from all three pentagrams and shewed her Marks, consisting of a large brown nevus running transversely between her legs, close to her genitals and on the left leg, and a tiny, biro tattoo on the Fool's Finger of her left hand on the lowest joint.

Dropping her apron, Esbial knelt down, resting her buttocks firmly against the right heel of her crossed feet and, with the palm of her left hand uppermost, she clasped the forefinger of her left hand with the thumb of her right and at the same time inserted the Fool's Finger of her right hand into the clenched fist of her left and closed the remaining fingers of her right hand, and the whole she let rest in her lap.

In the attitude of the Rood and Rose, Esbial began to pray.

— Almighty and Everlasting (here Esbial pronounced a Tetragrammaton which, although it superseded the usual Kabbalistic Twelve, is unprintable), whose Kingdom is Everlasting and whose Power is Infinite; have Mercy upon this Thy Nevoc and so rule the Heart of Thy Chosen Servant Esbial that she may above all things seek Thy Honour and Glory and that she may faithfully Serve, Honour and Obey Thee according to Thy Blessed Word; through Beelzebub our Saviour, who with Thee and Asmodeus Liveth and Reigneth, for ever One God, World Without End. Eman.

Esbial remained with her head bowed in silent contemplation for some considerable time before she rose to her feet.

Making strange hopping movements on alternate legs, she circled the three pentagrams in an anti-clockwise direction nine times in order to enhance The Work. Kneeling in front of the small right-hand pentagram and facing The Corner Stone she sealed the Work with the piece of chalk after the Instructions and Manner of Our Lady Rebis — making sure it was complete upon the finishing.

— Bow down Thine ear, O Rebis, and hear Esbial, for she has come to Work Thy Miracle. Give Strength unto Thy Servant and help Thy Daughter Esbial to her Desire. Shew some Token upon her for she has made a Coven and is sworn unto Beelzebub. If Thou so doest she will stablish Thy Seed for ever; and set up Thy Throne from one generation to another. For Thou art The Glory of her Strength; and in Thy Loving Kindness Thou shalt Implant Thy Sister. O Prosper Thou this Our handy-work. Eman.

Having described the circle and closed it with the finishing there remained only the opening through which the Spirit might enter before the setting of The Great Seal.

— Daeh ruoy morf llaf sriah eht dna enots of nrut traeh ruoy ytinrete rof delaes eb sgninepo ylidob ruoy yam Nedwob Evilo.

So saying, Esbial set The Great Seal upon her Work and it was done.

— Such things as are said in the Temple of Natas, Lord of Esbial, shall come to pass and from this shall we know Him.

Crawling over to the left-hand pentagram, she knelt in front of it. Taking some spittle from her mouth with the tip of her Physic Finger on her left hand, she transferred it to The Corner Stone of her Work and, taking up the chalk, began to seal the circle after the Instructions and Manner of Rosier, Prince of Dominions, making sure it was complete upon the finishing.

— Bow down Thine ear, O Rosier and hear Esbial, for she has come to Work Thy Miracle. Give Strength unto Thy Servant, Harlot of Carnivean, Prince of Powers, and help her in Thy Great Work that she may, through Thy Honeyed Tongue and Wondrous Power, conclude her Desire. Shew some Token upon her; for she has made a Coven and is sworn unto Asmodeus. If Thou so doest she will stablish Thy seed for ever; and set up

Thy Throne from one generation to another. For Thou art The Glory of her Strength; through Thee she will do Great Acts; for Thy Testimonies are her Delight and her Counsellors. O quicken Esbial in her Wickedness and in this her handy-work. Eman.

Having described the circle and closed it with the finishing, there remained only the opening through which the Spirit might enter before the setting of The Great Seal.

Keeping the first two fingers of her left hand astride the description and her right hand within The Residual of Virtue, Esbial directed Rosier.

— Rehto on rof seye evah lliw uoy taht dna god gnitnap a ekil reh retfa nur ot uoy esuac lliw erised Pu Gnitae eht nopu taht. Laibse rof ylno erised htiw eslup dna ecnadnuba ni nemes htrof gnirb dna denekciht eb ti yam. Gnorts edam dna denehtgnel eb sullahp ruoy yam Nedwob Yelnats.

So saying, Esbial set the Great Seal upon her Work and, it being finished, she kissed her Venus Thumb.

Rising with dignity, she walked solemnly into the Great Pentagram and, picking up The Source of Light, placed it upon The Corner Stone which she had described to The Great Architect.

Immediately, she stopped shivering, even though the turbulence in the air bent the flames of the flickering candles and it was noticeable that the temperature had dropped considerably.

Very carefully, trying not to miss any portion of her body, she wiped herself with the soiled handkerchief on which was her beloved's sweat and his sperm which she had secretly caught up on it. Satisfied she had covered her body, including the soles of her feet, face, ears and hair, she passed it through The Residual of Virtue in her apron — from the rear, and then screwed it into a ball which she laid at her feet.

Taking up the small, green apple, she polished it on the flesh of her stomach before passing it through the opening of The Residual of Virtue — from the front, and then between her legs from the rear. Finally, with much fumbling and grimacing, her legs apart and squatting, she managed to insert it into her vagina and, once there, retain it.

Cautiously, Esbial knelt down in front of the toads. With her hands resting on her lap, clasped in the form of The Mystic Rose, she bowed her head and intoned.

— By the Matrix of Esbial which is in Hell, Hallowed be Baphomet. His Kingdom come. His Will be done, on Earth as it is in Hell. Give Esbial this day her Magick Rood that her Mystic Rose may Flower. And lead her into Temptation. Eman.

— Almighty Baphomet, unto whom all hearts be open, all Desires known, and from whom no Secrets are hid; Foul the Thoughts of our hearts by the Inspiration of Thy Holy Spirit, that Esbial may perfectly Love Thee, and Worthily Magnify Thy Holy Name; through Asmodeus Our Lord. Eman.

— I believe in The Serpent and The Lion, Mystery of Mystery, and his name is Baphomet. And I believe in One Gnostic Catholic Church of Light, Love and Liberty, The Word of whose Law is Hevhma. Eman.

Esbial made the sign of the Reversed Cross over her naked breasts and with her left hand within The Residual of Virtue and her right raised in the sign of The Horned Hand, bowed her head and remained motionless for several minutes.

Taking the screwed-up handkerchief, she shook it out and laid it over the squirming toads. Picking up The Source of Light from The Corner Stone, she sat back on her heels.

— Let Your Light so shine before men that they may see Your Works and Glorify Baphomet.

She made the sign of The Left-Handed Cross with The Source of Light over the soiled handkerchief and returned the candle to The Corner Stone. With her fingers, she parted The Residual of Virtue and began her confession.

— Almighty Serpent, Mystery of Mysteries, Universal Architect and Divine Inspiration of all men, I acknowledge and rejoice in all my Wickedness, which I have joyfully committed, by Thought, Word and Deed in Adoration of Thy Divine Majesty. I do earnestly obdurate all sense of guilt and am heartily jubilant for these my Excesses; grant that I, even hereafter, may Serve and Please Thee in Lewdness, to Honour and Glory in Thy Name, through Asmodeus Our Lord. Eman.

Esbial made the sign of the Horn and kissed her thumb to show that she had reverted to her impersonal state — having made her First Degree Affirmation — never to reveal, ever conceal, any part or parts, art or arts.

Rising to her feet, Esbial twisted her apron round so that it hung over her buttocks and then, holding in the apple, slowly sank to her knees.

With her elbows in front of her and resting on the floor, the palms of her hands upwards, she rested her chin on the heels of her wrists. In this State of Mortification and in imitation of The Two Pillars, she began to breathe rhythmically. With each deep, long-drawn breath she silently appealed to Rosier to favour her with His presence, and with each noisy exhalation dispel any Worldly thought which might deter his materialisation.

Persisting with her breathing, she sat back on her heels and delivered a lewd and obscene kiss into the Divine Rose which she had hurriedly shaped with her hands.

— ENTER ROSIER! FILL ME WITH THY DIVINE BEING THAT I MAY HAVE STRENGTH TO PERFORM THY MIRACLES!

Going down on all fours like an animal, Esbial began to breathe rapidly; her chest and stomach alternately caving and swelling as she gulped in the air and expelled it through her slack, puffed lips on which her spittle was beginning to collect.

After a while, small grunts began to accompany each exhalation and, convulsed by her rapidity of breathing, she became slowly possessed. Her jaw slowly opened and out of her slack face her tongue, wet and ridged, emerged; protruding, while her eyelids rolled back uncovering the bald whites of her eyes — eyes which seemed to be enlarged and pressed outwards; bulging.

As the frequency of her rapid breathing increased, like the panting of an exhausted dog, Esbial's moan, issuing from the back of her throat as if mixed with quantities of phlegm, rose in pitch and became a continuous wail which went shrieking and gurgling round the Temple.

Caving her back, she threw back her head and, quivering from head to toe, stretched her mouth open as the copious saliva streamed out and ran dribbling down her neck.

With a stupendous effort, Esbial beseeched Rosier.

— O O Rosier reehti otiri esnep esori citasymari yoma adoori kacigami yohtre hatiwa remi ecreipa!

Sensing His presence, Esbial groaned and agitated her hips. — Rati leefori imra! Tiro leefori tiro hara! and she tilted up her buttocks.

— Deifositasi emo evaelori udna gonudo etymo etullopori. Egassaro trayalohi etymo ruocorsi eriseda ruoya fori selacso delochii egrhoto leefori emo teleri. Ecanesse rudoya hat hatiwari ganiebra etymo doolorfo, emo Mori! she gabbled.

Squirming, Esbial raised her voice and shouted.

— Eromari! Eromari!

And she strained; caving her back until, seemingly, it would crack.

— Niaga ereraheti dona ereraheti semit ereraheti niatonacci onaco io!

In desperation, Esbial raised her voice and shouted even louder; fattening and thickening the veins which bulged in the side of her neck.

— REVERI ROFORI GANUDORA YMO XIFASINARATRI. YATORSI! NE-THOTO YATORSI!

Disappointed, because she felt her possession had been incomplete and the iciness in her entrails, which she had hoped would flow to the very limits of her being but which had merely cooled her desperation, frustrating it, Esbial bowed her head down and laid her flushed cheek against the cool flagstones and, totally subject, uttered the two words of The Mystery.

— OVRAMMUAUM.

In unison, the flames of all the candles shrank; dimming, until only their wicks glowed bright orange in the blackness of the Temple. The instant they were snuffed out, The Source of Light burst into flame and sent streaming from its tip a pencil-thin column of bright blue smoke which, clinging, billowed and went rolling about the ceiling.

Esbial looked up and her expression changed to one of ecstasy. Pushing herself up onto all fours, she began to pant violently and buck her body rapidly.

Suddenly, the flame of The Source of Light dimmed and became static; motionless; giving off a deep, dark blue light which barely penetrated to the corners of the Temple.

Esbial, hardly illuminated by this central, unwavering blue flame which transmuted her dull flesh into a translucent blue marble so that she appeared to glow from within, slowed her movements until only the undulating contractions of her stomach were discernible — for she had arrested her breathing in joyous anticipation.

In the silent Temple, now like some satanic, subterranean grotto, an almost undetectable shape passed swiftly in front of the blue flame. Then another. And another; crisscrossing in disorder; slowly filling the pentagram and obscuring Esbial as more shapes jostled and crowded round her, assembling in an agitated preparation for the commencement of The Five Ways.

In the blue gloom they laboured; shuffling their positions while an abominable stench, as if from the soggy middens of Gomorrah or the putrid swamps which rot the base of Monte Leano, rolled outwards from the pentagram like a luminous fog; hugging the damp flagstones. Attracted by this putrid smell, divers worms and slugs and little things wriggled their way up from between the cracks in the loose-fitting flagstones and, followed by all manner of hideousness which had lain coiled in the indigestible earth, turned their blind eyes towards the pentagram and in silent phalanxes crept and wriggled on trails of slime and disappeared into the mist of stench.

The sounds from the darkness were no less spectacular than the beastly shapes which, seemingly coming from nowhere, converged on the pentagram. There was the clap and flurry of beating wings; the constant scratching of unsheathed nails on the flagstones; the grating and gnashing of powerful teeth; the grunt of pigs or swine; growls, a twittering and croaks. Some things squeaked whilst others thumped the ground with their tails. A few barked but all, breathing heavily, and panting, filled the Temple with the sound of a constant, liquid, churning motion.

The Temple, filled though it was with excessive turmoil, became colder. So cold, that the flame of The Source of Light turned to ice and the driblets of damp which had oozed through and run down the perspiring walls, froze; glazing the walls and turning them into sheets of bright glass.

Only Esbial's voice was intelligible. It droned on interminably; express-ive of each Act as she dedicated them to The Glorifying of The Chosen Way.

As the inevitability of Disorder and Chaos presented itself to her; of Blessing her Great Work; of participating in the Assembly of The Five Ways, Esbial began to intone the dedication and manner of her sub-missiveness.

— Esbial setacidedo sithori io esrati dellaco Citsym Esor roti bebeheto Bubezleeb, tatharo buohateri toseyami erusaemo ethoto hetegenelli fori ruoyari Kcigam Door oni yam tefosori tiahos.

— Esbial setacidedo sithori io dellaco Laudiser fori Eutriv roti bebeheto Reisor tatharo buohataro toseyami ecreipera otani io yarevo slewobori donari nowwordo io nia ruoyari marepsi.

— Esbial setacidedo sithori reho hatuomi, dellaci Elbaitasni Nolemahc otori eehato Suedomsa tahet ruohato taseyamoni Ilifo tia hatiwo yehut deesa osi taheto ehas yamo wollaworsi yehut hetganeritissimo.

— Esbial setacidedo sithori reho tafeli denahori otori eehato Naevinrac taheto ehas yamo waredro hetarofurini ruotyo deeso oteni retho seyelo-mino, soratea denai seliratossono.

— Esbial setacidedo sithori reho tahigioro denahori otori eehato Retsis Htebazile taheto ehas yamo ganirabori hetrofonum ruoynis deeso denai ecoreiponii ahatoni gunudum fori rutoyum salewoburim.

Then, in a louder voice before she was smothered, she exhorted them with all the magical strength left to her.

— Nigeribuggari heccatra silohit tarergamm kerowum oso tahetra nil emita hecareth oiyam esil dellifalufoni denar yehut retohaguadel dellifiori hetiwon ehato nemesi fori tahigiledoni. Abecy litonuo tibis hatennuri morafoni rehmun esonno denabali reaho tishosol sexiamo hetiwani yehot deesi denran sebilo neveno noputono rethoi efuganotuum hasilpemoccatii ebahet ehaviffa sayawa!

At this, Disorder and Chaos, in forms which were recognisably human, descended upon the pentagram and set about accomplishing The Great Work.

Above the grunts and groans and cries of painful ecstasy, rose a shouted logorrhea of all the known and unknown obscenities; jumbled and streamed together in an uncontrolled, continuous expression of gross lewdness.

From under the mists of stench which had become blown and wispy and from the very centre of the pentagram, obscured by a great, undefined mass of turgid matter, the consistency of boiling porridge, there appeared the beginnings of a slimy rheum. It came in surging, thickening limp jets which spilled over the sides of the pulsing matter and dribbled down to mingle with the copious extrusions oozing out beneath it; sucking and tacky. At moments, great gashes appeared in the glistening wet matter, like muscled wounds, and there spilt out the same milky white mucous which fell in beaded strings like glutinous spittle.

The gathering pool of rheum, scumming the floor, rolled quietly outwards; steaming, cloying and viscous; adhering to everything as the turgid mass within the pentagram quivered, altered its form yet again and continued.

At first thick, the moving discharge, no longer opaque but pale and translucent like thick water in which was suspended small globules of jelly, changed colour; but slowly, and became marbled. From under the mass and dribbling down over the sides, slim fingers of colour, brown and red, conjoined with the colourless rheum, twisting and eddying, dividing and turning circles upon and within themselves; marbling the terrible discharge and making it seem dense and full of matter.

As this transformation took place, the temperature rose rapidly and the clotted rheum began to steam so that, as the slime condensed, the

Temple was filled with a dense, unbreathable vapour in which it was impossible to see.

From somewhere within the pentagram, a single moan — not the sound of one, lonely voice, but of many, expressing not a moment's anguish but the agonies of all time, in a single, sustained groan of dissolution which, as it echoed round the Temple, seemed to petrify the very vapour suspended in the air — rent the sudden stillness.

Immediately confusion filled the Temple.

Wings beat, claws scratched and there was a desperate scurrying, as of beasts surprised in some act of theft when the bright torch of sudden daylight is turned upon them. Shapes dashed hither and thither, hooves clattered and the hurrying little things squealed out as they were trampled; and all the while a pitiful wail accompanied their frantic haste.

In an instant there was silence.

Complete and utter silence.

And stillness.

The thinning vapour crystallized and fell, tinkling, onto the flagstones, and was gone. The stench rolled inwards towards the pentagram and was drawn down, in between the cracks where the last of the slow-moving worms and slugs wriggled out of sight, and the Temple, as the candles mysteriously glowed bright again, appeared much as it was before; but with two exceptions.

The pentagrams and the descriptions Esbial had so carefully drawn were rubbed and, in places, entirely obliterated — as if milling feet had scuffed the stones and rubbed out the markings. Of the charms not one thing remained where it had been placed and Esbial herself, prone and naked, her arms and legs spread wide, lay outside the pentagram; her apron ripped, soiled and thrown up over her left shoulder. The nevus on her upper leg was bleeding and she was smeared with dirt from the floor. Only the circle containing the three pentagrams remained untouched; a visible demarcation line, respected.

It was intensely cold but Esbial, lying insensible on the flagstones, scarcely breathing, looked flushed and pink and warm. When she stirred, she only grunted, swallowed and changed the position of one of her hands.

Half an hour later, still insensible but her skin white and blotched with blue, she rolled onto her back; murmuring.

Seconds later she sat up and shook her head. Rubbing her face and opening her mouth wide — stretching her jaw muscles — she gave an involuntary shudder. Crossing her arms over her chest, she rubbed herself, sniffed and, grunting, struggled to her feet. Untangling the apron, she looked at the torn Residual of Virtue, sighed, folded it and placed it carefully on the floor near to the door.

Standing, holding her sex within the palm of her hand, she looked round The Temple for the apple. Spying it near to the wall she went and picked it up. Having inspected it for bruises and satisfied that there were none, she polished it with the palm of her hand before laying it on top of her Regalia.

Shivering violently, her teeth chattering, she squatted down in the Main Pentagram. The two toads, pinned to the pair of underpants, were dead; squashed, their entrails burst out of their stomachs. Gingerly, with distaste, Esbial unpinned their remains and, getting up, carried the pants over to the wall where she shook the toads off onto the floor. Turning the underpants inside out, she put them in a plastic bag which she placed near her Regalia.

Palsied with cold, her legs turning bright purple, Esbial slipped her woollen dress round her shoulders and went to the right-hand pentagram. Picking up the clay image of Mrs Bowden, she set it astride a rusty nail in the wall. Assuring herself it wouldn't topple over, she picked up the aiguillette and tugged the knots tighter. Still holding it and straining it across her breasts, she walked to the altar and, giving the rope a final tug, laid it on the floor.

Stooping, and using both hands, she strained at a metal ring attached, by means of an iron link, to one of the flagstones in front of the altar. Dragging the stone aside, she revealed the opening of a well. The well which, in 1900, Sister Catherine F . . . e had calculated was the well used in

1756 by Novec 234 when, in all probability, it had stood in a wood close to the city's west wall gate. Screwing up the aiguillette, Esbial cast it into the well. An age seems to pass before Esbial, straining to listen, heard the aiguillette strike the water. Smiling, she dragged the stone back across the mouth of the well and let it fall back into place.

Her woollen dress having slipped off her shoulders, Esbial picked it up and tied the sleeves round her neck so that the dress hung down her back; warming.

Dusting her hands, palm against palm, she gathered up the small cakes and put them into her leather sling bag; the apple, too.

The tin containing the putrid image she manoeuvred with her foot until it was more or less beneath the clay image of Mrs. Bowden hanging on the wall.

The erect phallus she threw against the wall amongst the fallen plaster and discarded images after removing the swallow's heart — which she put, together with the charm looped round her neck, into the sling bag.

Swivelling on her heel and slapping her numb thighs, Esbial looked round the Temple to see if she had forgotten anything. Satisfied that she hadn't, she lit the stub of yellow candle from The Source of Light and placed it near her clothes. For some reason — perhaps because she was so elated with the success of her Work — she failed to perform The Ritual of Darkness; contenting herself with the snuffing out of The Source of Light and the other black candles with a spittle-wet thumb and forefinger.

In the gloom, while she busied herself drawing on her cold, damp clothes and buttoning her suspenders, Esbial did not see the beady eyes of an albino rat watching her intently as he sat on the rotting altar cloth; his whiskers quivering in agitation.

Dressed, she squirmed her feet into her stiletto heeled, black court shoes, stuffed her Regalia into her bag, pulled the drawstrings tight and humped the bag onto her shoulder. Removing the besom leant against the door, she drew back the bolt and dabbed out the flame of the yellow candle with the sole of her shoe.

At the top of the basement steps, she glanced over her shoulder to make sure she had padlocked the Temple door, turned off the electric light and locked the door with a Chubb key.

Going to the end of the grubby passage, she stood in the orange sunlight filtering through the soot-caked fanlight over the street door and looked at her face in a small pocket mirror. Spitting onto a clean handkerchief, she removed most of the grime from her face, powdered her nose and lipsticked her mouth generously. Feeling presentable after she had given her hair a final finger comb and pat, she opened the door and stepped out into the bright sunlight of a cold, spring afternoon.

Immediately, Erowina was overwhelmed by the roar of the red buses, the intent and hurrying people barging past each other, the raucous posters and the poisonous smell of the city. Determined to feel benevolent towards those who would make her cringe, who would openly steal her confidence out there in the street, she set off with long strides, swinging her sling bag as a warning, and walked homewards, concentrating upon the mouthwatering expectation of toast and tea in front of the warming fire.

Stanley would be coming and she would offer him one of the cakes. Or the apple. If he took neither, there was all the other Magick she had worked. Should it fail, there would be other times, other ways. She was only thirty-three and still had half her life to live. The waiting had been worth it; as long as Stanley didn't keep her waiting too long.

PECTORILOQUY (9.ix.1962)

THE KARDOMA 3 p.m.

S he looks embittered — tight-lipped — can't keep her gimlet eyes still — shifty — probably self-opinionated and mealy-minded — he looks dishy — fascinating — Tammy would make a meal of that word — Freudian overtones Esmeralda dear — poor Tam — if only he'd been an outdoor man — he looks kind and gentle too — mature — wonder what it would be like to be kissed by him — his face is rough and weather-beaten — doesn't look browbeaten — still independent — I wouldn't mind him touching my thighs or something — must be married to her — ten years and you can be certain they think back to back — I'd just have eyes for him — I wouldn't dress like her either — not midday — why do the old wear their mother's jewellery — her fox fur's got the moth — I've never seen a face so plastered with make-up — probably to hide behind — I wonder if he thinks I'm attractive — or is it my frothy moustache — handkerchief — casually — just a dab and a quick wipe — there — nice coffee too — good — chest out a bit — he is looking at me — why not — compared to her I must look like Brigitte Bardot — he's looking at my bosoms — they're firmer than hers — he's probably wondering what they feel like — he'd soon know if I showed myself naked — I'd have to keep my back turned away so he wouldn't see my birthmark — he'd be unable to resist me — probably turn out wrong though — much better the wanting — the having's not so real — the wanting lasts an eternity — the having's too short — they always want to leave — to stay stopped up is an illusion — wishful thinking — they shy away from the eternal embrace — it's always off to find the same different somewhere else — if I was Queen of Siam I'd fill my harem with a thousand men — if only they'd stay still and quiet — filling — I'd remain young and mother what was left outside — I wouldn't feel guilty — fucking's only part sex — Giacopo never understood it meant more when I gave freely — I could have performed just to please but he humiliated me so often — he wasn't loving — Tammy was — he made me feel attractive again and wanted because I was so beautiful — he gave me back my self-respect — it was gentle loving — Giacopo went mad with jealousy probably imagining Tammy and me in situations which had taken force and tears with him — Tammy wasn't like that — and never jealous — nor me — I wasn't jealous of Nesta — I envied her — her way with men — but Adam was weak — he collapsed too quickly — he couldn't see she was unaffectionate — her sole reason for tempting him away was to get at me — it wasn't to prove her over-ripe love for him — but he grovelled for it — and she let him — naturally — you could tell it didn't mean a thing to her — she was shallow and unintelligent — I don't expect they had one sensible conversation together like we had — it wouldn't have taken the whisperings of other men to convince him she wasn't as good-looking as me and hadn't got my lovely eyes and smile and my nice legs — O she knew how to make the best of what she'd got — and didn't mind showing it — like at that party dressed as Salome — she'd seduced most of the men before she'd let slip her last veil — and that ridiculous jewel in her navel — Harry said he'd found two more and was passing them round — she must have had Adam that night — then at the Strand Hotel in January — why an hotel and not her flat like later — it must have been her guilty conscience — giving me all those mirrors in the bathroom -- I often think of him in quieter moments — must mean I miss him in some way — like playing sister to his brother but wanting children too — Giacopo accused me of being barren — if he'd put it in the right place often enough I might have had his child — I expect his pride was hurt when he heard I was pregnant by Tammy — knowing Giacopo he'd have gone straight home to Elsie if he was still living with her and she'd have wondered what on earth had gone wrong with the world when he took it out of her — queer how we all react differently — odder still the compulsion to do certain things — and the guilt — disappointment too — I'm sure Tammy was disappointed because I'd not got a penis he could play with — it never crossed his mind I might be just as disappointed — not that I am — now — it all boils down to the same thing in the end — except for the doom — our bloody eternal wound — I'd wish that onto a man any day and see how he reacted — they either behave in an offhand manner as if it was some trivial thing we'd taken in our stride when it had altered our whole world and think we have lived with it comfortably ever since or else they're unsympathetic and get into a rage as if we were deliberately trying to frustrate them — five days of being reminded of their castration complex Tammy said — perhaps he's right — living with Gloria helped — or did it — God knows — I know nothing — Tammy said I would be the greatest woman of the twentieth century if I could answer the question "Was will das Weib" — he said the woman who answered it would be revealed as a man when they undressed her — but there must be an answer — I'm sure we weren't meant to spend our time painfully swollen easing out the screaming child like Morag's been doing most of her life — yet she's very happy — more like me than anyone I've ever met — not womanly but intensely feminine — Gloria argued the opposite — said I was the one coping successfully with the difficult situations — if that's how she saw me she couldn't have understood — how could she — we all keep things hidden from each other and from ourselves — who'd have suspected Giacopo — the business of the stockings and those damned garters and always wanting to put it up my bottom — to disguise the image of the castrated female Tammy said — I don't see why — something to do with clothes and the way we dress — clothes are the outward expression of hopes and failures — and said my trousers were an attempt to pretend a penis — I asked him why I wore them tight to try and show off my feminine figure if it was just to pretend I'd got a penis — and wouldn't that put them off — he said that's exactly what attracted men — what about the zip down the back I asked, why was it there and not down the front or at the side and who designed them that way in any case — a man of course -- that foxed him — I should think so too — as if I'd spend all that money and time choosing and trying to find a dress which helped my figure and flattered me and made me feel good and had the right effect on the man I wanted or any other man for that matter only to be told all I'd done was to have very carefully selected myself an appropriate penis — I'd rather go about stark naked — daft — half the time we haven't got anything to wear anyway let alone waste time pretending we're men — that was Tammy's trouble — everything had to be explained — he was always wanting to find in the simplest gesture or the most innocent remark some dark motive or reason — and always sexual — it made life difficult — like having to walk on a wafer-thin sheet of glass and knowing at the slightest movement it would shatter into fragments — I cut him to the quick sometimes — really hurt him — poor Tammy — living by himself now Gloria says and doesn't get out at all — he's dirty and neglects himself — he wants to finish his book because he doesn't think he's got much time left to him — poor Tam-Tam — I never could give him the confidence he deserved — he probably hates all women now and will never trust them again, but it's his own fault if he wants to become a hermit — there's no need for it — I could easily have slipped into the same ways if I hadn't taken a hold on myself — and he did find himself a room all right — I've been lucky having the flat all along — that's been a steadying influence ever since I left home — how long ago is it now — must be nineteen years — nineteen years — that's a long time to stay in the same place — but it's been a comfort — knowing it's there — home — my home — a room — womb said Tammy forever rubbing and polishing and wanting it clean and tidy — I like things to hand — pretending he could never find what he wanted — I can't begin work until I'm satisfied everything's in its right place — polishing and dusting — putting off the time when he had to sit down and write — it's a compulsion — my masturbation complex — dusting and apologising like a housewife — it's not the way I'd like to be — as if it was me he was dusting and polishing and trying to rearrange — I don't know how you can live in such disorder — but I used not to — with Adam I spent all my time shining things and dusting in case anyone came — ashamed they might see it not looking decent — I can't think why or when it no longer seemed important or didn't matter and I wasn't embarrassed to be found living in the middle of all the dirt and muddle — I think it was Gloria who put me at my ease — yet Giacopo always insisted everything should be left in a mess — always rowing if he saw me with a dustpan and brush — I think he was the only one I ever turned on and reminded it was my bloody flat and if he didn't like it he could bugger off back to his studio — that shut him up — but he'd never let me rearrange the furniture — don't touch a thing — something to do with the shapes he saw — I'd been wanting to paint that for weeks — he boxed my head for clearing away the breakfast things 'cause he'd wanted to paint them — and always on to me to put up net curtains in the big room — what you put they in the kitchen for — and at the back of the house — it's the front we don't want people seeing into — seeing what we're doing — and I'd gone and put up those lovely red curtains — a gorgeous soft red velvet with a nice deep top frill that I'd paid for out of my own money — for all his artistry he couldn't see the window didn't need anything else — it was as pretty as it could ever be lovely — from the outside especially — inside too — bugger the curtain he said cover the windows with net — always telling me what to do with my own room — expecting they could have their own way with the room as well as with me — perhaps not Adam — he was quiet — at times you wouldn't know he was there — didn't seem to care how the room looked — he never changed things about — except in the beginning — but Giacopo would wreck the whole flat just to get me to leave everything where it was — even poor old Tammy had to have a reason why such and such a thing should be in a certain place — he'd talk for hours trying to convince me why it was so much more sensible to have the wicker chair to the right of the bed — much more practical — when it looked so much nicer by the window where the sun fell on it in the mornings and you opened your eyes and there it was — Gloria understood these things — she could have been my twin — we often crawled out of bed and got dressed in the wrong clothes or made to sit in the same chair — everything was almost too perfect — like living with myself all the time but loving the me she'd become — I hope she doesn't hate me too much — I'm sure she thinks I did it to get my own back — perhaps it's because Stanley's a married man — he's never stayed in the flat long enough to change it — I wouldn't mind — I wonder what his house is like inside — expect his wife makes it look like a dark old cavern — the way she drapes the windows it's a wonder Stanley can find his way about inside — might as well have no windows — poor Stanley — he gets so upset and cries like a child when he can't get it to stand up — I can just hear Gloria chuckling and rubbing her hands with glee if I told her he couldn't make it sometimes — our little Shunammite's not so hot eh? — he-he serve you right — jealousy that's all — but the thought of him going home and getting into bed with his wife makes me depressed — even if he says he doesn't do it any more — was it Pamela who said she'd seen Gloria and Stanley together — or was it a dream — must have been a dream — she may be jealous but she wouldn't be that spiteful — I'm sure it must have been a dream — I don't often dream of Gloria now though — she was the first to call him an old man — he is but it was the way she said it which made him sound ancient — he's only sixty-four — wonder how old his wife is — sixty — she looks older — he doesn't look fifty — his hair is still as black as pitch and he walks like a younger man — Gloria was being bitchy — wonder if he knows about Gloria and me — someone must have told him a thing like that — men don't seem to mind — seems to excite them — think it sensible to fall for a woman — Martin's the exception but at least he didn't become hysterical — some husbands might have — Gloria is fortunate being married to Martin even though she feels terribly guilty — if he'd slammed out of the house or knocked her about she'd have felt justified — as it is she's stuck with him and her conscience unless she finds someone else — anyone who looked and behaved less like a married mother than Gloria's hard to imagine — as for her being a lesbian Joan died twice when Gloria told her — not from horror but surprise — who wouldn't — a woman so feminine with a wonderfully pretty daughter and a good husband Gloria couldn't have been anything other than a female plus to Joan's way of thinking — I wonder how Joan rated me — it must have been an equal shock for her to discover I was Gloria's lover —

who does she think seduced who — probably that I was the weaker and was bowled over by Gloria — Joan's no fool though — at the party she and Harry gave and when everybody was high she pushed her way in between us and said in that thick low voice of hers did we know how lucky we were sticking in square one — what she knows isn't worth trying to cover with a sixpence but she's got that trying habit of uttering thoughtless remarks which always get home with a rush — two-edged often — you can never be sure she is scratching the surface or has her knife in the raw part and is twisting it deliberately — quick to cover up a lie too — has a sensitive insight into others' blind spots Gloria said — I remember her asking me what I did about wanting a child when I was with Gloria — how could she have known — Gloria never suspected — I'd love to have a child by Stanley — when it comes to the actual moment I get scared stiff and get him to wear a rubber — we didn't at first just damned lucky nothing happened — I'll get those pills though and there won't be any of that fiddling around and stopping and it'll be so much nicer without it — I'll go see Doctor Borges — Stanley wouldn't want a baby — it would give his morale a boost knowing he still could — with Gloria it seemed more sensible — less of a palaver — but I still wanted the baby — all wrapped up at the bottom of the bed like it had just happened without me knowing but mine — I don't think Gloria did — she'd got Leslie so why should she — wonder if Leslie ever realised her mother was in love with me — no — a happy little girl — never sulked or got cross — can't remember her ever crying when she came to stay with us — and full of life — running across the park with her kite exhilarating to see her so flushed and laughing and giggling and affectionate and all pink and smiling out of the bath and we rubbing her dry with a towel and Gloria's eyes on me and wishing she was mine to kiss goodnight and tuck up — Leslie didn't seem to prefer Martin to her mother which Gloria seemed to think she did — probably resented their happiness together — and a girl if Leslie had been a boy — a boy would have been nice but I don't think I could go through all that again — pity he died — and that blood clot — thank goodness I wasn't Catholic and them saving him — might have been both of us died — and the nurse all white and starched and smiling and stiff and crackling and leaning over me saying it's a blood clot just below your left knee — I'm sure I fainted — still come out in a sweat remembering — and that's why I've got that varicose — if anything was going to happen it would have happened before — it took three years for the clot to reach mother's brain — or was it her heart — I suppose I was lucky — it still hurts if I do a lot of walking or standing — and Tammy getting me to put my feet up and plumping up the cushions and fussing and wanting to marry me and saying he loved me enough and it wasn't because I was pregnant — and the argument about when it had happened — wouldn't believe I could tell without counting up on my fingers — on the evening he kept stroking my hair — and running his fingers through it — just stroking me — and all over — and over — I would have done anything just to have him keep on doing it — smoothing his hands all over me and stroking my temples and up the back of my neck — and — it was then — poor little mite — he'd have been so happy — a little boy — it would be lovely to have Stanley's boy — I wonder if he'd look like the children he's got off her — his daughters have got her looks — mean — all cramped — the boy's like him but with her pinched mouth — just to have his child even if I never saw him again would be heavenly — I'd call him Coronus and wheel him into the park so people could see how beautiful he was and let him run naked on the grass and show him how much I loved him with kissing and cuddling and let him sleep snuggled up in my bed and feed him my breasts — and — oh how I want a child — Tam knew this feeling we have — then his was born dead and each trying to cheer the other up — but I wasn't going to make another for all his I've got my book to finish but what have you got — I couldn't tell him I was scared stiff so he sulked thinking I blamed him — you're better off my dear Joan said even the cows come spring sleep out under the stars — God knows what she meant but I had a picture of me looking up at the stars with my mouth wide open and tears streaming from my eyes while I lay on the grass slowly filling with joy as I opened myself to surround the baby growing in me — mad — no wonder she goes to see Tuldorfy yet she's the sort who deliberately chose to get married and walked into it with her

eyes open or so she says — then sneers at me — you're avoiding responsibility — sour grapes I shouldn't wonder for all the bragging she does
about the size of her Harry's cock — because he's a dwarf I suppose — Tuldorfy would know if that's why she married him — all girls want to marry
but it's got to be easy when the moment comes for decision — otherwise
it's not love — God I'd marry Stanley tomorrow if he wasn't married — not
that he'd try for a divorce but I might back out when it came to the
crunch because he doesn't love me as much as I love him — I know he
finds it difficult to talk about — the only time he says it is when he thinks
he can make it without flopping — they think it needs proof when a kiss
was all I expected — I wish he'd ask more of me — outside of bed their loving grows cold 'cepting Tammy — only he had his food fads which I didn't
mind but he put me off cooking saying I had cooked such and such a dish
because of my emotional state — at the commencement of your menstrual
cycle you always start showing an interest in baking large puddings and
cakes and insist periodically on baking your own bread even when you
know your last seven attempts at bread-making have been a complete
flop — balls I said — pudding babies he said — then why this urge to satisfy my maternal instincts when it occurs during a period when I'm incapable of conceiving and he shut up — but it was uncomfortable to know he
was watching me so closely and perhaps noting it all down carefully and
using it in his book — his sublimation he called it trying to be honest because he wasn't so proud of his cock as Giacopo was — and was he — he'd
have had an epileptic fit if I'd suggested the soft joy surrounding his erect
cock was nothing but a geat behind which lay the mould of his image
which had first impressed me and into which I was urging his come so I
could have his double within me and eventually about my skirts to be
picked up and cuddled and was all I desired — he'd have vomited to think
it was a deliberate activity on my part — initially that's what my fucking
was — or any of us — an expression of giving not taking something by
force like they're always taking — even Stanley — and no woman could
give herself like I have to him without any thought of restraint and I've
given him presents — that scarf a cardigan tie gloves — the umbrella's the

only thing I've ever seen him with because he's scared his wife might suspect — God knows where he hides them all — I'm not selfish but I wish he'd give me something other than flowers in such an offhand way as if he was dutifully slipping a sixpence under the saucer — and never accepting anything with good grace as if he was loath to take anything from me when all the time he's itching to take the other whether it's in the car or back at the flat — I suppose I shouldn't sulk really — he's no different from other men in that respect and I should know by now he finds it difficult to say he loves me without the additional embarrassment of showing it by bearing a gift — they're all the same — different but basically similar — and all liars if their present loves are anything to go by — from the pleasing quiet intelligent woman me they've all gone over to the loud stupid and demanding as if in defiance of their first love — me — I wonder what Stanley's wife was like in her younger days — when she attracted him — she must have done I suppose though it's hard to imagine looking at her now — once you know what it's all about and how damn easy it is if you can bear to put up with it which I can't just to get your own way like she probably did because she rode about on a motorbike which in her day means she must have been a bit of a daredevil — that's the type she was — never trust them because they're only after one thing — she would have seen he was a good catch — good-looking and tall and young and going to be successful and he'd have been daft enough like Adam to think it was because she loved him — the young fool — he's still like a little boy — most men are — it's because they're no longer ashamed or they're not aware they've regressed in their old age — he's in his second childhood they say — you never hear of a woman in her second childhood — either she's neurotic or they snigger about her spinsterhood or the more kindly blame her menopause and excuse her odd behaviour — as likely as not to spend the rest of her life in an Institution living out the madness men have never understood — when that man masturbated himself like the monkey in the zoo — God — yes — I'd forgotten — Saint Dympna's — they'll never get me in there as long as I live if they thought I wasn't all there like my Aunt — no — men just decline — all their energy and drive ending up under a Sunday newspaper and snoring while the women work off their energy on committee meetings or polishing key holes and the like or lay on their backs finishing myself off while they sleep quickly afterwards when it's over so quickly — a pity men don't have the energy to get out of the flat of an evening to round off the day together somewhere with friends or at the theatre or something — a career woman wouldn't flop out behind her newspaper and keep Saturday evenings for boozing and a little exhausted sex — Joan said certainly not and I can't imagine her letting up for one minute as long as Harry was about or someone willing to listen to all her complaints about him when he's not doing it for her — bitter tirades which are no more than envious outpourings about some innocent acquaintance of Harry's who I don't know why he puts up with her constantly criticising him and everyone else — it's she who's at fault all the time — she'd never admit it if I dared to tackle her — never wrong — I'm sure if I was told I was wrong I'd be only too pleased to admit it if I could be convinced I was wrong so that I'd be right the next time — I'd admit to errors of all kinds — misjudgement shortsightedness or even social faux pas if I had them explained to me — it just happens I rarely make a mistake either intuitively, emotionally or rationally — I'm far too passive and slow in reaction to do anything hastily and have more time to work out a solution — people like Joan are far too ready to precipitate their own mistakes and are adamant in the face of proven truths — it can't be that Joan is stupid — evil yes — making an alchemy of confusion and lies to make others doubt or confess to a nonexistent weakness or fault — like men — they're the worst and more successful because they're determined to lay any blame at the feet of a woman by tricking her and trying to get her to admit to some quaint make-believe error — it seems universal men continually blame us women for all sorts of things — it must be because he's so imperfect himself he feels guilty and that's why he's hostile towards us — we have to be perfect — he makes us his ideal and we have to live up to it otherwise he wouldn't tolerate us for one moment — no man goes around with a woman whom he doesn't think of as perfect — even Giacopo — he must have seen me as his ideal girl — once — he might have been cunning and preyed on me imagining my weakness made me especially malleable hoping he could molten my resistance and cast me in the role of a lewd bitch — poor Giacopo — he failed miserably maybe somewhere there is a corrupted female waggling her bum for the honour of his embrace although I doubt she exists — if she does it's only in his turgid imagination — I must have been his visual ideal of beauty once though — up until the time he realised he couldn't corrupt me or wouldn't willingly partner him in his nasty practices — he'd probably be bitterly disappointed if he met me now and found that after all his efforts I am still the same me — a little older — wiser — confident too and totally unaffected by his attempts to pervert me — of course he'd bring up Gloria and probably say I was two-faced and like all women rotten at heart — that would be the man talking — I can just see his sneer smudging up one side of his face as he said it — I'm sure if he'd have met Gloria he'd have been bowled over by her looks and would have tried hard to make a pass at her in front of me just to get his own back and prove his masculinity — I'd love to have seen Gloria deal with him — it would have been wonderful to have seen his face when she turned on him and in that quiet voice of hers told him exactly why she wasn't the slightest bit interested in men — she'd have known just what to say to wound his pride and masculine vanity and to make him feel as small as a worm — he'd have wriggled for a while even shouted but he'd have slunk off in the end as transparent as his boasting always made him — and he still hasn't got anywhere with his paintings — I can't remember when I last saw a painting of his in any of the mixed exhibitions — he hasn't had a one-man show for ages — if he spent more time working and less preening and trying to make himself look like a young mod he'd get somewhere with his painting and one would at least be able to respect him for that — I'll never forget Tammy saying how nicely he thought Giacopo had arranged the paint on his sweater and jeans — that was so true as to have been one of the cruellest things anyone could have said about Giacopo — yet Tammy never took the slightest interest in how he dressed himself — others yes — he said he could find a clue in their outward appearance which gave them away and revealed the very essence of their person — he didn't care what he had on — I continually had to persuade him to put on something presentable otherwise I felt like a street hawker with a bundle of old clothes over my arm whenever we went out together — never mind — let's hope he gets somewhere with his writing — and soon — he deserves success — and good luck to the woman who manages to get him — if she can clean him up stay adoring she'll have married a near genius — it's a pity if he has really gone queer and stays shut up by himself all the time he's only forty-two and that's far too young for a man to go cutting himself off from everybody like that — I ought to go and see him — when — no — better not — seeing me so happy and knowing how sensitive he is it might upset him — I could get Gloria to go — she's good at that sort of thing and gets on well with Tammy — the last time she saw him she said that he'd made me one of the main characters in a book — she couldn't understand why I wasn't flattered and didn't want to read all about myself — I'd like to know but I'm scared of what he might write because he was always making his women so neurotic and he might have become bitter like Strindberg was about his Siri in his Fool's Defence — so I'd rather not know until people start giving me queer looks — even in our happiest period when he wrote The Straw Popinjay I found it so depressing I couldn't finish reading it — he was irritable for weeks saying I hadn't understood — I did — but he wouldn't explain why he felt compelled to write such misery-making books when we were so happy together and making me feel it was all my fault — God knows what he's writing now if he's shut himself away and is as miserable as I'm told he is — as long as he doesn't dedicate it to me I don't mind — it would be his way of saying he still loved me and that would make me feel terribly guilty — now I'm depressed — why should I be — it's Saturday and I'm seeing Stanley tonight — I feel good — I know I look attractive - I smell delicious or will do and I've got a beautiful dress he's never seen before lying on the bed ready to slip into the moment I've had a bath — I feel sexy and everything's going to be marvellous with him tonight — but I'm depressed — nervous too — of what — it's anticipating things will go wrong — thinking it will be O so nice but feeling guilty — so what — no one is without a feeling of guilt of one sort or another — even father — spent hours at Mummy's grave quietly weeping until Nancy fetched him home to get drunk and falling all over that misery-making house to end up tumbling Nancy into bed — with Mummy dead — and before on the floor — how long have you been standing there — up in my room he would have been surprised to know what that hateful Nancy did to me — and she him — as if being a father is any different — because I looked like Mummy — he said she would forgive him — or turn in her grave I said — and left — it was too late to think of marrying her — a cook — a Nanny she insisted — silly woman — stole worthless trinkets and fled to Brighton to have her heart attack — which is an unhappy but satisfactory conclusion to a most unsavoury and obsessive relationship he wrote — come home and look after your father who misses you — or mother — I am not coming — until his illness — and since without strings attached if only to collect my allowance — to be paid in cash from now on will ensure I see you at least once a month — or Mathew if you cannot bring yourself to walk upstairs and see your father — who has been less than kind to me — I — you — and weeping — and him saying there there but not able to wipe away the tears which fell inwardly for all the harm done me by that hateful Nancy and your betrayal of me — your mother — no no — me your daughter who saw — you are a grown woman and know — not what but when I saw — and since — I have become a recluse — but imagine I am Elfreda — and that got him weeping and pleading saying I was cruel and he weak and prey to all sorts of emotions over which he had no control — nor I — but I saw the look of disbelief and had to tell him — which was worse than any confession told to a priest — how Gloria would have revelled in my outpouring — telling everything and demanding he compensate for the harm done to me — how — by having him grovel and down on his hands and knees swearing I could come and go as I pleased or I would lay a complaint with the police for all his filthy activities — known and unknown — thinking I had a black power over him and regretting my use of the library — which was nonsense — I am your daughter — in darkness he said — in revenge — then take it — I will and had to get him to promise not to interfere —

where — under this roof where I was born and where I might find the self I was before you and that hateful Nancy spirited it away — and he agreed with more deference than I expected of a man who I thought did not understand motivations — which shows how wrong one can be — perhaps if I had confronted him sooner — but I have matured slowly — unable to stand my ground — unlike Gloria — when I repeated what Joan had said about her being obviously a man's woman — Erica darling when will you understand Joan is devious and bitchy and went on to explain it was Joan's way of saying I was masculine and that was why she Gloria was attracted to me — which was the silliest thing she could have said but it made Gloria so furious for my sake she went to Joan's party dressed like a man in slacks with flies and wearing a shirt with a collar and tie and her tweed jacket and using her low sexy voice tried to seduce Joan — Joan's laughter went very thin after her initial embarrassment because Gloria persisted with her charade until I was as upset as Joan and quite as bewildered and both of us nearly in tears — the extraordinary thing was for a brief moment I was overwhelmed by the possibility that Gloria was a man — yet it was so unlike Gloria to behave like that — she wasn't ashamed and shrugged her shoulders saying it would teach Joan not to be bitchy to me in the future — and she wasn't — well not so much — quieter — I'm sure she never connected Gloria's behaviour with the remark she'd made to me — still Gloria let her off lightly compared with that time at Aldeburgh when she'd gone back to the car to fetch her coat because the breeze coming off the sea was sharper than we'd expected and I went looking at the shops and that old lesbian followed me — dressed in a grey uniform — St John's Ambulance if I remember — she had nicotine-stained fingers and short grey hair and very blue piercing eyes — Gloria turned on her straight away and threatened to call the police if she didn't stop pestering me — I never felt so ashamed in all my life — Gloria made it worse by telling me I was naive if I didn't know what she was after and ranted on about loathsome professionals who went around trying to seduce any girl who took their fancy — it wasn't long after that we had our terrible row — I'm still not sure how she found out unless she went through my clothes that night when I got back late and she found my knickers in my overcoat pocket and put two and two together — I'd wanted to tell her sooner but delayed so as not to hurt her — perhaps I imagined it would just peter out and she'd lose interest in me instead of ending in that terrible scene — Giacopo behaved like a man possessed but Gloria was from another world and I was far more frightened of her than I have ever been of a man — I suppose if I hadn't said she was getting the best of both worlds seeing she was living on and off with Martin as well as with me she wouldn't have lost her temper — if she'd been stronger I know she would have killed me — it was my own fault — I was very cruel — one day I suppose I'll apologise to her but I've only just about got over the fear of seeing her in the distance on the odd occasion and there are all those long letters she keeps sending me although there haven't been so many recently — I suppose it's wrong of me to tear them up without reading them but I'd only get in a state if I did — I wonder if it was Stanley's wife who found out about him and me and told Gloria — no — she wouldn't know about Gloria — more likely it was Joan — even Martin — he could have seen me in Stanley's car on more than one occasion and slipped his suspicion to Gloria hoping it might be his chance to get her back — she'd let him gather her to him if there was any truth in it — she must have had her suspicions — why go snooping otherwise — as if she didn't trust me and twigging I was up to something — could have been intuition — yet it had to be that one night — all those months of wanting him — being so close to him — knowing it was bound to happen given the opportunity — in the car — I got my knickers off so quickly when he started to fiddle about I might have put him off me for good but he was trembling so — both of us were dying to — what it must have been like in the old days with all those petticoats and things — happens so much more quickly nowadays — speed up even more some say — who cares — what I object to is everything being expendable — it's cheaper to rep lace them than having them mended — most things are made to throw away — where's the sense — women are accused of spending money like water — at least husbands resent their wives spending money — with me it's the women who resent me buying — because

I've got my own and make it go a long way — Joan's bitchy enough to think I use it as bait — bait for what — Giacopo thought he could trick me out of it and thought I was deliberately humiliating him by insisting he provide the money we lived on — even Tammy — with his slow smile pretending surprise when he realised I wasn't going to part with it for the privilege of loving and living with him — he was so disorganised he never guessed he didn't even earn enough to pay for the food — I was soft — he was always so proud of the amount he had earned as if it was an achievement of great significance — never hesitated to hand it all over to me or ask me to account for the spending of it — money never impressed him — only how much drink it would buy — he never asked how much such and such a dress cost — always so pleased it made me look pretty and me happy — Gloria too — never once did we talk money — not emotionally — she was the easiest to live with — never resentful because the other was too demanding or wasn't prepared to give — it seemed natural one dominated the other when the mood was on one and the other willing to be enfolded — at least Gloria understood women are passive creatures and conditioned to surrender by being submissive — two negatives don't make for harmony so one or other always had to be more submissive — and we were intensely happy — wonder whether it would be like that with another woman — never regarded Gloria as man or woman — she existed for me as an emotion — that first time I saw her in the Turkish baths I had a feeling she loved me and I wanted to be loved by her — it was her confidence — and her beauty — it never dawned on me that such a beautiful woman could be unhappy and not know what it was like to be loved fully by a man — how wrong I was — it was strange it happened to us at one and the same moment and that for months we went about thinking of each other — ashamed of our thoughts but hoping we'd bump into each other again — hoping — getting worked up — beside myself — choked with a peculiar emotion like that poor old lesbian at Aldeburgh who was obviously overcome — like Sonia Linton — it was Tammy said she was in love with me — blushed right out there in the street she did — when we were passing — I should have guessed from the way she threw open her legs when she laughed and deliberately exposed her knickers — I thought it odd at the time but never connected it with what she was thinking — it wasn't as if it was a sight which would seduce me — like Judy tried — she was outspoken — not embarrassed — straight out with it over a cup of cocoa in her room — she wasn't aggressive either — just in earnest and wanting terribly badly to touch me — like Sidony to look at — not so ready with her laugh — or openly randy — it was as if she was frightened of men — of them slipping into her — of having it in nice and deep — holding it in there — holding it in — keeping it in — goodness — what am I doing — dishy man gone — three — no — less than two hours — I shall have to hurry if I am to get home bath set my hair get into my new dress and be in the Perseverance by six — tip — sixpence — my allowance is not enough with rising prices — to ask for more means going and asking — please — and acting the good girl I'm not — coming and going as the mood takes me — because I'm a grown woman and please myself — I'm not under any obligation blood may be thicker than water but it's my blood my inheritance my home when I wish it to be and for reasons which haven't got anything to do with my allowance being due — are you what they call deeply disturbed he said — what the fuck's that got to do with you — I'm your daughter and do as I like — play as I like make up for the childhood I never had — you never let me have — and I'm here — what more do you want — but no — he had to move it down into the chapel — the roof leaks — and the rest of my things where were they — gone — like me — but I'm back — visiting — what more do you want — but he never answers — cries — cries — wanting to know if I was living with a man — I could have told him — will — a bigger man than you ever were and I'm meeting him tonight — I am meeting him tonight — he said — sometimes he makes excuses — the council meeting went on and on — and on — and tonight — he promised — it's been arranged — I have arranged everything — but if he shouldn't — he must — if not — I — he must — he's got to — otherwise — I — what — run home to dad — yes — run home — you began — finish it — get it over with once and for all — end it.

For God's sake, Stanley, BE there. Otherwise.

NIHIL EX NIHILO FIT (28.iii.1964)

Erowina — if that is who she is, reaches up, rings the bell, and waits.

She has the relaxed stance of one who is familiar with the ominous door and who knows and appreciates that Mathew will take an age to rise from the stool in his gloomy cupboard and begin his long climb up from the basement; pausing every fourth step to swallow sips of hastily caught breath into a chest awash with sticky fluid and battling with an arthritic hip until he stands on the other side of the door fumbling the chains, bolts and locks in answer to her shrill summons.

Erowina turns her back on the dark door and glances up and down the bright, sunny street. In the spring-like morning, it is luxurious with fresh, white paint; polished Bentleys; Nannies heading for the park with unnaturally quiet, odourless children in sunshaded prams the size of wagons rolling on noiseless wheels; mysterious, aproned maids opening windows to let out the fug of cigars and rearranging ruffled net curtains; confident, tall gentlemen who nose the air before ducking past chauffeur-held doors to gather up their crisp papers, deep in the leather interiors of their sparkling limousines; purring electric delivery vans off-loading their squeaky, wickerwork laundry baskets at the tradesmen's entrances where the dustbins overflow with cut flowers, empty bottles and banquet scrapings; and, above all, luxurious with the hush of wealth.

The residents who pass Erowina keep their heads erect but, narrowing their eyes, screw them round in suspicion and bitter distrust of the raincoat-belted, good-looking woman who stands waiting with confidence on the steps in front of the house sinister.

Number Thirty is an affront to their arrogance and pride. It stands black and medieval in the smart, sharp street; like a warted toad. The house's grimed windows, mantled with soot, the black, mossed brickwork, the bevelled, spiked and weirdly fashioned rusting railings and the sharp, black turrets needling the sky forebode doom while its shadow darkens the street and fingers its way up their respectable, newly-painted façades.

Erowina remains passive and indifferent while she waits. She is so familiar with the large, grimed door, where the soot lies like felt along the moulding, with the greasy finger marks round the pocked bell push and with the dumb, corroded letter box, that she is at ease with herself and, knowing what lies beyond the blind door, feels she has an advantage over the distrusting, suspicious elite who, on well shod heels, click past her on the pavement below while she stands on the second step; waiting.

For them, wealth should be displayed; it was a means of identification; of proof. It meant respect, solidarity, reliability, unshakable superiority and unquestionable morality. To be otherwise was a betrayal; an eccentricity which was a spurious luxury; an outward, indelible, visible stain of the abandonment of ideals and standards and a flaunting of enjoyable corruption. Mismanagement, adultery or a whiff of perversion were only regrettable but understandable lapses which were either tolerated or became effectively suffocated if overlaid with the visible symbols of respectability. In their exclusive coterie, an unshakable loyalty and a sense of historical dominance cemented an indestructible and impregnable class structure which they were prepared to defend with honour at the slightest provocation. But an outward, uninhibited intent, like a Jew emotionally squeezing out a percentage, was an abasement; a complete abandonment of self-respect and ideals. Their gates were never opened to the usufruct who failed his obligations. It didn't matter to them that the owner of number Thirty had a lineage which commenced with the beginning of time, that he was wealthy enough to buy the whole street; it mattered only that he had failed them miserably. So they had cast him out for being inexplicable and for betraying them.

Erowina turns slowly on her heel when she hears the chains being slipped from their housing, the bolts drawn and the latches clicked back. In the widening crack of the opening door is Mathew's green felt apron and his bald, bowed head. He looks up and, as recognition slowly dawns, he leans his frail body against the massive door and drags it wider for Erowina to pass through, into the house.

She stands in the silent hall while Mathew closes the door and fiddles with the locks, chains and bolts.

"Good morning, Miss Emily. Shall I take your raincoat?"

Erowina shakes her head, smiles and waits for Mathew, bent almost double, to shuffle away, down, limping, into the bowels of the house; his breath like a tired file rasping damp wood.

Alone, Erowina stands in the gloom and, cut off from the outer world, allows the silence and atmosphere of the house to seep in through her pores until she is absorbed into and becomes part of the house, and the unreality becomes reality. It is as if she awakes from a dream only to consciously re-enter a tactile world of the imagination; to be surrounded by, and to move amongst dream objects. Unlike Alice breasting the looking glass, Erowina knows what lies beyond, is able to control the situation, the time and the inevitable climax, into a long, drawn out, personal, satisfying subtleness. Her eyes half closed, she bathes herself in silence.

The hall is complex and dark. Closed doors guard impenetrable stillnesses sealed with smothering, clinging dust, making ominous the catacombed rooms. A heavily carpeted stairway to her left, broad and majestic, rises slowly, twisting away above her, the walls crowded with Hambucks; vain, glorious, beautiful and forgotten; cobwebbed, opaque with grime, mildewed and rotting; their dead faces disintegrating in a second and final death.

Erowina somnambulates to the foot of the stairs, scuffing the friable, dust-filled carpet while a tap drips rusty water into a minute porcelain bowl secreted in a dark, cold alcove somewhere behind her. Enclosed by the eyeing Hambucks. Erowina sees herself ascend against a background of the jigsawed dead while, dustily mirrored, she rises to her own image;

reduced to a small, grey, defenceless being. The ghosted, pocked reflections, moving with her, accompany her silent tread, stare back, miming each tired gesture, peering from another background, another age; gesticulating, mute; aping her trance while she climbs the stairs. When the stairs turn, the images fall away, retreating into their grey, complicated labyrinths and a second, Gothic hall, vaulted in darkness, spires above her head; cluttered and crowded with more Hambucks. Their pale, bleached faces, cracking, gathering dust, wrinkling with dryness, stare out of their gilt paradises; reminders of human frailty, of wasted endeavours, of long, busy lives reduced to a fraction of time, and then discarded. Instinctively, Erowina looks at a fragile, sad-eyed woman who sits wilting, defenceless; the brittle image of hopelessness; and thinks of herself relegated to a similar high, dark corner, laced in by the busily spun cobwebs. She sighs and, having reached the first floor, turns to her right; wiping away a cobweb which nets her face.

Walking down a broad passage, she restrains an impulse to run her fingers along a marble-topped bureau and gather on the tips of her fingers a soft, clinging scoop of dust; recalling her footprints on the library floor when, eight years previously, she had ventured down into it only to discover that her footprints still remained as visible depressions in the grey dust. Noting that the ornate gilt clock on the bureau, whose hands have fallen to half past six but whose hidden wheels still grittily tic-toc, is in its usual position, she walks towards the large double doors.

Grasping the cold, brass doorknobs and feeling the intricate patterning in her moist palm, she senses the weight of the massive doors as they swing slowly open on their grotesque hinges.

The room she enters is vast and ageless. It is as if it had always been, not that it had once been different.

Masking the large windows yellow with soot, darkening the corners, barring the light which presses snub-nosed to the opaque panes in dumb bewilderment, are mirrors large enough to contain the reflections of a complete warrior army, shielded and breast-plated astride their jangling mounts with their colours unfurled and streaming in the wind. Retainers of every image set before them since Doomsday, the mirrors, now filmed and grey with dust, curtain the watcher from his image and reflect only the ghost of his disembodied movements like their sisters, the watchers of the dread stairs, terraced and mazing the stranger's direction.

In the gloom, an even greyness pervades the deepest recesses. Tapestried, upholstered chairs, once ablaze with intricate imagination, squat in the gloom, powdered with thick, grey dust. The pianos, the settees, the tables, the armchairs, the ornaments, the books, the statuary and the ever present Hambucks, high in the vaulted darkness, have the same grey felt clinging and suffocating their shapes. It is as if they are overwhelmed, smothered by a great eiderdown of dust; motionless and immovable; entrenched. Cobwebs, vast as hammocks, fill silently with soot and sag from the ceilings and walls. Impossible cobwebs, strung between ornaments, senseless in their intricate lacing of objects which have become unrecognisable inside the cocoons woven with spidery patience. Incongruous cobwebs which have parcelled the room's bric-a-brac into stalagmites of monstrous proportions, and cobwebs so evenly spun that they hang like the gossamer curtains a blushing, young and home-loving wife might have hung to discreetly veil the inner, raised rooms whose pierced, intricate lattice screening already evidenced modesty. Retiring rooms where one could imagine a young lady, with the delicacy of nature born of breeding, lain on a couch nursing the faintest of headaches or sat picking at her gloves whilst a young man stirred her blood as he knelt at her feet evidencing his love and rising passion. But now, within these rooms, jungled with cobwebs, the couches, their coverlets felted with dust and which crack when they are turned back, silently let drop onto the floor their ruptured innards while greedy woodworms bore and burrow; powdering their homes and doing battle with nightmare spiders. Past the furthest of these latticed rooms are the twisting wooden steps which lead down to the library where each shelf is sandwiched tight with close-packed books, slowly solidifying in the yellow half light. It is an accumulated labyrinth of fused paper, tunnelled and riddled with book tics who suffocate while the settling dust, ingraining, tarnishing and obliterating the wide-backed, once gilt spines, seals them into their morbid ecstasy. Erowina, reassured that the room exists in her moment of time, turns to her left and walks the length of the room on a trodden path, scuffed bald over the years, to yet another door which stands open; rigid on seized hinges which are pocked with verdigris.

The second room is as large as the room behind her and is filled with yet more chairs, sofas, bureaus, tables, ornaments and statuary; with yet more paintings of the Hambucks adorning the walls, all coated with grime and dust and laced together with giant cobwebs. Beyond, Erowina can see through successive, open doors, more rooms, each dimmer, each gloomier, each shrouded in dust and cobwebs, until the darkness snuffs the grey perspective and there is nothing but blackness beyond the stillness.

Erowina hesitates before turning right, and nods her head.

Reclining on a chaise longue, a table near his elbow, is Mr Hambuck, removing, with the tip of his little jewelled finger, some blackcurrant jam which is clinging to the corner of his soft red lips.

Mr Hambuck nods in recognition and Erowina passes him.

He is a large man in his early sixties. His complexion is fresh; too fresh, as if he had just emerged from an exceptionally hot bath or had had a particularly close shave — all over, for he has no facial hair; even his eyebrows are depleted and bare. His bright pink face is soft and puffy; his nose arrogant and pinched; his strawberry lips plump and sensual.

Mr Hambuck watches Erowina cross the room and enter the chapel. Sucking the jam off his little finger, he crosses his legs; baring a naked leg which protrudes from his Tibetan wrap which crackles when he moves; like paper. Sensing his hammer toe squeezed into his exotic sandals, he wriggles his foot and, turning to a shining, silver coffee pot, pours himself a second cup of coffee and picks up the Financial Times in his pink, feminine hands. Before he reads, he glances over to where a photograph in a silver frame, gleaming and polished, stands amidst the dust and confusion of an open bureau. The photograph is of a very beautiful, dark-haired woman who is gazing over her naked shoulder towards the camera through what appears to be an encircling mist. She is Mr Hambuck's dead wife, Elfreda. Scratching his naked forehead with his nails, Mr Hambuck sighs, opens the newspaper and makes an effort to concentrate upon his static shares.

Erowina stands with her back against the closed chapel door and shuts her eyes. A feeling of peace, of being home, floods through her entire being and, inwardly, she glows. Stepping forward, she sits down facing the altar and closes her eyes again.

The chapel is small and has seating for only nine people. The altar, like everything else in the house, is festooned with cobwebs.

They shroud the baroque gilt cross, askew on its worm-eaten plinth, the painted Byzantine tabernacle whose door has groaned open on its broken hinge, and they blanket the dried, yellow candles which have cracked and lean crazily forward on their ornate brass sconces. A Bible, its gilt-edged leaves stuck together with damp and age, solidifies under a layer of dust while a heavy, ornately embroidered altar cloth, tarnished and brittle, sags to the floor, silently rotting and tearing under its own weight. Behind the altar, on the two side walls and covering the ceiling, are hung or nailed a profusion of gilt angels; sealed reliquaries; medallions, crucifixes onto which are nailed the painted, sagging bodies of a tortured Christ; broken, carved, child-less Madonnas; cherubs, motionless in flight with outstretched, trembling, broken wings; limp rosaries; stiff, mute icons; appealing infants with upturned eyes and fat little, well-fed tummies and plump, dimpled fingers — all wired, nailed or hung from the walls and ceiling, as well as sconces; oddments of carving; painted hands and arms; parts of heads haloed in brass; bits of carved and gilded ornaments; odds and ends; all tacked in confusion in an attempt to create the carefully-wrought ornateness of a Mexican baroque church. But the resulting muddle is garish and vulgar, pious and profane; with the idolatrous imagery writhing in mock ecstasy to the Glory of God and smothering every inch of the cobwebbed walls.

Because of the dust it is impossible to tell whether or not some of the objects hanging from the ceiling, cocooned and webbed, are not the bodies of lifeless, mummified bats or that the suspended heads, painted and eyeless but black with grime, were not once the heads of martyrs whose gaping mouths uttered and affirmed their belief before an axe descended and their heads were raised on pikes for the multitude, only to be stolen by the faithful and secretly passed as venerated relics from hand to hand, like half-inflated leather footballs, to be finally wired to the ceiling of this grotesque Aladdin's grotto.

Scattered about the floor, bursting cassocks, lying higgledy-piggledy, spew out their sawdust contents; religious paintings yawn great rents whilst rotting vestments and prayer books litter the skewed chairs and the rucked, carpeted floor.

Only the chair on which Erowina is sat is polished. Everything else scarcely breathes under the centuries of dust and cobwebs; the one bright chair emphasising the years of neglect.

Erowina, after thoughtlessly picking at the cuticle round a nail and chewing off the sore, freed end, rises and, taking off her macintosh, throws it over the back of an over-stuffed armchair which is behind her and which is jammed against a tall cupboard. When she begins to struggle with the armchair and to drag it away from the cupboard, a shaft of sunlight, thin and weak, glows into the chapel, revealing an oval window high up in the wall which is coated with soot and almost obscured by imagery. For an instant, the pale yellow shaft of sunlight, alive with glittering dust, illuminates the gloomy chapel, giving life and depth to the confusing clutter. It is as if someone has spread their hands over the yellow keys of a hidden organ and, in a minor key, played and held an octave of sound; stirring and vibrating the chapel with a resonant, almost tangible, atmosphere. For a moment the sunbeam glows brightly, spotlighting the orange teddy bear sat in the armchair, then dims and, as if defeated, shrivels and retires, leaving the chapel to the cold and gloom. Erowina hopes that the sunlight striking little Mister Piggy-Buck is not an omen; and she heaves the chair away from the cupboard.

The cupboard is almost as broad as it is tall and when Erowina has opened both the doors, she drags the armchair back to it and, turning, sits facing into the cupboard. But the cupboard is not a cupboard; it is a doll's house, some six foot high and proportionately wide. It lacks a front wall, but in every other respect it is perfect.

For the next ten minutes Erowina busies herself with rearranging the furniture in the doll's house, blowing away the dust, making the beds and closing all the doors.

There are four floors in the doll's house; five if the basement is included. A replica of an over-furnished, Victorian dwelling, each room is exact, down to the smallest detail. The brass coal scuttles are filled with real coal; the tiny hair brushes on the dressing room table are bristled and silver-backed; there is real scent in the toiletrie; the piano keys work and the individual books arranged on the shelves in the library have readable titles as do the magazines scattered on the drawing room table; even the tassels on the draperies and the monogrammed pillow-cases are unbelievably accurate, as are the details on the copper and iron utensils in the basement kitchen where each hammered rivet is exact. There is nothing lacking. One has only to open a cupboard door and search for a needle box, a thimble or an old letter, and they are there; and more besides.

When Erowina is satisfied all is tidy, she stoops down and pull; open a drawer in the bottom of the cupboard. She appears undecided while she turns the fragile dolls over very carefully.

Except for a few wax dolls, the majority, some three dozen if all, have exquisite china hands and faces. They are all about nine inches high. Each doll is wigged and the females have rosy cheek or are wrinkled to look old. The men are whiskered with heavy eyebrows. All the dolls are dressed in clothes dating from about 1880 and the details of the jewellery and the contents of their individual pockets are as exact as patience, a keen eye and delicate needlework will allow.

Erowina discards a gentleman in a brown Biedermeier tail coal and selects another dressed in a very dark, high-buttoned frock coat and matching trousers. She removes his top hat and stanch him in the hallway of the doll's house, as if he had just entered hanging his hat on the ornate hall stand. Bending over the drawee again, she removes a doll wrapped in tissue paper. Slowly and lovingly, with the greatest of care, she removes the wrappings to reveal an exquisitely-made young girl who is wearing a dazzling white, muslin ball dress which has a flounced skirt and sleeves.

The young girl is carrying a posy of flowers and round her neck is hung a locket in which is a curl of blonde hair. After Erowina has re-arranged the doll's skirt, she seats her on the largest chair in the first floor drawing room and props an open magazine on her lap. Lastly, Erowina takes two female dolls from the drawer. One represents an ageing but beautiful woman whom Erowina puts in the large double bed in the master bedroom; pulling the bedclothes up to the doll's chin so that only her pale face and hair are visible. The other doll, which is dressed as a cook and, from constant and rough handling, is much the worse for wear, she places down in the kitchen amongst the bright copper pans; making her look as if she is stood at the table preparing dinner.

The dolls arranged, Erowina closes the drawer, cuddles her orange teddy and begins to play.

The downstairs door slams and the young girl puts aside her magazine and hurries down the stairs to greet her father. His coat removed, his daughter drags him, protesting, upstairs. In the drawing room, the father stands with his back to the fire.

'Don't I get a kiss?'

They kiss.

'And a hug?'

They hug.

'Come, sit on my knee.'

She straddles his thigh.

'And who is it Father loves?'

'Me.'

'You are his favourite. What are you?'

'Daddy's good girl.'

'Can you keep secrets?'

'I'll not tell.'

'Good girl.' And they embrace. 'No harm will come of it. It's Daddy's way of showing he loves you. What is it? '

'Daddy's.'

'Good. Gently, then.'

The slovenly cook puffs her way up the stairs from the basement and, without knocking on the door, enters the drawing room.

'What's all this, then? It's time you were in bed, young madam.' She tweaks Emily's ear. 'Bed is the place for you,' and she hustles Emily out.

Stood on the landing, the cook points.

'Up.'

Emily stands her ground.

'Do you want me to paddle your backside? Up. I'll be with you in a minute.'

Emily climbs the stairs towards her attic bedroom.

Looking over the banisters, she sees Nancy open her mother's bedroom door.

'You asleep? '

There is no response from within.

Nancy closes the door quietly and labours up towards Emily's bedroom.

'Why aren't we in bed? Get into bed.'

Emily snuggles down under the bedclothes and Nancy settles herself.

'Once upon a time . . .'

'When I'm older . . .'

'Yes, dear. Hush. Once upon a time . . .'

'There will just be Daddy and me.'

'Yes. Yes. Go to sleep. Once . . .'

'He said so.'

'Did he now? Did he indeed? '

'Yes.'

'Then you're in for a big surprise, young woman. Now. Once upon a time. Are you turning on your stomach? Oh, very well.' And Nancy withdraws her hand. 'If you can get to sleep without me . . . So much the better. Goodnight.'

Nancy tiptoes from Emily's room, down the stairs and past Elfreda's bedroom; on towards the living room.

Mr Hambuck places his hand on Erowina's shoulder.

"Do you want a torch?"

Erowina nods and Mr Hambuck goes off to find one.

In the darkness, Emily, having woken with a start, crawls out of bed and, sucking her thumb, gropes her way down the darkened stairs towards her mother's bedroom. The chill night air strikes chill through her thin nightdress.

'Is that you, Sidney?'

'It's me, Mummy. Emily.'

Emily fumbles her way to Elfreda's warm bedside.

'Emily, I'm dying. Fetch Daddy, will you? And give me a kiss.'

They kiss.

'Now hurry, child. Hurry. And turn on the light.'

"This isn't very bright. It needs a new battery."

"Thank you."

"One day, I'll get someone to rewire the house."

"Yes."

"Yes."

'Are you going, Emily?'

"It's nearly eleven o'clock and I've got an appointment at one."

'Hurry, child. Run to your father and tell him . . .'

"Will you be here when I return?"

"Go away."

'Mummy . . . ?'

' Emily, I . . .'

"Emily!"

She tiptoes to the bed and feels for her mother's silent face.

'Mother?'

Her mother's mouth is open. Emily feels inside it.

'Mother?'

Silence.

'Mother!'

She runs to the door.

'Daddy! Mummy's dead!'

But Daddy's bedroom is empty.

'Daddy!'

Running downstairs, Emily races towards the brightly-lit crack of the partly opened drawing room door.

'Daddy! Mummy's dead!'

No answer.

She pushes open the door.

In the brightly-lit room, cook rolls over onto her back, closes the lid of her one good eye and opens her legs wider.

Erowina kneels.

Emily stares.

And she goes down on all fours.

'Daddy, Daddy!'

Exposed, the draught strikes chill.

"I said, stop it."

'Daddy, Daddy!'

And Emily, with her small hammering fists, pounds cook's face; crushing the red, explosive laugh and crazing the enamelled cheeks.

"What are you doing?"

Pummelled, the split head falls in half like a broken coconut and cook's one good eye drops from its socket and falls into the back of her empty skull.

Her anger unleashed, Erowina crushes the breaking face into the carpet; grinding it into the dust.

"Stop it ! I said, NO," and Erowina tries to twist from his clutching.

The furniture rocks and a single chair topples, losing its seat.

"Elfreda. Please. PLEASE!"

A blackened dove, its wings wired in full flight, swoops from the ceiling and into the drawing room.

Emily screams and Nancy, clawing down her clothes, runs into the chairs; upending them and scattering the cassocks.

"What's got into you? STOP IT!"

Another chair crashes and splinters under her weight.

'Daddy, Daddy.'

And tears begin to course down her face, clearing channels through her dirty cheek pressed into the carpet as she sobs dust into her mouth.

'Daddy. Daddy.'

SLAP.

'Nancy! Come back!'

"Hold still."

Burdened, she crawls towards the altar and tries to haul herself up. But the cloth tears under her crabbing hand and from the toppling tabernacle a tinkling bell clatters to the floor, followed by a shower of dried Eucharist wafers which confetti her hair, like cornflakes.

'Daddy. Daddy.'

A dull black, once-silver cup falls, striking her elbow, and dents; its yawed lips crusted with dried wine as dark as blood.

"NO, Daddy, NO!"

And she makes a grab at the crumbling wood of the altar as her skirt rents.

'Daddy. Daddy.'

As she heaves herself up, the altar groans and begins to collapse sideways; tugging the cobwebs. Emily falls across it screaming as it crashes to the floor, powdering and filling the air with a swirling dust.

"Oh, Elfreda, my love. My love."

'Daddy, Daddy.'

With cobwebs streaming from her hair like a bridal veil, Erowina, looking for something with which to strike the beast fastened onto her back, drags herself towards an iron crucifix.

"I only want."

'Daddy. Daddy.'

'You're hysterical, child. Stop it!'

SLAP.

An angel, a nail through its throat, falls with outstretched arms; striking her in the middle of her bared back.

Cowed amidst the softly falling cobwebs, a froth fills her mouth and bubbles from between her clenched teeth. Gripping the crucifix, she twists and strikes at what she cannot see.

"God — HELP me!"

And He obliges.

But it is too horrific.

The walls slowly bulge and the ceiling sags. As dislodged ornaments begin to fall one by one, she protects her head with her crossed arms and awaits the disaster.

It comes with a roar as the walls and ceilings collapse inwards; showering her with loose plaster and centuries of jumbled bric-a-brac.

Obliterated, the two figures embrace in the holocaust of rubble and thickening, dense dust.

"Good God, deliver us . . ."

Grimed, in disarray, her cheek pressed to what had been a rose-patterned carpet, she peers through the settling dust while her spittle falls, stringing and glistening; to be absorbed into the brown, smelling carpet.

Emily, stood in the doorway dressed only in her nightie, gazes at Erowina in mute recognition. Erowina smiles back.

Why not?

The heat and the smell rise warmly in shaming familiarity while Sidney roots for the hard-edged stone with his tongue and, desperate with greed, breaks open the peach with his fingernails.

'Help me, for goodness sake.'

And Nancy's nails fill with juicy pith while her blood-red stone erupts and the hard peach tears.

'Emily? Is that you?'

"No, it's me — Elfreda," and, with her gristled knees grinding into the gritted carpet, she pushes backwards, watching Elfreda, coy behind her bare, rising shoulder.

"Then let me."

Fixing Elfreda with a hateful look, Erowina extrudes her tongue; poking. But Elfreda remains passive, indifferent while Hambuck, under his photographer's cowl, snorts his way forward all of a tremble.

Seeing his inverted, dazzling image framed and pulsing, he bares his tongue as he sinks his fingers into the fat-handled kaleidoscope of his terrible-smelling compulsion.

"Elfreda . . ."

The blood surges into Emily's face, fattening it, and her lips balloon. Pop-eyed, still dribbling, her hair in disarray and dandruffed with plaster, she swallows; oblivious of another avalanche of bric-a-brac sliding from the wall and clouding them both.

Hambuck tries to save his collapsing cabinet and up-ends it before heaving the smothering image into his snorted desire amidst the chaos of the crumbling chapel. But his other need is greater and upon him. Kneeling in the clutter, half obscured by the swirling dust, he directs his compulsion with a guiding hand.

Instead of screaming her protest and trying to wriggle out of his perspiring grip, Erowina looks back at him over Elfreda's shoulder. But it is Emily, smiling, her teeth cracked black and her lips scummed with dust, who slowly, deliberately, fattens her image; proffering paradise.

Hambuck, gluttonous and trembling, about to enter a pulsating paradise, winking and extruding a smell of dung, hesitates. He looks up, streaked with dirt and perspiration.

"Is that you, Emily?"

And he pitches forward.

Erowina extricates herself and stands.

Hambuck, watching her, turns slowly purple and his feet begin to drum.

Of the chapel, nothing remains; only the doll's house, swirled with dust.

"Sidney?"

Mr Hambuck stiffens, collapses and expires with his mouth open. Lying on the rubble, powdered with plaster, he looks as white as a corpse.

Erowina, picking her way carefully through the rubble, absent-mindedly brushes the dust off her clothes. Picking up a piece of broken, grey mirror, she wipes it with her hand and looks in it to pick the crushed Eucharist wafers and cobwebs out of her hair. Taking off her laddered stockings, she rolls them, finds and shakes out her macintosh and puts the stockings into the pocket. Twisting her split skirt, she tucks in her blouse, slips on her macintosh and draws the belt tight. Satisfied, she turns and looks about her.

Spying the orange teddy bear, she picks it up and steps over the purple-faced Hambuck, lying on his back, dead. His gown is in disarray; opened, revealing his small sex which is slowly hardening: rising up against his hairless stomach.

"Poor Piggy-Buck. Poor little Piggy-Buck."

Leaving the chapel, she wanders into the room adjoining. Absent-mindedly picking up the remains of a piece of half-eaten toast spread with blackcurrant jam, she bites into it and looks across to Elfreda.

"Bitch," and she turns the photograph face downwards. Swinging the teddy bear, she runs through the rooms and hurries down the stairs.

In the hall, Erowina struggles with the tap until a trickle of rusty col-oured water runs into the dusty bowl. Wetting her handkerchief, she dabs and wipes her face clean while she looks in a tiny pocket mirror. Having lipsticked her mouth generously, snapped shut her handbag, she walks to the street door and starts to fiddle with the locks and bolts.

"Going so soon, Miss?"

"Yes, Mathew; but I'm locked in."

"This is the lock, Miss. Just turn it, like this, and it opens the door."

"Thank you, Mathew. There are so many, I don't see how you remem-ber which one to turn. I was beginning to panic when I found myself locked in."

"We wouldn't want anybody thinking we tried to lock you in, Miss. They're for locking people out. Nobody likes being locked in."

And he unlocks the door for her.

"Thank you, Mathew. Goodbye."

"Good day, Miss Emily. Miss Emily!"

"Yes?"

"Your father . . . I have been in his employ for . . . Since you were this high. And . . ."

"Yes?"

"Nothing."

"Goodbye then, Mathew."

"Good day, Miss."

"Goodbye."

In the taxi, Erowina, disturbed and feeling contaminated, "I am the disease, not the diseased," formulates a conclusion.

"Pardon, Miss?"

"What?"

The taxi driver faces his front.

"You said?"

"Did I? I was thinking aloud. Reminding myself to have a bath when I get home."

"Yes, Miss."

It would be a ritual cleansing. A ceremony. It would be akin to an absolution.

"Do you know where one might secure an abortion?"

"Miss?"

Why bother. They declared her gonorrhoea cleared but requested she return for further checks. "And it would help us to know your contact." But there are other forms of revenge.

The fare paid, Erowina tips the contents of her purse into the taxi driver's gloved hand.

"Honestly, Miss, I don't know. I'd help if I could."

"Would you?"

"They do say if you drink gin and take a hot bath . . ."

"Really?"

"So I've heard tell."

"Have you also heard tell it is less painful if you cut your veins under water?"

The taxi driver watches the raincoat-belted, good-looking woman let herself into number ten and looks up to the windows tightly curtained against the pale mid-morning light. He gears into first and U-turns his taxi, unaware he is carrying a non-paying passenger, Mister Piggy-Buck, the orange teddy bear, sat on the back seat grinning.

SPECIFIC (MAUNDY THURSDAY, 1964)

Miss Emily Hambuck wipes the condensation off the mirror
>   where nubile Nesta, ogling Adam, compensates her guilty infatu-
>   ation with impulsive generosity and, forsaking her naughty ways,
>   donates a millennium of reflected attitudes-cum-caresses, fired in
>   the kiln of her lonely flat
with her soiled knickers
>   Scamel waits in his white-walled, cubicle womb, exhausts the bone-
>   dry jet of his excitable imagination and balls the black-laced, elast-
>   icated bandage
and throws them
>   with a satisfactory left-handed green bullseye
into the basket.
>   A rubiginous moth claps its dusted wings and settles upon the offer-
>   tory while Omm, receiving the obligations from the mahogany altar,
>   goes creaking and slippered into the apse.
She glances at herself
>   seeing a Holy Hambuck ghost revealed as a bloodless penitent of
>   mostly odoriferous putty
in the full-length mirror
>   where scrubber Nesta, kneeling to the hospital floors down under,
>   attitudinises the supplicant woman from Magdala
and begins to sort through her discarded clothes.
>   Mary Anna Portabella, forever fingering soiled snips, bemoans His
>   passing while she darns dead holes and counts the missing flies.

She throws her stockings,
>   into the fairy wind where dandelion wishes seed; snagging the
>   creaking willow
brassiere,
>   moulded to the blessed bread fruit which chime Agatha's passion,
>   dished for the noble, gluttonous Quintian.
vest
>   chasuble, alb white and crutch high for summer
and jumper
>   of Dalmatian wool, tunicled
into the basket.
>   Old Ma Mead's bending corsets creak when she kneels reverently in
>   the silent aisles of black bottles, snug in their Gothic recesses, her
>   eyes searching the iconic labels.
She inspects her skirt, folds
>   the starched stiffness of the parcelled winding sheet, dampened by
>   droplets of water from Nancy's flicking fingers to await the steam
>   under the creasing iron, soot wiped when the spit bobs, bouncing a
>   crackling dance, shrivel and the flat apples her hot cheeks just so
and puts it on top of the basket.
>   The Divine malt-fat mice prick their ears and petrify on the cornices
>   of the barrel vaults while the creaking candle below them in the
>   damp crypt, goes muttering to herself, tapping and sounding out
>   the empty shells; marking them with chalk white crosses.
Miss Emily Hambuck straightens her back
>   bent to the ending of the bloody harvest
and
>   one black, dead kidney and the other like Daddy's wrinkled prune
stretches.
>   and the risen Peter flaps his scapulary wings and flies up and away
>   from the murderous hook.
Reluctantly and with a sigh, she bends down to
>   Pazzeroni who gratuitously performs his impulsive liturgy
>   while she intones the rubric on her ten little toes to . . .

pick up her suspender belt
>ridged with porpoise bone to corset her abducted thighs
and hangs it on the back of the door.
>She kicks a side her shoes
>>buskined, red and oak stilettoed
and a shoe horn
>pearl stiff, comely and infertile
falls out.
>The assembly notes the omen and the women amongst them turn
>their flaccid buttocks into the pale wind, hopefully.
Turning,
>knees bending,
she goes
>North
to the wash basin
>shrined and lapping with black, oracular blood.
She wipes the condensation off the oval mirror
>while the stiff hairs prickle the soft inside of Nessie's thighs and the
>heat of the galloping animal beneath her starts her desire, she
>glances over her shoulder at her myopic cobber who, not contend-
>ing her grey, one-eyed horse, manoeuvres his tractor with less than
>an inch to spare
with the palm of her hand
>wherein five weapons have stiffened in mortal combat
and looks at herself.
>"I say unto you, face, that the more I behold you so do you become
>less of a face. The face out of which I look is not the face into which I
>gaze. I say unto you, that I am you. That, thou art me. She, he or it is
>I. We is me. Yet I do not know the I you be, for I am that I am, and
>that is all I know."
Turning away from the mirror
>where A Silent Snow falls in a dead faint; her gaping slackness un-
>sullied but weeping pearls of frustration
she reaches up to the glass-fronted cabinet

ting
and opens it. She takes out a wide white ribbon
    to posy the wife caught goat dressed as lamb for slaughter
and, leaning over the bath
    patiently awaits Bannik's soft palm to rosy her naked back and, in-
    heriting the reaper's relieving, headless skin
peers through the steam
    for Cecily
and inspects the level of the hot
    oak-logged, need fire boiled
water. Turning
    knees bending
to the oval mirror,
    where Agnes's pendulous bubs with oracular, phosphorous nipples
    — blood red as carbuncles — gleam their kneading above the shy,
    pearling waterfall,
she ties the ribbon
    of decayed roses
about her head.
    'Arise, you Mongol hordes. Kupala, your little water mother, lives.'
She scratches the purple cellophane off a cube of bathsalts with a finger
nail
    leeched to heart
and sprinkles the crumbled cube over the surface of the water.
    'May my tears not flow in the open field nor my sobs sound over the
    dark blue sea. May my speech be firm for centuries and centuries.'
A heavy scent
    of sexifragencima
fills the bathroom while the steam condenses
    for Cecily, whose boiled head bursts
and trickles down the walls. Miss Emily Hambuck stirs
    out the fire and wishes in frosted
water

circling the flowering midnight bloom and avoiding the brilliant
gaze of the beasts embedded in the wall
and shivers. Uncapping a jar of oil
for the tired old virgin lady Rhea and certainty of Mary
into the swirling water, Miss Emily Hambuck sees in the oval mirror
she who is spelt Nion, Eadha, Saille, Tinne, Ailm seeding her Divine
Child — the second Adam, in her cavernous, dusty womb, lapped by
the sea
where the sweat is gathering on her forehead. Gathering up a
fair white linen cloth
towel, she pats herself dry,
retaining veraiconica et scamelscum
and looks down into the bath,
liquid with marbling matricidal blood.
While she stands waiting for the bath to fill, she absentmindedly rubs her
forefinger
(humming a divine paean quailery to Artemis)
up and down the furrow between her buttocks.
'O Julian, ferry poor me on this the twelfth and expunge the guilt
from my homeless soul.'
Miss Emily Hambuck turns off the water and returns
knees bending
to the oval mirror
Silent Now As imitative of bride Isis and Minos's watery execution-
er, she drowns Adam in rivulets of excess
and taking from the cabinet
ting
a wooden spatula
spelt S—A—I—L—L—E
and a crinkled tube,
of boned Palladium
she squeezes a worm of paste

sperm, mummified in the dark labyrinthed Penis of the Vestal
Temple on Banal Holidays to seed the Virgin womb to bear the
crippled King of Kings,
onto the spatula
spelt D—U—I—R but cursed as the waning Tinne
and spreads the paste about her mouth and chin and up over her cheeks.
She gazes at her reflection.
'Hail, Uncumber! risen from the Hermaphroditic Cross.'
Taking a
fair white linen cloth
face flannel, she wipes the paste from her face and, under the running
water, washes away the adhering hairs.
With a clap of thunder her departing soul gurgles into the waste
hole, safe from the sun and moon; never to be resurrected.
She examines her new face
and the late Mr Mead senses Marina's cleft whilst his daughter pats
her bloated stomach and dreams another monkish frolic
in the mirror
where Salome, slipping-veiled and navel-jewelled, squats to the
thumb where her reflections in the puddles she has painted and
sees Snails Wet On Adam's Bride,
and sits down on the ash-rimmed lavatory. Seated
on the sovereign throne to await the year's death
she inspects her upper lip and chin in the hand mirror
where Nelson waits in the arms of Emer for his Agamemnon.
She lets loose an amphoric fart
— a departing breath of life carried on a pig wind
and closes her
little Lucy Little lost her little Little
eyes while she urinates
milk and is become a bleeding Katherine. Albigenses (al-, -z), n.pl.
She is only vaguely aware of the sound she makes
of emetic cymbals announcing the maintenance of the Eucharist
fast

and thinks of happiness. Getting up
    a moon-shaped hoof imprinted upon her Barley Mother's rosied
    fury
she pulls the chain
    scattering her mirrored soul to the midden tributaries of the River
    Styx
and goes to the washbasin.
    Knees bend.
While cleaning her teeth
    thieving Holiness from the spiritual Da(e)ira in the clay-based paste,
she spits
    into the mouth of Easter Sunday, dispelling with her sovereign
    spittle a sleeping Holiness
and, having finished, stands in front of the full length mirror
    where Nates clenches her buttocked aversion and holds on high the
    stolen teraphin containing the severed oracular head of Adam.
She fingers the long hairs
    safe from the heady bird's nest
of her pubes
    dyed and testeless for Totytoc, but slit transversely in similitude of
    a goatish eye
and, in a dream
    of proleptic thought, equating Gervas's Tav, Resh, Yod Vav and Nun
    with D C L X VI in beastly revelry
reaches into the cabinet
    ting.
No sooner does she take up her small, gold-plated razor
    when Maidhdeanbuain bares her shorn dolly and emasculates her
    father's father's Daddy
than she lays it down
    under the hidden sun where the half-sheathed sword heralds sleep.
Biting her lip,
    cloaked in a dazzling red of kerm scarlet to gamaruche the netted
    King of his severed sperm

she glances under her arms where the golden hair
>   shining tears of sun for Emain
is growing anew
>   in groves of service or else and dropping cyderous sorbs
walks
>   erotically, like a booted Salmakide — rolling eyed and jutting but-
>   tocked
towards the mirror
>   where the Virgin Saten, guised as Sophia the Holy Spirit, grasps
>   Adam's nuzzling horn and wisely contents herself with samadhi
and contemplates her figure.
>   White as soaked barley.
She strokes and squeezes her flesh
>   and becomes all glorious milk-hard marble; erect and hung about
>   with wild asparagus,
imagining the delight, under another's touch,
>   of Ollave tipped, mnemonic trances while the Moon heel kneads the
>   beheaded Christmas fool who resurrects the wise prophylactic jewel
>   which heals the iron phallus fortunately guiding the secret whispers
of her plumpness. She presses herself against the mirror
>   where Mother Senta, rowan-lipped, intones — 'ab ovo usque ad
>   malium', and inserts the egg and crushes it in her womb when Mad
>   Adam, in the month of Quert, bites on the proffered crab as a morti-
>   fying shaft of illumination splits his skull
and tries to embrace the image
>   of Enlil, who covers her with his waters so that she, Ninlil, is im-
>   pregnated and moon-swollen with Nanna-Sin;
contenting herself by implanting a kiss upon the glass and, with her
flattened tongue, licking her reflection. She goes
>   tiptoeing, mincing and cave-backed
to the bath where she cocks one leg over the rim
>   until the buck rug slips, and, sliding, tilts and parts her splitting
>   buttocks. Summoning the Lame God of Light to lance her bidding,

she points to her forked crutch where the hawthorn blossoms
    odourise her sexuality
and cautiously lowers her foot into the water. Lifting the other, she stands
    drowning her immortality
in the bath. Kneeling, she goes down into the
    illuminating
water on all fours and,
    inventively cowed, her feet hoofed, proffers all the broad fullness of
    her shining moon to the risen Pazzeroni who, white-spurned, cov-
    ers her unnatural lust, squashing the mistletoe berries as the lech-
    erous white dove
in the steam
    for the beheaded Lucy
waits; puffing and blowing.
    'Exi ab eo immunde spiritus.'
She licks the perspiration
    'Exorcizo te, creatura salis.'
from her upper lip and looks at her pendulous breasts
    abundantly milked, spurting into the albescent water while Pan,
    suckling the dripped excess, snuggles into her flayed skin
swinging above the stinging water. Gingerly, she lowers her taut buttocks
into the water.
    And her hymen slowly reseals its fifth virginity.
She stretches herself
    lustral for baptism
full length in the water.
    Evoking Lusios.
She begins to wash herself
    holy stoning her sabbatarian whiteness
and, after letting more water
    streaked black and red as it falls from the slate cliffs like alkahest
into the bath, she submerges herself
    deep into the unconscious boughs
so that only her head, her black nipples and breasts

likening the paps of Anu
and her knees, jut out of the water as islands. Her navel
seat of wantonness
is submerged and her mass of pubic hair floats below the surface
like a drifting net set above the Golden Elysium to trawl and snare
the limping King.
She
who muscles virility, casts out the alder twig and, wallowing in the
corruption,
scoops the water over herself, sighs,
conceives,
smiles and sucks the warm wet
amice
flannel placed over her face.
To await the waning year.
For come it will.
Already the leaves are underfoot; soggy, brown and clinging and the
sorbs are dropping rotten for the last wasp's insistent bussing while
the fertile wind smells of sperm and tannin, and virgins, heated and
agape, examine, with their blind fingers, the coming spring.
Over the surface of the water, in a mist opaque as milk, the blind
boatman ships his oars and, in the drifting silence, rooting pigs
wrinkle their snouts in muddy paradise; scenting the tumescent
acorn with their eyes.
Strained, a sound, thin and faint, from an alder whistle, willow
tapped and stripped, dies in the mist and settles gently on the lapping shore.
The hidden beaters, ghosted and crackling the invisible under-
growth, encircle and converge upon their carnal King; with goatish
thoughts erect within their bellies and sharper than their golden
sickles.
Emerging, splashing through the gaseous marsh from under the
dripping alders, comes Bodwen; his hands and face stained crimson,
hobbling through the mists with the shrieks of the chase wilding his

Royal eye. To which, from the depths, slowly rising in monstrous contortion, lifted above the net and set about with dripping maidenhair, attracting his erratic steps, the rotten snare-sorb heaves itself above the waters and muscles a welcoming, erotic dream.

Attracted, intent and stooping low, he burrows to the brown and purple corruption which, at his touch, splits, gapes and reveals the immortality, strung about with slime and froth, buried within its elytron core.

Feverishly he fumbles the acorn tip of his silver thumb between the liquid lids and pressing, finds the soft bone arching the goatish eye. Captive in the entangling net set under his hardening limpness, he slaves to the demand and energises the fusion which rolls quietly on juicy waves, exhausting his year's vigour with seemingly endless voluptuousness. Stained in swollen purple, pulsing his anniversary coronation, he mounts his sacred throne and, in an ecstasy, enters the hollowing catacomb which sucks him greedily into his second watery birth.

The assembly watches; noting. Humming like a hive of bees, fingering their tiny sickles in expectancy; sharing the moment, they await the drawn out shudder.

Then, upon a scream, amidst the climactic gallop as the crushed, milk-white berries burst — secreting limp jets of viscous rheum — the stooping assembly sally and joyously hack the shrivelling testicles.

Below, the Queen, snaking to the glistening, empirical, ashen sceptre, engorges the molten geat and gnaws her golden teeth through the very root and gristle of Bodwen's sceptre — severing with utter finality his crippled reign. Reverently, trailing silvered strings, the wand and bulbous oracular tip is drawn free and laid beside the draining sacs, made ready for launching.

His image used, the Queen, imprisoned in the sprouting ashen thicket gorged on blood, at the moment of her madness, rides her desperation upon the emptying traceries of disbelief until, inevitably, her sweetness drains into the commingling waters; flowing in waves of silence as imperceptible as the urgency of necessity but with breathless, sweet relief at its slowing termination.

Gasping, her rolling eyes bulging from her puffy face, she watches the silent boat, laden with its shrivelling load — still quicksilvered and sheaned — float between the isles of Anu, whispering with its tadpole mouth those Elysian prophecies which lie like pearls embedded in the spongy tissues of the inflamed Godhead, deep in the subterranean depths, and on into the mists where the waters fall like alkahest.

Miss Emily Hambuck opens her eyes,

    and the youth, his cheeks soft and downy, buskined but game, steps forward, hands on hips, and surveys his year's kingdom, while the old Queen

wipes her crutch

    where the eclipsed penumbra of her periodic moon gently glows

with the

    fair white linen cloth

face flannel; pulls out the plug

    while the sanguine Cosmocrater shrieks his departure

and stands up.

    Lustrated, white and faint with cleanliness and spiritual with relief.

Stepping out of the bath

    borne upon a curving shell of fertile wind, virginal, pure, serene and proudly carrying the secret pearl embedded in her womb, light stepping the carpeting trefoil magically blooming her footsteps

she takes up the

    fair white linen cloth

towel and pats herself dry. After having slipped into her torn nightdress, she shakes

    ground white alphiton

talcum powder inside;

    ministering the scaly leprosy of her puff-white breasts;

switches off the light

anally

and pulls open the swollen, oak bathroom door.

And the priests of Janus raise their voices in lauding praise of Her.

Emily Hambuck.

Cleansed, under three blankets and her great sheep-skin coat, Erowina curls up into a tight ball and, pulling her nightdress down over her ten little toes, lies curled, waiting for Sunday and the necessary courage.

THE SUNDAYS (29.iii.1964)

Quos Deusvult perdere, dementat prius.
(Those whom God wishes to destroy, he first makes mad.)

Warmly snuggled, propped and desk-kneed, sponging hot tea and jubbly poofing a mouthed bubble; and then ease. Sucking from the tongued, holed tooth a soft, dissolving toast crumb, sweetly marmaladed, and sliding it with a sucked mouth swallow into the grubbling tum-tum. Patting the smelling warmth back under the tucked-in cosiness; stretching deliciously and reaching for the crackling Sundays — that's how Sundays should begin.

BAN THE BOMB MARCH FLOPS. DEMONSTRATORS REMOVED BODILY TO WAITING POLICE VANS

Decently slacked; not droopily drawered, trailing her rub-a-dub.

BAN THE BUM!

Sit up straight, Emily, and pull your skirt down. Anyone would think I hadn't brought you up properly. And stop jiggling.

MARCHERS' DEMONSTRATION FRUSTRATED BY PROMPT POLICE ACTION

I'll fetch the police to you. That's what I'll do. You keep out of my wardrobe! Bloody little thief. What are you? (Nancy closes the strange-smelling box and puts it back into the wardrobe and locks the mirrored door.) And don't think you'll find the key on top of the door again . . . (she conceals the key in the palm of her hand) . . . because you won't. Now get out of my sight, and stay out! Little pest.

yesnancyofcoursenancyimmediatelynancysorrynancyneveragainnancwillipryintothatboxwhereyoukeepyouruneatablewaxpessariesandthoseunrolledcondomspowderedwithfrenchchalkandthatwoodenstickforrollingthemontonevereveragainipromise.

YOU HAVE NO RIGHT CLUTTERING UP OUR HIGHWAYS PREVENTING THE VAST MAJORITY OF LAW ABIDING CITIZENS FROM GOING ABOUT THEIR RIGHTFUL BUSINESS

Arm in arm, with heels clicking on the deserted pavements, Eunice and the bearded Giacopo walked briskly home; their coat collars turned up against the chill night.

Baaa, baaa.

What's it like being shagged by a goat, Mrs?

What did you say?

Ignore them, Giacopo.

Four Teddy boys, dark and malevolent, with shining, slicked back hair and a rolling, exaggerated gait, full of indolence, blossom from a darkened doorway and confront Giacopo.

You talking to us?

I asked you to repeat what you said.

We asked your Mrs what it was like to be fucked by a goat.

Then you're more stupid than you look.

The one with the exaggerated sideburns dragged Eunice into the shop doorway where he tried to molest her while the others beat Giacopo to the pavement and there proceeded to kick him until he was unconscious.

Thrown onto the pavement, Eunice saw the four louts climb into a parked car, start the engine and go roaring away, up the street, shouting and laughing and waving their arms out of the windows.

BRIDES RUSHING TO THE ALTAR THIS EASTER

Damn fools they. Ninnies for the Chancellor's Easter Egg. Spoon cracked; the lot of them.

FREE. SPECIAL EASTER OFFER. ONLY 39 GNS. A SUPER HOOVER WITH TOUCH-TOE CONTROL

Vacuumed clean, with his beat as it sweeps all over me. Oh, no, not again. Sniffing carpet dust as Giacopo thumbs his way in. Don't have a cylindrical one; there's all that tubing. Get the other sort. Much better for the carpet if you rub it in. What's good for the carpet is sauce for you. Smack!

POLYGRIP HOLDS FALSE TEETH

Stop staring at your aunt like that. It's rude.

Smack.

Aunt Henrietta, having removed the plate, licks off the crumbs.

Pop peeth.

Pot teeth, she means.

And Aunt replaces the dentures in his mouth and snaps on them as they click back into place.

FAMILY REUNION IN BLACKPOOL. MOTHER AND DAUGHTER RE-UNITED AFTER THIRTY YEARS

Clive. Do you remember Clive? He was Harper's little boy. His Nanny used to bring him all the way from Chelsea to play with you. No? You must. A nasty little boy. Was. He's dead now. Joined the guards and was killed in North Africa. A Captain. Awarded the Military Medal, so I'm told. I always thought it was from him you picked up your dirty ways. Remember when he pushed a caterpillar up his nose? And there was Daphne Capper. She stayed occasionally during the holidays. Do you remember her? You and she filled your knickers with coal. Why, I'll never know. She never did have a coming out. Had to marry by all accounts. Lives in Wiltshire now. Breeds dogs. Do you remember Aunt Henrietta? We used to visit her at the asylum. He's dead. And Aunt — what was her name? Helen! Yes. Nicknamed Dodie. She's dead too. Remember the Christmas she stuffed the turkey with a teacloth? She was as dotty as Henrietta. And the Toths. Do you remember the Toths? They had a son called Sidney. Nice boy. He works in the City — a Merchant Banker, I think. Anyway, he lives in Surrey. Do you remember Vera Warbley? She was discovered by Rank and changed her name to Yvonne something-or-other. Been divorced twice, but never made it as an actress. And Sandra Luker? Do you remember her? She's Lady McArdle now. Her husband's in the Diplomatic Service. Who else? Oh yes! The Feldts.

NO!

In the Foreign Office, he was. But their son. What WAS his name? He studied law and became a High Court Judge. YOU remember.

NO!

The first summer after the outbreak of war you went and stayed with his family in Derbyshire. He had little piggy eyes and a mind to match. You remember. Maurice!

AAAaaaaaiannmeieeeeeeee!

The long boring day umbrella parachuting from the back of the birch carved, gilt, and upholstered Beauvais tapestried setteeeeeeeee!

Thinkofsomethingelsequickly.

Roses.

On the rug under the brolly overlooked by the muddled black backs of silhouetted chairs in the darkening log-fired room waiting tea-time with whispers and tickling snigger-snorts.

Thinkofsomethingelse. Quickly.

Knickers.

No. Yes. No. Please. All right then, and showing Maurice my wee-weeeeeeeee!

Thinkofsomething else.

Worm.

What? Watch. And watching it grow and growing within his frigging enlarging and lengthening.

Think of something else.

Rhubarb.

Stick-hard and bright red the skin rolled back and out popped a purple head with a tadpole mouth and. Now you. Me? You. How? Like. Like? Yes. Keep? Yes. More? More. Enough? More. Longer? Quicker. Faster? Harder. Why? Nice. Nice? Lovely when. What? Watch. For? It, stupid. Where? Oh, give it here. No, me. Get going then. Well? Yes. Nice? Soon. How soon? Soon. Now? If. What? You. Me? Suck. It? Yes. Like?

Silence.

YOU!

It pulsed at the same moment a hand dug deep into my neck and drew me up, up, up to be shaken and beaten and screamed at.

You dirty, filthy, little.

And I was dragged screaming; the roots of my hair tearing.

You . . . !

SMACK.

And the bucket vomited into the sink, filling the bowl.

Dirty little . . .

SMACK.

The water syphoned up my nose and, filling my mouth, gushed into my stomach; swelling and suffocating.

I've a good mind to drown you! You filthy . . .

My eyeballs floated about in the bowl as the water closed over my head and my ears became blocked.

Nancy, in the clear air above, shouted: Bad a pappy berl by boo bud bo aboun gambin pappy boys ad bor abe! Bugh!

Death rose up, hooded and cowled in black and clapped his wings, twice.

But the water regurgitated all over the stone floor; mixed with mince-meat and chopped carrot.

And you stay in there 'till I say you can come out. And you'd better get down on your knees and pray! You little horror!

The blank door slammed shut. And locked.

And so two long days lay heavily on the bed, clothed in a long white nightdress of hirsute torment while shame stole as slowly as a snail; sliming my flesh.

THE FALL OF THE ROMAN EMPIRE

A-n-d, another little shake. Same old faces. Same old new films. Astoria? Ah yes. Charing Cross. Years gone by. Squeezing giggles in the old 'phone box with lubly Adam. And London bedded quiet. The last train gone while the cold, old woman did a standing piss on the other side of the steamed up glass and flooded the cobbled alley. And a tiptoe home, giggling, through the stale frothed beer which fingered its way right, pointing homewards, following us.

Happy, mad nights.

ANIMAL TRAINERS ACCUSED OF USING CRUELTY

Which one? That one? The blue one? In the middle? I can't hear anything. Are you sure?

Listen, will you!

The budgerigars sat in a row. All ten of them. They sat on their perch, fluffed with pride and fat with seed. And silent.

Listen. Keep quiet. He'll say it again in a minute.

And he did.

Quietly.

Help! he said. Help! Help — I'm a robin.

THE SCHOOLGIRL AND THE MUSIC MASTER

Open your mouth wide. Wider. Come on, much wider than that. I want it open as wide as it will go. Wide. Until you feel the muscles stretching.

That's it. Keep it open. Don't close it yet. Keep it wide open. Good. Now that's how I want it when we get to the word Lord. Watch me make with my mouth.

AFTER THAT IT OCCURRED SEVERAL TIMES A WEEK AND ONCE AT HIS
HOME WHEN HIS WIFE HAD INVITED SOME OTHER CHILDREN IN

Use your handkerchief — and stop snivelling. Now, put your fingers into my mouth. See? There's plenty of room inside, isn't there? So there must be in yours. Good. Now. Watch my mouth as I make the words, Lord, have mercy upon us. Watch my mouth on the word, Lord. And then we'll do it together. Right? Right. Be-gin. And one.

UNMARRIED MAN AGED FORTY-FIVE TERRORISES LOCAL GIRLS
It's time that a stop was put to this sort of thing once and for all.

youl	etme	last	nigh	twhy	nott	onig	htit
hurt	nons	ense	youe	njoy	edit	idid	notl
iari	amno	tali	arno	frig	idwh	ybec	ause
idon	tlik	ebei	ngbu	gger	edno	woma	nlik
esto	have	itpu	tuph	erbu	mnig	htaf	tern
ight	wron	gthe	rear	ealo	tofw	omen	whoa
reon	lyto	oeag	erto	take	itup	thei	rars
enot	meye	snoa	ndif	youa	rego	ingt	omak
eani	ssue	outo	fity	ouca	nblo	odyw	ells
leep	onyo	urow	nint	hest	udio	iwil	lgoo
dthe	soon	erth	ebet	tera	nddo	ntth	inki
llch	ange	mymi	ndbe	caus	eiwo	ntmy	dear
iwou	ldnt	puti	tupy	oura	rsei	fyou	paid
meth	atsn	otve	ryli	kely	soyo	udbe	tter
getu	sedt	othe	idea	ofbu	tter	ingu	psom
eone	else	orst	icki	ngit	upyo	urow	nbum
nowg	etou	tand	dont	ever	dare	come	back

SHE'S THE TOAST OF PARIS. THIS CURVY, VIVACIOUS BOMBSHELL WITH THE MEASUREMENTS 38-24-38. CALLED REGLISSE, MEANING LICORICE, YOU'D NEVER GUESS FROM WHAT YOU CAN SEE OF HER (BE-LOW) THAT THIS CURVACIOUS DAME WAS, UNTIL AN OPERATION TWO YEARS AGO, A MAN, KNOWN IN THE AIRFORCE AS BOMBER ROY!

You know, my dear, I've always wondered. Tell me — which of you two. Well. You know. I mean. Who wears the pants? I'm not being nosey. It's just that. Not that I think it wrong. I don't. I mean, you're entitled to get your thrills anyway you like. It's not as if you're corrupting little girls. Are you? Besides, you're adult, and what you do in private is your own con-cern. Nobody else's. But I was wondering. After all, you're both my friends. Aren't you? And so who better to ask, than you. I mean. Where can one read about such things? Mmm? You can't. And I'm curious. Tell me. What do you actually DO? Mmm?

PETER KING GOES TO THE INQUEST ON SWEETLIFE GIRL, YVONNE FRENCH (PICTURED ON THE RIGHT WITH KING)

A real *joli homme*. Probably yummy tall, too. Must have faller for her navel by the look of her dress. Damned silly. Even if had the figure. Which I haven't. Unlike Nesta.

TO ANYONE WHO KNOWS ANYTHING ABOUT THESE SWEETLIFE GIRLS, THE INQUEST GAVE A CRYSTAL CLEAR PICTURE OF THE FINAL DESPERATE HOURS OF ONE OF THEM

I want to turn now to those of you who are leaving us at the end of this term. Whilst you have been with us, you have, to a certain extent, been shielded from the world outside. I'm sure you know that I, and my staff, from the many frank talks we have had with you, have done our best to prepare you for this eventuality. Despite our guidance it is possible you will find life different from what you had supposed. Indeed, many of you, when faced with the world outside, may come to regard the years spent here as some of the happiest years of your life. (Hear, hear.) Some may not. (Laughter.) Those of you who, for one reason or another, find that life is harsh and seems bent on breaking your will, take heart, for I am sure you will be able to overcome and surmount any difficulty if you follow in the ways I, and my staff, have tried — not only in our teaching but also by example — to infuse into your spirit; so that with clearness of eye, steadfastness of purpose, no difficulty will be insurmountable; no problem a healthy mind will be unable to solve. And if, too, you pay heed to the counsel, the wisdom, which your parents, with loving concern, may wish to impart, there is no reason why all of you shouldn't live good, useful, and happy lives. (Hear, hear.)

SHE BECAME A HOSTESS AT THE MOST FAMOUS NIGHT CLUB IN LONDON

I expect that most of you will fall in love (suppressed sniggering amongst the lower third), marry (a few blushes amongst the upper fifth) and are looking forward to this.

LIKE MANY OTHERS, SHE COULD NOT BE DESCRIBED CORRECTLY AS A PROSTITUTE. SHE WOULDN'T DREAM OF PLYING FOR HIRE

Many of you — I hope all of you — will enjoy the sacred and rewarding experience of motherhood.

IT WAS FOUND THAT SHE HAD GIVEN BIRTH TO A BABY IN NINETEEN FIFTY THREE WHICH HAD SINCE BEEN ADOPTED

Motherhood, I hope — I know — will be, for many of you, the greatest joy and the purpose in life. Others may, in the careers they have chosen, find an equally satisfying reward. But all of you will, I hope, however your life may shape and proceed, find happiness in living a full and useful life. I'm sure I speak for all my staff when I say that nothing would give us greater joy than to hear of your progress from time to time, and, if you can spare a moment in your hectic lives to pay us a visit — bring your children with you (laughter), and husbands (more laughter), you will be made most welcome. AND given tea. (Laughter and ironic cheers.) It only remains for me to wish you all a life full of happiness, and rewards far greater than you had ever dared to dream.

THE PATHOLOGIST FOUND SOFTENING OF THE BRAIN CAUSED BY A PREVIOUS PERIOD OF PROLONGED UNCONSCIOUSNESS. THE VERDICT WAS THAT SHE DIED OF SECONAL POISONING WHICH WAS SELF-ADMINISTERED WHEN NOT IN HER NORMAL STATE OF MIND

Serves her happy if she was so miserable. Forgive me, Mummy, for what I am bound to do.

WHAT THE STARS HOLD FOR YOU

I wonder if they'd foretell death? They wouldn't dare.

GEMINI

That's me. The twins. Two faced. A double morality. Up one minute, down the next.

BE THE ONE TO SET THE PACE

Right. Drinks on me, everybody. Stanley! Kiss me. Kiss me, you cock poxed man, you.

LOTS OF LAUGHTER AND GAIETY IN SOCIAL QUARTERS

That there will be. Oh, yes. Laugh themselves sick to the grave, they will.

THIS WEEK SHOULD LAST LIKE A TONIC

Just gin, Stanley. Not a 'pinky '. Straight gin. The quicker to get me drunk, you jinn, you.

LISTEN TO YOUR ELDERS

It is your duty, Emily. As only daughter, you are under an obligation. Tedious as this may seem to you now, when you are older you will appreciate the significance of your inheritance.

Besides, over-taxed and understaffed, how am I to cope on my own? It's not proper that Nancy should have sole responsibility for the running of the house. You are of an age when you should be interesting yourself in such things. I've no intention of turning you into a maid of all work, but ask that you shoulder your responsibilities. Were you my son, I would be just as adamant. More so. It is your inheritance, Emily. You would be breaking tradition by leaving. And leaving to go where? To do what? I'll not support you. And remember, you are under age. Cock a snook at twenty-one if you like, but not at eighteen. And at eighteen — what do you know of the real world? Who would employ you? And where would you live? In a bedsit? They cook their meals on a gas ring in the hearth. Or didn't you know that?

Be sensible. Reconsider. If you like, I'll make over the whole of the upper floor to you. Come and go as you choose. Entertain. I'd welcome young people. But don't leave. You're loved, Emily. I love you. Imagine the effect your going away would have on your mother were she still alive. Then consider me. Alone. Here. My daughter gone. Could you be so insensitive?

And I'm warning you, if you do leave, I shan't hesitate to involve the police.

LUCKY NUMBER — NINE

The Devil's number, Father. If A equals one and D, four, twice four is eight and one is nine. NINE, Dad. NINE. The Devil's number.

COLOUR — GREEN

Left-handed green. Lesbian green. It would be. Just my luck to be given hateful green for a colour. And Gloria?

AQUARIUS

Yes. Lubly eighteenth of Feb-ru-ary, is Gloria. Eighteen? Grief! One plus eight is bloody nine again. NINE! And her forecast?

A NEW INTEREST GAINS SURPRISING POPULARITY WITH YOU THIS WEEKEND

The vixen, sharp-eyed, snout pointing, hackles rising, glares up the blocked, stopped track; the blood, fresh drawn from the kill, staining her panting, long-tongued, grinning wet mouth (she wrote).

YOU ARE EXTREMELY SUCCESSFUL WITH THE OPPOSITE SEX

When the piercing fox secures his mount, the vixen turns and buries her teeth in his neck. A cry whistles from his wounded throat; bubbling sighs. Without turning, the vixen scuds back along the track, drag wiping her rump, up to the lair where a sleek, sister vixen lies panting her happy re-turn; her festering leg still clamped in an iron snap-shut trap.

They spend the afternoon together; snapping at flies and licking pus from the wound. (1958.)

YOUR LUCKY NUMBER IS SIX

Six! Now let me see. Born on the sixth of the sixth of the twenty-seventh. Two and seven is nine. That's, six plus six plus nine, therefore her birth number is twenty-one which, added together is three which added to her lucky number is — NINE! Six and Nine, sixty-nine. Soixante-neuf! Well,

well, and who said there wasn't significance in numbers!

YOUR COLOUR IS BLACK

Black! Gloria's naked pink fleshy tartness veiled and putty-coloured under a black diaphanous wisp? Death suited. In black? Never. Black indeed. What's that for a colour?

SUNDAY PUZZLE No. 3,033. SET BY PYTHAGORAS

IF TODAY IS THE 29th OF MARCH, 1964, WHAT DAY IS IT AND HOW DID YOU ARRIVE AT THAT SOLUTION?

Erowina consulted the table which contained as much of the Calendar as was necessary for the determining of the solution; to find which, she looked for the Golden Number of the Year in the First Column of the Table, against which stood the Day of the Paschal Full Moon. Then, looking in the Third Column for the Sunday Letter, next after the Day of the Full Moon and at the Day of the Month standing against the Sunday Letter, she saw it was Easter Sunday. She remembered that if the Full Moon happened on a Sunday then, according to the first rule, the next Sunday after was Easter Day: but which did not apply. She then found the Golden Number, or Prime, by adding One to the Year of our Lord and dividing by Nineteen; the Remainder of viii was the Golden Number. Having found the Dominical or Sunday Letter, according to the Calendar, which extended to, and was inclusive of, the Year Two Thousand and Ninety-nine, and adding to the Year of our Lord its Fourth part and the Number Six, she divided the Sum by Seven. The Number Four, which was remaining, she found in the small annexed Table standing against the Sunday Letter D.

She checked her findings with the Calendar in her hand-bag and saw, to her great satisfaction, she had solved the puzzle and that it was, indeed, Easter Sunday.

WIDOW BRUNDLE PLANS MORE HOLIDAYS FOR THE LONELY OF DAR-

LINGTON

The first and positively the last blind booking into a bay-windowed sea-fronting house with a room vacant sign hung in the window.

Come in. Come in.

Was it party time?

In the glad hall were a clutter of buckets and spades, and rubber wings and rings and things.

We followed the slippered feet up the sand carpeted stairs and were shown the gritted bath where the water would be hot, tomorrow, Saturday, glimpsed the toilet splattered with unflushed crap and followed up stairs become linoleum to an attic room where the three of us stood bowed beneath the weight of the sloping roof.

With the door propped shut, we eased our excitement between hard, crackling sheets which sanded our sin-burned backs but refrained, not daring to jangle the quoits of the hollowing, lump sprung bed and stain the starched white of our linen yellow.

In the morning, we breakfasted on thick haddock, mugged tea and pappy, margarined bread sat at a separate table while the rest of the glad, mad regulars supped and gawped and sniggered at us, the luggageless couple.

Who cared? The sun was up.

But rain came streaming, obscuring and isolating; sealing in the cabbage damp smell while dice rattled on a ludo board and children with sticky fists thumped the yellow keyboard of the mildewed upright. So we fled and sat outdoors huddling our cold misery in a rain lashed promenade shelter; our one holiday passing.

But it was Adam who suggested we take the last train back, to London.

UP-TO-THE-MINUTE TWIST DRESS. TAILORED IN SOFT, WARM LUXURY BRUSHED SOFTVALLA. IDEAL DRESS FOR THE COMING SEASON. NOTE THE ATTRACTIVE CONTRAST STITCHING AND THE DEEP INVERTED PLEATS. 19 in. ZIP, OPENING TO WAIST FOR SUPER FIT. ONLY 19 /

11d. p /p ex. C.O.D. 2 /6 ex. ROSE PINK, MINK, PETROL, LEMON AND OAT-
MEAL

Put your arms around me. Round me. Round. All round me and gather me
closely.

Oh, press yourself against me. Up against me. Hard against me. Let me
feel your thigh in my groin.

And give me your cheek. My cheek to your cheek. Our cheeks together
while we drift in dance; warm cheek to warm cheek. Pardon? Oh, yes. Yes,
it is crowded, isn't it?

The old, cold, grey face with the bitter smile and the almond eyes narrowed to a beadling squint, watched me closely; twisting her golden wed-
ding ring.

Hold my hand tighter. Much tighter. Squeeze reassurance into my fingertips across this void. Squeeze. Please. And hold me tightly. Tighter.

Oh! It's all over. Thank you. I enjoyed it. Very much. Dismissed to crawl
past the smirking, hurtful, gruesome hunchback who took hold of my
arm.

Don't think I don't know. I do.

Her five, carefully graded children danced onto the floor and she
smirked with pride while she twisted her ring and glanced over the bare-
shouldered, twittering women to catch sight of Stanley stood at the bar;
safely ringed by men.

AT FIFTY-FOUR SHE FOUND LIFE BORING. MRS B., FASHIONABLY -
DRESSED WIFE OF A COMPANY DIRECTOR AND MOTHER OF THREE,
POSED FOR A PHOTOGRAPHER

Why?

It was his need I fulfilled, not my desire.

Such an excuse is totally unacceptable.

It is not an excuse. By confining his attention, I was able to divert his
energies from other women.

It is mere speculation to suggest your non-co-operation would have resulted in the corruption of other women.

I submit that the same is true if, as you have suggested, a person or persons looking at the photographs would have been corrupted. Such a statement is speculative, incapable of corroboration and is deserving of the same disrespect as lavished upon my own statement of opinion. Furthermore . . .

You will confine yourself to answering the questions I put to you.

I object to the word corrupt if, by inference, you are ascribing it to my own moral behaviour.

Madam, in law, moral wickedness is established if the person arraigned has failed to reach the moral standard approved of by this court which bases its judgement upon the generally accepted and approved moral standards of this country at this particular moment in history. It is not sufficient for you to believe that because you acted within the confines of your own conscience—albeit sincerely, though misguidedly — that blame cannot be attached to you. This court's assessment of your moral conduct is a true one and, as such, will be upheld against an individual's attempt to force upon the court a moral standard of his, or her, own invention. Do I make myself clear?

Your words are understandable, but not your intention. From the beginning of your cross-examination you have insisted upon my wickedness. This, I can only think, is intended to inflame and stimulate prejudice which will allow you to suggest and to justify an unwarranted, and severe punishment.

This is the twentieth century, madam, not the sixteenth . . .

Yet you are attempting, by showing that my conduct has transgressed a modern code of ethics, that such immorality is proof of my criminal guilt. Not only that, but by suggesting yourself that the court's moral standard is a true one, you at the same time admitted that it is capable of variation because it is dependent on the climate of public opinion. Therefore, what you, the court, may consider a venial transgression now, may, at some future date, excite deep, moral reprobation whereas, before, it was condoned as a minor transgression because it infringed an unpopular rule of law.

Madam, I am fully acquainted with the principles of criminal liability and it is with this object in mind that I am pursuing my prosecution. Now, will you please confine yourself to answering my questions. Did the accused, Pazzeroni, at any time threaten to use force if you refused to pose for him?

I do not like being beaten.

Are you saying that you were?

I was not beaten.

Was your bodily person threatened?

Yes, it was.

Earlier, you stated you were a willing participant.

Correct.

But now you wish the court to believe that it was the threats to your person which forced you to succumb to indecency.

I did not say that.

Then you are saying your indecency was not engendered by the threat of bodily assault?

I am.

You wish the court to believe that these threats to your person did not influence your decision?

I was not intimidated.

You admit that you wilfully, and knowingly, allowed yourself to be photographed in a degrading and indecent manner?

My actions were not degrading and not indecent.

I fear the majority of citizens would be of that opinion.

Opinion is not law, although, as you have gone to great pains to point out to me, a majority opinion may become moral law.

I do believe we are beginning to understand one another.

On the contrary, when it comes to explaining why I posed for those photographs, it will be found you are prejudiced because of the inflexible moral standards of this court.

Which is as it should be.

I disagree.

Silence. It has already been explained to you how the court arrives at a moral standard and you will have to be content with that. Unless you can influence public opinion, the Church and other respectable and responsible bodies, you will have to be satisfied with, and live up to, the moral standards that we, the majority, are content to abide by. Now, in your own words, will you tell the court why you allowed yourself to be photographed in these indecent poses?

As I stated earlier, it was Pazzeroni's need I fulfilled, not the satisfying of my own erotic desire. My first duty lay in confining his activities. Would the court accept this?

The court will take note of it.

Secondly, in the confines of the intimate privacy of our relationship, it was also my duty to re-channel, if I could, the childish retrogression which demanded that he take photographs of women — in what you term indecent poses.

By posing in these lewd photographs for him?

To wean a baby away from a bottle is not to snatch it away.

That you showed concern for his activities surely denotes that you foresaw that your participation was what amounted to an act of gross lewdness.

Not at all. With patience, it could be shown to Pazzeroni that what he was doing was a very infantile occupation for an adult man to be engaged in. To suggest that my part in the affair was lewd is to suppose that I felt lewd, or was attempting to be lewd whilst posing. I was not. Any more than I would be were I asked to submit myself to a medical examination.

The two activities are in no way comparable.

I have no means of knowing if a doctor's appraisal of me as a patient lying on an examination couch is lewd unless it is made clear to me in some tangible way. He would be less than human if he did not have some sexual thought — however fleeting.

Did your feelings for Pazzeroni amount to an infatuation?

If you mean, was I in love with him, the answer is yes.

To the point where you were willing to do anything to please him?

No.

Then was it in the hopes of monetary gain that you posed for these obscene photographs?

HUNDREDS OF PEOPLE WHO PAID TWO OR THREE SHILLINGS A TIME HAVE SEEN YOU IN THESE DISGUSTING PHOTOGRAPHS. THAT SHOULD MAKE YOU THOROUGHLY ASHAMED OF YOURSELF

No. It was never my intention nor was it hinted these photographs were to be sold for money.

Did it never occur to you that such a thing might happen? At the time, it seemed an irrational fear.

If it entered your head that such a thing was possible, why did you continue to pose for these photographs?

By using the word continue, you are implying that there was more than one occasion on which I posed. This is not the case.

I will put it to you another way then. Did it occur to you before you took up your first pose that the photographs might be copied and sold to the general public?

Yes.

Then I will repeat my question. Why, if you thought the photographs might be sold, did you persist in posing?

I have already explained.

Did it never occur to you the disastrous effects these photographs might have on people who bought them?

In all probability, the people who would purchase such photographs would be men whose erotic immaturity expressed itself in masturbation — the end result of which is not disastrous.

You don't seem very concerned.

I have already said I think this erotic outlet is indicative of regression.

Did you never stop to consider that these photographs might find their way into the hands of children?

No. But now you put it to me, I would draw your attention to the photographs themselves and ask you whether or not they are detailed photographic explorations of a female body and, as such, could be instructive to the inquisitively ignorant — of whatever age?

These photographs are both obscene and pornographic.

No, sir.

Yes, madam, and that is not only my opinion but the opinion of this court.

The court should take into account that such photographs as you hold may be found amongst the illustrations in medical books.

Medical books do not find their way into the hands of minors. Such books are for the instruction of medical, or would-be medical practitioners.

You have made my point for me.

The jury will decide if the point has been taken. That is all.

THE DOCTOR'S WIFE WHO WAS INTERESTED IN MEN

No.

Cheeks were scuffed by rough scaled soles.

No more.

I was adamant.

But the dung pungent image pressed down.

NO! Please!

My marbled eyes rolled back as the jigsaw cracked and, parting steadied on the diminishing edge of my focus before the two halves fell away; the one, exhausted with frustration.

I can't any more. I'm sorry. But I just can't.

A furious lower lip was bitten into, before she bared her teeth.

WHY? she hissed.

The boneless flesh collapsed into a heap in the chair.

Why? What have I done? Said?

Her audible heart pumped in agitation.

Just tell me why, for God's sake!

The clock ticked in the noiseless room; matching my silence.

Is it because of Stanley Bowden — or whatever his name is?

Closing my eyes, I curled into myself, shrinking.

Well? Is it? Tell me!

A mashed book collided with the wall and fell onto the bed.

I know it bloody well is! It's him! Isn't it? (Sniff.)

A hollow handbag snapped open.

(Mine?)

GOOD GOD!

HER HUSBAND FOUND CONTRACEPTIVES IN HER HANDBAG AND CON-
TRACEPTIVES HIDDEN IN THE INSIDE BAND OF HER HATS. ACCORDING
TO THE CHEMIST, SHE HAD PURCHASED CONTRACEPTIVES EVERY WEEK
SINCE SEPTEMBER

How could you!

The handbag spewed out the contents from its pink satined mouth; and grinned.

GOD! To think you've been . . .

A gristle-white knuckle of a word thumped into a floating kidney; crippling. And I cringed.

I could kill you! (But she said: You little whore!)

She could have bruised my undefended breasts, but chose to go direct.

D'you hear? I could kill you! (But called me a tramp and a slut.)

Kill you!

Her spittle strung down onto my curling back; necklacing my bareness humped against her stinging slaps.

You bitch!

Bone and flesh collided, and hair was pulled.

Been deceiving me, have you? You bloody little tart! Well, I'll show you.

And, yes, she actually slapped me. ME!

A painful tear fell onto my bent back; bruising.

Worse than the words, that was.

Ashamed, a subsided temper grovelled on the floor; begging.

Forgive me. Forgive me.

But her turned circles led nowhere.

Truly, here was a dog in a manger.

Oh, forgive me. Forgive me. Dear, dear Erica, forgive me.

Please. Please forgive me.

And it went on and on.

My pummelled ghost rose up and regarded a prostrate love become disgustingly dwarf.

I forgive you, I said, stepping over her.

It had ended.

Forgive me . . .

My warm flesh tingled, grew blue and turned black. I could have whipped her; trod on her neck; forced her to grovel, but I contained my-self.

Get dressed and I'll make some tea.

Forgive me . . .

The tea was made and drunk in silence.

Forgive me, Erica.

But I had spoken and held open the door; waiting.

Dressed, she left; passing in silence, forgiven.

But why did she have to hurt me? Why must all of you hurt me. Why? WHY?

What have I done?

What have I become?

THE WOMAN DESCRIBED HERSELF AS A PHOTOGRAPHER'S MODEL

THE INCREDIBLY HANDSOME JEW DISGUISED AS A REPORTER: FOR GOD'S SAKE, WOMAN! WHAT'S SO SPECIAL ABOUT YOURS? (He focuses his un-capped one-eyed Hasselblads bishop packed with unexposed Tri-X Professional Goy goo.) Come ON. OPEN THEM UP! (His eye fills with blood and he snaps. Plop!) WIDER! Copy's no good without cheese cake. Say, cheese.

THE BEAUTIFUL EROWINA: With what?

THE CANES, SHE SAID, WERE FOR HER OWN, PERSONAL USE. MY BOY FRIENDS, AND SOMETIMES MY GIRL FRIENDS, USED THEM TO WHIP ME

THE INCREDIBLY HANDSOME JEW DISGUISED AS A REPORTER: Whip YOU? (He savours the combination of soft red wood and lead in the moist tip of his pencil.)

THE BEAUTIFUL EROWINA (bent to her life's task of tying knots in a neverending tube of latex rubber): Would I be so stupid as to scourge myself?

THE INCREDIBLY HANDSOME JEW DISGUISED AS A REPORTER: I'll write, sensitive. (He writes, "thick".) Now. Let's have a look at the scars. (Eunice exposes herself.) No. The scars. Lash marks. Stigmata. You're a Christian, aren't you? Show me blood. If you're a bleedin' Katherine, milk.

THE BEAUTIFUL EROWINA: Is it necessary? My underclothes are . . .

Let's begin again, says the reporter who looks like THE INCREDIBLY HANDSOME JEW.

HER HOUSE WAS A BROTHEL AND VISITING SEAMEN, STRANGERS TO THE CITY, ASKED FOR IT BY NAME

In the waiting room of the EXCELSIOR, there is a strong smell of carbolic. The atmosphere is moist, the light, bright. Condensation runs down the white tiled walls on which enamel posters, urging personal hygiene, are screwed. Bolted to the floor are rigid wooden benches. A plaque on the door leading into the well-upholstered room of appointments reads, IT IS

PERMITTED, and signed, in facsimile, by the Minister.

THE INCREDIBLY HANDSOME JEW DISGUISED AS A REPORTER: You allowed yourself to be whipped. (He spits out a bit of pencil.)

THE BEAUTIFUL EROWINA (shrugging her shoulders): Frequently.

THE INCREDIBLY HANDSOME JEW DISGUISED AS A REPORTER: Pleasurably humiliated or permissively punished?

THE BEAUTIFUL EROWINA: The men inflicted the wounds; the women kept them open by rubbing salt into them.

The male clients in the EXCELSIOR who are not smoking nervously, eye the women sat on the benches waiting their turn.

MADAM BRUTT (née "Whippy" Tuffold, called Grimkrak by delinquent teenagers who oblige for a giggle, cash and a high tea): I'm not letting anyone in until the doctor's seen the new girl and the reporter's gone. And use the ashtrays, you slobs.

THE INCREDIBLY HANDSOME JEW (making copious notes with his broken pencil): Tell me, in your own words, Miss Eunice, when did you first notice this tendency?

THE BEAUTIFUL EROWINA: I was first made aware of pain at a very tender age.

THE INCREDIBLY HANDSOME JEW: A-cross — my-father's — knee.

THE BEAUTIFUL EROWINA: No, no. Lying on a luxurious and flowered — a rose-patterned, carpet. In my night dress. But please don't quote me.

MADAME BRUTT (withdrawing a scented, lace-edged handkerchief from her ample, powdered cleavage and sniffing it): If there is to be a grand bum-feagle, I don't want the whole neighbourhood to know. I'm not unmindful, but keep it orderly. Otherwise. OUT. The lot of you.

THE INCREDIBLY HANDSOME JEW: One more photograph, Miss Eunice, and, who knows, it might be next month's pull-out centre spread in *Craphouse*.

THE BEAUTIFUL EROWINA (opening her soft, satin-lined purse wider and revealing all the improper contents in the salmon-pink interior): How much do I owe you?

MADAM BRUTT: I don't do it for money. (Fluttering the hanky under her warty nose.) For old times' sake, in the hopes you might . . . (sniff) . . . let me. (Two black tears ooze out between her puffy lids and escape down her rouged cheeks.) I'd do anything for you.

THE BEAUTIFUL EROWINA: It was your uniform. I was frightened.

MADAM BRUTT (delicately scratching the corner of her (pen mouth with the long nail of her little finger): It was only a St John's Ambulance Service uniform. It suited me. I thought I looked very smart. (Sniff.) I wanted to be in . . . Maternity, but . . . (Sniff.) I recognised you as one instantly. I did. (Sniffing and patting her bosom.) It's not as if I'm old. (Vigorously brushing dandruff off her shoulders.) Well — too old. They (nodding towards the waiting room of the EXCELSIOR on the other side of the padded and buttoned satin door) won't respect your person. It's like a circus out there. Scrofulous lot! And that goes for the women. (Folding her hands in front of her.) Well, doctor? My clients are becoming restive.

DOCTOR TULDORFY (smelling of Dettol and rubber): From what Penelope tells me, satyriasis. Without a doubt.

MADAM BRUIT (clapping her hands): Mother of God! To think I might have . . .

DOCTOR TULDORFY: Sexual madness, madam. Not contagious. (He raises a gloved hand.) You may turn on the fluorescent. Advertise. Do your duty by the State, and by Miss, er, Miss. This lady here.

He opens the door into the waiting room and a sigh of relief, smelling of tea, chips, lipstick and pudding, buffets him in the face.

Quickly, several spittle-wet, hand-rolled cigarettes are stubbed out on the wet tiles; trousers hitched up and scrotums eased to the left; skirts smoothed; knicker elastic fingered comfy; seams straightened and throats cleared of phlegm in expectation.

MADAM BRUTT (her eyelashes sticking together as she rubs mascara trails of disappointment from her cheeks): Now don't all push at once. There are ladies present. (And she breasts the pressing crowd and guards the door with her back.)

THE INCREDIBLY HANDSOME JEW: Bugger the women. (Effectively using his elbows and taking advantage of the clapping and laughing.) Is she virgin?

MADAM BRUTT (turning down the corners of her mouth and sniffing the crapulous odour filtering through her moustache): An unnatural virgin — yes. (And she bursts into tears.)

THE INCREDIBLY HANDSOME JEW: Take heart, Madam Brutt, like Raphael de Sainte-Marie-des-Bois, I shall not tread your particular road but confine myself to the verge. (He gives her a reassuring hug.) Now. Am I to be first? I'll leave the door open.

MADAM BRUTT (quite recovered): I can see no objections. (Tapping lightly on the door.) Are we ready, my dear? I've got a Jew here. Very clean, they are.

In the silent waiting room, everyone strains to hear.

MADAM BRUTT (in an undertone): Perhaps she's had second thoughts. I hope. (In an audible voice.) May we come in?

THE BEAUTIFUL EROWINA (from within): Enter.

MADAM BRUTT (turning, with a broad smile, which reveals her aluminium teeth): I declare the EXCELSIOR — open.

A bell, hidden somewhere in the dark warmth beneath Madam Brutt's skirt, tinkles. With great dignity, her movements majestic, she slowly opens the door leading directly into the inner sanctum.

MADAM BRUTT: Mister . . . er . . . umm. A Jew — and incredibly hand-some, my dear. (Putting her hand affectionately beneath Pazzeroni's rump and patting him forward.) An ORIENTAL Jew. (And whispering to him as he passes.) And don't forget your bloody promise. (Aloud.) Remember there are others just as eager as yourself to have a go at her, so don't go tiring her out.

Eunice is naked except for a wide, black, patent leather belt buckled round her tummy; bright red, silk garters, which pinch into the soft flesh of her thighs, and black, patent leather shoes with exaggerated cuban heels. Her face is gaudily made-up and her hair hangs down to the middle of her back.

THE BEAUTIFUL EROWINA: Come in, you incredibly handsome Jew you. And close the door.

PAZZERONI: I'm not ashamed to let people know what I do. Let them see.

THE BEAUTIFUL EROWINA: I don't mind giving an exhibition. It will encourage the others. Is this to your taste? (She indicates the tight belt and gartering.)

PAZZERONI: You know my preferences. Let's get down to it.

THE BEAUTIFUL EROWINA: How can I please you best? Like this? (She totters on her high heels towards a hard, wooden bench; taking tiny, tip-tapping, ridiculously short steps. Lying face down on the bench, with her legs astride the seat and her feet on the floor, she wriggles her bottom enticingly and smiles up at him over her shoulder.) Well, come on then. Whip me. (Stacked untidily in the corner are several canes.) There's a Hairy Mary amongst that lot. Most of the prickles have fallen out but you can bum-baste me with that if you like. Or would you prefer a Four Stand Flogger? A fire-hardened leather thong, then? No? A vinegared Slim Jim? I am not averse to a toughened Autumn delinquent Birch or the Rowan whip to correct my bewitched horse flanks. But you choose. This is your night.

PAZZERONI (snuffling and grunting like a pig but resembling a goat): Do you think I've waited an hour just to paddle your lard? Ye Gods! Talk about being undersexed! (Eunice winces and grips the edges of the bench as a bright red weal grows scarlet on her fleshy bottom.) The trouble with you, Eunice, is that you haven't the remotest idea what sex is all about. (She smiles through the pain as the sound of her smacked flesh hangs in the tingling.) Here you are — what is it? — twenty-three years old, behaving as if . . . (THE BEAUTIFUL EROWINA tenses herself in anticipation.) as if . . .

THE BEAUTIFUL EROWINA: Oh, you incredibly handsome bastard — GO ON!

PAZZERONI: Like an adolescent schoolgirl!

THE BEAUTIFUL EROWINA: HARDER! LAY ON, FOF CHRIST'S SAKE!

PAZZERONI: You should have been a man.

THE BEAUTIFUL EROWINA: YES, YES.

PAZZERONI: Do you know what? (He jabs his forefinger into her soft, brightening bottom.)

THE BEAUTIFUL EROWINA: TELL ME, TELL ME! (He: smile is ecstatic; her teeth clenched and bared.)

PAZZERONI: It wouldn't surprise me one little bit if you turned lesbian!

Eunice fights back tears of hurtful joy while she bucks up am down on the bench, wriggling her bottom furiously.

PAZZERONI (with all his remaining strength): If any man ever finds you attractive — especially in bed — I'll take my hat off to a prize idiot! GOODBYE!

Eunice collapses over the bench exhausted; her flanks scarlet. Touched by the scene Madam Brutt dabs her eyes with her handkerchief and the incredibly handsome Jew acknowledges the applause.

Raphael Arlington enters the room quietly, a grave look on his face. Closing the door he leans his back against it and folds his arms. His face, luxuriantly bearded, is expressionless; the twinkle in his eyes obscured by the blank discs of light reflected from his gold-rimmed glasses. He coughs, gives his hairy tweed jacket a masterful tug and refolds his arms.

RAPHAEL ARLINGTON: Well, have you made up your mind yet?

Emma is dressed in a dull, khaki green suit. The jacket has wide revers, square, padded shoulders, and a pinched, natural waistline. The skirt drops to within six inches of the ground and is slightly flared. Her hair is short, like a boy's, giving her an impish look. She has little make-up on but is wearing long, dangling earrings. Under her arm she carries several thick books.

THE BEAUTIFUL EROWINA: Just give me time, Adam.

Putting the books on the floor, she shivers violently although the room is very warm and there is a gleam of perspiration round her nostrils.

RAPHAEL ARLINGTON: If you don't hurry, it will be too late. (And he lets out a sigh of impatience.)

Emma, trembling, unbuttons her jacket, slips it off and places it carefully over the back of a chair. Unzipping her skirt, she steps out of it, folds and lays it over her jacket, and turns to face Adam wearing a white brassiere, pale blue lawn knickers, a frayed suspender belt, emerald green stockings and flat black shoes.

THE BEAUTIFUL EROWINA: How much shall I remove? (Adam regards her in silence.)

Biting her lip, Emma, with her legs pressed close together, unbuckles her brassiere and drops it onto the floor. With her arms crossed in front of her bare breasts and gripping her shoulders, she stands waiting; embarrassed by her hidden nipples which are slowly erecting.

THE BEAUTIFUL EROWINA: Shall we? (Her legs trembling.) I think I'm ready.

RAPHAEL ARLINGTON (tiredly mocking): As ready as you are able, or as ready as you are willing to be?

THE BEAUTIFUL EROWINA: Oh. (And she gropes inside her knickers and unbuckles her suspender belt. Releasing her stockings, she draws the suspender belt out and drops it onto the floor. After she has taken off her stockings, she puts her black, flat-heeled shoes back on again.) Now? (Adam fills his lungs with air, and exhales it; slowly.) I do wish you'd say something.

RAPHAEL ARLINGTON: I find conversation with you very difficult. You have a certain intuitive understanding but that alone will not be enough if you intend to keep abreast of my intellectual ability.

THE BEAUTIFUL EROWINA (smiling now): I'm glad you want to. I'll take my nixies off. (Stooping, she removes them and then stands; waiting, with her rumpled knickers pressed hard against her pubes.)

RAPHAEL ARLINGTON: You're not just doing this to spite Nesta, are you?

Warming to his punitive agression, Emma feels her breasts fill with blood. A welt appears across her eye and cheek.

THE BEAUTIFUL EROWINA (eagerly): Do go on.

RAPHAEL ARLINGTON: Oh, be your age, Emma. (Emma claps her hand over the pain.)

THE BEAUTIFUL EROWINA: Keep at it!

RAPHAEL ARLINGTON: Well, dammit, either you like it or don't; either want it or hate it. Even you, Emma, wouldn't argue with that!

Stinging pleasantly, Emma, her arms clasped round herself hugging the smart, rocks on her heels.

The door opens and Blind Dutt pokes his head round.

MOT NAMMIO (BLIND DUTT, friend and confidant of Adam): You in?
RAPHAEL ARLINGTON: I'm here.
MOT NAMMIO (BLIND DUTT): I said IN. IN!
RAPHAEL ARLINGTON: I shall soon be finished with her.

Emma bites her lip in anticipation.

MOT NAMMIO (BLIND DUTT): Has she taken off her knickers? You said she'd lay like a plank and you didn't even get your finger . . .

Emma, receiving it upon her face, turns and runs into the wall.

MOT NAMMIO (BLIND DUTT): You told me . . .

The colour-blind Raphael and Mot (Blind Dutt) Nammio leave with their arms about each other, oblivious of Emma who is threshing about in the corner of the room, delirious with convulsions.

TAMMY LAMLIN (knocking): May I come in? (He puts his head round the door.) May I? I appreciate that the others, er, have only just left but . . . I only want to talk to you. I promise I won't try and . . . (He closes the door behind him.)
THE BEAUTIFUL EROWINA: Oh, but you must. YOU MUST!

Esmeralda is elegantly dressed in a loosely bloused silk dress which is exotically printed with unusual flowers in shades of aubergine, violet and orange. Perched on her short hair is a vivid purple capline hat which is trimmed with pale mauve chiffon. Her stockings are white and her shoes, which make her feet look small and slim, are deep blue, green and scarlet, bound with patent black leather. She carries a matching green handbag and gloves.

She runs to Tammy and, throwing her arms about him, begins to kiss him, passionately; thrusting her thick tongue into his mouth and rubbing her body up against him lasciviously Tammy, gently, pushes her away. Esmeralda stands looking adoringly up at him trying to hide her disappointment.

TAMMY LAMLIN (looking at the floor and scratching behind his ear): I find this all very embarrassing, Esmeralda. I'm not exactly certain as to what . . . in these circumstances . . . er . . . what is expected of me.

THE BEAUTIFUL EROWINA (running her painted nails up and down his jacket collar): Most of my other boy friends like to whip me.

TAMMY LAMLIN: OH, no. NO. No, I couldn't do that.

Esmeralda, secretly, sweetly, deliciously feels herself beginning to flood with expectation.

THE BEAUTIFUL EROWINA: Oh, but please, Tammy, PLEASE do.

TAMMY LAMLIN: Naturally I'd . . . er, if it would please you.

Esmeralda starts to pull at her beautiful dress, tugging at the fasteners and zips, trying to disrobe as quickly as possible. The dress tears.

THE BEAUTIFUL EROWINA: OH, it would. It WOULD!

TAMMY LAMLIN: I wouldn't for a moment suggest that you did anything which was contrary to your nature — I would very much like to be able to turn to you and say — do what you want to do; but I can't. I suppose it's because . . . I find this most difficult to say . . .

THE BEAUTIFUL EROWINA (who, in her desperation to denude herself, is ripping and tearing her dress to shreds): Oh, for God's sake — GO ON! GET STARTED!

Tammy stares at her breasts and at the lipstick she has applied to her nipples.

TAMMY LAMLIN: But I don't want you to think I am bringing pressure to bear upon you. YOU MUST BE FREE TO DECIDE FOR YOURSELF!

THE BEAUTIFUL EROWINA (her eyes wild and staring): That's it! THAT'S IT! GO ON!

TAMMY LAMLIN: But that's the very reason why I can't tell you what I came to say!

THE BEAUTIFUL EROWINA: Oh, but you must! YOU MUST!

TAMMY LAMLIN (shrugging his shoulders): Very well, then. I love you.

Esmeralda's knees give way beneath her and she slowly sinks to the floor.

THE BEAUTIFUL EROWINA: Oh, my God. Say it again. Again!

TAMMY LAMLIN: I love you.

Esmeralda, tearing off the last shreds of her dress, kicks off her shoes and, lying stark naked on the floor at Tammy's feet, arches her back; and groans.

THE BEAUTIFUL EROWINA: AGAIN!

TAMMY LAMLIN: I love you.

THE BEAUTIFUL EROWINA (her eyes rolling back as she begins to writhe): Go ON! AGAIN. Say it HARDER!

TAMMY LAMLIN (his head bowed in shame): I LOVE you.

THE BEAUTIFUL EROWINA (making a wrestler's arch as her body, from her feet to her cheeks, becomes suffused with bright red patches): GO ON. AGAIN!

TAMMY LAMLIN: I'm sorry; but I can't help it. I LOVE YOU. I LOVE YOU!

Esmeralda, writhing and knotting her body; twisting and groaning, suddenly heaves up her flesh into a last, desperate, monstrous contortion.

THE BEAUTIFUL EROWINA: HE LOVES ME HE LOVESME, LOVES-MELOVESMELOVESME!

Sadly, Tammy turns away and makes a quiet exit; unnoticed.

MADAM BRUTT (flushed by all the excitement and her eye red and watering from the draught which blows through the peephole): I think you'd best have a bit of a breather. (Confidentially and indicating the door with her thumb.) So I've got an old one for you. (She opens the door and beckons.) Come in. Come on. Don't be shy. (Stanley Bowden enters.) Up from the country, are we? (Leaving and winking.) Don't forget to take off your boots, will you?
THE BEAUTIFUL EROWINA: Close the door.

Stanley Bowden obliges and, with one hand in his pocket, his tall frame slightly stooped, puffs at a cigarette while he watches Evelyn through narrowed eyes.
Evelyn is dressed in a black, shiny patent plastic macintosh, knee-length glossy black boots and a small, matching black plastic sou'wester stuck cheekily on top of her head.

THE BEAUTIFUL EROWINA: You've time? I mean, you won't have to do a lot of explaining. Will you?

Bowden is silent. His shifty, calculating eyes narrow to a single line of lashes, wrinkling, and he drags on his cigarette.
Evelyn struts up and down in the rain. Her hair, which is not protected by the sou'wester at the back, sticks together forming snaking rats' tails whilst the escaping curls round about her face cling to her cheeks and forehead. Her face is alive and smiling and splashed with diamond raindrops which glisten and sparkle like her eyes. She is, and looks, radiantly happy; brimming with confidence and love. Tilting her head back she lets the rain splash down onto her face; revelling in the rivulets which run

warm off her chin. Laughing, she opens wide her red, wet lips, and catches raindrops in the hollow of her mouth; swallowing them down. Turning to Stanley Bowden she slowly begins to undo the tightly knotted belt at her waist.

THE BEAUTIFUL EROWINA: So. It's to be quickly, eh? Are you up to it?

Teasing him with a look which is wickedly naughty, Evelyn provocatively parts her black raincoat. Underneath she is naked. Keeping her eyes upon him, she fluffs up her pubic hair; scattering the raindrops which had clung like dew.

THE BEAUTIFUL EROWINA: What are you going to swish me with? (Her face flushed with energy and youthfulness, she closes her raincoat and giggles.)

STANLEY BOWDEN: I wouldn't dream of hurting you. What sort of a man do you think I am?

THE BEAUTIFUL EROWINA (doubling up, hunching her shoulders and thrusting her clenched palms between her legs): Oooh, delicious.

STANLEY BOWDEN: I have no intention of hurting you.

THE BEAUTIFUL EROWINA: They all say that. But they do. In the end.

STANLEY BOWDEN: I am not as others. The others.

THE BEAUTIFUL EROWINA: No. But won't you? Please.

STANLEY BOWDEN: No.

THE BEAUTIFUL EROWINA (bravely trying to smile through the tears which are spilling out of her eyes and running down her rain-washed cheeks; mingling and salty): Not just a teeny weeny little smack on my botty?

Embarrassed, but excited by her willingness, Stanley Bowden narrows his eyes until Evelyn can no longer discern his pupils. His smile, fixed and spread, covers his face.

THE BEAUTIFUL EROWINA (pouting): No? Even if I went down on my knees and said — please, nice man, smack by botty-bom; wouldn't you?

STANLEY BOWDEN (standing tall): I doubt if I'd be able to rise to the occasion.

THE BEAUTIFUL EROWINA (crestfallen): Oh. (Brightening.) Just a teeny weeny pat-a-cake? Here? (Half turning, she exposes her right buttock.) One pat?

STANLEY BOWDEN: No. I'm sorry. I'm not up to it, Evelyn. I don't know why. I just . . . well. I'm not aroused. There's nothing I — you, can do about it. I'm sorry, Evelyn.

THE BEAUTIFUL EROWINA (drawing her macintosh about her and shivering): Don't be. And don't worry about it. It's not unusual; so cheer up.

STANLEY BOWDEN: But . . .

THE BEAUTIFUL EROWINA: It's quite all right, Stanley. I'm not disappointed — in the least. And don't be so embarrassed! Next time, perhaps.

STANLEY BOWDEN: I don't. Well. You see . . .

THE BEAUTIFUL EROWINA (looking at him expectantly — anticipating; not concealing her mounting excitement): Yes . . .?

STANLEY BOWDEN: Sarah . . .

THE BEAUTIFUL EROWINA: SARAH!

STANLEY BOWDEN: Yes. Sarah and I . . .

Evelyn struggles with her macintosh belt which she has retied and, pulling it undone, opens her macintosh and exposes her breasts to the falling, warm rain. Taking them in either hand she lifts and pushes them forward.

THE BEAUTIFUL EROWINA: GO ON. SARAH AND YOU . . .

STANLEY BOWDEN: Me and Sarah . . .

THE BEAUTIFUL EROWINA: YES? Go ON! I thought you'd never get started. Sarah and you WHAT?

STANLEY BOWDEN: I didn't mean it that way. Not . . .

Evelyn, frustrated, lets her breasts flop, opens her arms wide and throws back her head.

THE BEAUTIFUL EROWINA: DAMN YOU! DAMN YOU!

STANLEY BOWDEN: But it doesn't mean a thing, Evelyn. Not to me.

THE BEAUTIFUL EROWINA: Don't lie to me, Stanley. Tell me. TELL ME! How often?

STANLEY BOWDEN: Once. Perhaps . . . well, — yes, once a month. Perhaps not as often.

Relaxing, her face flushing with a joyous smile, Evelyn slowly opens her macintosh and gives her body up to the rain. It falls, splashing onto her breasts and runs between them, down to her mysterious pubes where it drops, streaming and splashing, onto the pavement. So radiant is she that her body steams in the downpour.

THE BEAUTIFUL EROWINA: Say it again!

STANLEY BOWDEN: Twice a month.

Her mouth open, her teeth bared and the rain pouring off her chin, Evelyn begins to massage her stomach; taking it in great handfuls and kneading it like newly risen dough.

THE BEAUTIFUL EROWINA (who is now desperate): GO ON THEN! DON'T STOP! IDIOT!

STANLEY BOWDEN: Once a week, then. But only at weekends. I promise you.

THE BEAUTIFUL EROWINA: Tell me more. MORE!

STANLEY BOWDEN: But we've been all through this before, Evelyn! I keep telling you, if ONLY I'd met you ten years ago . . .

Evelyn, screaming with pain, falls backwards onto the pavement and pedals her legs furiously as the rain, falling ceaselessly in torrents, drums on to her exposed, bruising flesh.

THE BEAUTIFUL EROWINA: DON'T STOP NOW. CAN'T YOU SEE I'M NEARLY THERE! HURRY! SAY IT AGAIN! (Knocking the back of her head repeatedly on the pavement.) Go — ON!

STANLEY BOWDEN: If we'd have met ten years ago . . .

THE BEAUTIFUL EROWINA: That's it. That's it. Put more feeling into it. Bring your words down harder.

STANLEY BOWDEN: If I'd have met you ten years ago . . .

THE BEAUTIFUL EROWINA: WELL, SAY IT, MAN! TEN YEARS AGO YOU'D HAVE WHAT? (Clasping the back of her wet thighs and pedalling furiously.) WHAT WOULD YOU HAVE DONE?

STANLEY BOWDEN: I could have loved you.

THE BEAUTIFUL EROWINA (near to desperation): No, you wouldn't. You don't mean that, Stanley. You wouldn't have loved me, would you? You can love at any age. Be truthful, Stanley. Why do you wish you could have met me ten years ago? Say it. Go on. Quickly.

STANLEY BOWDEN: IF I'D MET YOU TEN YEARS AGO I COULD HAVE FUCKED YOU!

Gulping down mouthfuls of rain, Evelyn suddenly thrusts out her tongue and, doubling herself up, tries to reach her pubes.

THE BEAUTIFUL EROWINA (inaudible to all but herself and the back of her macintosh cut to shreds): Again.

Stanley Bowden, making a hopeless, dismissing gesture with his hand in the empty space above Evelyn, turns and opens the door. Several men who had been standing on the other side, their faces flushed and eager, press forward; their laughter coarse and explosive.

STANLEY BOWDEN (showing them his handkerchief): Easy. Dead easy. It was a piece of cake. A walkover. Come on. Let's go somewhere else. What about Betty's? (He slams the door behind him, unaware that Evelyn, overcome by hysteria, is rolling on the wet pavement unable to comprehend the ungovernable ecstasy and pain which she feels flowing from her wounded flesh and sees passing before her eyes, as blood; mingling with the rain in the flooded gutter.)

MADAM BRUTT (entering, with a cup of cocoa in her hand): How are we doing?

Erowina, dressed in marine blue ski pants and a white and red, loose knit, chunky sweater, is sitting curled up on the window seat.

THE BEAUTIFUL EROWINA (closing her book): It is all too much.

MADAM BRUTT: They've got together and want an orgy. (She opens her clenched palm and reveals a tablet.) Drink this aspirin down.

THE BEAUTIFUL EROWINA (taking the aspirin and sipping the cocoa): I've endured enough, Miss Brutt. I'm black and blue.

MADAM BRUTT: Once you put yourself under an obligation to your fellow humans you have to endure them. Once you're born, you're born. That's always been my philosophy. Anyway, it's all for the good of the soul.

THE BEAUTIFUL EROWINA: Don't you mean character-forming? Send them in.

MADAM BRUTT: Couldn't we . . . Just you and I. Nothing elaborate . . .

THE BEAUTIFUL EROWINA: Presumably there will have to be some preparation if I am to entertain . . .

MADAM BRUTT: Only with my hand. I assure you. (And she opens her palm.)

THE BEAUTIFUL EROWINA: An orgy, you said. I must be prepared.

MADAM BRUTT (angered): You ungrateful little puppy!

THE BEAUTIFUL EROWINA: Would you have followed me into the sea?

MADAM BRUTT: I followed you along the sea front.

THE BEAUTIFUL EROWINA: The pavements were crowded with wild dreams. It was only because I hesitated.

MADAM BRUTT: The promenade was always crowded with long bronzed legs and young bottoms stuffed into tight white shorts; holidaying. HOLIDAYING ! And the bleak, empty, winter days to be filled. (Sniff.) You might at least have thought of that. And it so cold; and chill; and only the odd lone old-age pensioner on the promenade. Or stumbling on the pebbled beach. What's that for a life?

THE BEAUTIFUL EROWINA: You had your fun in the sun; rubbing up against the crowds. Or didn't you? See how they would have treated you if you had. Open the door. Let them have their orgy.

Madame Brutt gathers up an armful of whips and canes, opens the door and distributes them to the men and women as they bustle into the room.

Erowina, her legs apart, is suspended upside down above the dance floor.

MRS SARAH BOWDEN (a small, grey-haired woman with a marked stoop, who is very unlovely): You're not the first, you know. (She stands close to Evelyn; poised.) Not by any stretch of the imagination. (Evelyn winces.) And I don't suppose you'll be the last. (Tears of real pain run up Evelyn's forehead and into her hair.) God knows why you all run after him. HE'S NO DAMN GOOD IN BED. (Evelyn cries out; struck to the quick.)

Before Grimkrak, who is breasting her way through the dancers, can stop her, Mrs Bowden unpins the rosebud on her bosom and strikes Evelyn's exposed crutch.

MADAM BRUTT: Stop it! Stop it at once! (Pinioning Mrs Bowden's arms, she steers her towards the exit.) I'm not having that sort of behaviour in the Town Hall. (Mrs Bowden is ejected.) These bloody Masonics.

The band help cut Erowina down and the crowd press round.

MISTER SCAMEL (ex-chief accountant at St. Veronica's hospital, who is a thin man with wattles under his chin like a turkey and a protruding, bright red, adam's apple): As it's Ladies Night, ladies first. (He blows into a wet, not snot-wet, handkerchief.) Knickers, anyone? (He opens his sample case.) What about you, madam?

BETTY: My pleasure. (She is the same age as Evelyn, has very dark hair and is an enthusiastic "Meals on Wheels". Erowina envies her middle-class confidence.) I'll soon have her whimpering.

Betty removes her knickers, hands them to Scamel, straddles Evelyn and, lifting the hem of her expensive dress, squats down on Evelyn's stomach. Putting her hand behind her, she grabs a fold of flesh and, grinning down at Evelyn, twists.

BETTY: Fancy you knowing Stanley. (Twist.) I've known him for ages. (Twist.) You reckon he fancies you, do you? (Twist.) He doesn't. (Twist.)

Before Evelyn can answer, another woman sits astride her chest and, clasping Betty, begins to rock backwards and forwards.

ALICE OLLEON: Tell me, was that Stanley's car I saw parked outside your house? (And she winks as she tweaks Evelyn's nipple.) Before he was councillor, he'd park anywhere. Did. Doing his rounds, we said.

The milkman, wearing only his blue and white striped apron, kneels down between Emma's legs and lifts his apron.

MILKMAN TED: Come on, love. Gis a feel. You ain't married to him, so where's the harm? (And he tries to struggle up a milk bottle.)

Erowina begins to thresh.

GORMUN O'CONNOR: Bear up, love. (His eyes moist and sad, he positions himself over Erowina's face.) No need to fret. No harm'll come of it. (He runs his nervous hands through her damp hair.) It's a schoolgirl's looks you have with that innocent face — and who'd want to spoil that. (He tries to struggle something into her mouth; probably a rolled magazine. Erowina grits her teeth and escaping tears go coursing down her cheeks and onto his busy hands.)

A NAVVY (stood in a trench, stripped to the waist, flings up a clod of earth): Move over, O'Hairy, and let's see what a lesbian fairy looks like. (He whistles.) She wants my pick up her funk hole. She'd bloody learn. Silly cow.

JEAN KING (her voice heard over the powder room partition): Have you noticed her hands? (Someone stamps on them.) MIDGE TREE: Her feet, you mean.

MADELINE COURT: Her ankles.

Erowina twists but Old Ma Mead, an elderly lady with rosy cheeks and currant-bun eyes, strokes the soles of Erica's feet with a beer bottle label.

O.M.M.: Take no notice, my dear. The other way only brings trouble. Take my daughter . . . (Marina bares her swollen belly.) A priest, she says. (And she chalks an empty barrel.) As if he would. (Sounding the staves with a knocking knuckle.) But no one questions what I do. Do they? Me being a widow, and all that. I'll be frank — I do. So if I found you and her in bed, you'd have my blessing. Far better to be finger foolish than penis pregnant, I always say.

Evelyn bucks violently and the grouping collapses.

MISTER SCAMEL: Wait on. Wait on. (And he masturbates into a pair of knickers.)

POLICEMAN: Come. Come.

MISTER SCAMEL: Wait on, will you. It's a present I have for her. (He strains.) With my. (And strains) Compliments. Done. (And his meagre of-fering flops.) For you. The last in my sample case. (And he proffers them across the counter of The Perseverance, under the watchful eyes of Old Ma Mead; exactly as it was reported in the newspapers.)

THE BEAUTIFUL EROWINA: I was embarrassed but saw no reason not to wear them.

TERRY: Are you wearing them now? (Parting Evelyn's legs still further.) Stanley won't mind. We've shared the same woman before.

Evelyn, unable to bear the pain, struggles and kicks her legs.

BETTY: Oh, no you don't! (And seizing Evelyn's legs, tucks them one under each other.) You're not having him.

TERRY: Lift her a bit higher. That's it. LOOK! Just where Stanley said. YAK. It does too. (Betty turns away in disgust and lets go Evelyn's legs.)

THE PEOPLE: STAND HER UP! LET'S ALL HAVE A GO AT HER! (They crack their whips and Erowina struggles to her feet.)

THE BEAUTIFUL EROWINA: One at a time. You first, Mrs Oberjee.

MRS OBERJEE (the upstairs tenant, clad in leg irons and her long, greasy hair sticking to her oily skin, offers Emma a black banana): Go on. Take it. There's plenty more down the Clubs. Once you've tasted that, you won't want no other. Watch. (She opens her mouth and the unbroken black banana slips down her throat.)

MRS ALICE OLLEON (her lips pursed as tightly as the mouth of her draw-string handbag, her chin pulled in, squints out of the corner of her ever-watchful eye): Do as she suggests. You're out of your class here, among us.

ALF STACK (a bum solicitor, his greasy hair hanging over his eyes like a broken raven's wing, kingsize cigarettes stuffed into his top pocket and his face flushed with drink, fumbles with his flies): Take no notice, but you might as well go the rounds while you're at it. You see, my wife doesn't . . .

THE BEAUTIFUL EROWINA: It is I who don't understand.

SHANE O'KEEF (a red-faced buffoon of a man with loose lips and a lecherous eye, shoulders Alf aside and stands holding a piece of lavatory wall from the gent's urinal): That's you, ain't it? (He points with a black, nicotined nail at the obscene drawing on the wall.) Your name, ain't it? And it says underneath what you done; who you done it with; and the dates. Well? What about adding my name?

PAMELA YEASON (grey and mousey-eyed behind her pale upswept spectacle frames, sidles up to Emma and, with marked acidity and an expressionless voice, whispers through her pot teeth): Why this false pride? We all know. Everyone knows. He's been seeing Nesta the whole of this past year.

Erowina is beginning to warm to the continuous assaults and her flesh glows bright crimson.

MRS BLATCH (looking up the well of the stairs and holding a white china pot full of her daughter's piss): Hey! YOU! Miss Stuck Up ! You was at it again last night. (Mrs Blatch's hennaed hair is frizzed and she has a nicotine stain on her upper lip which looks like a ginger moustache. Her excited Airedale, 'Beauty', is sniffing under her pale pink, washed out, wrap-round apron and wagging its tail.) Been at it for six days now, you and that bloody artist bloke. (The Airedale pisses against her wooden leg.) We heard. Hear everything as plain as plain down here, we can. (She rattles a tin half filled with dried peas.) You want to get those bed springs oiled, you and that, that JEW boy you got up there.

And Clarissa and Sullivan Bowden walk the length of Erowina's body, without looking down. And it hurts.

JOAN POLLOCK (tall and very elegant in a dark green silk dress with a choker of pearls at her throat, she stands head and shoulders above her husband, Harry, who is deformed and hunchbacked. He has an enormous carboard phallus tied round his waist which is marked off in inches. Holding it, Joan waves gaily to Erica and calls to her across the room): Heard you'd got a new boy friend, darling — or is that the wrong expression? Never mind — lucky you.
MISTER BROUSTER (the thick set, blank-faced cashier of the Co-Operative stores): Didn't I see you Sunday with brother Stanley? Out picnicking were you? (The gleam in his eye is wicked.)

MISTER MACHBONE (his hands as raw as the meat he sells, holds a sausage in a handkerchief. Looking at Evelyn from under the brim of his straw hat, he winks a pig eye): How's brother Stanley? (He bites the end off the sausage and chomps. His quivering cheeks, red and veined with broken blood vessels, look like two raw chops hung either side of his face.) Shall I fix you up with a piece of black pudding?

NESTA WILSON: May I? (She takes the black pudding.) You don't mind, do you? (She is dressed for the kill in a flame red velvet dress which is draped and pulled across her pliant body to reveal her immodest, outsize bust and ample hips. In her plunging neckline is a dainty, lace-edged handkerchief. She withdraws it.) I embroidered it myself. So satisfying — embroidery. (She shows Emma the twined initials R.A. embroidered in one corner, smirks and pushes the handkerchief back into her cleavage; poking it further and further down into the warming valley before she turns to her cobber husband.)

COBBER (in long-hand): "Seeing you and she was not close friends I am obliged for you not to write concerning her whereabouts as I and she is married since I give her a horse to make up for the time she spent scrubbing floors in Sydney where we met in hospital because of my eyes not being good and her being only a kindly orderly who washed floors and says she don't know no Adam so stop the writing."

NESTA WILSON (disrobed, she strikes a mannered pose, prior to doing the dance of the Seven Veils in reverse. Removing a well-sucked glass marble from her mouth she fits it into her navel): Who knows what it is a man sees in a woman? (And she lards her thighs.) Obviously, Adam thinks I have something you haven't. Could it be good looks? (She arranges three mirrors and regards her triple image.) Or . . . (Breathing heavily, she begins an Eastern dance.) Or because he thinks I'm sexy?

Emma reels and falls into a mirror which shatters.

Shane O'Keef, grinning and happy, shoulders his way through the jostling crowd, determined to join in the fun and hang the morrow. He approaches Erowina again.

SHANE O'KEEF: You, her? (Topping his long red neck, his congested face looks like a boiled beetroot. He is holding a sample bottle of urine — thinking, in his drunkenness, it is drinkable lager.) Her what Tam and Gor . . . (He clenches his fist and makes his forearm rigid.) Cor . . . (He staggers off in search of Nik-Nik and Yum-Yum.)

MRS PRISSY NIMBLE: Aren't men beastly. (Mrs Prissy Nimble's pneumatic figure is seemingly made of tremulous blancmange. She is wearing Erowina's too small, slim-line pants. The zip, which is down the back, is broken and Prissy's dimpled bottom, pinched and cleft, is plainly visible.) I can't think why you wear these things. Of course, I know it's difficult to see ourselves as others see us — but one should take notice. Imagine Betty wearing them! She's a bit like you, of course. Even she doesn't seem to realise she's all bottom.

Mrs Helen Arlington, dressed in mourning, a handkerchief in her hand and a long string of clicking jets hung from her neck, tiptoes up to Emma.

MRS HELEN ARLINGTON: Adam's been dead these two years. (She dabs her eyes.) I wish he'd married that Wilson gel. Now, she was nice. Very nice. (She sniffs and wipes her aristocratic nostrils.) His first gel was most unsuitable. Name of Emma.

Mrs Olive Gregson, a widow, pushes Mrs Arlington aside.

MRS GREGSON: I don't understand half of what is happening. Gloria's a good Catholic. And Martin's an excellent husband. I couldn't have wished for a better son-in-law. And now this ! If it wasn't for my granddaughter, Leslie, I'd sooner she lived with some nigger.

Tears of gratitude flow from Erica's eyes and she sinks to her knees hoping for more chastisement. But Mrs Gregson turns away to search for her son-in-law; who isn't there.

A waiter, specially hired for the occasion, bald, wearing a dicky and black bow below his rubbery face, approaches Erica on the balls of his feet, holding a galvanised bucket full of broken balloon glasses. Turning his head, he spits.

WAITER: I saw you. The both of you. Hard up against the bandstand. Kissing. (He spits again.) You couple of Leslies. You want this lot stuffin' up you. That'd cure you. (He walks away — towards the toastmaster.)

TOASTMASTER: LADIES AND GENTLEMEN ! (He raps his hard, ebony gavel on Erowina's skull.) PRAY SILENCE FOR THE BEAUTIFUL EROWINA!

THE BEAUTIFUL EROWINA (nudging him and pointing): There's still Sonia.

THE TOASTMASTER: MRS SWANSFRONT !

THE BEAUTIFUL EROWINA: NO. SONIA LINTON!

SONIA LINTON: I wouldn't mind so much, my dear, if I didn't think it so unexciting. I mean — a man can do the same thing for you better. And it's so much more satisfying. No? (She smoothes her pale yellow dress.) You can pride yourself on one thing — there's no one else in our little group who would have dared be so original. But, Gloria! I was surprised. I mean. All the men, but ALL the men, positively pant after her. (She shrugs her bony shoulders.) If I was in her shoes, I wouldn't waste my time . . . (She lays a hand on Erica's arm.) I didn't mean it that way. Perhaps I'm a teeny-weeny bit jealous. (She taps the ash off a dead cigarette she has wedged into an ivory holder.) Jealous of you. (She gives a disarming smile.) I'm surprised you didn't think I was a . . . I have the look of a man, don't you think? Now. (And she unbuttons her frock to the waist and reveals her flat and freckled chest.) Had my titties cut off. Cancer, you know.

Clive Harper, sitting on a long legged stool holding an open umbrella and giggling uncontrollably, pisses his short trousers and begins to rock backwards and forwards, laughing hysterically. Sidney Toths, also red in the face from laughing, pricks Maurice Feldt's contraceptive with a pin. It bursts, covering Emily and Madam Brutt with spunk.

MADAM BRUTT: How dare you! Get out! All of you! OUT! OUT ! Every-one out! Shoo!

Sheepishly, the clients all troop out and the door is slammed.

THE BEAUTIFUL EROWINA: On reflection, it wasn't much of an orgy. Perhaps I've become resistant to pain.
MADAM BRUTT: The imagination is more virile than reality, my dear. Believe me, I know. Now hurry. Have a good scrub. I want you looking as fresh as a daisy for the doctor.
THE BEAUTIFUL ERONWINA: Doctor who?
MADAM BRUTT: Doctor Ah-hum.

Evelyn scrubs herself clean. Twice. Inside, and out, using soapy water. And once more, to be absolutely certain.
Doctor Ah-hum, wearing a white face mask, a white skull cap and a long white gown, enters the room noiselessly in his white surgeon's boots. He holds his hands, which are covered by slimy, transparent rubber gloves, in front of his chest.
Evelyn is entirely naked. She lies on an uncomfortable, high, examina-tion couch which is inclined at about thirty degrees to allow her intest-ines to gravitate towards her diaphragm. Her legs are splayed and bent, and secured by the webbing of a Kelly's leg holder.

DOCTOR AH-HUM: The nurse is my witness.

Not only has the whole ward gathered round Erowina but, the news having spread, very many strangers have come and are craning their necks to look. And point.

DOCTOR AH-HUM: I'm very careful to have a witness. Now. Got into trouble using my exploratory finger once. (He inserts two.) Keep the heating turned off to discourage the warm blooded. (Using a speculum, he bends down and peers into Evelyn's exposed genitals.)

THE BEAUTIFUL EROWINA (smiling and excited): Is it cancer?

Doctor Ah-hum shakes his head but Evelyn suspects he is smiling behind his mask.

THE BEAUTIFUL EROWINA (scratching her navel): What then?

DOCTOR AH-HUM: Not cancer. There's no evidence whatsoever that you have a malignant growth up there. However . . .

THE BEAUTIFUL EROWINA (disappointed): Not cancer?

DOCTOR AH-HUM: NOT cancer. However . . . (An escaping tear runs down Evelyn's cheek.) We'll soon have it cleared up.

THE BEAUTIFUL EROWINA: You're hiding the truth from me, aren't you? It is cancer but you won't tell me.

DOCTOR AH-HUM: I repeat — you haven't got cancer. You have a form, a very mild form, of gonorrhoea.

Evelyn shrieks with delight, twisting her body this way and that; trying to release herself from the contraption which holds her to the table.

DOCTOR AH-HUM: In cases like this, it would be a great help to us, in order to prevent further spread of the infection, if you told us — in the strictest confidence, of course — especially as I see from your form that you are unmarried . . . (Evelyn, in anticipation of his question, is unable to conceal her mounting excitement.) . . . the name, or names, of the gentleman with whom you have been associating. Sexually, that is. With your co-operation . . .

But Evelyn is not listening. She has heard enough. Convulsing her body, she strains her mounting ecstasy against the webbing. As her frenzy increases the table gives a groan, creaks and begins slowly to fall sideways; collapsing. Lying amidst the debris of the equipment, Evelyn, unable to control the involuntary spasms which puppet her body, succumbs; while a thick spittle oozes out of her mouth and dribbles over her cheeks, and the welts on her body bleed.

MADAM BRUTT: Serve you right. Serve you damn well right. Little minx. That'll teach you to go rutting.

THE BEAUTIFUL EROWINA: That certainly was something. Wow.

MADAM BRUTT (dressed as a callboy with a pill box hat): You're on in one minute. The sofa's on stage.

THE BEAUTIFUL EROWINA: Who am I playing to?

MADAM BRUTT: How should I know? They tell me the King of Siam's out front, so you'd better put on a good performance.

THE BEAUTIFUL EROWINA: Not a public performance, surely.

MADAM BRUTT: Gormun's stage hand. (Esmeralda begins to excite herself as the glow of the slap brightens her cheek.) Not now! WAIT! (The band oompahs into Rose's Stripper and the curtains part.) You're on!

Alone on stage, a thousand faces turned towards her, Esmeralda, naked from the waist down, begins. The King fixes her with his eyes and the fantasy drains from her.

THE AUDIENCE: Go on! Get going! (And they boo and begin to stamp heir feet. Esmeralda's agitation is mechanical. She looks appealingly towards Gormun who is stood in the wings with his eyes closed.) Stop teasing — or get off! One or the other!

Esmeralda covers herself with an orange blanket. Hidden, she tries her hardest — with no notable success.

GORMUN: Could I be of help? (And he slides his hand under the blanket.)

THE BEAUTIFUL EROWINA: No need. (And she is suddenly past helping when, trembling at the knees, she is transported on downy wings of voluptuousness by her own efforts. As one, the audience roar their approval when the rhythmic convulsions of her gluteal muscles betray her sweet agony.)

The curtains closed, Esmeralda turns on her side. But. Gormun takes hold of her hand and kisses her fingertips.

GORMUN: I'll not tell.

The knock sends Esmeralda sprawling, and she lies blanched and rigid.

MADAM BRUTT: There. That wasn't so bad, was it?
THE BEAUTIFUL EROWINA: Not when I saw I wasn't the only one.
MADAM BRUTT: It was that damned coachload of lunatics who started the others off. It's their sort which gives the rest of us a bad name. (Going to the door.) There's some kids outside wanting a go. Are you ready for them?
THE BEAUTIFUL EROWINA: Children?
MADAM BRUTT: Look. When you start, there's no stopping. And who's to say when it starts? At most they'll want to look, and go away laughing. (She opens the door.) Come on in, you lot. And remember, there's others waiting. Say, see, do what you want, and off home. And no telling.

Into the room troop three children. Maurice, Sandra and Vera. Clive, too, who runs in, slamming the door behind him.
Emily is dressed in a white cotton blouse with long sleeves, a dark blue serge skirt, white ankle socks and brown sandals. Her brown velour hat is pushed onto the back of her head and the elastic securing strap cuts deep into her chubby cheeks. Her face is framed by unruly, long brown hair.

THE BEAUTIFUL EROWINA: Goodness — aren't you all a little young to be bum fiddlers? Shouldn't you be home in bed? (Emily sits down on the floor cross-legged; revealing her bleached elastic-legged knickers.

Maurice lies down on the floor and looks between her legs. Emily pulls her skirt down over her knees.) You wouldn't want to get me into trouble, would you? (The children look crestfallen and are on the verge of tears.) Do you really want to? (They nod their heads vigorously.) Wouldn't you rather we played fathers and mothers? (The children are silent.) Have you all lost your tongues? Never mind. There are canes in the corner. Go and get them. Only one each, mind. (The children return and face Emily.) Who's going to start? Vera?

MAURICE: What's that? (He pokes his stick between Emily's parted legs.)

THE BEAUTIFUL EROWINA (looking between her legs): My knick-knicks.

MAURICE: No. THAT!

THE BEAUTIFUL EROWINA: Oh . . . you want to see my ringerrangeroo in the nuddy. But Vera and Sandra have got one like mine.

VERA and SANDRA: We haven't either! Not that! (And Vera Warbley jabs her cane into the soft flesh on the inside of Emily's thigh.)

THE BEAUTIFUL EROWINA: Oh, that.

VERA, SANDRA, MAURICE and CLIVE: Yes. THAT! What's that?

THE BEAUTIFUL EROWINA: That's my birthmark.

CLIVE: That's shit.

THE BEAUTIFUL EROWINA (clapping her hands with delight): Again!

CLIVE, SANDRA, MAURICE and VERA: SHIT!

Emily leans back, spreads her legs wide and the children, joining hands, dance round her shouting, 'Shit, shit, shit '.

THE CHILDREN: What is it?

But Emily is beyond recall and is revelling in an almost continuous orgasm of pain.

The last child out of the room turns off the light.

NANCY SEDOLOID: Isn't little Emily bye-byes yet?

Emily shakes her head and sucks on her thumb. She is lying in an elaborately draped, antique cot. She is wearing a long nightdress and is cuddling her favourite teddy bear — Mister Piggy Buck.

Nancy tiptoes up to the cot, settles herself and slides her hand beneath the bedclothes. She begins.

NANCY SEDOLOID: Yan — tan — tethera — methera — pimp-a-sethera — lethera — hovera — povera . . .

THE BEAUTIFUL EROWINA: Must you?

NANCY SEDOLOID: Tyan-a-dick — tethera-a-dick — methera-a-dick . . .

THE BEAUTIFUL EROWINA: It doesn't make me sleepy afterwards, you know. Not any more.

NANCY SEDOLOID: Tethera-bum-fit — lethera-bum-fit — fit-a-giggot. What dear?

THE BEAUTIFUL EROWINA: I said, it won't send me to sleep.

NANCY SEDOLOID: Yes, dear. Close your eyes. There's a good girl. Hush now. Rub-adub-dub-a-dub-a-dub . . .

THE BEAUTIFUL EROWINA: I won't come. You can't make me come, if I don't want to.

NANCY SEDOLOID: Rubba-dubby-dubby-dubby-dubby-dubby . . .

THE BEAUTIFUL EROWINA: Will — you — STOP — it!

NANCY SEDOLOID: Dubby-dubby-dubby-dubby . . .

THE BEAUTIFUL EROWINA: I said . . . (She seizes hold of Nancy's hand and bends her plump fingers back as far as they will go.)

NANCY SEDOLOID: OUCH! You little beast!

THE BEAUTIFUL EROWINA: That's better. What am I?

NANCY SEDOLOID: An ungrateful little girl.

THE BEAUTIFUL EROWINA: Mmmmm. Lubly. Do go on, Cook-Nanny.

NANCY SEDOLOID: You're spoilt, that's what you are. Spoilt. And too precocious by half.

THE BEAUTIFUL EROWINA: Oh, yum-yum. Tell me more.

NANCY SEDOLOID: There are names for filthy little girls like you.

THE BEAUTIFUL EROWINA: Oh, DO tell me.

NANCY SEDOLOID: Per-verts.

THE BEAUTIFUL EROWINA: Again.

NANCY SEDOLOID: PER-VERTS.

THE BEAUTIFUL EROWINA: Yes, but what sort of pervert? Tell me. Go-on. Quickly!

NANCY SEDOLOID: A dirty pervert.

THE BEAUTIFUL EROWINA: But how dirty? Tell me how dirty I am.

NANCY SEDOLOID: Dirtier than dirt. Filthy. You and that Maurice did the filthiest of dirty things.

THE BEAUTIFUL EROWINA: Oh, yes. Yes. Yes, yes, yes.

NANCY SEDOLOID: So indescribably dirty, I could have drowned you! D'you hear? DROWNED YOU!

Emily, drumming her feet, tosses her head from side to side in an ecstasy of agony. Eventually, she is still, and a calm, satisfied look glows from her half-shut eyes in a face suffused with warmth and colour.

THE BEAUTIFUL EROWINA: Thank you, Nancy. Thank you. I shall be able to sleep now. Goodnight. (But there is blood running from between her teeth and from her nose.) And don't worry, Nancy. The bleeding's internal. No one will know. I'll not tell.

MADAM BRUTT: Goodness! Gracious! To a child? Have you left leave of your senses, woman? Get out before I inform the police. (Nancy leaves and Madam Brutt leans over Emily.) There's an elderly gentleman in the waiting room. Very distinguished. But hairless. He's crying and insists on seeing you.

THE BEAUTIFUL EROWINA: Come one, come all.

MADAM BRUTT: That's my beautiful Erowina. (And she exits.)

Emily is dressed in little pink knitted bootees and is wearing a nappy. On her head is a pink bonnet secured and tied under her chin by a wide, silk ribbon. Over her breasts, to hide them, she has arranged a bib on which is embroidered a duck. She is just finishing tying this round her neck when Sidney enters.

THE BEAUTIFUL EROWINA (surprised): Oh! Hello.
SIDNEY HAMBUCK: Hello, my dear. How are you? Keeping well? (He lays his hat and cane on the table and walks to the armchair.) May I?
THE BEAUTIFUL EROWINA: Please, do.

Sidney seats himself, crosses his legs and flicks a piece of imaginary dust from his knee. Taking a silk handkerchief from his inside pocket, he pats his forehead and wipes either side of his nose.

SIDNEY HAMBUCK (returning the handkerchief to his inside pocket): Come here, my dear. Come and sit on my knee.
THE BEAUTIFUL EROWINA: I'm not your little girl any longer. I'm a big girl now. (And she takes a deep breath and swells her chest.)
SIDNEY HAMBUCK: Let me see. Both of them. Come nearer. Yes. YES. (And he kisses her nipple.) But I think of you as my little girl. I always will. Sit. (Smarting pleasantly, Emily seats herself on his uncomfortable knee.) Put your arm around me, my dear. Like you used to. Show your father you love him
THE BEAUTIFUL EROWINA: Do you know what you're asking of me, Father?
SIDNEY HAMBUCK: I came all this way, just to see you, my dear. I only wanted to see you. See you were happy.
THE BEAUTIFUL EROWINA: But, Father, don't you understand?
SIDNEY HAMBUCK: As long as you're happy, my dear, and occasionally spare a thought for your father, that's all I ask.
THE BEAUTIFUL EROWINA: Father, it would be incest!
SIDNEY HAMBUCK: Words, my dear. Words. Just tell me you're happy. That's all I worry about — whether you're happy or not. Just tell me you're happy. Say you're happy.
THE BEAUTIFUL EROWINA: I'm happy.

SIDNEY HAMBUCK: As long as you're happy, then everything's all right. I know your mother would have wanted you to be happy. (Emily squirms down onto her father's hard knee — beginning to enjoy herself.) But your mother wasn't. She wasn't happy. God rest her soul. Not after you were born. (Emily feels her flesh goosing.) It took Elfreda badly, you know. Your birth. A blood clot formed. It was the blood clot which killed her. Poor Elfreda.

THE BEAUTIFUL EROWINA (wriggling on her father's knee): Was I to blame?

SIDNEY HAMBUCK: In a way, I suppose. Yes. (Emily bears down; hard.) If you hadn't been born, she wouldn't have got the blood clot. Yes. (Emily tugs at her nappy and rubs her open palms up and down her bare thighs; trying to contain herself and not anticipate the question she must ask.) You're so like your mother, Emily. (He slides his hand down, into the nappy.) The same eyes. Nose. Mouth. Your profile. Even the texture of your skin. Just like your mother's . . .

THE BEAUTIFUL EROWINA: In every way?

SIDNEY HAMBUCK: Ev-er-y way.

THE BEAUTIFUL EROWINA: But?

SIDNEY HAMBUCK (withdrawing his hand). Of course, having Nancy helped. You won't remember, but she was a fine, strapping woman when she first came into our service. And handsome. Not intelligent. A sort of dull-witted amazon. I don't know what I would have done without her. (He puts his hand inside his jacket pocket and fingers the photograph in his wallet.) I suppose I should have married her. She put it about I had, thinking the mock ceremony in our private chapel legal. It wasn't. I did it to satisfy her exaggerated sense of respectability. (Emily swallows in anticipation of more revelations.) A highly developed sense of respectability which was completely at odds with her passionate nature. And she was quick to exploit your father's weakness, my dear.

Sidney begins to jiggle Emily on his knee.

She rides his thigh like a hobby-horse; rocking backwards and forwards, urging on her mount.

THE BEAUTIFUL EROWINA: Show me the photograph.

SIDNEY HAMBUCK: What photograph? (And he cleans his hidden nail on the corner of the print.)

THE BEAUTIFUL EROWINA: You know — THE photograph. Please?

SIDNEY HAMBUCK (withdrawing the photograph): Do you mean this?

THE BEAUTIFUL EROWINA (urging her mount into a canter): Yes. Yes. That's the one. Let me have it.

SIDNEY HAMBUCK: It's an old photograph, my dear. Taken when you were young. You couldn't have been much more than three.

THE BEAUTIFUL EROWINA (her mount galloping so fast over the rugged terrain, she is forced to throw her arms about his neck): Please, Daddy. Please. PLEASE let me have it.

SIDNEY HAMBUCK: You don't want this one. I've much better ones at home. The library is tilled with illustrated books.

THE BEAUTIFUL EROWINA: But it's that one I want. Give it! (And she snatches the photograph and runs to the corner of the room. Trembling, she stands, the photograph held close to her face. devouring the details.) Tell me about it, Daddy.

SIDNEY HAMBUCK: What is there to tell? I hardly recall the incident.

THE BEAUTIFUL EROWINA: TELL ME!

SIDNEY HAMBUCK: What? That that is how life is? You're a grown woman. YOU KNOW.

THE BEAUTIFUL EROWINA (unfastening the safety pin and threatening her father with the point as her nappy falls to the ground): Unless you repeat, word for word . . .

SIDNEY HAMBUCK: I can't !

THE BEAUTIFUL EROWINA: You must! Otherwise . . .

SIDNEY HAMBUCK: Otherwise?

The beautiful Erowina, letting drop the opened safety pin, goes and stands before her father. Burying his face in his hands, he sinks on his knees before her.

SIDNEY HAMBUCK: As it was in the beginning . . .

THE BEAUTIFUL EROWINA: So it shall be for ever and ever! (And said with vehemence) I KNOW! SOD YOU!

SIDNEY HAMBUCK: For me, too ! (He reaches up, snatches the photograph and tears it into pieces.) For me, too. For me, too. DON'T YOU UNDERSTAND? FOR ME TOO! OH . . . (He seizes Emily in a monstrous hug.) . . . Elfreda. (And he squeezes and squeezes.) Elfreda. My darling, Elfreda.

Erowina disengages herself, apologises and helps her weeping father from the room. At the door he turns, looks and is about to depart.

SIDNEY HAMBUCK: I too bear them. (He unbuttons his silk shirt and shamefacedly bares his scars.) To whom should I appeal for understanding or a just retribution? (Embittered, his hairless face close to that of his daughter's, he whispers.) It has been our inheritance. (They stand for a moment staring at each other.)

THE BEAUTIFUL EROWINA (taking hold of her father's hand): May I? (And she takes the torn scraps of the photograph.) Thank you. Goodbye. (And Erowina kisses her father's tear-stained cheek.)

Alone, Emily carries the torn photograph to the corner and kneels. Spreading out the pieces, she searches through the jigsawed photograph for some detail she might have missed. Alternately weeping and laughing, she turns the pieces and hurriedly reassembles the photograph. And it is all there. The act of betrayal. The father feeding and being fed. The rose patterned carpet. The curly silhouettes of the chair legs. The white skin, stretched and taut and alternately slack and bulged, running rivers of veins. The damp hair curled and glistening with sweat. It is all there. The sounds. The colours. The movement. The unutterable smell. All there. The cries of delight. The moans of a turgid ecstasy amidst slime and swallows and unending grunts of animality. All plainly visible and remembered. Her father pigging it with Nancy on the carpet.

Emily begins to butt the wall with her head and to claw the plaster. With her hand, she scatters the torn fragments, but the photograph reassembles itself on the retina of her imagination.

Moaning, rocking backwards and forwards on her heels, Emily allows the ache embedded in her being to take wing and express itself in an unearthly wail. While her agony unwinds, there appears on her back, her legs, her arms, across her breasts and stomach, long red welts, witness to her terrible scourging.

Pazzeroni, THE INCREDIBLY HANDSOME JEW, bursts into the room. His tie is askew and he is breathless.

Eunice is dressed in a black leotard with a gold belt drawn tightly round her middle. The leotard has openings in it which reveal her breasts, bottom and sex. She is reclining upon a white, long-haired goatskin rug, posturing as obscenely as the openings in her costume will allow.

THE BEAUTIFUL EROWINA: Did you hear me screaming and come running?
THE INCREDIBLY HANDSOME JEW: No-no. No. I'd got half way down the street when a thought occurred. Tell me. Be frank. (Eunice squirms and her eyes brighten in anticipation. Pazzeroni takes a deep breath.) Is is because of something your father said to you? Did to you? (But he slams out of the room without waiting for an answer.)

Eunice stands with her mouth open, struck dumb.

MADAM BRUTT (putting her head round the door): Goodness, he was quick.

THE BEAUTIFUL EROWINA: He's a sly one, that Jew. (And she chews off a piece of broken nail.) Better shut up shop.

MADAM BRUTT: There's a woman in the waiting room.

THE BEAUTIFUL EROWINA: Blonde?

MADAM BRUTT: Could be Swedish.

THE BEAUTIFUL EROWINA: With mauve eyes?

MADAM BRUTT: It was her eyes which attracted me.

THE BEAUTIFUL EROWINA: Not her figure?

MADAM BRUTT: I DID notice her figure, dammit.

THE BEAUTIFUL EROWINA (perambulating): And her manner of walking.

MADAM BRUTT (sinking to her knees with a moan and clutching Erica): Stop goading me, the pair of you.

THE BEAUTIFUL EROWINA: You recognise her?

MADAM BRUTT: How could I forget. You both look alike. Identical.

THE BEAUTIFUL EROWINA: Then you should not object to my refusal if her answer is in the affirmative.

MADAM BRUTT: You think . . . ?

THE BEAUTIFUL EROWINA: I have no objection.

MADAM BRUTT: None?

THE BEAUTIFUL EROWINA: I would be saddened. That's all. But she won't agree. Might not. Probably will. I hope she does. For my sake.

MADAM BRUTT: You despise me. I know you do. (And she begins to weep.)

THE BEAUTIFUL EROWINA: You are making yourself look ridiculous, Miss Grimkrak.

MADAM BRUTT: You'd soon discover I was anything but childish. I'd . . .

THE BEAUTIFUL EROWINA: You've got your peep-hole. Content yourself with watching and . . send in Gongyla.

MADAM BRUTT: Don't you get all hoity-toity with me, young lady. And fetch her yourself. I'm going. (Walking towards the door.) I'm not interested in what you two get up to. (Turning, with her hand on the door knob.) I'm going home. My friend may be young but she's consistent. And adoring. Good night! (Leaving the door open, she walks through the waiting room with her head held high; sniffing back tears.)

Mrs Gloria Sansum is sat on the bench; her elegant legs crossed. She is composed and the glitter of her costume accentuates her desperate beauty.

THE BEAUTIFUL EROWINA: Have you been sitting there all this time?

MRS GLORIA SANSUM: The passing of time is of no consequence if it can be filled with thought.

THE BEAUTIFUL EROWINA: No memories?

MRS GLORIA SANSUM: I have disciplined myself against my own indulgence.

THE BEAUTIFUL EROWINA: Oh. Well. You'd better come in. That's if you want to.

MRS GLORIA SANSUM: You were expecting me.

THE BEAUTIFUL EROWINA: No. Hoping you would come.

MRS GLORIA SANSUM: I am here.

THE BEAUTIFUL EROWINA: And I invite you in.

MRS GLORIA SANSUM: Please bear that in mind when, in the future, I am blamed.

THE BEAUTIFUL EROWINA: An alternative would be for you to leave.

MRS GLORIA SANSUM: I have never tried to conceal my grosser instincts, but I have always attempted to control them. (She smiles and slips her arm about Erica's slim waist.)

THE BEAUTIFUL EROWINA: For one who is so reluctant, you have a delicious habit of making the most innocent gestures positively debauched. Do come in. (Together, they enter Erica's crib and close the door.) You can stay as long as you like. I don't propose to do any more entertaining.

Erica is dressed in grey, tight fitting, woollen trousers and jacket, a white shirt and bright red tie, and calf length boots. Her hair is cropped short, combed back and dyed blonde.

MRS GLORIA SANSUM: Cigarette?

THE BEAUTIFUL EROWINA: Thank you, darling. (Taking the black, gold tipped cigarette, she inserts it in a long holder and leans towards Gongyla who is holding a silver lighter she has thumbed into flame. Erica throws back her head, blowing out smoke.) I like your suit.

Mrs Sansum is dressed in a dazzling silver suit which rustles when she moves.

THE BEAUTIFUL EROWINA: How's Martin?

MRS GLORIA SANSUM: Moody. I am back with him.

THE BEAUTIFUL EROWINA (withdrawing, as if stung): I admire his tolerance.

MRS GLORIA SANSUM: I'm fortunate. Of course, Leslie plays link.

THE BEAUTIFUL EROWINA: Your darling daughter.

MRS GLORIA SANSUM: Do you know, Martin had the audacity to ask if you encouraged her to join in our games.

Erica gives under the blow.

MRS GLORIA SANSUM: Actually, Joan mooted the same question. (And she lifts Erica who has fallen to one knee.) So did her husband, Harry. I said no.

THE BEAUTIFUL EROWINA: I think I had better take off my jacket if you are going to start.

MRS GLORIA SANSUM: You want me to?

THE BEAUTIFUL EROWINA: It is inevitable.

MRS GLORIA SANSUM (sighing): On your own head be it. (And she helps Erica undress — occasionally caressing and drawing Erica towards her.) But there's really no need.

THE BEAUTIFUL EROWINA (pushing Gongyla away): You will have to bind me. Tightly. There must be no escaping, this time.

MRS GLORIA SANSUM: I have no stomach for such an act.

THE BEAUTIFUL EROWINA: Nor I. Bind me! You must. For safety's sake.

MRS GLORIA SANSUM (taking a length of rope and beginning to bind Erica, who is now nude, to the end of the iron bedstead against which she has positioned herself): Must you stand like that?

THE BEAUTIFUL EROWINA: I am about to die.

MRS GLORIA SANSUM: I'm not going to crucify you.

THE BEAUTIFUUL EROWINA: You will. This time I shall force myself to listen. How many men have you had? Begin at the beginning.

MRS GLORIA SANSUM (securing one of the knots): Since I have known you?

THE BEAUTIFUL EROWINA: Beginning with the dwarf.

MRS GLORIA SANSUM: It was at a party. We were drunk.

THE BEAUTIFUL EROWINA: Say it!

MRS GLORIA SANSUM: Stop torturing yourself.

THE BEAUTIFUL EROWINA: His name ! Say his name!

Gongyla yanks the remaining rope round Erica's flank, pulls it tight and ties the final knot. Before she rises to her feet, Gongyla implants a tiny kiss upon Erica's buttock.

MRS GLORIA SANSUM: Harry. Harry Pollock.

THE BEAUTIFUL EROWINA (jerking back her head and wincing): Again!

MRS GLORIA SANSUM: Harry Pollock. Joan's husband.

THE BEAUTIFUL EROWINA (on an intake of sucked breath): You wouldn't lie to me.

MRS GLORIA SANSUM (while Erica strains against the rope lashing): Did I lie about Pazzeroni? (A welt, bright red and snaking, raises itself on Erica's back.)

ERICA: Pig!

GONGYLA: Not a stuck one.

ERICA: Yes!

GONGYLA: No. Drooled over like crackling.

ERICA: Ah, that hurt.

GONGYLA: Not a bit. I enjoyed every frigging moment.

ERICA: Doing what?

GONGYLA: Use your imagination.

ERICA (whose back is criss-crossed with lashes): No. Not that . . . not that.

THE BEAUTIFUL EROWINA: Where are you?

MRS GLORIA SANSUM (from the depths of an armchair): Here.

THE BEAUTIFUL EROWINA: Well, don't stop.

MRS GLORIA SANSUM: You're forcing the pace. Besides, it's not natural.

THE BEAUTIFUL EROWINA: Who's to say? YOU? Keep at it. Who else? WHO ELSE!

Gongyla, standing close to Erica, blows smoke into Erica's face.

MRS GLORIA SANSUM: Tammy Lamlin.

The bed squeaks as Erica struggles against her tight bonds. Her back, but more especially her buttocks, are slowly becoming suffused with blood and turning bright pink.

THE BEAUTIFUL EROWINA: Again! Don't stop.

MRS GLORIA SANSUM: Tammy Lamlin.

THE BEAUTIFUL EROWINA (panting): Again. Say it again.

MRS GLORIA SANSUM: Tam-my Lam-lin.

THE BEAUTIFUL EROWINA: Ooooh, yes. YES. Yes. More.

MRS GLORIA SANSUM (exasperated): Oh lots more.

THE BEAUTIFUL EROWINA (gyrating her hips): How many more?

MRS GLORIA SANSUM: Oh, for God's sake, Erica. How the hell should I know? I don't keep count. Stanley Bowden!

Flinging her head from side to side, Erica pulls and tugs, arching her back against the pain.

MRS GLORIA SANSUM: Honestly, Erica . . . (Gongyla opens and rummages about inside her handbag; searching for something.) What does it matter how many? (Erica's face congests with blood and from between her stretched, open lips, her tongue — a vivid purple and blue — slowly emerges; stiff and rigid.) The way you keep on asking me what I do, what I don't do; the way you probe into my affairs — yes ! affairs . . . (She finds and looks at herself in a small mirror.) . . . anyone would think we were married. (Looking at herself in the mirror and kissing her image.) I'm not a lesbian, am I, darling? Nor so silly as to fall in love. (And she kisses herself.) Never so silly as to fall in love.

The bonds binding Erica fall away. And.

A low moan, bubbling from the back of Erica's throat, is carried on the spittle which, like a thick mucous trail, dribbles from her nose and mouth; suffocating. Erica coughs up the phlegm in bursts — bulging the blood vessels in her neck as she strains against the asphyxiation. Alternately moaning and coughing, she fights against drowning in her own copious saliva. Gripping the bed rail, she bows her head and feels her enlarged eyes being pressed outwards by the pressure of the blood flooding into the sockets behind them. Her body and limbs, where the rope has chafed her soft flesh, are rubbed raw and ooze tiny droplets of blood as if her skin had been sucked until the minute blood vessels had ruptured through the delicate skin. Covered in her own gore, she clenches her bright red buttocks together in an agony of pain until the ridges and depressions in them blanch and reveal the outline and strength of the two great encircling muscles; now gristle hard. White patches appear on her flayed skin and her entire flesh becomes blotchy. Matching her strength to the bed, she arches and becomes iron; rigid and unyielding.

Suddenly, there is a short, sharp sound.

To Erowina, it is like an explosion. A sudden and drastic roar at the base of her skull. It splits her head and the great cavity of her skull retains the unbearable resonance; which booms and rolls about in the expanding membrane which balloons from the top of her head; becoming larger and larger.

Clapping her hands to her ears, Erowina tries to compress and obliterate the roar which overwhelms her senses.

Squinting sidelong through her frightened eyes, she sees the long, pearl tipped hat pin; an heirloom from her dead Aunt, Harry. Seizing it, she works the point through the maddening gristle — into the balloon of sound.

A sigh escapes her when, in an instant, the boom goes pop and she is finally released — for ever.

CLARE 1962